ALSO BY
EMMA SCOTT

LOST BOYS

The Girl in the Love Song

When You Come Back to Me

The Last Piece of His Heart

FULL TILT DUET

Full Tilt

All In

CASTLE HILL ACADEMY

Little Pieces of Light

Everything We Couldn't Say

Everything WE couldn't SAY

EMMA SCOTT

Bloom books

Cover design by Antoaneta Lisak/Sourcebooks
Cover images © myshkovsky/iStock, Iana Kunitsa/Getty Images, AlanMardi/iStock, PepeLaguarda/iStock
Internal art by Neeraj S.

Published by Bloom Books, an imprint of Sourcebooks
1935 Brookdale RD, Naperville, IL 60563-2773
(630) 961-3900
sourcebooks.com

Cataloging-in-Publication data is on file with the Library of Congress.

The authorized representative in the EEA is Dorling Kindersley Verlag GmbH. Arnulfstr. 124, 80636 Munich, Germany

Manufactured in the UK by Clays and distributed by Dorling Kindersley Limited, London
001-364815-Jul/26
10 9 8 7 6 5 4 3 2 1

For Robin. They're all because of you, but this one belongs to you. With love.

PLAYLIST

Prelude in D Major // Sergei Rachmaninoff
Nocturne in C Sharp Minor // Frédéric Chopin
Ballade No. 1 in G Minor // Frédéric Chopin
Beautiful Things // Benson Boone
What Was I Made For? // Billie Eilish
Gaspard de la Nuit // Maurice Ravel
back to friends // Sombr
Cosmic Love // Florence + The Machine
Étude-Tableau Op. 39 No. 5 in E-flat minor //
Sergei Rachmaninoff
Stargazing (Take My Heart Don't Break It) //
Myles Smith
All the Things She Said // Harrison
Use Somebody // Mae Stephens (Kings of Leon cover)
Bad Liar // Imagine Dragons
Eldest Daughter // Taylor Swift
Spectrum (Say My Name) // Florence + The Machine
Noticed // Mutemath

CONTENT WARNING

Poverty shaming, sexual assault (inappropriate touching of hands, arm, and face), alcoholic parent, drug overdose, mention of suicide, mind shame, courtesy stigma of child by parents, misdiagnosis of learning disability.

MEN'S EIGHT ROWING CREW

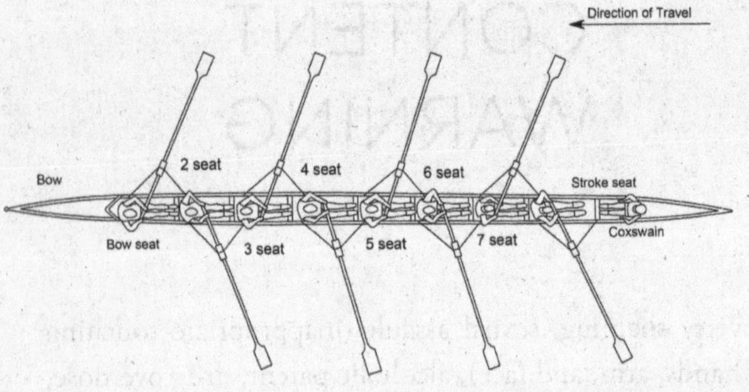

Prologue

ORION, AGE 15

I tell my piano the things
I used to tell you.
—Frédéric Chopin

Castle Hill Academy filled the window of my father's limo, looming like a huge, angular monstrosity. Futuristic and ultra-modern, like something out of an episode of *Black Mirror*.

"I know it's far from home," Mum said, "but you'll love it here. Just like your brothers did."

I kept a smile plastered on my face, thinking, *This place will try to break me like a nightmare.*

"Impressive, isn't it?" Father said. Rockwell Mercer was the walking definition of *impressive*—big, imposing, dressed in a gray Brioni suit with diamond cufflinks at the sleeves. His dark eyes regarded me from across the seat. "And it ought to be." British accent was still touched with Nigerian. "We funnel enough money into it."

Many Castle Hill Academy students hailed from wealthy families and gave generously to the school; mine and four others gave the most. We were known as the Big Five, and our endowment had funded renovations that made my last school in London, Alistair Morton Prep, look like a motorway hotel.

"Turn the fan up a bit, would you, darling?" Mum asked, gathering her ash-blond hair off her neck. Celeste Mercer looked every bit as impressive as Father in her pink Chanel suit and A-line skirt, though she'd never cared for Rhode Island humidity in late August.

"Yes, Mum." I hit the power button on the AC and switched to a brash Cockney accent. My palms were already sweaty but not from the heat. "It's a bit close 'ere, innit?"

Father frowned. "Best behavior, Orion. You need to start on the right foot. Morton Prep will seem like child's play compared to the next four years."

He sounded like a judge handing down a prison sentence. My stomach tightened, and I just managed to hold on to my smile. "Well, Father, given that I *was* a child during my time at Mort—"

"You did a good deal of playing around," he snapped. "The antics you got away with won't be tolerated at Castle Hill."

I tried not to roll my eyes. Translated from Father's lofty Queen's English, *antics* meant *workarounds*: the daily dodges and weaves I used to hide my struggle with ADHD.

Father downplayed my condition, treating it more like a personality quirk than an actual diagnosis. Getting by in school was exhausting. The few times I'd asked for help, I was told, "Take your meds and try harder."

What a crock. The meds made my heart feel like it'd been possessed by a jackhammer, and then I was so depressed and tired the next day, I could hardly move, so I'd secretly stopped taking them. And if I tried any harder at work, my brain would leak out of my ears. But talking about "troubles" wasn't something we Mercers did, so I kept that to myself.

Gravel crunched under its tires as the limo skirted the school's front doors and glided down the curve of the circular driveway to the back of the building. From my previous trips to Castle Hill when my brothers were students, I knew this entrance was reserved for faculty and visitors.

"There they are," Father said.

Dr. Vincent Sterling, the Academy's president, seemed to have gathered his entire staff to greet us—at least fifteen people.

I shook my head. "No red carpet or paparazzi? I'd dock a million pounds from next year's endowment for this egregious slight. The *audacity*."

Mum laughed, and even Father gave a reluctant grin as our driver opened his door.

"Mr. Mercer," Dr. Sterling said. "Welcome back."

He was a tall man, with dark hair going silver along

the sides, dressed in an impeccable suit. He shook my father's hand as if he were greeting royalty. I was surprised he didn't bow. Rockwell Mercer was CEO of Mercer Chemicals, one of the largest manufacturers in the world. The entire UK and half of the US used Mercer products to clean their ovens and wash their clothes. Father had created the business from nothing. My brothers graduated early from CHA and were well into their tenure at Cambridge, both being groomed to enter the family business. I would follow in their footsteps.

No one asked me if this track was what I wanted—not even me—but working in the family business was safe. Or would be, once I was done with essays, tests, exams…

I stared up at the behemoth of a school.

Four more years. And then another four at Cambridge. God help me.

"This must be Orion," Dr. Sterling said, breaking me out of my thoughts. "Delighted to meet you, young man. Your brothers were exemplary students during their time here. I gather we can expect great things of you as well?"

I widened my charming smile, the one that ought to be trademarked. A grin that got me through excruciating years at Morton Prep, wooing teachers and headmasters. They all marveled at how smart I was but lamented how I never *applied* myself. Not even a diagnosis of ADHD could explain a brilliant mind that struggled with the basics. Hence the arsenal of workarounds—tricks to keep teachers fooled or distracted with a patented smile…

"Orion?"

I blinked. The welcome committee was waiting for an answer.

"Oh, my brothers are the brains of the family," I said. "I'm just here for the food."

Dr. Sterling laughed, and his staff joined after a beat, a little too loudly.

"He's quite the wit, is he?" Sterling said to Father.

"Indeed." Father gave me a pointed look above a thin smile, laying a heavy hand on my shoulder. "But he has big shoes to fill. Big shoes. I presume arrangements have been made?"

Understanding passed between the two men.

"Yes, of course," Dr. Sterling said. "This is Mr. Jameson, one of our best test proctors." He gestured at an older, white-haired gentleman. "He'll be presiding over Orion's exams. *Privately.*"

Mum and Father exchanged approving glances.

I gazed at Jameson, my one and only accommodation for the disorder diagnosed when I was ten years old.

I crouched behind one of Mum's gigantic vases, listening hard. My brothers and I were forbidden to even breathe on these antiques, but from this hiding spot, I could hear the adults in the sitting room.

"I've finished my evaluation of your son," Dr. Billings said. "I have to say, Orion is an extraordinarily intelligent

child, with an even more extraordinary gift for the piano. And his reading comprehension is incredible."

"Yes," Mum said. "He reads seven or eight books a month, at least. He's far beyond his brothers' level when they were in Year Five."

"But his test scores are abysmal," Father said. "And dear God, his penmanship."

"Orion has classic attention deficit hyperactivity disorder," the doctor said. "ADHD. I've seen cases like it many times. He's a bright boy, but he can't sit still during the exams, yes? That would account for his wonderful aptitude, but poor test results."

I frowned. I could sit for exams no problem. It was the words that wouldn't sit still.

I loved to read, but I didn't understand a story until I'd read the whole thing. A book was a puzzle that only made sense when I had put all the pieces together, and then it came together in my mind like a tapestry. Or a film.

Short chapters in textbooks were hard. When teachers asked me to stand up and give a summary, I completely fell apart. Even math problems were hard if I had to explain my work. Writing was the worst. I couldn't make the thoughts in my head into words on the page. But I could draw the images. I could draw really well, actually.

And music…

Music made sense in a way that nothing else did. It was air and water. It was light and breath and my own heartbeat. When I played piano, my hands worked perfectly, as if they heard the music coming from somewhere else and channeled it through me. The notes on the page didn't have holes in them. They made patterns that I understood without even trying. And when I looked at the black and white keys, I saw sounds and melodies and could play them right out. It was as if the piano and I were not two separate things but connected somehow, and I never wanted to be apart...

"I'll prescribe him some medication," Dr. Billings was saying. "You should see improvement in his schoolwork immediately."

The leather couch creaked, and then Father spoke. "I don't need to tell you that discretion is paramount here."

"Of course, but I assure you, ADHD is quite common."

"Not in this house," Father muttered.

"We just don't want to make a fuss," Mum said. "If it's quite common, let's not make more of it than we ought."

Dr. Billings cleared his throat. "Well, it would be good if you spoke with your son about the challenges he's been having. How he's been feeling—"

"I'm sure your medication will do the trick," Mum said.

"Indeed," Father said.

A pause followed, and I could feel the doctor's confusion. He didn't understand that my parents didn't discuss challenges or feelings. Not in this household. I'd never heard my parents so much as raise their voices to each other.

"We don't rock the boat," they liked to say.

When my brothers and I got mad or sad, we were meant

to keep it to ourselves. Displays of intense emotions were messy. Distasteful. Growing up, we were like boats floating on the surface of Loch Ness, desperately trying not to plunge into the depths where feelings lived like monsters. But sometimes, even when the boat was still afloat, my feelings came bursting up from down below.

When that happened, I went to the piano. But even that wasn't allowed. While Mum and Father said I was a gifted player, they insisted my talent was just a hobby.

"Must you bang like the devil?" Father complained when I played angry.

"That's pretty but so gloomy, Orion," Mum would say when I created something sad. "Play something cheerful!"

But even if I wasn't allowed to show the feelings, they were still there. Way down deep beneath the lake's surface, dark and murky and confusing.

Was this part of having ADHD?

Was I broken? Was something wrong with me?

A tap came on my shoulder, and I nearly toppled the vase. Odin, my fifteen-year-old big brother, caught it. He grinned and motioned me away from the living room.

"Spying on Mum and Father? What gives? And hey, how did your appointment—?"

I threw my arms around his waist.

"What's this all about?" He laughed and knelt in front of me.

"I don't want you to go away to school," I whispered. "I'm…scared."

Odin's brows came together. "Honestly? So am I," he whispered back.

My eyes widened. "You are?"

"But what can I do? It's always been the plan." He waved a hand. "Anyway, what did the doctor say?"

"I have ADHD."

Odin frowned. "Oh. Okay. Well...I'm sure he'll help you. He give you medication?"

I nodded tearfully. "But Odin—"

Voices grew louder. Our parents were seeing the doctor out. Odin gave me a quick hug.

"You're going to be okay, Orion. Promise."

I wanted to tell him that I'd miss him too much, and that I was scared that I was broken. But Odin was going out with friends and I couldn't tell him. I didn't want to bother him about it anyway.

Better to keep it to myself.

At dinner that night, I sat at the table with my family, while servants moved between the kitchen and dining room. Odin sat across from me, Octavian next to me. He was twelve and very serious and quiet. Basically, the opposite of me.

I waited for Mum or Father to ask me about my evaluation with Dr. Billings, but they never did.

"So, Odin," Mum said. "Are you getting excited for Castle Hill?"

"Yes," Odin said, not looking at me. "I'm sure it'll be fine."

Not scared, not nervous, not anything but fine.

Everything was always fine in our house. Just how they liked it.

The next morning, our housekeeper dosed out my medication. Almost immediately, my heart started to race, I couldn't breathe very well, and I felt jumpy and jittery. Whatever this stuff was, wasn't it supposed to make me the opposite *of jumpy and jittery?*

Maybe it was just excitement. I was psyched to get to school for once. Finally, I'd be able to read short chapters. The meds would make me focus and everything would make sense.

During history, Mr. Mooney asked me to read a passage about the daily life of the first Anglo-Saxons in Britain. But the words still had holes in them. The paragraph wasn't long enough for me to get the gist.

"Sorry, Mr. Mooney," I said, squinting and making funny faces. "I think I need glasses."

The class laughed. I made a lot of jokes in class. Making my friends laugh was the part of school I liked best.

Mr. Mooney frowned but tried not to smile. I could see that all the way from my seat because my vision was perfect. "Orion, you do not need glasses."

"I think I do. Everything looks blurry." I turned to the girl beside me. "Asha? Is that you?"

She laughed while Mr. Mooney rolled his eyes. "Today it's glasses. Last week, you left your book at home. Two days before that, you had a stomachache." He crossed his arms. "What do you have to say for yourself?"

"I don't know, Mr. Mooney," I said. "Maybe I'm allergic to the daily life of the Anglo-Saxons."

Everyone laughed, fooled again, but I was right back where I'd always been. The doctor hadn't helped. The medicine didn't work. My parents didn't want to hear it. Down below, in Loch Ness, the monsters of sadness and anger were boiling up.

I raised my hand. "May I use the restroom, please?"

"If you can see your way there, yes," Mooney said.

I held my hands out in front of me, pretending to feel my way out of the room. The laughter roared in my ears while the blood was pounding in my head. My skin was hot, my smile stiff on my face like it was nailed on.

The boys' room was empty. I gripped the sink and took deep breaths, trying to remember what my brothers and I had been taught. We were Mercers. We were practically royalty. We were always calm and in control. We didn't embarrass ourselves. Ever.

The glass in front of me cracked like a spiderweb, and pain radiated out of my fist the same way. I stared at my reflection; my own face was fractured like my mind. Then I looked down at the droplets of blood staining the white porcelain sink. Instantly, my anger was replaced by fear.

I'd punched the mirror. I'd damaged school property.

I'd rocked the boat.

Panicked, I ran water in the sink, rinsing the blood down the drain. Then I wrapped my hand in paper towels, pressing hard on the little cuts. From knuckles to wrist, it stung and ached. I might've ruined my fingers for piano forever, but what if someone saw what I'd done? Any second now, the door would open, and they'd see…

I tucked my hand into my jumper pocket. Put my smile back in place. Then quickly left the bathroom.

No one would know I broke the mirror.

No one would know I'd rocked the boat.

I'd go home tonight and have my text reader read the chapter to me. I'd memorize it and tomorrow recite the whole thing word for word. Mr. Mooney would be impressed, and no one would know how hard it had been.

I'd done it before. I could do it again.

"Orion?" Mum smiled and linked her arm through mine. "Ready?"

As the entourage filed inside the school, I flashed Mum my trademark smile—the one that charmed teachers, disarmed girls, made me popular and untouchable.

I was last to go through the doors, gazing up as the building loomed up high. I was a Mercer prince, groomed to be a king, facing this dragon of a building with nothing but wit, jokes, tricks, and charisma.

My hand sought the brass coin in my pocket. A parting gift from Odin before I left, hurriedly pressed into my hand at the airport. It was engraved with the constellation, Orion, on its smooth surface.

"So you never lose your way."

I'd taken the coin with me and left piano behind. It

was a hobby, nothing more. My parents had told me I was good at it, but I wasn't made for it. I was a Mercer, made to join the dynasty. Over and over, they told me, and the music faded as the effort I had to put into keeping up at school and not be an embarrassment to the family took all of my energy. Drained me. Exhausted me, until I had nothing left.

I rubbed my thumb over the three stars on my namesake's belt and heaved a breath.

Four more years.

I'd done it before. I could do it again.

Part I

I would rather write ten thousand notes than a single letter of the alphabet.

—Ludwig van Beethoven

Chapter 1

HARPER

SEPTEMBER, THREE YEARS LATER

"Here it is." Mom unlocked the front door of our new house, beaming at me. "What do you think?"

I glanced around the small, shabby living room, and my heart sank. Not because it was small and shabby but because of a visceral feeling that some unseen calamity lurked behind the walls. Termites, maybe, or a crack in the foundation Mom didn't know about because she'd passed on doing an inspection when she'd made the one and only trip to Rhode Island earlier this summer.

Either I was quiet a half second too long or Mom read my face.

"Gee, thanks, Harper," she said. "You know, I worked really hard to buy this place instead of renting some shitty apartment from another shitty landlord that—"

"Mom, it's fine," I said, smiling. "Really. You did good, Maeve Bennett."

"Yeah?" Her face filled with dubious hope as she brushed a lock of hair out of her face. Once it was sandy blond, but now it was full of gray.

"Yeah," I said. "My eyes just needed to adjust to the dark."

She blew a sigh of relief and rallied her enthusiasm.

"Thanks, baby. You're gonna love this place. Trust me. I mean, wait till you see *that school.* It doesn't matter how much money I have in the bank or what neighborhood we're in. What matters is how much smarts you got in that brain of yours. You're finally gonna be at a school that deserves you."

Then I felt like shit for being so pessimistic. As usual.

"Thanks, Mom," I said, giving her a hug and a kiss on the temple. "This is going to be great."

I was excited about Castle Hill Academy, but a bit intimidated. Ninety percent of the student populace weren't living in shabby houses with foundation problems. But Mom was right—where we lived didn't matter. The Academy was my gateway to MIT, or maybe NYU. Then I could get a great job in the field of chemistry, and my family's next house would be the opposite of shabby.

My little brother—half brother, technically, though I never thought of him as half of anything—had been tearing around the tiny front yard. Now he burst inside and pushed between me and Mom, singing, "I love it. I love it. I love it!"

He started racing around the tiny living room. Mom had been prescient to name him Dash—the kid loved to run. He made a circuit around the whole house, then jumped on the furniture that came with it. Mom had done well in that department too. The furniture we'd had in our crappy Pittsburgh apartment hadn't been worth the price of the U-Haul, so we abandoned it. We piled everything we could in a storage bin secured to the roof of Mom's ancient SUV and crammed the rest in my old blue Prius.

"Do I have my own room?" Dash asked with wide-eyed, seven-year-old enthusiasm.

"You sure do," Mom said. "Look upstairs. Yours is the smaller one. Harper gets the big one because she's the big sister."

"I thought you said this was a two-bedroom," I said, while Dash thumped upstairs to investigate.

"It is," Mom said. "I'll sleep down here on the couch."

"Mom..."

"You're going to need your own space to study. I'll be fine. Plus, with my jobs, I'll be coming and going, so this will make it easier."

Easier. I clenched my teeth. That was the thing about Mom. She was admirable yet frustrating as hell. Adamant I have my own space to study and not get a job, so I could focus on my grades and get into a great college. To pay the mortgage on this new house, she'd work nine to five as a receptionist at a local dental office, and clean Airbnbs in whatever time she had left over. But the bulk of my "study time" would be spent babysitting Dash, getting him to and from school, supervising his schoolwork, cooking meals and taking care of the house. Just like I did in Pittsburgh.

Like I did when Mom was drinking.

She went into the postage-stamp-size kitchen with its old linoleum flooring and splayed her hands on the counter that faced the living room.

"I can't believe it. This is all ours, Harper. We're homeowners. Wow, we've come a long way, baby. *I've* come a long way." She shook her head, disbelieving. "What a road."

Like a movie montage, my mind played out that road. Long years of pitfalls and potholes that nearly sent us off a cliff more than once: Mom struggling as a single mother because my father split before I was born. My grandparents dying and Mom struggling harder, a parade of nameless friends and neighbors stepping in. I might've been three when the struggle became too much and suddenly there were a lot of bottles lining the counters and littering the floor of our tiny apartment.

Here the montage turned bleary, steeped in whiskey-and-beer uncertainty, watching my mother stumble around drunk. By age six, I was either helping put her to bed when she came home smashed or cowering under the covers, alone and terrified, when she didn't come home at all.

More pitying neighbors helping me get her off the front lawn because she was too loud to ignore and too heavy for me to lift.

There were stints in foster care when it got really bad, and periods of relative normalcy when she'd dry out. But it never lasted. When I was ten, she took up with a fellow alcoholic, and Dash was the result of that blessed union. That guy didn't stick around either.

Then the movie tried to find a happy ending, showing a room full of clapping people as Mom got sober, went to night school, and got her AA degree.

"An AA degree to go with my AA meetings!" she liked to say.

She'd been clean and sober for four years now, but the damage had been done. No finish line crossed as far as I was concerned. My trust in her was built on a shaky foundation and she knew it. I tried my best to forgive, but when you're eleven years old and hiding your one-year-old brother in a closet because some rando boyfriend is on a drunken rage and your mom just makes excuses the next day...

I still had nightmares and took stairs instead of elevators.

Buying this house *was* a big step, and I was proud of her, but doubt gnawed at the corners of my mind. While our apartment in Pittsburgh may have been shitty, at least we had Benny the landlord. If the toilet clogged, he fixed it. If it required a plumber, it was on him. We may have been one disaster away from eviction, but repair bills weren't why.

Stop being so goddamn pessimistic, I thought. *Be happy for once in your life. Let a little bit of hope in.*

Hope wasn't in my nature. My default setting was *stressed to the fucking max*.

But I could try. Castle Hill Academy held the key to unlocking a lot of doors for me. Our new neighborhood, the Bend, was surrounded by lush trees, and we had a yard Dash could play in, instead of a cracked concrete parking lot.

I smiled at my mother—a real smile. "Thanks, Mom."

Her expression turned perplexed. A little wary. "What for?"

"Working so hard. Both for us and for yourself."

Tears filled her eyes, and she put a hand on her chest. "Oh, baby. I needed that."

She came to me and gave me a hug, then held me away by the shoulders, her expression brighter than Dash's on Christmas morning.

"Our luck has changed. I can feel it." She kissed my cheek. "Let's unpack."

I heaved a sigh and glanced around our new, old place.

Please let her be right.

The first day of school arrived.

As predicted, Mom wanted to be at the dentist office early to make a good first impression, so I drove Dash to Castle Hill Elementary where he was starting second grade.

"Are you excited, bud?" I said, glancing at him in the

rearview where he was cheerfully kicking his feet against the booster seat. He was such a happy kid. God, I loved that little bugger. He looked nothing like me—sandy-blond hair to my dark curls, blue eyes to my brown. Whoever my father was, his genes beat out Mom's. Hers won with Dash.

"I'm super excited," Dash said. "I hope my teacher is nice. I hope I make lots of friends. I hope they have tetherballs on the playground. I love tetherball. Do you think they'll have tetherballs?"

I laughed. "I have no idea, buddy. I hope they do."

I hope they have everything you could possibly want.

"What about you, Harper?"

"What about me?"

"Are you nervous about your first day of school?"

"A little."

I was more than a little nervous. I wasn't normally preoccupied about other people's opinions, but back in Pittsburgh, there'd been hundreds of kids in the same socioeconomic range as me. At Castle Hill Academy, I'd be in a very obvious minority.

So what? Might not be a big deal. Don't get defensive already.

"Why are you nervous?" Dash asked. "Because you're going to be new?"

"Exactly," I said. "Doesn't that make *you* nervous, Dash?"

"Nah," he said. "I like meeting new people. If you get

nervous, all you do is turn to the person sitting next to you, and say, 'Hi, I'm Harper. I'd like to be your friend.'"

I grinned. "That easy, huh?"

"Yup."

"Where did you learn that?"

"*Sesame Street*, of course."

"Of course."

I pulled up to the car line and helped Dash out of his booster. "You know where you're going?"

"Yup."

"Good man. I'll be here after school to pick you up, okay?" I ruffled his hair. "Have a great day, buddy. Love you."

"Love you, Harper."

He waved his little starfish hand at me and jogged eagerly into the school.

Brave kid, I thought. I wished I had half of his courage and a fraction of his optimism. I'd long ago decided my real job—more important than making good grades or getting into a good college—was to preserve that spirit in Dash for as long as I could.

My minority status was made evident before I even left Castle Hill Academy's student parking lot: Every other car was manufactured in this decade. I headed for the white-winged, angular building that looked more like someone's idea of the future. As I passed by clumps of students basking in the early September sun, my clothing stood out as much as my car did.

Out of necessity as much as fashion sense, I preferred thrifting clothes, or even making my own. Today I wore a red, orange, and blue-striped apron-style dress over a short-sleeved white blouse and chunky shoes. Unbeknownst to me, the girl dress code at CHA seemed to be short-shorts and tight tops that showed ample cleavage, preferably in white or pastels.

"Ooh, a new Bender," said one such girl, leaning against a Mercedes with a bunch of jocks. She twiddled her fingers at me. "Hi, Bender."

I hunched my shoulders.

Bender. Got it. Because I live in the Bend. *How droll.*

It was on the tip of my tongue to ask how long it had taken to come up with such a witty and cutting insult, but I wasn't even out of the parking lot. Making smart-ass remarks probably wasn't something they taught on *Sesame Street.* Even if Dash wasn't around, I wanted to set a good example.

Inside the Academy, I tried not to gawk like a tourist, but…damn. Its gleaming hallways were lined with trophy cases, each one bursting with cups, medals, bowls, and plates, and draped in the school colors—black and gold. Sports were a religion at CHA, which had an Olympic-sized gym at the center of its hexagonal layout. No football team. Instead, the Castle Hill Lions competed in rowing, lacrosse, tennis, water polo, and gymnastics. *Royal Pride!* was the rallying cry *and* school ethos.

The whole place screamed *money and success*, and I actually felt my pulse kick up that I might be standing at the starting line of an entirely different life.

In the STEM Wing, I found my first class, AP Calculus. I took an empty seat toward the back-left corner. The seat to my left remained empty until after the bell rang, when one of the most beautiful girls I'd ever seen sauntered in. She had long blond hair with Sabrina Carpenter–style bangs. She sat down in a cloud of expensive perfume and a haughty expression. Upon closer inspection, I saw something like fear glinting in her blue-green eyes.

The teacher, Mr. Greer, smirked. "So glad you could join us, Miss Wallace."

This was the Queen Bee. I would've staked my entire college career on it. But ten minutes into class and it was obvious that she was out of her element, so lost in the equations and formulas, I wondered why she was in this class in the first place. I thought about doing what my little brother had suggested and asking if she needed help. I wasn't a shy person by nature, but I was on guard and didn't put myself out there.

These Richies—*so* original—didn't want me there, so they could fend for themselves. I was here to get a world-class education and get the hell out. I left Emery Wallace to her struggles.

At the bell, my stomach was growling. In my hurry to make Dash his lunch, I hadn't had time to eat breakfast. Between all the gleaming trophy cases, I found a vending machine that sold nutrition bars, protein bars, and trail mix. No junk here. I found a bar that looked relatively palatable and fed the machine two dollars. The coils spun and the protein bar started its journey toward me. Then stopped.

"Oh, come on," I murmured under the cacophony of students passing by, a hundred conversations and laughter echoing off the walls. Two dollars was absolutely nothing to most of these students, but it was something to me. Everything was something to me.

I glanced around, then made a fist and gave the vending machine a small bang or two.

Nothing happened.

"Dammit."

"Ah, this one is temperamental," said a tenor voice beside me, wearing a British accent. "The moodiest of the lot."

I looked up.

Okay, so he's beautiful.

The thought slipped into my mind like a cat through an open door.

I was 5'6", but the guy towered over me, easily six feet and probably one of the most handsome guys I'd ever seen in person. The kind of handsome that made you forget your own name. He belonged in a Hollywood movie or TV show instead of standing in front of a busted vending machine.

I must've been staring because he grinned at me, a blinding smile of perfect white teeth. It hit me full force, warm and electric, like a spotlight. His light-brown skin was, in a word, flawless, and his rich dark-brown eyes were full of intelligence, and yet twinkling. *Twinkling.* I would never in my life use that word and expect to be taken seriously, but this guy's eyes *twinkled* with humor and more than a touch of arrogance. He wore jeans and a polo shirt that screamed *money*, as did his fade haircut—short on the sides, a mop of loose dark curls on top.

Definitely not a Bender. Not by a mile. Which meant he was a Richie. The opposite end of the social spectrum from me, which meant the social gulf between us was a mile wide.

No, Britain/Rhode Island-wide.

That didn't stop me from gawking at him like an idiot.

He eyed me, amused. "Like some help?"

"What?" I blinked. "Oh. The damn thing ate my money."

"You must be new or else you'd know to steer clear of Bandit. He's a thief."

"You name the vending machines?"

"Of course," he said, as if it were natural to name inanimate objects. "I've been here three years. This school has six vending machines, and I know all of their quirks and foibles."

Foibles. Good word.

"Bandit, as you've learned the hard way, loves to chew up your money."

The guy leaned in, drawing me into his aura of cologne, soap, and designer clothes—all of him expensive and clean but not overdone. Not like the clouds of Axe body spray the guys back home wore. His scent was…

Sexy. It's sexy and I must be losing my mind.

"But I'll let you in on a secret," he continued with a grin. "Bandit's a bit of a masochist. He likes when you rough him up a little."

"I'm sorry, what?"

"I'll show you. What were you after?"

"F-3."

He squinted, searching the rows of snacks.

I pointed. "That one."

"Ah, yes. Come now, Bandit, do not steal this lovely girl's quid. You want a bit of a beating, do you? Perhaps a good spanking?"

And now I was blushing. I never blushed.

He made a fist and pounded the glass over F-3, whacked the side, then grabbed the whole machine and gave it a good rattle. My protein bar was jostled loose, as well as another stuck bar from a different coil.

"There we go. Bandit always gives up the goods. You just have to know what he likes." He shot me a wink as he retrieved the bars. "There you are."

"Uh, thanks. I appreciate it."

He grinned, and *my God*, he had to have the most beautiful, blinding smile I'd ever seen in my life.

And that is the second time you thought something ridiculously hyperbolic about this guy in the space of three minutes.

He raised his brows expectedly.

"Oh, sorry," I stammered. "Did you want one?"

He chuckled. "No, but perhaps your name. I'm Orion Mercer."

"Harper Bennett."

He held out his hand. "A pleasure."

I juggled the two protein bars into my left hand, so I could shake his. Holy hell, this guy was scrambling my circuits as if he were shooting electric shocks directly into my brain.

"Harper," Orion mused. "That's not one I've heard before. Unique."

"Says the guy named Orion," I said, struggling to maintain *some* semblance of my own personality.

"My parents went on a tear with O names. Odin, Octavian…" He laid a hand on his broad chest. "Orion. Good thing they quit at three boys, or later siblings might've been Olaf. Octagon. Ozone…"

I laughed, and it sounded dangerously close to a giggle.

Girl, run.

"Well, anyway, thanks again," I said. "I better go. I have class," I added, like a dolt. As if he didn't.

"Of course. Nice to meet you, Harper Bennett."

"You too."

The bell rang. Not a normal school bell clang but the elegant tone of an elevator taking you to the penthouse. I stepped out of Orion Mercer's atmosphere, away from his expensive cologne and whatever made him, *him*, and strode down the hall feeling…disappointed?

Oh my God, you have got to get a grip.

Orion was exceptionally handsome and witty. Tall and built and, yes, the whole package, but it was no reason to lose my mind. I didn't lose my mind with guys. Ever.

You're a red-blooded human. You're allowed one moment of embarrassing girly girlness.

Even so, Orion was a Richie in this ecosystem, and I was a Bender. I couldn't even get out of the parking lot without being informed of my social status. The thought was sobering and kind of sad too. My last school in Pittsburgh might've been loud and crowded, but everyone looked out for each other.

Orion had probably only helped me out of pity—the poor Bender who couldn't afford to lose her snack money. The thought stung more than I wanted to admit.

He's beautiful but arrogant. No care in the world while you're carrying a hundred in your backpack. Focus. He's not for you.

English class came next, where the same beautiful girl from AP Calculus, Emery Wallace, sat beside me. Again.

Beautiful Richies in my face to exploit my inadequacies.

I brushed off the pitying thoughts. English had always been a favorite subject, and this teacher—Ms. Alvarez—was a winner, but I couldn't wait to get to third-period chemistry.

There, the classroom didn't have desks but twelve heavy two-person lab tables. I took one front and center, relishing the periodic tables on the walls, the shelves of beakers, test tubes, and Bunsen burners. Here was my future. My dream. It was where my career lay, and nothing could distract me.

Of course, the universe heard me and laughed its ass off.

I was pulling materials out of my bag when I smelled the cologne and heard the smooth British accent: "Harper Bennett. We meet again."

I looked up. Orion Mercer and his megawatt smile beamed down at me.

Shit.

Chapter 2

ORION

Harper's eyes flared in alarm. "What are you doing here?"

She hit me with the question like she wanted to shove me off my lab stool, but I didn't miss the little flicker of…something in her eyes. A tiny spark. And while I was used to girls *sparking* around me, usually I didn't spark back.

Usually.

I tapped my chin, pretending to consider it. "What am I doing here, what am I doing here… Ah, I remember now. I've been assigned third-period chemistry with Dr. Langford."

Harper faced forward stiffly. "I meant, why are you sitting next to me?"

"Shouldn't I?" I glanced around. "Too late now, love. The tables are full."

The word *love* made her blink.

"You're stuck with me," I continued. "And to avoid further nasty surprises, I'll share that I have History with Callister next, and then Advanced Piano with Wolfe to finish off the day."

"You're joking." Harper had beautiful brown eyes. They softened for a heartbeat, then hardened again, as if my class schedule was both the best and worst news she'd heard all day.

"No," I said. "If I were joking, I'd have said, a priest, a nun, and a whore walk into a bar…"

She shook her head, soft dark curls falling around her shoulders. "*I* also have History with Callister and Advanced Piano with Wolfe."

Despite the sour look on her face, the news made me surprisingly happy.

Spark, again.

"Do you?" I mused. "Isn't that lucky?"

"*Lucky* isn't the first word that comes to mind," she muttered.

"Not luck? So it's on purpose, then? Are you stalking me, Harper Bennett?" I heaved a dramatic sigh. "Story of my life."

She tried not to smile but failed. "You're a lot, aren't you?"

"I've been told."

"I can see why."

She faced forward again with a distinctly *conversation over* manner.

"Have I offended somehow? I seem to recall heroically securing not one, but *two* protein bars from Bandit's claws just a few hours ago."

She laughed a little—almost against her will, but her gaze was wary and untrusting.

"Sorry," she said. "It's my first day here, and I'm out of my element."

For a brief moment, her walls came down, and I saw a flash of uncertainty. Vulnerability. The kind I liked to pretend didn't exist in me whenever I stepped into a new classroom. When I didn't yet know the teacher's methods or moods, the workarounds I'd have to deploy, the shit I could get away with…

"I understand," I said.

Harper's expression softened. "You do?"

"Sure. I was a new face in these dusty old halls, once upon a time."

She smirked. "Dusty?"

"This'll be my fourth year. Anything can get old if you give it long enough. Where do you hail from?"

"I *hail* from Pittsburgh, Pennsylvania." She arched a brow. "Now I live in the *Bend*."

"Should I take offense?"

"Shouldn't you?" she countered. "I didn't get three steps away from my car before I was labeled a *Bender*."

I frowned. "Ridiculous, isn't it? An actual caste system in this day and age."

Harper organized her materials. "Your heroic disapproval from the heights of privilege is duly noted."

I grinned. "I like you, Bennett. You've got some fire to you. Some real spunk."

"Orion, do *not* say spunk."

"Why not?" I asked, the paragon of innocence, but when she'd said my name…

Spark in the prick, if we're being honest.

"Because," Harper said, "on this side of the Atlantic, it doesn't mean what you think it means."

"Perhaps I know *exactly* what it means."

She rolled her eyes, but color came rushing to her cheeks. "Are you always this crude to girls you just met?"

"You're right," I said. "That was crude. I suffer an acute inability to govern my tongue."

She narrowed her eyes at me, studying me. A wayward curl fell over her cheek, and I itched to brush it away.

"Fancy British accent aside, you've got quite the vocabulary for a high schooler."

I shrugged. "I read a lot. Always have. You?"

"Not as much as I'd like lately, but yes."

"Why not as much?"

"Well…" She toyed with her pencil and glanced at the door, as if looking for our still-absent teacher. "I have a brother, Dash. He's seven. My mother works two jobs, so I spend a lot of time taking care of him."

My facade slipped a wee bit at that. She was right; I did perch on the heights of privilege, and while I believed my fellow Richies were too hard on the Benders at school, I never much thought of their lives and struggles *beyond* the walls of Castle Hill Academy.

"And your father?" I asked, then waved my hands. "No, never mind. That's personal. See? I *am* capable of behaving myself. But I promise I won't make a habit out of it."

Another laugh escaped Harper, sounding rusty. "Here's a British word for you: incorrigible."

"Yes! Incorrigible. Intractable. Irredeemable. If only there were someone who could put me in my place." I wagged my brows. "Or your place? I'm not picky."

"Oh my God." She covered her eyes with one hand.

"I was quite nearly well-behaved, wasn't I?" I sighed. "But I *blew* it."

She was outright laughing now. "Stop."

I didn't want to stop. I was used to making people laugh. The sound of it wasn't uncommon music to my ears, usually as a deflection or diversion. But Harper's laugh…

I might be addicted already.

From the sound alone, I knew she didn't laugh often. Her heart-shaped face was made for it, but from her first defensive glance at the vending machine, I knew she was more accustomed to frowns and tension. Her large eyes were soft around the edges but hard within. She was on her guard. Defenses up.

I could relate. While I had a different set of defenses, I recognized a fellow soldier when I saw one.

Maybe if we shared war stories…

"So sorry, so sorry," Dr. Langford said, breezing in at last. "It's rude of me to be this late on our first day but…" He heaved both a sigh and a briefcase onto his own big lab desk. "Hello, class."

The students offered enthusiastic hellos. Dr. Ian Langford was the most popular professor in the STEM department, if not the entire school. In his mid-thirties, he was handsome, friendly, and *almost* as witty as me. Everybody loved him.

He scanned the group. "Wow. You may have heard I say this to every class, but don't believe it. *You* are the most attractive, and obviously the most brilliant, group of students I have this year. I can tell already."

Appreciative laughs. I glanced at Harper, whose brows were furrowed.

I leaned toward her. "Not charmed?"

She shrugged. "Chemistry is what I want to do for a living. I want a serious education from a serious teacher."

"He's the best, don't worry."

"If you say so."

"Before we begin," Dr. Langford said, "I have a major announcement. This year, Castle Hill Academy has partnered with major universities, both at home and abroad, for a very special contest that has been years in the making."

Harper sat up straighter.

"It's called the Novus Prize for Scientific Innovation, or NoSci. The winning student must come up with a science project of epic proportions. Something original, innovative, and groundbreaking. First prize is twenty-five thousand dollars cash and priority status in the admissions pool for universities such as MIT, Harvard, Stanford, Caltech, NYU, Oxford, Cambridge, the Imperial College of London… Shall I go on?"

I noticed Harper gripping the edge of the table, her fingers white.

Shit, bollocks, fuck.

She really wanted this. She might *need* this, and I… did not. But as one of three heirs to the Mercer Chem dynasty, my parents would expect me not only to enter this contest but win.

Given their pull with the Academy, a win might be all but guaranteed.

They don't have to know about it. I'll hope the deadline passes before they get wind of it across the pond.

Doubtful given the close tabs Father kept on me, but worth a shot.

"I'm on the panel of judges for the NoSci prize," Dr. Langford was saying, "so if you want to start sending me your bribes now, I'll post my office hours after class."

The class laughed. Harper did not.

"The contest will consist of three steps, the first being the most perilous," Dr. Langford continued, holding for dramatic effect. "You must sign up."

More laughter.

"Step two: Submit your entry. Step three: If your entry is chosen to continue, you will present your project before the judges in April. I'll put email links for more information, full contest rules, requirements, and deadlines in our class notes on your iPads." Dr. Langford gave us all a sly smile. "Now, down to business. I hope you chose your seats wisely because the person sitting next to you is going to be your lab partner for the entire rest of the year."

I solemnly offered my hand to Harper. "Congratulations."

She smacked me away without looking.

"Careful, Bennett," I whispered. "You keep flirting with me like that and I'll think you're in love with me already."

"You wish."

I rolled my pen across my knuckles, a small smile on my lips.

"May I have a volunteer?" Dr. Langford asked.

Out of twenty-four students, twenty hands went up.

Langford grinned. "I love your enthusiasm. You, sir," he said, picking a student. "First lesson in my class: Never volunteer for anything."

Everyone laughed as a student came up the aisle only to be loaded up with heavy chemistry textbooks. He plunked them down on our desks one at a time.

"All of the information contained in these extraordinarily heavy textbooks is also in your iPads," Langford said. "But these are for you to take home in case of technological malfunctions...and our icebreaking assignment today. Introduction, page three."

I stiffened. Harper pulled her book toward her and opened it to the intro. I left my book untouched.

"Most everything we do in chemistry begins at the atomic level." Langford gestured at the huge periodic table on one wall. "I thought it'd be fun to begin by examining how our understanding of atoms and molecules evolved over time. Please read the paragraph on the different atomic models as described by five different scientists."

Shit, bollocks, fuck again.

"Your icebreaker assignment is to read how each scientist imagined atomic structure and then sketch a model based on their descriptions. Please label your work with a brief description." Langford glanced at the wall clock. "You have ten minutes. Go."

When I didn't move, Harper glanced at me. "Ready?"

"Always."

"You sure?" She offered a tight smile. "Tick tock, partner."

Translation: Hurry the fuck up.

Feigning a bored sigh, I opened the book.

Day One. Let the games begin.

The paragraph was short, no more than four lines. I set about the arduous task of forcing my ADHD brain to stay focused on the letters, building them into words, and then building the words into sentences. The letters blurred and slid sideways, like fish beneath the water's surface. I could catch their shape, but there weren't enough of them to build meaning, so I gave up. I rested my cheek on my fist, pretending to nap while the tension in my gut coiled tight.

Like the rest of the class, Harper was done reading in moments. Every pair broke out in discussion.

"How do you want to split it up?" Harper asked. "Do you—Orion?"

"Hm?"

"We have only a few minutes. I'll take Dalton and Thomson. You take Rutherford and Bohr. We'll collab on Schrödinger."

"How about you read the paragraph to me, and I sketch?"

"Why?"

"Perhaps because I like listening to your lovely voice?"

She shot me a withering stare, and I could feel that whatever little bit of something was between us—that little spark—would snuff out if I wasn't careful.

"I'm a crack visualizer and can sketch like a pro," I said. "You label."

"That doesn't give me much to do."

"My handwriting is like that of a serial killer, and I don't want to frighten you so early in our partnership."

Another joke. Another shield. Another shot fired in my endless battle.

Harper looked about to protest. I clenched my jaw. "Tick tock, *partner*."

"Okay, fine. But sketch fast."

As Harper quietly read the paragraph out loud, her voice turned the chaos in my head into pictures I could actually use—a bowling ball, a muffin, a single nucleus, a solar system, a cloud—and I drew what I saw.

"Your sketches are amazing," Harper said, "but they don't have to be this good. We're running out of time."

"Two minutes," Langford said from the front of the classroom, as if to confirm.

"Relax, love," I drawled, keeping the irritation out of my voice. "It's too early in the day to be this intense."

I slid the drawings to Harper, and her eyes widened in shock at the detail. Then she got busy labeling with something like panic, as if this were a final exam and not a meaningless assignment.

"Label," Harper said with urgency. She tapped two of my drawings without looking up. "I can't get to them all."

"'Fraid not," I said. "All that sketching wore me out."

"Can you please be serious for one minute?"

"Possibly. But only for a minute."

"Orion."

But it was too late.

"Time."

Langford collected our work and gave them a once-over.

"Wow, Harper and Orion. The sketches are worthy of the Louvre. Conceptually brilliant. Too bad I have no idea what they represent."

He moved on, and I could feel Harper's exasperation buzzing beside me.

"Easy, love. It's just a—"

"Don't *love* me." She stopped, her cheeks pink again. "I mean… You know what I mean."

She gave me the silent treatment the rest of class, which made my bloody skin itch. When the bell rang, she abruptly gathered her things and strode out. I followed, feeling guilty for giving her a hard time while the old anger and exhaustion boiled below. I was so damn tired of this dance.

"Harper, hold on," I called.

She turned around, inhaling to steady herself. "Look, chemistry is my life. We're stuck together for the entire year. My grade is tied to yours, so I need you to take it seriously."

Her tone was calm and collected but beneath was fear. Pressure. Survival. It glinted in her dark eyes. I recognized it because I had it too. A different shade and flavor, but a similar, incessant anxiety to succeed despite the mountain we had to drag behind us.

"I can pull my weight," I told her. "My father is CEO of Mercer Chemicals. Perhaps you've heard of us?"

Her brows shot up. "Am I supposed to be impressed?"

I gritted my teeth. I'd meant to reassure, not brag. Now I was just annoyed too.

"*Yes*," I said. "My background is in chemistry. My brothers are at Cambridge as we speak, learning the trade, and I'll eventually be there too. Point being, I know what I'm doing and like to have a bit of fun while doing it. No harm in that, is there?"

I tossed her my trademark grin that helped me charm my way out of dodgy situations.

Harper saw right through it.

"Orion, you may have everyone wrapped around your finger with that smile of yours, but I don't have time for games. My father is CEO of Walked Out the Door, and I have no direct line to Cambridge or any other college. I can't afford to fuck around, so do me a favor and cut the BS, okay?"

Four years at the Academy and no one had dared speak to me like that. And she had no idea what she was asking. How much BS was required for me to survive this place. Heat crawled up the back of my neck, and my jaw clenched.

Harper shook her head. "I'm sorry. I don't mean to come off like a stony bitch, but I'm under a lot of pressure. I don't expect you to understand, but—"

My eyes flared, a sudden, shocking flood of anger killing my smile. "Oh, is that a fact?"

"Yes." She crossed her arms. "Unless you have something real you'd like to share? Or just more credentials? Maybe your bank statement?"

There it was. The biggest spark of all. Not just attraction, but a flare threatening to light a dark place no one ventured into. Including me.

But what should I tell her? The truth?

Not going to happen.

I pushed it all down, found my smirk. "Apologies. I'll make sure to be on my best behavior from now on. Apparently having a personality is overrated."

The moment the words left me, I wanted to snatch them back. Hurt flashed across her face, and her jaw tightened.

"Sorry to disappoint," she said in a low voice, then turned on her heel and walked away.

"Well, that was bloody brilliant," I muttered and rubbed my eyes. "Ace job. Truly."

If I'd been in the boys' restroom, I might've ruined another mirror. Instead, I took a few deep breaths and waited until all the emotions sank back down beneath the surface. Because letting them out did no bloody good, did it? You rocked the boat, you said stupid shit you regretted, and for what? Over some pointless sketches for a meaningless assignment?

And anyway, that girl is wound up tight and nothing but a headache. Forget her.

But I knew, even then, that was impossible.

At lunch I sat with my mates: Emery Wallace and her boyfriend Tucker Hill. Rhett Calloway and his girlfriend Aria Kingston—who looked more like vampire siblings than boyfriend and girlfriend—Gideon Foster, and

Elowen Blake. Elowen was a pretty blond whose expression turned borderline predatory as soon as she saw me. She'd been pursuing me since the end of last year, and I'd considered giving in. She was beautiful, popular, and had made it abundantly clear I'd never want for her *affection*.

But after the fiery introduction to Harper Bennett, Elowen—and everyone else at the table—seemed like characters in a book I'd read one too many times.

"Orion, my man," Tucker said. We clasped hands, and he pulled me to him for a hard thump on the back. "Ready for crew tryouts this Saturday?"

Of course I am, I wanted to snap. *I'm always ready. My entire life is being ready.*

I flashed him a grin. "You know it."

He grinned back. "Fuck yeah."

Truthfully, crew was one of the best things I had going at CHA. Being out on the water, the exertion of rowing, the teamwork, the freedom from all the mental strain of school… It shut off the noise of grades and the expectations of everything I was supposed to become.

And piano?

My pulse quickened just thinking about it, but whether out of fear or excitement, I couldn't tell. I'd avoided the Arts Wing for three years until this year, when my schedule allowed room for an elective. Piano was a door I'd closed on purpose, a version of myself I'd buried, and now I was opening it again. Why? Would I even know how to play anymore?

But even as expert as I was at burying feelings, I knew the answer to that. And I only had to make it through one more class before I'd be sitting at a baby grand.

With Harper…

"It's fucking ridiculous," Rhett snarled, cutting into my thoughts. "Why is Coach making *us* try out for crew if we were on the team last year?"

"To ensure we haven't slacked off all summer, mate," I said, half hoping Rhett had done just that. Technically, he was a friend, but I also suspected he'd knife me in the back if it came down to him or me getting a seat.

"No worries," Tucker said. "There's nobody new this year that's good enough to steal a seat from our crew."

"Hm," I said noncommittally, glancing around the cafeteria.

I spotted Harper's striped dress immediately. I'd just vowed to keep everything still and calm, and yet I itched to go talk to her. To set off another round of bangers and fireworks, explosives and pyrotechnics. To have a different conversation from the one I'd been having with this group for the last three years. Perhaps one that blew down walls, and plumbed the depths until it found something…

Real.

I looked around the table. None of these friends knew the first damn thing about me. I was one of the most popular guys in school, with no shortage of female attention. A "manwhore," as the Americans liked to say. Everyone knew my name, yet I was close to no one. They only knew the fun guy who made them laugh, not the guy with the messed-up brain and crushing loneliness…

Shut it. You have everything. No one likes a whining wanker.

I found myself scanning the cafeteria again, but Harper was gone.

"Two more classes to make a better first impression," I muttered.

But I arrived late to history. She was in front. I was in back, sitting next to the pretty actress, Tessa Carlyle, whom I began flirting with immediately. Like a program I couldn't override.

Strike two, Mercer.

I hustled to piano class—almost ran, actually—but arrived to find the dozen or so others in the class gathered around the door and a messy, scrawled note that was taped to it. Professor Wolfe had cancelled due to "unforeseen circumstances."

Disappointment sank sharp teeth into me. This new professor, Ezra Wolfe, was rumored to be someone famous too. Legendary, even. But perhaps the delay was for the best. It was day one, and I was already bloody beat.

I caught Harper's eye as she turned to go. She went one way while I went another. When I turned to look over my shoulder, heat swept over the back of my neck again, this time pleasant. Wanted. Her eyes flared. She quickened her step and rounded a corner, out of sight.

Strike three.

"It was lovely to meet you, Harper Bennett," I murmured.

Back at my two-person apartment in Atlas Hall—the international dormitories—my roommate remained absent as well. I'd been told his name was Easton Locke and that he was a junior, but I'd yet to see him in the flesh.

Maybe he's an actual vampire, currently sleeping under his bed.

All I knew of him was that he played guitar and rode a motorcycle. This I deduced by using my exemplary powers of observation: He'd left an instrument case and a motorcycle helmet on his side of the bedroom.

I opened my chemistry book and used my iPhone's Spoken Content function to read Chapter 1 out loud. I committed all of it to memory, then all of Chapter 2 for good measure.

I was exhausted by the time I'd finished. But Harper needed me to not let her down, so I wouldn't.

Chapter 3

HARPER

"So? How is it?" Vanessa Gerard asked over the phone. "Gold toilets and a personal butler to walk you to class?"

"Not quite, but you're not far off either," I told my best friend back home. I tapped my pen and looked out the window from my desk. Only a few scattered lights from my neighborhood. The forest was quiet and dark. Lonely. "I miss you guys."

"Please." Vanessa snorted. "We'd all give our right tit to go to the gleaming castle on the hill."

She sounded bored. Or pissed off. Almost eager to get off the phone, and we'd been talking for a grand total of four minutes.

"I'm serious," I said. "Yeah, it's a great opportunity, but—"

"Great opportunity? Bitch, you practically have a golden ticket to MIT or NYU or wherever the hell you want to go. The rest of us are wallowing in the dirt, hoping for community college at best."

I swallowed a sudden rock in my throat. "I thought you were happy for me."

"No, I'm sorry. I'm PMSing like a fiend. I am happy for you, Harp. We all are. Just jealous as fuck. Anyway, tell me all the things. Any hot guys? Any hot, *rich* guys?"

On cue, Orion Mercer's face floated in front of my vision.

"I suppose."

"Rich as hell, I bet," Vanessa said. "Way better than the scuzzy guys hanging out at the E-Z Stop parking lot." The bitterness was back in her voice again. "Any prospects?"

"I don't know. There's this one guy who's sort of infuriating—"

"Oh shit. Speaking of E-Z Stop, I promised Micah and the gang I'd meet them in ten. I gotta go. Call me later, okay?"

"Oh. Sure." Before I could say another word, the line went dead. "Okay, good talk."

I stared at my phone, part of me wishing I could crawl into it. Go back to Pittsburgh and hang out with my old friends. The guys too, but that had to be the homesickness talking, because I'd sworn them off forever. Or until I could have something meaningful and real, which felt like the same thing.

I'd never had a real boyfriend. I'd been too busy studying and taking care of Dash and *doing life* to be able to focus on a boyfriend and so had only awkward, uncomfortable, fumbling encounters in backseats or hangouts in parking lots. No dates, only hookups. Doing things—doing *all the things*—because it seemed like that's what I was supposed to be doing. Not necessarily because I wanted to. No real connections. Never rounding emotional bases, only physical ones.

Never again.

I'd compromised myself one too many times and vowed not to do *casual* ever again. The next time I was with a guy, it was going to be serious.

Not that I had time for serious. Not with the NoSci contest dropped in my lap and the schoolwork and the pressure I was under.

I'd been hoping to talk to Vanessa about it all, and maybe about Orion too. But I guess those would all sound like first-world problems. I may as well have been a Richie in her eyes.

Maybe she's right. This is a tremendous opportunity, and I should suck it up and get to work.

So I bent my head over my desk and got to work.

The next morning, I parked in the student lot. No sooner did I step out of my car than a group of seniors—three guys and a girl—surrounded me. My heart clanged in my chest, but I inhaled deep and lifted my chin.

"Hey, Bender," one guy said. Big, beefy, blond. "This your sweet ride?"

"Obviously," I replied.

He and a dark-haired guy with black eyes and an equally wicked-looking girl hanging off his arm grinned. "We wanted to let you know that this is our parking lot. The Bender lot is down there."

He pointed to a rocky patch of dirt on the other side of a chain-link fence where the school's industrial arts and stagecraft classes dumped their old lumber and metal. My cheeks burned.

"I'll try to remember," I said, pushing past them.

"First warning, Bender," the big blond called after me. "Park here again and there will be consequences."

I ignored him and the snickering that chased me into the Academy.

Forget it. They're losers who have nothing better to do than hang around a parking lot being dickheads.

Still.

It was ten minutes into Calculus before the knots in my gut loosened. Beside me, Emery Wallace was drowning in derivative equations. Given the shit I'd just taken, I was inclined to let her, but…

You're not doing so hot either, you know.

Vanessa was going to stop returning my calls and texts, the connection between us attenuating until it snapped. I could use a friendly face. Some kindness. Who said Richies didn't too? I could cross enemy lines. What did I have to lose? *Be the change*, and all that.

I leaned over. "Hi, I'm Harper. If you ever need help—?"

"I'm good, thanks," Emery snapped back, fixing me with a syrupy sweet smile that didn't touch her eyes.

Okay, then.

My cheeks burned as if I'd been slapped. My eyes wanted to sting too, but I didn't let them. No fucking way.

And because no good deed goes unpunished, when we left class, a bunch of her friends fell in step behind me like a wake of vultures, picking apart my clothes, my hair, and the fact I was a Bender.

Emery picked at me too.

Fuck them, I thought lifting my head up high. *Fuck all these Richies if they think they're going to get the better of me.*

But goddamn. This was day two.

"You've been through worse," I muttered, remembering ten-year-old me trying to drag my drunk mother off the kitchen floor to put her to bed. Surely I could handle my best friend ghosting me with a side of bullying. I was a "tough cookie" after all.

"You're a tough cookie, Harper," Mom would say after a rough night. "That's what I love about you."

But that's the thing. Being resilient is overrated. I don't know anyone who *wants* to be tough. I'd have liked to have been a soft little girl playing with her dolls, but you make the best with what you have.

In English, Ms. Alvarez had us analyze a poem by Sylvia Plath—"Mad Girl's Love Song." A poem about a boy who seems so perfect, the speaker must've made him up inside her head. One who didn't seem real.

Don't go there… I warned my brain, but it conjured up Orion Mercer. Because of course it did. This boy with a smile that turned my insides to mush and who slid into my thoughts like a burglar.

"A bandit," I murmured.

Emery said something quite beautiful and profound about the poem. It nearly made me soften to her—she obviously had a lot going on inside she was keeping locked away.

The old me would have left her alone, but I was raw and bleeding and not going to keep taking any shit.

I was a tough cookie, after all.

I leaned over to Emery and whispered, "That was really good."

"Thanks—"

"Too bad you're a total fake."

As soon as I said the words, I wanted to snatch them back. They didn't make me feel any better about being mocked. I'd only spread more bad vibes, like a sickness.

If Dash had heard me…

Shame burned my cheeks. I could do better. *Be* better than that, and not let this school dig roots down into me and plant more rotten fruit.

The Academy had a ton of student-run clubs and extracurriculars that would all look good on a college application. At midmorning break, I went to one of the many patios and found the booth for the Math & Physics Club. It was manned by a handsome guy with dark hair and green eyes. Also a Bender, if I had to guess by his plain clothes and worn-out shoes.

"Dean Yearwood, secretary," he said, introducing himself.

"Harper Bennett."

"Pleased to meet you, Harper," he said, handing me a clipboard. "Answer me these questions three."

That rang a bell. Sure enough, the last question was the quote from *Monty Python and the Holy Grail.* I answered the other two correctly.

"Congrats," Dean said, shaking my hand. "Welcome to the Math and Physics Club."

"Thanks," I said, relief flooding me. As if I'd been shipwrecked, clinging to a piece of driftwood until Dean hauled me onto dry land.

"New here?" he asked. "How are you liking our humble school so far?"

"To be honest, it's a lot."

"I get it. It can feel overwhelming, especially for those of us not quite as *privileged* as our fellow students."

Dean's gaze went a group of Richies, Orion among them, gathered on the deck, talking and laughing. Orion had at least three girls hanging on his every word. His smile was as brilliant as ever, his laugh quick and easy, just as it had been with me.

Why wouldn't it be? I wasn't anything but a new recipient of his charm. With Orion was the big blond guy, the sinister-looking darker guy, and his girlfriend from the parking lot this morning.

So he's with that crowd. Good to know.

I used the info like ammunition. Or fortifications against him for chemistry and history class, and piano, if the teacher ever showed up.

"They're practically blinding, aren't they?" Dean asked with a laugh, and I realized I was staring.

I jerked my gaze away. "I almost wonder why they let us Benders in here at all," I said. "Oh, shit, sorry. I don't mean to presume—"

Dean chuckled. "It's okay. I'm a Bender through and through." His eyes dimmed slightly. "I may be the bendiest of them all. But we're all one big happy family."

As if to illustrate his point, Orion's group of Richies caught sight of Dean and waved. I quickly looked away.

Dean waved back. "That's Tucker and Orion, my boys on the crew. Both Big Five."

"Big Five?"

"Their families give the most money to the Academy. Kings of the school." Dean smiled. "But they're good guys. Most everyone is, once you get to know them. Give it time, and you'll feel at home."

"If you say so."

I must've sounded more pathetic than I meant to, because Dean put a hand on my arm.

"Come find me at lunch," he said kindly. "You can meet the rest of the club, and you're welcome to sit with us anytime. There's safety in numbers."

I smiled gratefully. "Thanks. I'll do that."

"And you're coming to the bonfire this Saturday, yeah? It's the first big social event of the season. The whole school will be there."

"Not sure that's the selling point you think it is."

Dean laughed. "Castle Hill Lighthouse. Eight p.m. Give me your number and I'll text you the details."

Dean was handsome, sweet, funny. Perfect boyfriend material. As we exchanged numbers, I waited for a spark of attraction to ignite and drag my fixation away from Orion Mercer. But the energy between us remained stubbornly brother and sisterly.

But I did it, Dash. I made a friend.

"A volunteer?" Dr. Langford said, holding up a cardboard box in one hand and a list in the other. "Who would like to get acquainted with the chemistry storage room, just down the hall—code 353—and refill some of our classroom supplies?"

Several hands went up. Mine was not one of them. Storage rooms, in my experience, tended to be small, dark, cramped places with no moving air. Hard pass.

"Harper Bennett," Langford said. "If you'd be so kind."

Shit.

But the last thing I was going to do was show weakness, not so early in the game at a place like this. Get in, get out.

Not to mention, here was an opportunity to extract myself from Orion Mercer's orbit. From the moment I'd arrived in class, I was inundated with all that was *him*, and I wondered just how in the hell I was supposed to survive an entire year like this.

I took the box from Langford and strode out of the classroom. The storage room was clearly marked, and I plugged in the keycode and propped open the aluminum door. It started to slide shut under the heavy weight, but the door stand held.

Get in, get out.

The room was small and cramped, lined floor to ceiling with non-chemical chemistry supplies, stored in neatly labeled shelves. A bulky, counter-like table stood in the center. My pulse quickened, and I took a deep breath.

"Nope. You're fine. You can do this."

I studied the shelves for a second and then realized…

"Forget something, Bennett."

I nearly jumped out of my skin. Orion leaned in the doorframe, arms crossed, Langford's list dangling from one hand.

"You ran out of there too fast, love."

"You scared the crap out of me," I said. "And stop calling me that."

"Apologies…*love*."

Orion pushed off the wall and hopped onto the table, long legs dangling. Today he wore black jeans, boots, and a cream-colored hoodie with a black zipper. I didn't know designer labels, but my instincts told me the hoodie alone probably cost more than my entire closet.

He looks like a model…

I clenched my teeth, as if that could shut up my inner voice, and glared at him.

"Well? Are you going to help or not? I'd like to get this over with."

"What's the rush?" Orion said. "We have a break from class. Let's enjoy the dim ambience of the storage room."

"No, thanks. I don't like it here."

"What's not to like? Just you, me…" He glanced around. "Graduated cylinders for days…"

Outside the door, footsteps, a man's voice grumbling under his breath, and then the door shut with a *thunk*.

"What…?" I rushed at the door and pushed at the long bar handle, but the door wouldn't budge.

You've got to be kidding.

I spun around. "Did you do that?" I demanded, glaring at Orion, who was in the middle of the room, nowhere near the door. Panic was already making me stupid.

He frowned. "Clearly…*no*. But I'm not mad about it. Trapped together. It's fate."

"Don't start." I gave the door handle another shake.

"I'm not starting anything." Orion leaned back on the counter and shot me a knowing grin. "But I'm here if you change your mind."

I ignored him and took a deep breath against the tightness in my chest. The room was small. The air thin…

"It's fine," I murmured. "We just have to wait for Langford to realize we've been gone too long. A few minutes, tops."

"Or," Orion said, "we could make the most of this time together."

I rolled my eyes and snatched the list out of his hand. "It's cute you'd think I'd call that an upside. Let's get the required supplies, as instructed."

He tilted his head, cocky smile dialed up to eleven. "You know, most girls at this school would be thrilled to be locked in a room with me."

"Is that a fact?"

"That *is* a fact."

"Good for them."

I set about what I came to do, putting beakers, boxes of test tubes, and filaments into the box and trying to ignore Orion's *presence*. His charisma was so strong, it practically glowed around him like an aura. Against my will, I could see *exactly* why most girls would want to be locked in a room with him. Orion was also keeping the smallness of this room from feeling menacing, and so I was glad too.

Not that he needed to know that.

"Are you going to sit there, or are you going to help?" I jerked my chin at a shelf. "Clamps, stands, stoppers. Go."

Orion turned to look at the labeled shelves, his brows coming together. "How about I hold the box and you fill it with aforementioned items."

I sighed and set the box on the counter, then slid it toward him. "If it gets you to do actual work..."

"Careful, Bennett." He grinned. "I could get used to you bossing me around."

"Oh, really? You want to be treated like the vending machine?"

"Depends," he said, eyes *twinkling*. "Will there be spanking? Then, yes."

"Ugh. You're impossible."

Orion held the box, while I filled it with the supplies from Langford's list. I was acutely conscious of his nearness again, his gaze on me. Worse, I didn't mind.

"So, Harper Bennett. Tell me your life story."

And then the lights went out.

A small *tick* plunged the room into black, and my chest seized. Instantly, I was ten years old, in the closet, on the floor. Dash—barely a toddler—was huddled against me, his face buried in my side, my arms wrapped around him tight while some drunken monster raged outside…

"Harper?" Orion's voice was empty of its playful swagger. "Hey. Talk to me."

I swallowed hard. "I—I'm fine."

"Like hell."

I heard the rustle of cardboard as he put the box somewhere, and then his hand was on my arm.

"Come here."

I took a step closer, my pulse pounding between my ears. The dark was like a huge hand wrapping me in its grip and squeezing.

"I can't see…I can't breathe," I whispered.

"It's okay. I'm here." Orion's hand on my arm slid down to clasp my hand in his. "We're fine. The lights are on a timer. You're not in danger, okay? Give me a second…"

I heard another rustle, and then he turned on the flashlight function on his phone. He set his phone face up on the table, close to us. In the sharp white light of the flashlight, his face was a mask of concern, his eyes locked on mine.

"Breathe, Harper. In…and out."

I nodded rapidly, but my breath was stuck in my throat. "I'm s-sorry. I don't—I don't like small spaces."

"You don't have to be sorry," he said. "Just breathe. And sit down. Here…"

He helped me up onto the counter and then hopped up to sit beside me. I realized I was clutching his hand like a vise.

"Sorry," I murmured, but didn't loosen my death grip either.

"Stop saying that. Breathe. In…and out."

He repeated that several more times while his thumb drew small, steady circles across the back of my hand. I concentrated on his voice, the rhythmic feel of his touch, and the fist in my chest began to unclench.

"Better?"

I swallowed. "Yeah. Better."

"Good," he said. Gently. Softly. "Keep breathing. In… and out."

I did as he said, and he breathed with me. My grip on his hand loosened, but I didn't let go, and neither did he.

"This can't be safe," I said, still taking deep breaths. "What if there was a fire?"

"If a fire alarm goes off, every door in the school automatically unlocks," Orion said. He smiled at me, not flirty or cocky, but reassuring, taking my mind off the dark. "If you really want to get out of here, we could light the box on fire and use the list to get it started. Serve Langford right for taking so bloody long."

I nodded gratefully. "Good idea. This much security feels like overkill."

"Right? You'd think I'd know better by now."

"You've been in this situation before?"

He cleared his throat, brows raised meaningfully, and I chuckled, despite everything.

"Oh, right," I said. "You and the hordes of girls lining up to be locked in storage rooms with you."

"There she is," Orion said, giving my hand a squeeze. "Thought I'd lost you for a second."

I rolled my eyes, but warmth flooded me, as if in a conduit from him to me, and I was acutely conscious of all the ways we were close: shoulder to shoulder, his chest rising and falling in concert with mine, his steady hand like an anchor I clutched to keep the panic from running away with me. The Ghosts of Drunken Rampages Past faded away.

"I'm sure this isn't how you wanted to spend your first days of school. Helping the new girl wage war with vending machines and being stuck in storage closets."

"I don't mind being stuck with you, Harper."

I looked over to see his dark eyes watching me, still no trace of the flirty arrogance of earlier.

I scoffed weakly. "That's because you're an *incorrigible* flirt."

"I *am* a tremendous flirt," he admitted. "But I don't hold just anyone's hand."

My eyes widened, and Orion must've thought my panic was coming back for round two.

His hand tightened around mine. "We're okay, Harper. I've got you."

I've got you.

No one had said that to me before. No one had offered me what those words meant: safety, security, protection. I'd been the bulwark for so long, holding Dash and sometimes even my mother under whatever meager shelter I could provide, and now here was Orion, providing me the smallest taste of what it felt to be the one sheltered…

With sudden shock, the door scraped open and the blinding fluorescents came back on.

"I thought so," Langford said, his brows wagging. "Naughty, naughty, you two."

My cheeks went scarlet. I let go of Orion's hand and jumped off the counter.

"Someone shut the door on us," I said, my skin itching at Langford's knowing grin.

"Ah, yes. Likely victims of Mr. Blandford," he said. "His nemesis is an open door, and in twenty years, he's never bothered to check for occupants. Come on."

Langford shot Orion a wink I didn't like and held the door for us while we finished gathering the supplies. Back in the classroom, he gestured dramatically at Orion and me.

"I have found the lovebirds."

The students laughed and applauded, and my cheeks burned hotter as we took our seats.

"It's all right, love," Orion said under his breath. "He's a jokester."

"It's inappropriate," I whispered back.

"Nah. It's all in good fun."

Dr. Langford gave us the day's lab instructions. I tried to listen but kept glancing at Orion sitting beside me. His usual grin was back in its place. He'd donned his King of the World slouch, and his pen spun in his fingers, all of it like a costume.

He felt me staring. "Yes?"

"The Orion who helped me through that panic doesn't feel like the same Orion sitting beside me right now."

The smile tilted. "What do you mean? There's only one *me*, love." He cleared his throat and nodded at today's lesson. "Shall we?"

Maybe he was right. Maybe he was just really good in a crisis. But as we got to work, the warmth I'd felt in the storage room slipped away by degrees until, by the end of class, there was none left.

Chapter 4

ORION

The Orion who helped me through that panic doesn't feel like the same Orion sitting next to me right now.

The bell rang, and Harper gathered her stuff and went out. I watched her go, a strange ache in my chest. A nostalgia for the storage closet. I wished we were back there, locked away from the rest of the bloody school for a hundred more hours. In there, in the dark, I'd felt…

Honest.

My phone buzzed in my jacket pocket. I pulled it out and a grin spread over my face.

"Odin," I said, heading toward the cafeteria for lunch. "How badly do you miss me? A lot or a whole lot?"

"I cry every day," my big brother replied, but his voice

sounded a little tight under the din of the crowded CHA hallways. "I know you're in class now, but do you have a minute? It's about Octavian."

"Give me a second."

I exited the nearest door, into the coppery September afternoon and found a bench overlooking the Narragansett Bay, where white-winged sailboats and gleaming yachts cut wakes on the deep-blue water.

"What is it?"

"Don't mean to alarm you," Odin said. "I wondered if you'd heard from him lately."

"Have I communicated with a member of our family?" I said dryly. "It's not a holiday or birthday. Whyever would I do that?"

"Bloody facts," Odin agreed.

He and I were the only ones to text or call somewhat regularly, and that meant once a month, if that. It just wasn't in the Mercer blood to reach out. We'd been trained well to keep to ourselves.

"But why do you ask?"

"He's acting strangely," Odin said. "Not at all himself."

"Drugs?"

"I don't think so. Maybe. He's jumpy and flies off the handle at the smallest slight, and that's not like him."

"Definitely not," I said. Our middle brother was a quiet, almost shy fellow. I'd never seen him get upset, even as a wee kid. "But you're at uni with him while I'm over here. I'm not going to be a good judge."

"I know. I just wondered if he'd called you and told you something. Anything."

"No," I said. "Have Mum or Father noticed a change?"

"I'll say. Tav demanded Father up his weekly allowance. Threw a fit about it until Father agreed. It was surreal."

Tension coiled in my stomach. "I hate to say it, but that sounds like drugs."

"I know, but my gut tells me it's something else. He doesn't look strung out and his grades are exceptional as always. Anyway, reach out to him, would you? Check in and see if you can't pry something loose?"

"Of course."

"Thanks. Oh, hey, I know it's early days of senior year, but how are things?"

The usual struggles, headaches, stress. And one girl like a light in a dark cavern…

"Fine," I said.

"Right. Talk soon."

We ended the call and I pulled up the text thread with Octavian. To my shame, the last time we'd spoken was back in June.

Hey, Tav. Just checking in.

Too obvious. Octavian was a genius who'd graduated from CHA two years early. I backspaced and tried again.

My roommate is a motorcycle-riding vampire. Did Camby give you a werewolf? Let's compare.

No answer.

I sighed, put my phone away, and added worry for my brother to the teetering stack of stress, then trudged my way to world history.

Professor Callister was a stiff, no-nonsense teacher with a gray beard and gray suit to match, who—much to my horror—cold-called students to read aloud from the text. I sat through class, flirting with Tessa Carlyle and pretending I wasn't about to puke. This wasn't history, it was *The Hunger Games*, and any second now, I'd be called as tribute.

Halfway through class, my number came up.

"Mr. Mercer. Top of page forty-seven, please. Royal Commission on the Employment of Children…"

Shit, bollocks, fuck.

I leaned back in my chair, spinning my pen over my knuckles, and pretended I hadn't heard him. When the silence stretched, I glanced around. "Sorry, me?"

Callister frowned. "Unless there's another Orion Mercer in the class?"

"Oh no, Professor. I'm one of a kind."

The class chuckled appreciatively. Callister sighed. "Page forty-seven."

"Right." I looked down at the text and tried to focus. The words danced on the page, and my brain stumbled along, three steps behind.

"The...uh...Confession—sorry, the Commission established..."

Humiliation burned my skin.

Nope. Try again.

My pen spun as I scanned the paragraph for context clues. Seconds ticked by. The silence grew uncomfortable, then excruciating, but I got the gist. Barely.

"Mr. Mercer?"

I tossed my pen down and sat back. "Basically, they made new rules about factory child labor."

"That's a summary. Please read—"

"I'm just trying to save us all some time," I said, beads of sweat rolling down the middle of my back like crawling insects. "Parliament decided toddlers should only work fifteen hours per day. Ten, tops. Certain cell phone factories have yet to get the memo."

Another round of chuckles from the class and another scowl from Callister.

"Orion, you were tasked with *reading* what's printed, not to editorialize it."

The class was entranced by the standoff, waiting to see how far I could push Callister so early in the year. Waiting to see what I'd do next. The jokester using his elevated status as prince of the school to fuck around when I wanted to scream. To run out of the room or slam my head into the desk until my stupid fucking brain just *worked.*

Just when the silence verged on not being funny at all, Harper cleared her throat and began to read.

"In 1833, the British Parliament established the Factory Commission to investigate the conditions of child labor in textile mills. The resulting Factory Act limited the number of working hours of children and required basic education for those employed therein."

"Thank you, Ms. Bennett." Callister fixed me with a stern glare. "Next time, Mr. Mercer, just read the damn text."

I let out a breath, and the anxiety in my head eased off like a pressure valve.

"I could never back-talk a teacher like that," Tessa whispered from beside me with a flirtatious smile. "You're awfully brave."

She was an actress, the star of all the school musicals and plays. A sweet girl, and extremely beautiful. Destined for Hollywood. But I couldn't take my eyes off the girl in the front row. The one who'd just saved my arse, even if she didn't know it.

Harper must've felt my gaze because she turned around again. I expected irritation painted on her face for my "antics," but there was only confusion. Our eyes met, and she stiffened and turned back around.

I see you, Harper Bennett…

But she was starting to see me too. I was feeling *seen*. Found. Whatever that meant.

Class let out and as we stepped into the hallway, I caught Harper's eye again, only because I was watching her. Couldn't take my eyes off this girl. In that half heartbeat where our gazes clashed, my pulse quickened, and her mouth parted slightly before she looked away.

I didn't want her to look away.

And what, pray tell, would you do if she doesn't?

I had no answer. I'd never been affected by a girl beyond bodily lust. If I wanted to get laid, I could. I never treated anyone poorly, but I made it clear that the evening would be just that—one evening.

But Harper wasn't one evening.

So what is she?

I had no answer there either. Little glances aside, she didn't like me very much. Or at least she didn't fall at my feet like everyone else did.

I like that she doesn't like me. Make of that what you will.

When Professor Wolfe was a no-show for Advanced Piano again, the disappointment verged on wrath. The first week of school wasn't over, and the year was shaping up to be a real shit show, as my American mates liked to say. Callister and his cold-calling were bloody dangerous—I was good at deflecting, but not *that* good—and the one class I actually looked forward to was taught by a teacher who didn't know how to read a fucking calendar.

I forced the anger down into the depths and found a study room where I used my text-to-speech to commit the first three chapters of history to memory, just like I had with chemistry. All the new information crowded my memory circuits, but I got it all in there. I had to; I couldn't afford another cockup with Callister.

As I was packing up, my phone read me a text from Tucker.

Parking lot ASAP. We got a live one.

What fresh hell…?

I went to the parking lot where Tucker, Rhett, Aria, and Brent Reynolds from crew were crouched behind Tucker's huge truck. They all watched as Harper Bennett walked to her little blue car where *SECOND WARNING BENDER!* was soaped onto the back windshield.

"What the bloody shit is this?" I demanded.

"Shhh." Tucker elbowed me in the side. "This year's senior prank."

"We had other fresh meat picked out," Rhett said. "Some nerd named Xander, but he's *so* much of a Bender, he doesn't even own a car."

"Only a bicycle." Aria giggled. "Sacrifices had to be made."

My hands clenched into fists. "So you're going to pick on a girl? How chivalrous."

Tucker gave me a strange look. "Since when do you give a shit, Mercer? This is the senior prank."

Harper glanced around. Goddamn, my heart ached at the anguish on her face. Then something like fierce pride roared up in me as she held her head high and climbed into her car with dignity.

"That," Rhett said, "is a fine piece of automotive engineering."

The others snickered, and I fought to keep my tone even. "Leave her be. We have nothing better to do?"

"She's not allowed to park in our parking lot," Brent said.

I nearly put my fist through the whiny wanker's teeth. "Where the bloody hell is she supposed to park?"

Rhett grinned, loving that I was upset. "Touchy, touchy, Orion. What's this all about?" He cocked his head. "You've got your own senior *prank* with her, is that it?"

Tucker's eyes widened. "Oh shit. Has the hunter gotten bored with all the usual prey?"

I ignored him, sucking in calming breaths as Harper drove away.

"Well?" Tucker said, relaxing against his truck, arms crossed.

"Maybe," I said. "Don't fuck with my game."

He chuckled. "Damn, Mercer, I got game too. I have the hottest girlfriend in the school."

"I can understand why Orion would get bored," Rhett said as if I weren't there. "He's got Elowen drooling all over him every time she sees him. Where's the challenge?"

Aria busted out laughing and then clapped a hand over her mouth. "Rude, babe. That's my friend you're talking about."

Rhett shrugged. "Am I wrong?"

"No. It's pathetic, honestly."

Tucker gripped my chin and gave it a wag. "With a face card this lethal, who could blame her?"

I knocked his hand away. "Piss off," I snarled, but managed—just barely—to lighten it with a laugh.

Tucker laughed too, rubbing his wrist where I'd whacked him.

"I don't blame Orion," Rhett continued. "He's hunting for sport outside our own kind because the buffet is too easy."

"This is all very enlightening," I said, casual as hell. "Please. Tell me more."

Tucker shrugged. "Why else are you so defensive about some little Bender?"

I had a witty denial ready to fire but found my jaw clenched shut.

This is ridiculous. I don't care.

Yet a voice whispered if he called her "little" again I was going to put him on the ground.

"She's pretty in a witchy kind of way," Aria said. "I mean, her fashion sense is atrocious, but she's not…*ugly.*" She glanced up at me. "But she's also way beneath you, Orion. It's weird you don't get with Elowen. Like, really weird. You've hooked up with everyone else."

I shrugged and smiled tightly. "Maybe I like to be the prey sometimes too."

The group laughed, and we went our separate ways:

they to their big white houses on the Narragansett Bay, and me to Atlas Hall. Once inside my student apartment, I sagged against the wall.

"No wonder Harper hates you, mate," I muttered to the empty apartment. "You're utterly full of shit."

I rubbed my eyes and headed for the bedroom, intending to crash.

Lo and behold, it turned out the apartment wasn't so empty after all. My roommate, Easton Locke, had finally seen fit to grace me with his presence. He sat at his desk, in the dark, blinds drawn, working intently on a laptop that was covered in an array of artsy stickers.

"So, we meet at last," I said. "Mind if I turn on a light?"

"If you must," Easton said without looking up.

I flicked on the overheads, and he swiveled in his chair. Good-looking fellow, if a bit pale, with a mop of dusty blond hair, thick brows, large blue eyes. He wore torn jeans, Converse, and a black V-neck T-shirt revealing various necklaces, including a chain choker. I'm sure the girls—or boys, or both—in his class were all over him.

I offered my hand. "Good to meet you, Easton."

He stared at it, sizing me up with a lot more balls than I'd give a junior credit for. "Likewise."

"Okay." I withdrew my hand. "Where are you from?"

"California."

"Doesn't quite narrow it down, mate. I'm not aces in geography, but doesn't California possess a vast array of cities and towns?"

Easton went back to his screen. "I'm from Los Angeles. And to spare us the getting-to-know-you chitchat, I applied here on my own, was accepted, forged some paperwork, and here I am. But because my parents have a shit-ton of money and are the literal scum of the earth, they followed me and are moving to Newport next year." His gaze flickered to me. "So. We good?"

"Um…sure," I said, completely unsure what I was supposed to do with all that. "Are you coming to the bonfire tomorrow night? Maybe I could—"

"No."

Okay, good talk.

I took a shower to wash off the ugly shit I'd witnessed in the parking lot. When I came back out, Easton was gone. I hoped he wasn't going to be this much of a killjoy all year, but I felt bad for the guy. I'd been shipped clear across the Atlantic, and while my parents weren't exactly warm fuzzy types, they still loved me. I'd never not known that.

Easton spoke as if he'd tried to *escape* his parents and they'd given chase.

He's being dramatic, surely.

No matter. I vowed to have him laughing by month's end. It's what I did, after all. Make 'em laugh, keep 'em charmed and happy so they'll never know. Never suspect…

Harper suspects. Hell, you might even tell her…

I shelved the thought before it could finish forming. She didn't need the poor little rich boy dumping his problems in her lap. My brain might struggle with short text, but *SECOND WARNING BENDER* came in loud and clear. They'd already harassed her twice now. Third time was the charm because I knew what "senior prank" meant.

Now I had another job to do.

Chapter 5

HARPER

FRIDAY MORNING.

I paced the primary bedroom of our little house—my bedroom, technically—feeling the minutes stack up. Mom was in the attached bathroom, showering, running late for work, which was making Dash late for school, which was going to make *me* late for school.

"I know, I know," Mom said, finally coming out in a towel and a cloud of steam. "It's all yours."

I gritted my teeth and took my turn. I had about three minutes of hot water.

"One more day," I muttered, dragging a comb through my hair while frantically looking for something to wear. "Just one more day, then two glorious days off from the madness."

Dressed and packed, I raced downstairs, thanking the gods of foresight that I made lunches the night before.

"Dash, let's go."

"I'm ready," he chirped from the door, backpack and shoes on, bless his little heart.

"Mom, don't forget," I said, grabbing my keys from the hook on the wall. "I have the bonfire tomorrow night. It's kind of a big deal. My new friends will be there."

"I remember, baby," she said, shouldering her own purse. "The little man and I will watch a movie. Now scoot. Have a good day."

I heaved a breath. A good day wasn't outside the realm of possibility.

I was late to Calculus, where Emery Wallace kept shooting me weird looks, as if she was trying to work up the nerve to talk to me. The same thing happened in English class. I couldn't take Emery's stare any more, or any more Richie bullshit, so while Ms. Alvarez was busy getting organized for the day, I asked Emery flat-out, "Can I help you?"

"I'm sorry."

Okay. Didn't expect that. But after all the shit I'd been through in the last three days, I wasn't about to let her off that easy.

"For?"

"You know what for," Emery said.

Nope. Sorry, honey.

I arched a brow, waiting, which she seemed to appreciate.

"I'm sorry for talking shit yesterday," she said. "And for not speaking up when my friends talked shit."

"Apology accepted."

"Do you want to hang out sometime?"

I glanced at her twice. "Are you serious?"

"One hundred percent. Maybe we could go to a movie sometime or grab a coffee milk." Emery bit her lip. "I mean…if you want. No big deal."

I was on high alert, positive she was fucking with me. She hung out with Aria, and her boyfriend was Tucker Hill, both Parking Lot Assholes.

"Why?"

Emery recoiled as if I'd slapped her. "Never mind, forget it."

"No, I mean, why do *you* want to hang out with *me*? You don't have enough friends?"

She shrugged shyly. "You seem cool."

I studied her, searching for signs this was another Richie prank, but Emery wasn't good at keeping her mask up. Her eyes burned with a desperate desire for me to say yes, and I had exactly one friend so far—Dean Yearwood. And while he was a good guy, he was also a *guy*. I missed having a girlfriend to talk to *about* guys.

One guy in particular…

"I'm very cool," I said. "I'm so cool, in fact, that I go all the way off the charts and come back around to uncool. But…okay."

Emery's relief was so great it was almost sad. "Great!"

Great, I thought as Ms. Alvarez got down to business, though *great* wasn't how I'd describe anything about my time at Castle Hill Academy so far.

At the bell, Emery gathered her things, shy again. "So, should we exchange numbers?"

"Unless you can speak to me telepathically, yes," I teased. "Haven't you done this whole friend thing before?"

She gave me a nudge. "Shut up. Not with someone new. Not in a long time."

"Me neither."

We exchanged phones, and I plugged my number into Emery Wallace's—much newer—iPhone.

This is surreal. Just a bit.

"Great!" she said, as we headed for the door, then laughed sheepishly. "I say that a lot, don't I?"

"It's okay," I said. "I say *fuck* a lot. Yours is safer in mixed company."

She laughed, this time for real. "You have a good sense of humor."

"Thanks," I said, glancing around the crowded hallway for her Parking Lot BFFs. "Um, I should get to my next class."

"My friends can be bitches, but I don't care what anyone thinks, if that's what you're worried about," Emery said.

I managed a smile. That was the thing about privilege. You could afford not to care. Some of us didn't have that luxury.

"My class is all the way in the back in the STEM Wing," I said. "Don't want to be late. But we'll talk later?"

"I'd like that," Emery said sincerely.

"Great!"

"Oh, *ha-ha*."

I started down the hall and she called after me, "Hey, Harper."

"Yeah?"

"Fuck!" she shouted, then clapped her hands over her mouth.

I laughed. "Thattagirl."

Okay, Dash. That's two.

In chem, half my attention was on Dr. Langford's lecture about oxidation and ionization, and the other half was on Orion. I hated how *aware* I was of him. As if my senses were trapped in his gravitational pull against my will.

He's friends with assholes. How's that?

The thought wouldn't take.

It was an exercise in self-restraint to keep my eyes on my notebook when his left hand was inches from mine. Then I noticed he had his phone out, recording the lecture. A strange look was on his face, almost as if he were half asleep. Not bored or lazy, but something I couldn't quite place.

He shot me a cocky smile. A mask-smile. I was starting to tell the difference.

"What am I doing wrong now?" he whispered.

I nodded at his phone. "Didn't know that was allowed."

"You don't approve?"

"No, just seems...easy."

"Easy. Right," he said, his smile tightening. "It listens better than I do. And I told you, my handwriting is like a secret code, except not even I can crack it."

"I don't care," I whispered. "You do you."

"You don't care? *The* Harper Bennett doesn't care about something school related? Bollocks."

"Okay, so I walked into that one," I whispered back. "But no, as your lab partner, as long as you get the material down, I don't care."

He narrowed his eyes playfully. "I don't believe you."

I started to retort then shut my mouth. Damn, this boy. Everything about him was maddening. Impossible to ignore. Impossible to dislike. Impossible to miss he had something intangible behind his eyes that his charming smile couldn't conceal.

"It doesn't matter what you believe," I said. "It's the truth."

Watching me squirm, Orion's amused smile deepened, and I felt my cheeks heat. I started to retort again when he leaned close, rested his cheek in his fist, his beautiful dark eyes boring into mine. Dammit if my heart didn't skip ten beats.

"So Bennett, you do think—?"

Dr. Langford stopped his lecture. "Orion, Harper, you seem very chatty. Do you have something to add?"

I jumped. "No, sorry." I'd forgotten there was anyone else on the damn planet but Orion and me.

This boy…

This boy was going to ruin my focus, my plans, my everything if I didn't get my shit together.

Enough with the fawning and blushing and melting like a fucking moron.

Langford peered closer at Orion's phone. "Mr. Mercer, is this how you take notes?"

Orion shifted in his seat, his smile dimming to a second-rate knockoff. "Yep. I'd be bloody heartbroken if I missed a single word of your fascinating lecture."

Langford burst out laughing. "Clever, Mr. Mercer, but not surprising. I expect great things from your NoSci contest entry."

Orion had the decency to look sheepish at such a blatant nod to his family's legacy, but if the Mercers were Big Five, then they were all but signatories on Langford's paychecks. I might be competing for second place, and I hadn't even come up with an idea yet.

What did you expect? Fairness? At a school like this?

The thought helped me build up the defenses Orion had a knack for bulldozing right over.

The bell rang. Over the bustle of twenty-four students packing up, Langford announced our homework.

"I expect both you and your partner to have a full grasp of oxidation and ionization, as we'll be putting those to the test in the lab tomorrow. Enjoy the rest of your day."

I inspected my notes to ensure I'd taken down Langford's definition of the terms accurately. My hand had cramped trying to get it word for word.

Orion turned to me and flashed me that beautiful smile of his, instantly disarming me, setting my insides fluttering and turning my thoughts to mush.

Fucking stop it. This can't happen. Nothing can happen, nothing will *happen…*

"I was going to say before we were so rudely interrupted," he said. "I feel like we got off on the wrong foot this week. We are, after all, stuck with each other all semester."

"I'm stuck with you, you mean," I snapped, the words flying out like a slap. An automatic defense cultivated by a lifetime of good things in my life that never lasted and that taught me to never get my hopes up because they always came crashing down in the end.

I instantly regretted it—instantly *hated* that I'd said it—but it was too late.

Orion's beautiful smile vanished. A cold sliver of silence slipped between us. Then he put on his jacket, shouldered his bag and nodded at my notes.

"Oxidation is the loss of electrons, while ionization is the removal of electrons from a neutral atom to form an ion, which is a type of oxidation that requires an input of energy." He shot me a cold look. "I do things the *easy* way."

Then he walked away.

Dr. Langford's definition. Word for word.

My shame chased me into history class and all the way to Advanced Piano, where Professor Wolfe decided to show up for a change. At least, we assumed class was happening; the door to the auditorium was unlocked and there was no cancellation note, so we all filed inside.

Anticipation buzzed in the small auditorium where the twelve of us sat in curved wooden rows, waiting for Ezra Wolfe's grand entrance. A child prodigy like Mozart, he'd toured Europe, then spent his teens and twenties drifting between major symphonies, never staying long. Scandals and rumors hounded him; he'd vanish for years, only to reemerge to perform legendary performances and sold-out tours. He had an elusive and almost mythical aura, and yet, Castle Hill Academy had somehow locked him down for one year.

Orion sat on the other side of the auditorium, me on the other, not looking at each other as the class waited for this legend to walk in the door, all of us holding our breath…

And then the back door to the auditorium door banged open, and Ezra Wolfe strode down the aisle like a giant in black. A cloud of strong liquor trailed after him, and a lot of cologne to cover it up.

The class stared.

He was shockingly handsome and young—late thirties—and tall, with disheveled chestnut hair. I imagined a piano virtuoso in a suit, but Wolfe wore a unisex sort of outfit: a black pants-skirt combo, and a black silk shirt, the sleeves rolled up. Black tattoos inked his forearms, his fingernails were painted black, and black leather bracelets were strapped to his wrists. Silver spikes pierced his ears. Blue eyes regarded us like icy daggers but were bloodshot to hell.

Ezra Wolfe looked as if he hadn't slept in days, and was either hungover or possibly still drunk.

"So here we are," he said with a British accent, rougher than Orion's but slightly gravelly and melodic. "Advanced Piano. I call you up, you play, we discuss. If I work one-on-one with someone, the rest of you fuck off to the practice rooms next door. Got it? Any questions? No? Good. Let's begin."

The students exchanged glances and a few nervous snickers.

Piano was something I'd always been good at. Benevolent teachers and YouTube videos kept me sharp through the years, but it wasn't anything I wanted to pursue seriously. I just liked to play. But the students in this class obviously wanted to make a career of it. They took their turn at the piano and poured their heart and soul into the keys. But no matter who sat at that bench in front of Ezra Wolfe, his reaction was the same: bland, disinterested irritation. He listened, unimpressed, without making a comment, except to bark, "Next!" when he'd heard enough.

Until Orion.

"Your piece?" Professor Wolfe asked.

"Rachmaninoff, Prelude in D Major," Orion said.

The professor arched a brow at Rachmaninoff, and I thought it was either really brave or really stupid to choose something so difficult. Maybe Orion, being the son of a Big Five family, had been given lessons as part of his pedigree—like foxhunting or yachting. Not a serious musician. Certainly not *Rachmaninoff* serious.

Wolfe waved his hand. "Go," he said, clearly not expecting anything that he hadn't already heard from the rest of us.

And then Orion began to play, and any preconceived notions went up in flames.

Even to my unprofessional ear, Orion was different. In a different league. In a different *stratosphere* than the rest of us.

Firstly, he had no sheet music. He sat down, put his hands on the keys, and something astonishing poured out. Rachmaninoff was known for being insanely hard, but this piece was softer, more emotional. This was the composer like none of us had ever heard before. Certainly not like Ezra Wolfe had ever heard before, because instead of bland disinterest, he stood straight, his head whipping to stare at Orion.

Orion, for his part, just played. He didn't put on any fancy manners or flourishes, he just closed his eyes, and it seemed like he and the piano were one entity, channeling the composer's spirit from 120 years ago and bringing it into the room.

"Stop, stop, stop," Professor Wolfe said after a few moments. "Where did you learn to play like that?"

Orion shrugged, his fingers lingering on the keys as if he were becoming reacquainted. "I don't know. That's just how I play."

Wolfe nodded, and then there was a silence where no one knew what to do next.

"Where is your sheet music?" the professor asked finally.

Orion's shoulders hunched; I could see it from where I was sitting.

"I don't have it."

"You played from memory?"

"I play by ear, mostly," Orion said.

I stared. *Rachmaninoff by ear? Holy shit.*

Wolfe wasn't impressed. "Do you not know how to read music?"

The class stiffened as a group, tension running through us like an electric current. I felt my own cheeks redden on Orion's behalf.

"I can read the notes," Orion said. "But…it's complicated."

"What do you mean, it's complicated?"

"Can we speak about this privately?" Orion asked in a low voice, but the auditorium was designed for sound to carry. We all heard every word.

Wolfe frowned as if the question made no sense. "Nothing spoken here is private," he said to the class. "You, Orion, play with technical perfection but no feeling."

I gasped. Audibly.

Wolfe pointed to another girl, Carla Salazar.

"That one," Wolfe said. "She poured herself into her piece, but her metering and timing were absolute shite. Yet if I had to choose between terrible metering or passion, I would pick passion every day of the week. Can you not hear that, class? The void in Orion's playing? The emptiness?"

The room was silent and cold as space. My hands felt like ice in my lap.

Wolfe paced, his own hands behind his back. "The truly great pianists master the craft, and then they bleed into the music the way a writer bleeds into their words. The way an actor weeps over their lines, and if you think what I'm saying is melodramatic, or that I'm being a cruel bastard, then you can leave this class right now because you're wasting my bloody fucking time."

More silence.

"Based on what I heard today, I'll email individually assigned pieces that you will play for us next time. Practice and come back Monday." Professor Wolfe waved a black-nailed hand. "I'm done with you. Go."

The students gathered their things and walked out, exchanging stares and mouthing OMGs to each other. Orion strode out the fastest. I hurried to catch up.

"Orion, wait."

Now it was his turn to stop and glare at me in the hallway, and it was almost heartbreaking to see him devoid of his smile, his humor… that *twinkle* in his eye.

"What?" he asked flatly.

"I just wanted to say that Wolfe is full of shit—"

"No, he's not. He knows exactly what he's talking about."

I took a step back, shocked.

"What? Do you think you know everything about me because I'm rich?" Orion demanded. "Do you think it's easy being me because of my last name?"

"I...I don't know," I managed. It was the most honest thing I could think to say.

"Hm." Orion looked over my head at the crowded hallway full of students, thinking, then flashed me his smile. Like a mask or a habit. It didn't touch his eyes, didn't light them up at all. "Are you going to the big bonfire this weekend?"

I blinked at the hairpin change of subject. "Oh. I think so. Dean Yearwood mentioned—"

"Brilliant. Perhaps I'll see you there."

Then he turned and walked away.

Chapter 6

ORION

I crawled into Saturday morning on my hands and knees. One short week of classes and my brain was already exhausted from the workarounds. It was a relief to go down to the docks for crew tryouts.

I wasn't too worried about making the team. Coach Daniels liked me. I was a strong two seat with the proper weight and skill set. Not big enough for the power needed in the middle of the shell, and not as important as bow or stroke. I figured I was safe.

I stood on the dock and listened as Coach bellowed instructions to newbies who'd never rowed before in their life, the poor bastards. Tucker, Rhett, Brent, and a few other veterans snickered, cocky as hell.

One new guy was a Bender in glasses and a sweatshirt

from some school in Maryland. When Coach Daniels went down the line taking names and positions, this guy announced himself as Xander Ford, bow seat.

Xander.

This must be the "fresh meat" with no car.

Given how Brent, last year's bow seat, was giving Xander the stink eye, I assumed he was one and the same.

Bow seat meant Xander would be sitting right behind me if he got a spot. We watched together as the first bunch of guys went out in a shell and proceeded to make complete arses of themselves.

"What a bloody shit show," I muttered.

Xander nodded. "Agreed."

Coach Daniels started calling out names for the next group. "Orion Mercer."

"That's me." I turned to Xander, and we shook hands. "Let's give 'em hell, mate."

We got into a shell with Rhett, Tucker, Kai Thornton, Henry Moore, Knox Whitman, Justin Wu, and Dean Yearwood as coxswain. We were the best of the lot by far, and I would've bet a king's ransom this was going to be the final team.

Back on dry land, Xander caught some shit for likely stealing Brent's bow seat right out from under him.

"Don't worry, Brent," Tucker said. "Your position is safe. Ford won't be able to afford the race goggles, never mind the uniform."

"Ease off, yeah?" I said. "Let's have some fun tonight and not worry about the roster."

One benefit to my popularity was it acted as buffer between the guys when they got too rough with the Benders.

That night, I met Tucker, Emery, and the gang at Cassidy's, a burger joint on the north side of Castle Hill, near the Bend. We took a booth big enough for all of us, but Elowen squashed herself up against me, tits flush with the shoulder of my black Armani bomber jacket.

The talk turned to the upcoming Halloween festival up at Bennington Farm—the second-biggest social event of the year with music, a costume contest, and prizes.

"Everyone got their costumes?" Elowen asked. Under the table, she trailed a finger along my thigh. "You'd make a fantastic Alfie."

I gritted my teeth and roughly brushed her hand away. Too rough. I had to make up for it. "What's that, love?"

As predicted, her eyes lit up at "love."

"From the show *Emily in Paris?* You'd make a fantastic Alfie."

"Never seen it," I said, knowing where this was going. She was one breath away from suggesting she go as Emily. Best Couple's Costume at the Halloween festival was a coveted prize, but the last thing I wanted was to get roped into a pairing.

"And I already have a costume," I said, pushing aside thoughts of chemistry partners who barely tolerated me.

"I'm going as Mr. Universe, and this"—I gestured at myself—"is my costume."

Elowen giggled and gave me a playful shove. The conversation moved on to Tucker's and Emery's costumes. They were going as Ken and Barbie and probably *would* win Best Couple, though Emery looked slightly green.

She looks like how I feel when Callister asks me to read aloud in class.

Gideon asked about crew tryouts, and Tucker's and Rhett's expressions darkened.

"Coach is going to shit-can one of our guys and replace him with a Bender," Tucker said. "The new guy, Xander Ford."

The waitress arrived, setting down milkshakes and sodas.

"Thank you *so* much," Rhett said, his smile oily. When she was gone, the smile vanished. "I bet that's Ford's mom."

"Probably," Tucker agreed. "We should make sure to tip her extra. If he makes the crew, he'll need the cash."

"Bloody hell," I said. "You're monsters, the lot of you."

"Or maybe we shouldn't tip her," Tucker said. "It'll keep her son from stealing Brent's seat."

"I humbly dissent," I said, keeping my smile bright, like a politician. "As two seat, I can tell you Ford is loads better than Brent. He's stable and smart. I could feel the difference having him at my back."

"Traitor," Rhett said. "I'm going to tell Brent you said that."

"The fuck do I care?" I said. "Do you want to win or do you want to defend your boyfriend?"

I clocked Gideon's immediate flinch, and something inside me recoiled with shame. Rhett laughed and tossed a packet of salt at me. I deflected it back with a grin, marveling at how easy it was to be as much of an arsehole as Tucker and Rhett. To be who they liked me to be.

As a kid, I once read a book about doppelgängers, creatures that could change appearance to blend in with their surroundings.

I could go the festival as one of those, I thought. *I wouldn't need a costume at all.*

At the Castle Hill Lighthouse—long abandoned—the bonfire was the same scene as last year and the year before: everyone drinking various hard teas out of coolers and harder liquor out of pockets. Parents paid off the cops to keep an eye on us and allow us our fun.

Tucker and the guys wasted no time getting pissed out of their minds. I wasn't a big drinker, but I thought about doing the same, to wash my mouth of the shit I'd said at dinner. Or to drown out what Ezra Wolfe had said at our first piano class.

My first time touching the keys in three years.

Why I'd picked Rachmaninoff, one of the most difficult piano composers of all time, was beyond me. To see if it was all still there, maybe. And it was.

Like coming home.

But harsh as he was, Ezra Wolfe had been right. I played without emotion because I'd buried it all, down in the depths and automatically, the way my family buried everything that wasn't fine. Losing control was an embarrassment waiting to happen. Even taking the class was a risk. Touching the keys again felt like breaking a rule I'd never been brave enough to question.

Why now?

I shoved the uncomfortable thoughts away with practiced ease and spotted Harper standing with Dean Yearwood and Xander Ford on one side of the bonfire, talking and laughing. When Emery Wallace headed to the lighthouse alone, Xander followed. I sent a silent prayer for his continued good health and well-being. That is to say, for Tucker to remain occupied elsewhere.

That left Dean and Harper. They made a good couple. They made sense. Perhaps the same way Elowen and I made sense. I don't know what she'd get out of being with me—she didn't know me, but who did? Being with her would be like scratching an itch, I supposed. What could I give her outside of an epic fuck and a laugh?

Not bloody much.

In moments, Dean was pulled away too, and Harper was alone. She wore a long maroon dress with some kind of gold pattern on it, and a sweater that was far too thin for a cool night on the Atlantic. She hugged herself, watching the black waves crash under a silver moon. I couldn't leave her by herself. Chivalry demanded I join her.

That's a proper excuse, right?

I approached slowly, hands up to show they were empty. "No assignments to be graded. No tests anywhere in sight."

Her eyes flared, and I could've sworn for half a second she was glad to see me. Or maybe it was a trick of the shadows.

"Sorry?"

"Just wondering if I'm allowed to be myself or if I have to be on my best behavior."

"Funny how being yourself and being on your best behavior are two entirely different things."

"Walked into that one, didn't I?"

Harper's expression softened, grew beautiful in the moonlight. "I'm sorry I was awful to you yesterday."

I waved my hand. "Water under the bridge."

She studied me. "Do you always do that?"

"Do what?"

"Forgive and forget so easily?"

"Should I hold a grudge? Doesn't seem karmically healthy. And I was rather dickish after piano."

"You had every right."

"Nah. It's not my way." I cocked my head. "Do *you* hold grudges? Will I be paying for my terrible first impression for the rest of the year?"

"You didn't make a terrible first impression," she said. "A confusing one, maybe."

"Confusing? Me?"

"Yeah, you." Harper studied me, started to say something, then changed her mind. A short silence fell, and my usual banter and flirtation that came so easily with most girls became tongue-tied and lost with this one.

"What do you think of Professor Wolfe?" I asked. "He's quite the character."

"I don't like him at all. How he spoke to you was completely uncalled for. You played beautifully."

"I don't know about that," I said. "But I steered this conversation directly into compliments about *me*, which was my plan."

Harper rolled her eyes but gave a small laugh too. A win.

"I'm serious," she said. "Why would he say you had no feeling or passion? And why would you agree?"

"Because he's probably right. I hadn't played in years."

She stared. "You haven't played in *years*, and so you just bust out with Rachmaninoff?"

Shit, fuck, bollocks.

"An exaggeration." I waved a hand. "I wasn't exactly in a stellar mood that day."

"Because I was a total bitch to you, as we've established."

"Ah, so you're the sole arbiter of my moods, Bennett? Aren't we full of ourselves?"

She gave my arm a shove. "Come on..."

"Maybe Wolfe picked up on something."

"Such as?"

I shrugged. "Something. Nothing. Who knows? He was drunk off his arse—"

"Okay, sure." Harper sighed, frustrated, and started to go. "Anyway, I should get back—"

I threw up my arms. "What the bloody hell have I done wrong now?"

"You haven't *done* anything. I just can't figure you out, Orion."

That makes two of us.

"Are you trying to figure me out, Harper?"

"Don't do that. Don't get all cute with me."

I waggled my brows. "Ah, you think I'm cute."

She turned to go again, but I grabbed her hand, laughing.

"Wait, wait, wait. Tell me."

For a long moment, her hand stayed in mine, then she pulled it back and crossed her arms tight.

"You *almost* answer questions with something honest, then back off. You screw around in every class, then you rattle off entire pages of text from memory. You play piano like a miracle and…" She shook her head. "I don't understand what you're doing."

"I'm not *doing* anything."

"I don't believe you."

I barked a laugh. "You don't *believe* me."

"No, I don't. I just… Never mind. Maybe it's me." She looked out over the water. "Maybe this fucking school is messing with my head. It's not what I thought it would be."

"What do you mean?"

"I thought I'd take the best classes and study and keep my head down, but it hasn't been that simple."

"How has it been?" I asked, though I already knew the answer.

"Hard," she said. "Really hard."

My jaw, chest, and fists tightened all at once. *Fucking senior prank.*

"Is there anything I can do?"

"No," she said, hugging herself tighter. "I'll be fine. It's growing pains or whatever. This is a great opportunity, so I shouldn't complain. I can manage."

I can manage. How many times had I said the same thing to myself? A hundred? A thousand? The battle cry of the lone soldier.

"You're right," I said.

She kicked at a piece of charred wood. "About?"

"I have…something of a secret."

"You do?"

"Yes. And it explains chemistry, history, and maybe even Wolfe's oh-so-gentle critique of my Rachmaninoff. But before I tell it, we have to find a place to sit and warm you up."

I found a fallen log suitable to my purposes, then took off my jacket and put it around Harper's shoulders.

"You don't have to—"

"Take my bloody jacket, Bennett," I said, before she could argue.

Harper looked like she *was* about to argue, clearly not used to being offered help or accepting it, but finally put her arms in the sleeves. The jacket was too big for her, which for some primal, manly, caveman reason, made me feel possessive. As if she were somehow mine now. Protected from the elements because of me, and… Fuck, I was going to get aroused if I continued this line of thinking.

Harper's eyes met mine. Her usual defensive composure fractured, and through the cracks, I saw the soft girl who had a hard time letting people see her real self too.

"Thank you," she said.

"You're welcome." I smiled. "Hey, we did it."

"Did what? Had a normal exchange of words like normal people? I noticed."

"We'd better not make a habit of it," I said. "Who knows where we might end up?"

Somewhere real?

The words hung in the air between us in a cartoon bubble as I guided us to the fallen log.

"So, out with my secret, yes?" I said. "I have ADHD. It's a complicated case. At least, I think so."

Harper's eyes widened, and she looked pained. Distraught. "Why didn't you tell me before? God, now I feel even worse for giving you a hard time about that stupid atomic model assignment. And recording Langford's lectures."

"No, no, it's all right. I have my own way of dealing with it."

"Your own way? You don't have accommodations? An IEP?"

"I get test accommodations. Not much else. My parents don't like to talk about it. In fact, my parents don't like to talk about much of anything. It's just not how we do it in my family."

Now Harper looked angry on my behalf, which was sort of sweet. And new. I wasn't used to having an ally in the trenches. My chest felt strangely heavy and light at the same time. Unburdened but self-conscious too.

She bit her lip. "Only test accommodations? But—"

I waved a hand. "It's fine. It is what it is. But I haven't told a soul in four years." I smiled. "You must have a way about you."

"Sure. A way of harassing you so *my* grade doesn't suffer." She shook her head. "I'm sorry."

"You didn't know."

"Thank you for telling me." She raised her eyes to mine. "It's not something you should be ashamed about. You know that, right?"

"I'm not ashamed, necessarily. It's just difficult."

"Telling others might make it less difficult."

I smiled. "I can manage."

"I see what you did there." Harper looked like she was going to reach for my hand, but then she tucked hers away in the pocket of my jacket. "But if you need anything from me, I'll help. I mean, not that you *need* help. But if you do, I will."

"Thank you. My brain's a nightmare with short stuff. Long books? Fine. A paragraph? Forget it."

"Is that what happened in history the other day?"

"Yes. You gallantly came to my rescue, even if you didn't know it at the time."

Harper nodded. "That makes sense. They call it an *attention* deficit, but I heard that if someone is really into an activity, they can focus for a long time. I mean, not to tell you about your own condition. I'm sure you know more about it than I do. Obviously."

She was so cute when she was flustered, which I suspected was a rare occurrence. I hadn't had anyone offer help or show concern in years. I'd forgotten what it felt like. I'd gotten so used to *managing* alone, the exhaustion of it became almost background noise. Right now, Harper was with me in this moment of confession, and I wasn't so alone…

I cleared my throat.

"I should've mentioned it earlier, seeing as we're going to be lab partners for the whole year. I really don't want you scolding me the whole time." I itched to brush a stray curl off her cheek. "You're much prettier when you're not scolding me."

It was too dark out to see her blush, but I felt it anyway. The moment grew soft, as if we'd drawn closer together without moving at all.

"You said ADHD explains Wolfe's tearing into your performance," she said eventually. "Absolutely not. Your

Rachmaninoff was truly beautiful, and I don't care what he says. You're not empty. I felt something listening to you play."

A warmth spread in my chest, and it wanted to wake up something long asleep, down there in the depths.

"Thank you," I said. "I suppose you're right. He couldn't know about my condition, but he *is* an expert about music. He can hear what most can't, so he heard *something*. Or nothing. Anyway, we don't have to talk about it anymore. I just wanted to clear the air."

Harper was smart enough to know I was done discussing the scene in piano class. "Well, I'm glad Wolfe's not a doctor," she said. "His bedside manner leaves a lot to be desired."

"I'll bet he knows how to get a good performance out of us," I said with a grin. "By sheer terror alone."

"Or drive us to nervous breakdowns." Harper looked up at me; we were so close on the log. Inches apart. "Do you want to do that for a living? Play the piano? You're more than good enough, and *do not* deflect."

"No, I'm going into the family business, remember?"

"But why not piano? If I played like you, that's all I would do, all day long."

"Nah," I said. "I think you're being overly generous."

"I think you're being overly modest. You could go to Juilliard or—"

I waved my hands. "I'm not going to Juilliard."

"No?"

"No, at the end of the year, I'm going back to the UK. To Cambridge."

"Oh. Gotcha." Something like disappointment flickered over Harper's face but then it was gone again. Maybe I imagined it. She cleared her throat. "It must be hard, being so far away from your family for so long."

"It was for years one and two, but I got used to it. Or numb to it. I go back every year for Christmas."

"That's it? Just Christmas?"

I nodded. "My father thought it would be a good way to build our moral character. Toughen us up. It was hardest for my middle brother, Octavian. He's a genius. He did CHA when he was two years younger than Odin or me."

"What's your family like?" Harper asked.

"They're good people. A little remote. Father's busy running his empire. Mum is busy running her galleries. They're kind but not effusive. I guess you could say they don't like to get their hands messy with all that lovey-dovey stuff. It's like being raised by benevolent strangers."

"That's odd, because you're so…" Harper shook her head.

"I'm so…?"

"Warm. You're very warm." This time there was no mistaking her blush.

"I'm *warm*," I said with a chuckle. "Like a cozy mitten."

"Come on," she said, elbowing me in the side. "You know what I mean. You're like Dean. Everybody loves you."

"They don't love me," I said, sort of shocked at the words escaping my mouth from down below. "How could they? They don't know me. They know the version of me that I show the world. I'm the guy that makes all the jokes. The guy who's everybody's friend." I gave her a rueful smile. "Well. *Almost* everybody."

Harper frowned. "But that's not the real you?"

"I don't know." I sighed. "Wolfe… He's going to try to play it out of me, I think. Because sometimes I feel like…"

"What?"

"I can draw and play, but my brain has turned my handwriting to shite, and I'm scattered and unfocused… I sometimes wonder if that's like some weird metaphor for me. As if I can't explain or decipher my own self." I laughed and shook my head. "That makes no damn sense."

"It makes perfect sense," she said. "You said your parents feel like strangers. So maybe it's hard to know who you are without ever having had a deep bond? Without them reflecting you back to you. That's a parent's job, isn't it? To validate their child's feelings, help them name and understand emotions, and model emotional awareness."

I stared with wide eyes. "Harper Bennett, casually forgetting to mention she has a degree in child psychology."

She laughed. "Al-Anon meetings. Some of it stuck."

"Al-Anon?"

Her laughter died a quick death. "That's short for Alcoholics Anonymous. I went to the family meetings. My mom's had some issues with alcohol. To say the least."

"I'm sorry."

"It's fine. I mean, it's not *fine*..." She waved a hand. "But anyway, I never knew my dad, so I feel that absence you're talking about. Like there's a part of me that will always be a huge mystery to me too." Harper turned to me, her eyes liquid dark in the dimness. "Maybe you playing the piano is trying to... I don't know. Feel into that absence and fill it with something beautiful."

Bloody hell, her soft words slammed into my chest, and then sank into my heart, making it ache with grief for something I never had, and long for something I wanted at the same time.

I swallowed hard. "It's just not in the cards for me," I said gruffly. "My brothers and I are part of the company. That's what we're going to do."

She nodded. "Okay."

A silence fell, and I cleared my throat.

"Now that we've thoroughly exhausted the subject of *me*," I said, "we're going to even things up and spend approximately fifteen hours talking about you."

Harper puffed her cheeks. "I don't know if the subject of me would fill up fifteen minutes, let alone fifteen hours."

"Bollocks."

"Seriously. I'm almost eighteen, but I haven't done anything yet. I've lived in Pittsburgh and now Rhode Island, so that makes a grand total of two places I've been to in my entire life."

"Really?"

"Really," she said. "I have an empty passport because some friends and I once planned a road trip to Canada, but my mother had a work emergency. I had to stay home and take care of my little brother." Her gaze went to the sand at our feet. "She's had a lot of emergencies."

I sensed the gulf between her experiences and mine stretching as wide as the ocean before us.

She glanced up at me. "I'm whining, right? Sorry, I just feel like… Nothing, never mind."

"Tell me."

"No, it's dumb."

"Hey," I said. "I don't know you all that well, but I can safely say 'dumb' is not a word I'd ever associate with you."

"Are you trying to flatter me into telling you something personal?"

"Did it work?"

"Seems so." Harper looked out toward the ocean. "My whole life has been nothing but stress. It runs through me like a current, all the time. I feel like I'm sitting in a sling shot and one day it's going to snap. I'll go flying into a bright, brilliant future of my own making, or straight into the ground. So I spend every waking hour on the lookout. Planning, studying, being vigilant. Because if I *am* going to get smashed to bits, I want to be prepared. As if it won't hurt as bad if I see it coming. The only thing worse than being smashed to bits is not seeing it coming." She shook her head. "That feels like death."

Her words hung in the cold air, but her trust in me

at that moment was soft and warm. She'd laid something deeply personal—and *real*—into my hands for safekeeping...but I didn't have the first idea what to say. I wanted to tell her I knew how she felt. That I had the smallest iota of understanding, but I couldn't. Any tightrope I walked had a safety net below it a mile wide. It's why I was going into the family business. Because it was safe.

And piano isn't.

The silence became too much. Harper hunched deeper into my jacket. "So *anyway*..."

"Doesn't matter," I blurted.

"Sorry?"

"It doesn't matter if you're catapulted into the dirt," I said. "You'll pick yourself up, dust yourself off, and go again. But for what it's worth, my money is on the brilliant future."

Harper studied me, gauging my sincerity. I held her gaze, the space between us growing shorter, the air warmer. Only the crashing of the waves on the shore and the moonlight. We both started to speak at the same time.

"Go ahead," she said.

"No, ladies first."

"I don't know what I was going to say," she said with a small laugh.

"Me, neither."

"You? At a loss for words?"

"Yeah, that was a lie..." My eyes roamed her delicate

face, her large eyes fringed with long lashes, her full lips. "I was about to say that I'm glad Bandit stole your money."

"You are?"

I nodded.

"We would've met in chemistry class," she said.

"It wouldn't have been the same," I murmured. "In the hallway, it was perfect."

My words disarmed her, defenses down, her beautiful face open. Her mouth too, lips parted, and I wanted to kiss her. Badly. Severely. A needy desire that wasn't born of lust but something else. Something real. For the first time, my heart seemed to be reaching for something real. Her. This girl…

Harper sat back and quickly looked away. "We shouldn't."

"Why not?" I blurted like a dope. Rejection wasn't something I encountered often, if ever. I was off my game. She threw me off my game because I liked her, and I never liked anyone.

"Why not?" She fixed me a look, her eyes glassy, fighting sudden tears. "Are you making fun of me too?"

"What? No, of course not."

"We just met, for one thing. And for another, I know the score. You're super rich and popular and I'm not."

"I don't care about any of that."

"I'm sure you believe that's true, but…" Harper stopped talking and looked at me, and I could see all the ways she'd been hurt this week reflected in her eyes. "You're a good guy, Orion. But I can't be some girl you hook up with on Saturday night and ignore on Monday."

I ran a hand through my hair, a knot of words tangled in my throat. Which had never happened to me with a girl before. I'd never *felt* anything for a girl before.

Harper smiled at my obvious struggle, but the sadness shone through, like cracks in the armor.

"You don't have to say anything," she said. "I get it. Believe me, I get it."

"What? No, I was just—"

A shrill voice cut through the air. "Orion. There you are."

Harper and I jumped off the log as if it were on fire. Elowen Blake came bounding up, drunk and unsteady. She threw her arms around my neck and planted a sloppy kiss on my cheek.

"What are you doing over here?" she said, her eyes on Harper. "We've been looking all over for you. Tucker wants to go on a packy run. Are you cool to drive?"

I should've gotten rid of Elowen. I should've told her to fuck off. I should've asked Harper to go with me somewhere quiet and private so I could tell her she was the first girl I shouldn't have tried to kiss right away, and that's why I tried to.

Try explaining that one…

"Sure," I heard myself saying instead. "I can drive."

"Let's go." Elowen eyed Harper up and down. "Can I help you?"

"Jesus," I muttered. "There's no need to—"

"It's all good," Harper said sharply. "I was just leaving."

"Harper, wait—"

Too late. She strode off, leaving me with Elowen, who was so drunk she could barely stand.

Fucking brilliant.

"Hey," Elowen breathed wetly in my ear, running her finger along my jawline. "You want to get out of here?"

"Yes, love. I'm taking you home."

"Mm, yes, please, *love*," she purred, and her fingers began a migration down my chest, southward.

"Keep to yourself, please." I removed her grabby hand. "I'm driving you home to sleep it off."

"Come on, Orion," she whined. "You're torturing me. Let's make us a thing already—"

A scream pierced the night.

I turned in time to see Jack Wallace, Emery's older brother, pull his fist out of the bonfire, his hand a flaming torch.

Elowen and I froze. It seemed as if the entire student body around the bonfire froze. Only Dean, Harper, and Emery rushed toward Jack. Before I even knew what was happening, the three of them had gotten Jack off the ground and were taking him to the parking lot.

"Holy shit," Elowen said. "Did you see that?"

"Yeah, I saw that."

Even from this distance, I saw Jack's burning hand. I saw his grimace of pain in the dancing shadows cast by the fire. And I'd seen the stony, impassive look on Harper's face when Elowen had staked her claim on me.

I'm not sure which was worse.

Are you making fun of me too?

Goddamn, straight to my heart.

As I disentangled myself from Elowen's octopus grip, I saw my jacket lying in the sand. Harper must've slipped out of it when she walked away.

"What is that?" Elowen asked, swaying slightly.

"That," I said, picking up my jacket and shaking the sand out of it, "is what literature calls *symbolism*."

"Huh?

"Nothing," I said, gripping her around the waist before she fell down. "This bloody night is over."

Chapter 7

HARPER

The smell of burnt flesh filled Dean's car because Jack Wallace's hand was a nightmare—a fist covered in angry red skin, some of it peeling off. I wanted to puke but figured that wouldn't be terribly helpful.

Propped between Emery and me in the backseat, Jack moaned, his head rolling on his shoulders, drunk off his ass. He was Emery's older brother but was in our senior class, having been held back for mental-health reasons. I didn't know the whole story, but clearly it was more of a nightmare.

"They killed him, Emery," he said again and again. "They killed him."

Emery shot me a look, panicked and horrified while

Dean drove to the Newport Medical Center. There, a team carefully extracted Jack from the car.

"What happened?" a doctor asked.

"We were at a bonfire at the Castle Hill Lighthouse," Dean said. He hesitated, glanced at Emery, then added, "I think he fell. He was pretty drunk."

The doctor took some more information, and Jack was wheeled away.

We pulled Emery aside. "I didn't know what to tell the doctor," Dean said. "Or if Jack could get in trouble or something, but you should know, he didn't fall."

I nodded. After leaving Orion and Elowen to enjoy the rest of the *beautiful moonlit night* together, I'd rejoined Dean. Jack Wallace had pushed between us, ranting and raving. He fell to his knees in front of the fire, and then…

I gently touched Emery's arm. "He said something about a train… Then he reached into the fire."

Emery paled, and I thought she might pass out. The three of us sat down, and I brought her some water while she called her father. When he arrived, he dismissed Dean and me as if we were his underlings. I was glad to go.

"Holy shit," Dean said as we walked back to the parking lot. "That was all kinds of fucked up." He shot me a smile full of false cheer. "And how was your night?"

The moment when Orion tried to kiss me flooded my thoughts. How we'd both shared something deeply personal, and then that gorgeous face of his was so close to mine, his mouth descending… I'd almost let myself believe it was going to be more than one kiss.

But I wasn't a fool. What else would it be but a casual hookup? What else could he and I be at a school like this?

Orion doesn't want anything real, I thought, my defenses running at maximum capacity. *He's used to girls falling all over him and assumed I'd fall all over him too—*

"Harper?"

"Oh, it was fine. Whatever," I said. "I mean, not fine, obviously. I hope Jack's okay. Emery too. Their dad seems like a piece of work."

"Yeah, no kidding," Dean said darkly. "I don't know if you've heard, but they had an older brother named Grant. He died a while back. Hit by a train up in Providence."

"Jesus." I shivered and hugged myself in my thin sweater. It smelled faintly of Orion's cologne, left over from his jacket. When I'd felt warm and safe—

Stop.

"Give you a ride home?" Dean said.

"I'm parked at the lighthouse."

"Right-o."

He drove me back to the beach—the last place I wanted to go—but there was no sign of Orion, thankfully.

Because he took Elowen home.

This whole night was a shit show that desperately needed to end. I drove home, ready to crawl into bed and dive into sleep. Instead, I opened the door and caught

Dash as he flew at me. He wrapped his little arms around my waist and burst into tears.

"Whoa, buddy, what's going on?" I cried. "What happened?"

"I was scared," he said.

I glanced around the living room. The couch was empty. The clock on the microwave said it was nearly eleven.

"Where's Mom?" I asked. "What are you doing up so late?"

"She got a call to go to work," Dash said against my middle.

My stomach tightened, stealing my breath. "And she left you here by yourself?"

I fumbled in my small purse for my phone to see if Mom had tried to call me to come home. Nothing. I squatted down so I was eye level with Dash. He looked so small and innocent in his dinosaur PJ's, his hair sticking up in the back.

"I don't understand. Tell me exactly what happened."

He rubbed his eye with the heel of his hand. "She said she didn't have a choice, and she was sorry. I should just watch a movie, and not cook anything or eat anything so I wouldn't choke. She said she'd be home soon, and it'd be okay."

Oh my fucking God…

"Why didn't she call me so I could come home?"

"She said she didn't want to ruin your night." Dash sniffled. "Are you mad?"

"Not at you, buddy," I said, trying my damnedest to keep my voice even. "Are you okay? Are you hurt?"

"No, I just got scared of being by myself in the new house."

"I'll bet," I said. "Come on."

I walked Dash up to his room, tucked him in and turned on his *Finding Nemo* nightlight. A blue-and-yellow glow filled the room as it slowly rotated, projecting Dory, Nemo, and Crush on the wall.

"Will you sit with me until I fall asleep, Harper?"

"Of course I will. Of course."

It didn't take long. He was so tired, probably from being scared all damn night.

I stayed with him until I was sure he was deeply under, then I went downstairs and sat on the couch to wait. Thirty minutes later, my mother walked in the door, dumping her linen bag of cleaning supplies by the front closet.

"Oh, Harper, good. You're home. Is Dash asleep?"

"What the fuck were you thinking?" I hissed in a stage whisper.

Mom flinched, then sighed. "Don't start with me. I've had a long night—"

"*You* had a long night? I came home and Dash was wide awake and scared to death. You just left him here? By himself? Why didn't you call me?"

"I was trying not to bother you. Your first social event of the year, right? Didn't you tell me you wanted to be with your new friends?"

"Yes, but it doesn't mean you leave a seven-year-old by himself."

"I didn't think it was going to be that long," Mom said. "The lady got a last-minute booking and needed a bit of extra cleanup. But the last guests used her white towels instead of the black ones she left *specifically* for makeup, so I had to do a lot of bleaching—"

"I don't care. You fucking call me so I can come home and take care of the *seven-year-old*."

Mom's gaze flattened, her lips pursed. She was tired from working two jobs and *goddammit*, I didn't want to feel bad for her. But I *did* feel bad for her while being ready to explode at the same time.

Or maybe that's *why* I wanted to explode.

"I don't appreciate your tone of voice, young lady," she said. "I don't appreciate being lectured, either, like you're the adult around here."

"Someone has to be."

Quick as lightning, her stinging slap exploded over my cheek. It took everything I had not to slap her back.

"I think you forget who you are sometimes, Harper."

"No," I said, teeth clenched, my cheek on fire. "I think you do. You're the mother. You're supposed to be taking care of him."

"I *am* trying to take care of him," she said, sinking onto the couch. "And this household. *And* make enough money so we can stay in it. I was *trying* to do you a favor tonight."

"Well, don't," I said. "He could've hurt himself. He could've started a fire. Did you think of that?"

Jack Wallace's burnt hand came to mind, and I thought I was going to puke. Mom's face fell, as a similar image must've come to her mind.

"He's a good kid," she said weakly. "He's smart. He wouldn't—"

"He's *seven*, Mom. If the neighbors found out and called the cops or CPS, they'd take him away. Again."

God, just the thought made me cold all over. I'd die first.

Her shoulders slumped. "You're right. No, you're right. I'm sorry, baby. I'm sorry. And I shouldn't have hit you. Come here."

I remained standing, arms crossed.

Irritation returned to her voice. "Harper, I've had a long day. I'm tired. He's fine. The house is still standing. Can we just forget this whole thing happened and start fresh? Please?"

Start fresh. Her favorite motto every time something like this happened. A hundred do-overs for her, while each one piled up in the back of my mind until I felt like I was carrying a thousand pounds on my back.

I started for the stairs. "I'm going to bed."

"How was your night?" she called after. "Was the bonfire fun, at least?"

"Oh, sure," I muttered. "Time of my life."

I sat at my desk, pulled out my ancient laptop, and

started brainstorming for the Novus Prize for Scientific Innovation. All that mattered now was winning that contest, getting the money for some kind of safety net, and getting a leg up at the universities. Everything else came second.

Everything.

Chapter 8

ORION

I DIDN'T DUMP A DRUNK ELOWEN BLAKE ONTO HER FRONT lawn, but I was tempted. By the time I arrived at her huge oceanfront house, I judged she'd sobered up enough to make the journey from my car to her front door on her own. She'd complained lucidly the entire drive because I wouldn't park at Brenton Park Point, a popular hookup spot.

"I don't get it, Orion," she said, as my silver Aston Martin Vantage idled in her driveway. "Are you gay or something? You've hooked up with every other girl in school but me."

"This contradiction brought to you by Tito's Vodka…"

"Huh?"

"Good night, Elowen."

"Whatever." She started to get out of the car, then stopped. "It's just that we make sense, right? Why were you hanging around that Bender? What do you see in her, anyway?"

She's pretty. She's also honest and brave and smart. Those things make her beautiful. She doesn't care about my money. In fact, she'd probably prefer it if I didn't have any. I told her and only her about my ADHD because I feel like I can be myself around her and it's okay. More than okay. Accepted...

Saying any of that would be wasted on Elowen.

"Harper's a good person," I said. "In fact, most of the Benders are, if you'd bother to give them half a chance."

Elowen's face crumpled. "Oh my God, you are the sweetest guy ever. And so *hot.* I'm not giving up on us, Orion." She kissed the tip of her finger and pressed it into the cleft in my chin. "I'll see you Monday."

"Can't wait."

When she was safely inside, I drove to Atlas Hall. Easton sat on the couch with his laptop, playing some sort of game.

"Fucking hell," I said, rubbing my eyes, sinking into the chair opposite.

"Fun night?"

"Brilliant. I fucked it up with the girl I wanted to take home and took home the drunk girl instead."

Easton's eyebrows disappeared under his mop of dusty blond hair.

"I didn't sleep with her. I'm not a complete scumbag.

Although I could have. She was more than willing. No, I fucked it up trying to make everyone happy. As usual."

"Serves you right."

I *almost* laughed. "I like her—the sober one. And I haven't ever liked a girl."

"Never?" Easton said. "I hear you have something of a reputation."

"Sleeping with girls and liking them are two different things."

His brows rose again. "Tell me more, O wise one."

"That sounded mercenary, didn't it?" I sighed. "I've never cared about a girl beyond sex, but in my defense, I've made sure it was clear from the start."

"But this girl is different," Easton stated.

This girl is different.

Four simple words and yet they clanged around in my damn mind and heart.

"Bottom line," I said, "I'm leaving for the UK at the end of the year. Stupid to overthink it, yeah?"

Easton shrugged. "Depends."

"On?"

"Are you going to try to repair it with this girl that you like?"

"I wouldn't have the first idea how," I said, recalling my jacket left in the sand. "She seemed rather done with me tonight."

"So maybe it's for the best. Since you're leaving at the end of the year and all."

My hackles went up at the idea of giving up on Harper, leaving her out in the cold again, fighting alone. "Or perhaps I could *try* to have one proper date with her before I map out the rest of my life?"

I stopped. Easton was watching me with raised brows.

"You're a wily one, aren't you?" I laughed.

"I try. That came for you," he said, jerking his chin at a package on our kitchen counter. "Birthday?"

"Not until next month," I said with a sinking feeling. The package was covered in international postage.

I got up and took a knife to the thick tape and unwrapped a leather-bound encyclopedia with gold sprayed edges, *Greatest Scientific Minds* embossed on the front. A note tucked in the pages, in Father's neat script. Cursive was my brain's least favorite thing to decipher, and I was too tired right now.

"Shit, fuck, bollocks."

"So it's good news," Easton deadpanned.

"You tell me. Would you do the honors?" I handed the note to him. "Aloud, please, so I can brace for presumption of success before I've even actually done anything."

He looked at me funny. "Um, sure."

Orion,

You will take your place among the greats, we have no doubt.

Good luck on the Novus Prize for Scientific

Innovation. We're counting on you to do our family proud.

Love,
Father, Mum, Odin, & Octavian

"Damn." I sank back into the chair. "I've been hoping to avoid entering a certain science contest. My parents, apparently, have other ideas."

"Isn't your family *in* the sciences? Or…chemicals?" Easton barely hid his smile. "Pesticides, wasn't it?"

"Do I detect a hint of smart-ass?" I snatched back the note. "So you *do* have a personality. You've been holding out on me, Locke, thank the gods. I thought I was doomed to spend the year with a stiff. And yes, we're *in chemicals*, but this contest has prizes in cash and a leg up at a university. Two things I don't need."

"You don't say."

"I'm a paragon of honesty." I tore the note into little pieces, making a neat pile on the coffee table. "They want me to win it for the prestige, but there are students who could actually use the rewards."

Harper Bennett, for instance.

Not only might Harper need the reward, she'd be offended if I didn't do my utmost to be a worthy competitor. But I already had a headache just thinking about the work I'd have to put in on such a project. And for what?

Another trophy in a case to gather dust. Another meaningless notch on the old Mercer bedframe.

Nailed another one, didn't we?

"But you're not going to enter," Easton said, eyeing the pile of scraps.

"I'm going to *try* not to," I said. "I'll conveniently forget to sign up and pray the deadline passes before Mum and Dad contact me again."

"You're one of those, eh? Beholden to the family?"

"You're not?" I leaned my arms on my knees. "Now that we've analyzed my love life and family pressures, would you care to have a little bit of getting-to-know-you chitchat? Seeing as we're stuck with each other."

Staring at me from across his computer, Easton looked so young—a baby face with hard-as-glass eyes that had seen a lot in his sixteen or seventeen years.

"Am I beholden to my family?" he mused. "If there was something I could do or say that would cause my parents to forever turn their back on me, I would do it in a heartbeat."

"Sounds ominous," I said. "Want to talk about it?"

"*No*," he said. Then softer, "I appreciate it. But no."

The barest flicker of a smile touched his lips, then he shut his laptop and got up. He put on his leather jacket, grabbed his motorcycle helmet, and split. I knew I wouldn't see him again until two or three in the morning. I didn't know where he went nearly every night, but I knew better than to ask.

I looked at what was left of Father's note and felt an unpleasant tightness in my gut at this small defiance. If the NoSci prize had come around last year, I would've already signed up for it. No waiting, no defiance. So why now…?

I had no answer. Just like I had no idea why I started up with piano again. Then I remembered Professor Wolfe had likely assigned our pieces for Monday's class. I opened my laptop and found it waiting for me.

from: ProfWolfe <ewolfe@cha.edu>

to: <omercerID58999@cha.edu>

re: Monday Assignment

Nocturne No. 20, in C Sharp Minor, Chopin.

Dig, Orion.

Chopin's No. 20 was one of the melancholiest of his works. I shut my laptop, thinking of Harper's face when Elowen stumbled into my arms, and how I might've had something real in my hands and I let it fall in the sand at my feet.

Maybe, for the first time in my life, I might not have to dig at all.

Instead of the piano practice rooms, I hit the Academy's immense gym first thing Sunday morning. Coach Daniels needed us in fit condition.

You don't even know yet if you made the crew but…sure.

I headed for the ergometers—the fancy rowing machines that mimicked being on the water. Tucker and Rhett and some of the other crew guys were there. Surprising, given how drunk Tucker had been last night. Dean Yearwood, our coxswain, was coaching Cassian Thorne—our singles guy—through some techniques on a mat.

"Orion, my man." Tucker's hand landed heavily on my back. "You finally did the deed."

"Which deed might that be? I've accomplished so much in my short life."

Rhett grinned. "I saw you leave with Elowen Blake."

"I only took her *home*," I said, adjusting the erg's settings. "She was drunk as shit."

"I fail to see a problem," Rhett said, curling forty-pound weights while admiring himself in the mirror.

"Bloody hell," I said. "Do you hear yourself?"

"Relax," he said. "I just meant she's made no secret how badly she wants you. Like a dog in heat. What difference does it make if she's drunk or not?"

"Oh, I don't know," I said, yanking on the erg's arm row. "I prefer my bedmates to be of sound mind and body, but that's just me."

"Well, did you do it or not?" Tucker asked, wiping his brow with a towel and looking slightly green. And not from this conversation.

"No."

"Christ. What the fuck are you waiting for?"

Chemistry class.

"Hey, listen," I said, ceasing my exercise. "You fucking arseholes are going to forget about your senior prank."

"Huh?" Tucker frowned. "You mean that Harper chick? Oh, come on—"

"I'm bloody serious. Leave her alone."

Rhett and Tucker exchanged glances, and I wondered just how much weight I actually carried with them after three years of friendship and countless hours on the water. Apparently enough.

"Orion here is a gentleman and a scholar," Rhett said. "It's the British propriety in him."

Tucker shrugged. "Suit yourself. It's not as fun when it's a girl anyway. Kind of feels unfair. I'd much rather it had been that Xander Ford fucker. Caught him with Emery last night, and I swear to God, he was about to put the moves on her."

"Coach is going to put him on the roster tomorrow," Rhett said. "Mark my words."

They continued to bitch about Ford, and I left them to it, satisfied Harper was safe. I'd worry about Xander later.

One gallant act at a time, I thought with a grimace, and rowed on the erg until I was about ready to puke too.

As I sat slumped over, toweling my face, Dean caught up with me. "Orion Mercer, hero of the little people."

"You heard that, eh?"

"I hear everything" he said. "I still maintain most people are good at heart, though they don't always make it easy. Rhett is especially challenging."

"Hey, you and Harper Bennett are friends, yeah?"

Fucking hell, that came out of nowhere, because I clearly had no game when it came to this girl. None. Naught. Zero.

"Yes." Dean grinned. "Why do you ask?"

"No reason," I said. "I just noticed that you guys helped Jack when he had his unfortunate accident last night."

Dean's smile fell. "Yeah, it was pretty bad."

"Is he okay?"

"Don't know. Haven't had an update."

"Well, it was a good thing you helped him, mate," I said, clasping his hand. "Quick thinking. He's lucky you were there. You and Harper both."

Perfect recovery. Now tell me everything you know, Yearwood.

He nodded. "She didn't hesitate to jump right in, even though it was pretty gruesome. Harper's a good one."

"Oh yeah?"

Dean's brows went up, amused.

"Right. Anyway." I coughed. "Any intel on the roster, since you and Coach Daniels are so chummy?"

Dean glanced around, making sure Rhett and Tucker were out of earshot, then pulled me close.

"Let's just say we're about to add another Bender to the crew who's going to appreciate having you watch his back." He chucked me on the shoulder. "Our very own champion."

"Oh, shut it."

He laughed. "Going home?"

"Shower, then piano practice," I said. "See you tomorrow?"

"Yep." Dean started to go, then turned and shot me a wink. "I'll tell Harper you said hi."

Chapter 9

HARPER

Sunday morning, Mom was all smiles, and Dash, being a kid, had forgiven and forgotten he'd been abandoned the night before. Still, too many nights like that would dim the light in his eyes. If that happened, I would *never* forgive my mother. No do-overs.

I remained distant, holed up in my room doing homework. It was nearly three when I realized I hadn't checked my email from Professor Wolfe to see what he expected of me for Monday.

from: ProfWolfe <ewolfe@cha.edu>

to: <hbennettID22335@cha.edu>

re: Monday Assignment

Für Elise, Beethoven

That was all. No greeting, no sign-off, nothing.

Charming.

My first instinct was to be pissed at being assigned one of the most cliché pieces in all of classical music, but I smelled a trap. Everyone and their mother knew the opening section of Für Elise, but few knew it took a turn for the difficult shortly after. Wolfe was trying to catch me being lazy or complacent—nail the first part, suck at the rest.

"Not on my watch, asshole," I muttered.

God, CHA was getting to me if I was hostile over Beethoven.

I printed out the sheet music, packed up my stuff, and went downstairs. Dash and Mom were curled up on thc couch watching *Bluey*.

"I'm going to the Academy to practice piano." I shouldered my bag and grabbed my keys from the hook on the door. "You guys have plans?"

Translation: Are you moving from that couch?

Mom shot me a dry look. "Nope, we're staying right here. You don't have to *hover*."

I clenched my teeth, then flashed Dash a smile. "See you, buddy."

"Bye-bye, Harper," he called.

"Bye, Harper," Mom said, her face now apologetic.

I turned away. "Be back in time for dinner."

It was only the first week of school, and yet Castle Hill Academy, on a Sunday, was active. The soccer field was busy, the track had runners. Most of the study rooms were buzzing, and when I passed by the massive gym, students were training and working out.

In the Arts Wing, I worried I wouldn't find an open piano room but got lucky. For two hours, I perfected my Für Elise, until the transitions were smooth.

Smooth, until I have Wolfe breathing down my neck while I play.

Heading out, I noticed all the practice rooms were still occupied with students from my class, striving to impress *the* Ezra Wolfe.

Or just plain scared of him.

One desperate student had even resorted to using our actual classroom. I froze as I passed by, listening. Coming through—no, *floating* through the closed door—was Chopin's Nocturne in C sharp minor. One of the saddest yet most beautiful pieces ever composed.

I knew without knowing. I didn't even have to look.

Orion.

I quietly pushed the door open. Orion was at the piano. His sheet music was in front of him, covered in strange tabs, like small Post-it notes, but his eyes were closed. His hands glided over the keys, and music was pouring out.

Wolfe called this emptiness?

Orion played it flawlessly, beautifully. The music moved from slow, melodic, and melancholy, into the faster desperation of a composer in agony—quiet moments of despair, then earthquakes of heartbreak. But it was as if Orion were a tool for the music, but not part of it.

Wrong. You're letting Wolfe get to you. He plays like a miracle.

Orion was a musical genius. No doubt about it. If he abandoned the piano to follow in his family's footsteps, it would be a crime against humanity. The music world would lose a tremendous gift and not even know it, because he carried his talent around in his back pocket like an afterthought.

Orion abruptly stopped playing. He picked up his phone and hit a button. The next movement in the Nocturne played, and he listened, eyes closed. Then he stopped the track, set the phone down, and played the same section. An exact replica, as if taking dictation.

I slipped away, trying to understand what I had just seen and heard.

It's none of your business. You shouldn't have been there in the first place.

That was true. I'd spent the weekend studying and fuming at my mother's negligence, but also strengthening my resolve that Orion and I would be working together as lab partners and possibly against each other for the Novus Science project. That's all. There was no earthly reason to do—or be—anything else.

But the beauty in his playing and the weight of his jacket at the bonfire—like borrowed armor—made me wonder if I'd walked away too fast. If I'd let old hurt pull up the drawbridge and keep Orion out.

I'd spent my life bracing for calamity, afraid even a crack of something good could break me.

As I left the Academy, one word followed me on the last notes of his music.

Maybe.

Monday morning, as talk about Jack Wallace filled the hallways, I used the restroom before chemistry. I stepped out of the stall to wash my hands, and suddenly Aria Kingston and Elowen Blake were behind me. My heart started to pound.

"Harper, right?" Aria said. Her eyes were like black glass. "You're new here."

"Yeah," I said, rinsing my hands and reaching for the paper towel dispenser.

"Let me." Elowen was faster, pulling two sheets and handing them to me with a fake smile.

"Thanks."

"Where were you before?" Aria asked.

"Pennsylvania," I said. "Pittsburgh."

"*Pitts*burgh," Aria said with a laugh. "That totally makes sense."

Elowen wasn't laughing. "I wanted to talk to you about Saturday night. About how I found you with Orion, all cozy on a log, wearing his jacket, no less."

Aria pulled out a tube of lip gloss and began applying it in the mirror. "Here's the thing, Harper from *Pitts*burgh.

I'll explain this to you because you're new and obviously don't know the deal." She smacked her lips together with a *pop* and turned to me. "Orion is up here." She reached her hand overhead, palm facing down. "He's Big Five. One of the kings of the school."

"Royalty," Elowen put in.

"And El and I, we're, like, here." Aria moved her hand slightly lower. "We might not be royalty but we're… How to put it?"

"Nobility."

"Exactly. And you…" Aria put her hand parallel to the ground at knee level. "You're down here."

I clenched my jaw, feeling my cheeks burn and hating it.

"What we're saying," Elowen said, "is that kings of the school do not associate so far down the ladder. It just doesn't happen."

"But it's okay!" Aria said, oozing false friendliness. "You didn't know. Which is why you were hanging out with Orion. He's a sweetheart and will often take pity on Benders, but it's not like he'd ever get serious with one. He's a fuckboy."

Elowen stared at her friend, indignant.

Aria shrugged. "Well? He is. Strictly a player. He doesn't get serious with anyone but definitely not with *Benders*." She looked to me. "You have to know that, right?"

Of course I know. Because this is real life. No maybes in sight.

Both girls stared at me with pitying, cringey smiles, actually waiting for me to answer. A wave of homesickness came over me. In *Pitts*burgh, I hadn't been the most popular girl in school, but I'd been comfortable. Confident. Here, I was out of my element. Naked and raw.

I balled up the paper towels and threw them into the wastebasket, feigning the courage I used to have. "I have a question. Because I'm new here and all, maybe you guys could help me out."

Aria's eyes flared with anger, catching on immediately. Her smile widened until it was all teeth. "Of course."

"Do you honestly believe all the royalty and nobility bullshit? Or do you have to work at convincing yourself of your own superiority?" I cocked my head. "Nah, never mind. If I were as ugly as you, I'd do my best to pretend I was better than everyone else too."

My heart thudded against my chest, sure I was about to get my ass kicked, hair pulled, face scratched. The two girls glanced at each other, and then burst out laughing.

"Oh my God, you are *so* cute," Aria said, though not one shred of humor touched her eyes. "Are you, like, some kind of philosopher or something?"

"That was really deep," Elowen said, nodding with mock thoughtfulness. "I'm going to go home and think about what you said for a long time."

Aria moved closer, eyes boring into mine. I could smell the peach flavor of her lip gloss. "Let me be plain. Stay the fuck away from Orion or we'll make your life at CHA a living hell." Her fake smile returned. "And honestly, it's not so much a warning but a favor. You don't want to embarrass yourself more than you already have, do you?"

My cheeks burned as Aria gave me one last appraising glance, taking in my overalls with a patchwork design.

"Cute outfit. Kinda like the Bratz doll I had when I was a kid. The one that liked thrifting, which was the only one I threw in the trash."

Then they turned and walked out, chatting about something else entirely, as if that whole entire conversation had never happened. As if I no longer existed.

I gripped the edge of the sink and took several deep breaths, my heart still pounding. I told myself it didn't matter. They were superficial Richies who cared about all the wrong things. Their bullshit didn't bother me. Still, it took me ten minutes to feel calm enough to leave the bathroom, which had never happened to me before. Even when my mother was drinking and some drunk asshole boyfriend was staggering around our apartment, I'd been in control.

If you can handle that, you can handle some rich-bitch bullying. You can handle all of this.

This.

Being uprooted, Dash being left alone, my mother's slap, the bullying, the pressure.

And Orion…

My *maybe* had been built on beautiful music floating on air, not solid ground. I'd been smart to protect myself that night after all. Even if Orion wasn't the manwhore Aria claimed him to be, we were too different. Guys like him didn't date girls like me. In stories, maybe, not in real life. Not in places like Castle Hill Academy. I'd almost let my guard down. I wouldn't be stupid enough to make that same mistake twice. Not here. Not when this place was doing its best to chew me up and spit me out.

"It's only been five days," I told the girl in the mirror. "Pace yourself."

I splashed cold water on my face, took a deep, steadying breath, stood up straight, and walked out.

Dr. Langford was ten minutes into explaining the lab for today, when I finally made it to chem.

"So glad you could join us, Ms. Bennett."

"Sorry," I murmured.

"Page twenty-one in your books," Dr. Langford said. "Chapter three on your iPads. Galvanic cells and Nernst equations. Enjoy."

The class got busy, talking in low murmurs. I pulled my iPad from my bag and flinched when I felt Orion's soft touch on my arm.

"Hey," he said in a low voice. "You all right, love?"

"I'm fine."

"You don't look fine," he said. "You look—"

"I'm *fine*." I pulled up chapter three on my device. "Do you want me to read this? It looks like we have to build a simple battery with zinc and copper, then measure its voltage—"

"Forget the bloody lab." Orion leaned closer. "About Saturday night..."

"What about it?"

"Well." He suddenly seemed nervous. "I thought it was quite lovely before we were so rudely interrupted, and I was wondering..." He cocked his head. "Are you sure you're all right? If it's because of Elowen, I'm sorry. I should have—"

I kept my eyes on the screen. "You don't have to be sorry. I get it."

"Get what?"

"Look, I'm not going to give you a hard time about it or expect anything. So don't worry, you're off the hook."

"Off the hook?"

"Yes. We can forget the whole thing ever happened."

"Maybe I don't want to forget it happened." His nervous smile returned. "Look, I'm bungling it. You may have heard, I don't normally do this—"

"Look, Orion, you don't have to make nice or pretend. It's just been made abundantly clear to me where I stand in the social order of things, and I'm not interested in playing Richie games, okay?"

His brows came together, and for the first time since we'd met, he looked truly angry. I sort of loathed that it had to be this way, but if he hated me, so be it. It was better—

"Who?" he demanded.

I blinked. "What?"

"You said it was made clear where you stand. Who made that clear to you?"

A fluttering in my stomach, like a hundred butterflies taking off at once. Same as when he'd put his jacket on me at the bonfire, and I'd been enveloped in the clean, masculine scent of his cologne and soap and the lingering heat of his body. Now the feeling came again, from watching Orion's handsome face turn threatening and protective. His smile morphing to a snarl. His *twinkly* eyes darkening with menace.

Dammit, this is not how this was supposed to go.

"No one," I said, looking away. "It's just the Academy in general. It's pretty obvious how it all works. The caste system. You said it yourself…"

"Harper. Tell me."

His stare was unrelenting, and the commanding tone in his voice nearly had me obeying. But I wasn't a snitch. I cleared my throat and recovered my sense of self. No, *stole* it back from this guy who had the ability to break through my defenses more easily than anyone I'd ever met.

All the more reason to build them higher and stronger.

"Just leave it," I said. "I've got too damn much on my plate. I'm your lab partner and that's all. That's all I'll ever be. Okay?"

"What? Why?"

"Because it's better that way."

"Says who? Harper, *what happened*?"

"Nothing. Everything. I'm…" I shook my head, willing my stupid eyes not to betray me. "I'm just done, okay? I'm fucking done."

Orion stared at me, a thousand thoughts playing over his features. For a moment I thought he might protest or tell me flat-out that this was unacceptable.

But he didn't.

"Fine," he said finally. "If it's what you want."

I swallowed hard and nodded. "Should I read the lab instructions?"

Another pause. His jaw ticked.

"Orion?"

"Sure."

So I did. All business. He and I, lab partners.

Just like I wanted.

All the while, Orion simmered next to me, a live wire throwing sparks, or a pot about to boil over. He flexed his fingers again and again, and when the bell mercifully rang, he gathered his things and stalked out.

I dragged myself through the rest of the day, feeling like an exposed nerve, dreading piano class where Wolfe would call me up to play Für Elise. There, I tried to find some of my usual fire and spirit, but I sat hunched in my seat, feeling small and insecure and hating how Rhode Island had doused me with one cold bucket of water after another.

Professor Wolfe strode in wearing jeans—against CHA

professor dress code—motorcycle boots, a Pink Floyd T-shirt, and a kind of long black tunic, open in the front and worn like a jacket. Without greeting or preamble, he started calling on students. Mercifully, I wasn't one of them. Orion was.

"Mercer," Wolfe said. "Where is your sheet music?"

"I don't have it," Orion said, steadily meeting Professor Wolfe's gaze. "I don't *need* it."

"Very well. Be my guest."

Orion sat down, laid his hands over the keys for a still, silent moment. Then he began to play the Nocturne. It was a short piece, but far more complicated than anything we'd heard from the other students. When it was done, the class started to break out into applause.

"Stop, stop, stop," Wolfe said, quelling us with outstretched hands. He looked at Orion. "Flawless, technical perfection. And you may as well have been a robot. Or a player piano. Take your seat."

But instead of returning to his seat, Orion turned back to the keys and began to play a few soft notes, then a slow, climbing of scales.

"What are you doing?" Wolfe said. "I told you—"

Orion kept playing. I didn't recognize the music until it took off and then it came to me: Chopin again, Ballade No. 1 in G minor. A piece that started slowly then erupted into a rainstorm up and down the scales.

"That's enough, Mr. Mercer," Wolfe shouted over the sound.

But Orion didn't stop. He kept playing through the highs and lows, his hands a blur, the music pouring into the room and over us like a beautiful tempest about to break free. Finally, Wolfe grabbed the piano's lid and slammed it down. If Orion hadn't snatched his hands away, his fingers would've been broken.

Silence then. All the more jarring after the astonishing thunderstorm we'd just experienced.

Orion shot to his feet, knocking over the bench. He and Wolfe stared each other down, Orion's eyes blazing, his breath coming out hard. I wondered for a second if the two were going to tackle each other to the ground, fists flying.

And then Wolfe laughed.

"That's what I've been waiting for," he said. "Class dismissed. Except you, Mercer. You stay with me."

Chapter 10

ORION

I'm your lab partner and that's all. That's all I'll ever be.

No doctor had ever told me it was part of my ADHD, but I visualized images out of words. Recognized patterns. When words failed me, pictures bloomed in my mind.

When Harper drew that line in the sand, I visualized my jacket lying abandoned next to it, something warm and good burning out, a pattern of hookups with girls I cared nothing about and who cared nothing for me but my status, continuing on until I went back to the UK at the end of the year.

But there was also Harper in the moonlight, her dark hair falling over her shoulders and her scrutinizing gaze, trying to decipher if I could be trusted, if I were someone *worthy* of her trust, while she didn't try to do or be anything but herself. I'd barely had a taste of who she was, but I'd liked everything so far. Everything.

But you cocked it up, and that's all you'll ever get.

Yet while my ego was not of inconsequential size, my actions on Saturday night couldn't be the only reason why Harper looked so broken in chem. But I wasn't about to challenge her in class when she was clearly at the brink. She had her pride.

But someone had hurt Harper.

Again.

A small storm had begun to brew in me, rising up from below. A fury for Harper piled on a lifetime of my own. All buried. Pushed down because that's all I knew to do.

When Ezra Wolfe started in on me in Advanced Piano, the storm began to rise. A tempest was still alive in me—decades' worth—ready to burst free. I shot to my feet, knocking over the bench, my breath coming hard. Wolfe stared me down, but I didn't blink. Didn't move—*afraid* to move—because every muscle was coiled and ready to spring, to tackle the fucker to the ground if I had to.

And then he laughed and dismissed the class.

As the students filed out, I fought for breath. For calm, pushing it all back down. Harper shot me a concerned glance as she went out, and it nearly all came back, a ferocious need to protect her…

Ezra Wolfe chuckled, bringing me back around. He and I stared each other down, the baby grand between us.

"Well, well, well," he drawled. "There he is. Or at least, a hint. You want to tell me where that's been hiding?"

"I don't know what you're talking about," I said tightly.

"Start with the basics," Wolfe said. "How is it you play so perfectly without sheet music? Rote memorization?"

"Sometimes," I said, fighting for calm. "I can hear a piece and play it by ear."

"The other day you said you can read music but that it's complicated. Explain."

"I see patterns in the notes, but things like tempo and dynamic notations are hard to decipher."

"Hard to decipher?"

"Yeah. Confusing. I have—"

He flapped a hand. "Actually, notes and notations, by ear or not… None of that interests me. What I want to know is, where did that come from? The fire just now. Or more importantly, where has it been and how do we keep it?"

"I don't know," I said, a small, strange ache in my chest. Like longing. "I don't usually…"

"Disobey?"

I nodded. The piano bench was tipped over, so I set it on its feet. "It's not how I was raised."

"Ah, yes," Wolfe said disdainfully, watching me put the bench back in its place. "The proper British stiff upper lip."

I crossed my arms. "You don't seem to have that problem."

Wolfe's eyes widened, and I thought I'd overstepped, but he laughed dryly.

"Indeed." He ran a hand along the shiny black surface of the piano that matched the lacquer on his nails. "I've swung quite far the other way, diving headlong into a deep well of vices. Nearly drowned once or twice, and I still take the occasional swim..." Wolfe looked pained for a moment, then dismissed the shadows. "But we're not talking about me. We're talking about you. I was lying when I said that you play without emotion or heart."

My head whipped up. "You were?"

He nodded. "I can hear it in your music, but faintly. A tap-tap-tapping of someone trapped in a cave-in and trying to get out. Your technical precision is astonishing, Orion. A talent like yours comes around perhaps once in a century. If only you could break out of that trap..." He shook his head. "You would put me to shame a hundred times over."

I scoffed, but that pang in my chest came again. The ache for the music I'd abandoned for so long. "That's a wild exaggeration."

Wolfe cocked a brow. "Have I presented myself as someone who lets compliments roll readily off his tongue?" He tapped his chin. "I must be giving a sweeter impression than I thought."

"Not exactly," I muttered.

"Aren't you at all curious about your extraordinary gift, Orion?" Wolfe asked. "I don't understand how you play like you do—emotional unavailability notwithstanding—and not do everything in your power to cultivate your talent. Make something of it. Hell, at the very least, show off and get paid for it?"

"I don't know," I said. "My family doesn't show off, Professor Wolfe. And it was never something I knew I could do as a *career*."

Wolfe's expression softened. "Did it ever occur to you *to ask*?"

The question hit me square in the chest. Because the answer was shockingly, stupidly, obviously *no*. I'd never asked because we never talked about what we wanted in my family. Hopes and dreams, aspirations and ambitions… they all belonged to the depths. We were never forced into our roles; we just accepted them because anything else was…

Rocking the boat.

I gave my head a shake. "It doesn't matter. I'm going into the family business."

"Ah, yes. Chemicals. Compounds. *Household cleaning products*." Wolfe enunciated each syllable with derision. "Riveting. When I spill one of my many weekly glasses of wine on my carpet, I reach for a Mercer product to get it out." He rolled his eyes. "Such a meaningful contribution to humanity."

I shrugged. "If you're trying to get a rise out of me again, it won't work. I'm not one of those tortured artists, Professor Wolfe, secretly trying to break free from rigid family expectations, or whatever clichéd bullshit you may think."

"Really?"

"Really."

"Hm." He tapped his chin again. "I doubt that."

I scoffed. "You think I'm lying?"

"No. I think you *believe* you're telling the truth."

A silence dropped heavy and hard between us. The professor met my gaze, unflinching, as if he were staring down into my soul.

I broke free. "Are we done here?"

"Almost. There is a spring music exhibition in April. I'm going to be choosing ten of the most promising students from my classes this semester to perform in it. Spoiler alert, as the Americans like to say—you will be one of them."

"Professor—"

"I will assign you a piece, and I want you and I to work on that piece together." He mimicked a hammering motion. "Tap, tap, tap."

I started to protest. To rebel. But apparently, I'd logged my one defiance for the decade.

Or maybe this is something you actually want.

"I'll think about it," I said. "Anything else?"

"Have you heard of the O-1 visa?"

"No."

"The O-1 visa is required for international students to remain abroad in order to attend certain universities such as, oh, I don't know." He waved his hand. "Juilliard? They require a mentor," he said, barreling over my protests. "It just so happens—despite my many, *many* aforementioned vices—I'm qualified to be one such mentor."

"Professor Wolfe, I told you, at the end of this year, I'm going back to the UK. I'm attending Cambridge and then I'm going to work for my family's company. End of story."

"End of story. End of *the* story," Wolfe mused. "Such a sad turn of phrase, don't you think?"

And to my shock, he reached out and put a gentle hand on my shoulder, the first soft, tender gesture I'd seen from him—this same man, who, not minutes before, might have shattered my fingers.

"It doesn't have to be."

The door clicked shut behind me.

I felt drunk. Or as if I were on a ship being tossed at sea—the ground beneath my feet suddenly uneven, the path no longer straight and easy. My hands were shaking, and I shoved them into my pockets.

What the hell just happened?

I'd walked into class prepared to keep my head down, play the Chopin, endure Wolfe's abuse, survive the day. But then the storm rose in me and I let it. *I let it.* Nothing had changed and everything had changed.

Tap, tap, tap. Someone trapped, trying to get out.

My chest ached. With a few sentences, Wolfe tore me open after a lifetime of silence.

I should've gone back to Atlas Hall, tackled my homework, and forgotten this entire scene. Pretend I didn't nearly break school property—or Wolfe's jaw—because something volcanic cracked open inside me. Pretend nothing had happened. That was the Mercer way.

But now questions were out there, floating in the air like echoes, and I couldn't unhear them.

Aren't you at all curious about your extraordinary gift, Orion? Did it ever occur to you to ask?

I never had. Not once. But nobody had ever asked me either.

Cambridge. Mercer Chemicals. A life mapped out, and I'd accepted it the way you "accept" the air you breathe or the language you grow up speaking—without question or protest. Why would I? You didn't question the weather or the tides, either. You didn't raise your voice. And you didn't rock the boat, but that boat was now a shipwreck after the storm I'd created…

I wasn't the same guy who walked into that room, and I didn't have the faintest idea what to do about it.

I thought about going to a piano room, but that felt too raw, so I ended up in the student lounge, pretending to study. Across the room, Aria Kingston and Elowen Blake were whispering together. I watched them watch other students walk by, sizing Benders up and down, then whispering some more, and a different kind of storm seized me.

I tossed my books in my bag and passed by, catching

my name from Elowen, followed by Aria's dismissive laughter.

"Please. He was bored. She's nobody."

My hands curled into fists before I even realized it. A hot, ugly rush of fury burned in my blood. Harper had heard some version of this. Of course she had.

She thinks I'm another spoiled prick who would use her, ditch her, and leave her with the fallout.

No wonder she drew that line and barricaded herself behind it.

"Aria," I said with a nod, a tight smile on my lips. "Elowen, may I speak with you a moment, love?"

"Of course!"

"Sorry about Saturday night," she said, moving to stand right up against me. "I can't believe I got so wasted. But I promise that if you give me a second chance to be taken home, I'll be much more *available*."

I crossed my arms. "Did you say something to Harper?"

The smile fell off Elowen's face like a mask. "Who?"

I cocked my head.

"Oh, the Bender from the bonfire? No, and why would I?" Her eyes narrowed in anger. "Why? Did she say something?"

"She didn't say a word," I said. I put on a dangerously lazy smile. "I was just curious, that's all. She's my chem partner and I don't like drama. In fact, I hate it. Nothing makes me more…turned off." My smile tightened. "So. Did you?"

"Oh, well..." Elowen looked uncertain. "I might've mentioned that you're a big deal at this school." Her smile turned flirty. "Because you are. That's no lie, right?"

I'm a big deal and Harper is not.

The picture could not have been made clearer if I'd been there. My stomach clenched.

"No lie," I agreed. "But I don't need anyone speaking for me, do I?"

"Um, no. Definitely not," Elowen said.

"Good. Then there's no need for you to talk to Harper ever again. Is there?"

"Oh. No, I suppose not—"

"Great. Glad to have that sorted." I turned my smile up to full wattage. "Hey, I've been meaning to ask. Are you going to the Halloween festival?"

Now Elowen's eyes widened with hope and no small amount of lust. I'd set the bait, and now she wriggled on my hook. I almost felt bad.

Almost.

"I am." Her smile turned coy. "I mean, I'd love to go..."

I opened my mouth to speak and then acted as if something dire had occurred to me.

"Shit, I forgot I have to get to the Hall. We'll talk more later, yeah?"

I gave her a light touch on the arm and walked away. I would never ask her to the festival or anywhere else, and leaving Elowen in purgatory wasn't very gentlemanly, but I wasn't about to intimidate her or threaten her with bodily harm, either.

Purgatory was punishment enough. Torture. I knew, because that's where Harper had left me.

But her time at CHA so far had been hell, and they'd made her believe getting close to me would only make it worse. If I pushed her now or tried to drag her back into whatever we almost had, I'd just be adding to her stress. She didn't need more tension; I refused to be just another rich bastard who made her life harder.

If what she wanted from me was space, then I'd give it to her. It was the least I could do. I had my own shit to sort anyway.

For instance, what I was supposed to do with the rest of my life.

Chapter 11

HARPER

END OF OCTOBER

"THAT'S IT," I MURMURED. I SAT BACK IN MY CHAIR AND hit *save* on my proposal.

It had taken me hours of brainstorming and many sleepless nights, but I'd come up with my Novus Prize for Scientific Innovation entry: an environmentally friendly, low-cost, portable water-purification system that could be used in underserved or disaster-struck areas. It wasn't sexy but seemed like it met the moment. *If* I could pull it off, given everything else I was trying to balance. Namely, taking care of my little brother while maintaining a 4.0 GPA.

And submitting the proposal was only round one. Langford said only 20 percent of entries made it to round two, where hopefuls had to put their ideas into action.

Let's hope the gods of chemistry are watching, I thought and shut my battered old laptop.

It was a Monday morning, and I could hear Dash and my mother moving around downstairs. I quickly finished getting ready for school, then packed up my supplies and headed down.

"Oh, Harper, there you are," Mom said, working over pans of eggs and bacon at the stove.

I froze, instantly on high alert. "Don't you have work at the dentist's office?"

Mom made a sour face. "I haven't lost my job already, if that's what you're thinking."

"Jesus, Mom, I wasn't thinking that." Except that's exactly what I was thinking. "It's just that you're usually at the office early."

"Dr. Hensley is very happy with me but doesn't need me until a little bit later today, so I thought I would make breakfast for the two of you and drive Dash to school."

Wow. Mom doing Mom Things. Hell hath frozen over.

I brushed the unfair thoughts away—she was doing her best, after all—and took a seat beside Dash on a stool at the kitchen counter. "So, things are going well over there?"

"They're going *great*," Mom said, setting a plate of scrambled eggs and bacon in front of me. "Dr. Hensley says he's never had an assistant who's as on top of things as I am. I may even be getting a raise soon."

"Awesome." I toyed with my fork. "Does that mean you'll be able to cut back on some of the cleaning?"

"I don't know about that," she said, sipping coffee from her favorite Pittsburgh Steelers mug. "But a gal can dream."

"The reason I ask is there's this big contest at school. It comes with a hefty leg up to my preferred universities and a cash prize. Twenty-five grand."

"What's twenty-five grand?" Dash asked. "Like the candy bar?"

"No, buddy. Twenty-five thousand dollars."

My mom put down her mug. "No kidding?"

"Yeah. A winner won't be announced until April, but I have an idea for an entry, and I think it's kind of a good one. If they accept it, and I move on to round two, I'll have to put in some late nights."

"This is exactly why we came to Rhode Island and Castle Hill Academy," Mom said. "For opportunities like this. We'll work something out, right, Dash?" She shot him a wink.

"Harper, I'm going to be a cowboy for Halloween!" he chirped. "What are you going to be?"

"I'm going to be a suffragette."

He scrunched up his face. "A what?"

"Well, buddy, it wasn't all that long ago that women weren't allowed to vote in elections. Suffragettes were women who fought for that right. Have they talked to you about elections in school?"

"Nope!"

"They will," I said with a grin and turned to Mom. "Remember that costume I made for the social studies project?"

"Of course. You worked so hard making that beautiful dress."

"I figured I'd put it to good use. There's a big Halloween festival here instead of a homecoming dance this Saturday."

"Saturday *is* Halloween!" Dash wiggled in his seat. "Candy, candy, candy."

I ruffled his hair. "Just what you need. More sugar."

Mom smiled coyly. "Any hot prospects for a date?"

Because my stupid brain—and heart—couldn't leave well enough alone even after all this time, Orion's face floated into my thoughts.

No, you shut that door. You don't get to open it, even in your imagination.

"I don't think so. I'll probably go with friends from the Math and Physics Club."

"Well, there's nothing on the books for cleaning, and I'll make sure I keep it that way." She leaned her elbows on the counter, coffee mug in both hands. "Anyway, Dash and I have some trick-or-treating to do."

He bounced in his seat. "Candy, candy, candy!"

Wow. Another Mom Thing I'd been stuck doing, three years running.

"Thanks, Mom."

"You don't have to *thank me*, Harper," she said, then quickly softened her tone. "We're all going to have a good time this Halloween."

She smiled apologetically. The Slap Heard Around the World was still hanging heavily between us after all this time too.

Her phone on the counter buzzed a text.

"Oh, it's Dr. Hensley. He needs me until 5:30 p.m. tonight." She looked to me as I was shouldering my backpack. "I'll drive Dash to school this morning, but can you pick him up today?"

I stared. I'd been hoping today could've been one of my late nights to finish writing up my NoSci proposal, but I guessed not.

"Sure," I said tightly. "No problem."

"Thanks, hon. You're a gem."

"Yep."

I ruffled Dash's hair again and grabbed a piece of bacon on my way out. "Have a good day, buddy."

"You have a good day too!"

A gal could dream.

As I crossed the quad from the parking lot, Elowen gave me the stink eye as if *I'd* bullied *her* in the girls' bathroom all those weeks ago, but she and Aria had left me alone since. I suspected that was Orion's doing, but I'd also obeyed their command and remembered my place in the food chain. I kept my interactions with him strictly chemistry-related.

Just like I wanted. Right?

Not that it was easy. Sitting next to Orion every day, being in his space, was wholly intoxicating. As if he had something in his very aura that bewildered the senses and turned normally rational girls (like me) into distracted, mushy-headed morons.

That day in chem, as Langford lectured about polymers, my eyes kept straying from my work to steal glances at Orion's profile. Each time, little jolts went straight down my spine. The fifth such time, he caught me. Or maybe he was stealing a glance too.

God, his eyes. Beautiful dark pools fringed in long lashes…

But Orion's eyes were tired lately. His smile was not as bright and seemed plastered on. Some days, he joked around with Langford, but that sounded tired too. Like an engine running out of gas.

Because he has no help. No accommodations.

My phone vibrated with a text from Emery Wallace.

Come with me to watch the boys' row after school?

Under the table, I typed back, Sure but need to be done by 4:15. Have to pick up the little guy.

No prob. CU then!

Emery and I had fallen into a "mismatched friendship," as she called it. She poured her guts out to me about her terrible home life and her authoritarian father, and I listened.

I wanted to spill my guts too, about Mom, Dash... certain boys that I could not evict from my thoughts no matter how hard I tried. But if I spoke Orion's name out loud, if I let any feelings out of the cage I'd locked them in, it would put cracks in my armor. I was holding my entire life together by dental floss and prayer, and I couldn't get distracted. I couldn't *be hurt* or the whole thing would come crashing down.

I risked another glance at the beautiful boy next to me.

Because when you fell for someone, you *fell.* Especially if it happened between a girl like me and a guy like Orion. There was only one outcome, and that was to hit the bottom.

But by the time the bell rang, all this chaos in my heart and brain was too much, and I decided to ask Dean Yearwood to the Halloween festival.

The sun was unusually bright and beautiful—an anomaly and probably one of the last truly beautiful days before the cold and rains of winter set in. At lunchtime, most students were taking advantage, eating on the quad. I sat with Dean on the grass, just him and me. I opened my mouth to ask him to be my date to the festival, and an entirely different question popped out instead.

"Dean, everybody loves you. You cross the invisible barrier between Richie and Bender so effortlessly. How do you do it?"

"Oh, wow. Wasn't expecting that, but okay..." Dean chuckled, then leaned back on his palms and tilted his head up to the sun, thinking. He was such a handsome guy, even in a simple jeans and sweatshirt...and I felt absolutely nothing but deep, sisterly affection for him.

"I don't know," he said. "I think it's because I know that everybody at CHA is facing severe pressure, Richie and Bender alike." He jerked his chin at a group of Richie girls not far from us: the Mean Girls, and Emery. "You see Delilah Winslow over there?"

"Yeah. The school's living TMZ."

"Her family is also one of the Big Five, like Tucker Hill, Gideon Foster, Emery, and Orion."

I clenched my jaw against the fluttering sensation in my chest that name never failed to create.

"She's one of the biggest gossips, and I think that's because she's insecure," Dean continued. "She tries to give people what they want so they'll like her. Because when you boil it down, isn't that what everybody wants? We're all wading through academic pressure or athletic pressure or performance pressure, but we really just want to be *seen*. I try to keep that in mind, so it doesn't matter to me if somebody is a Richie or a Bender. I try to see them for them, you know?"

I shook my head. "You're one of the good ones, Dean. No, one of the *rare* ones. The rarest."

"Nah," he said with a chuckle, as Xander Ford approached and sat down cross-legged between us.

"What are we talking about?" he said, adjusting his glasses with one muscled arm.

Xander was a super genius in an athlete's body, and in the short time I'd gotten to know him, he'd proven himself to be a good guy too...who happened to be smitten with Emery Wallace.

They're the best guys in my sphere, and one is taken-ish, and dating the other would be like dating my brother. I'm on a roll.

"I was just wondering how Dean maintains his status as a saint among us mere mortals," I said.

Xander chuckled. "Yeah, I've been wondering that myself."

"This one here," Dean said, jerking his chin at Xander, "handles pressure by getting out on the shell and rowing his guts out."

"Ah, yes. The classic Dean deflection," Xander teased.

"Bold of you to declare anything about me 'classic' when we met"—Dean pretended to check his watch—"a mere six weeks ago."

"I agree with Xander," I said. "You reek of modesty, Yearwood."

Dean muttered something and looked away, while Xander and I exchanged smiles, the three of us falling deeper, somehow, into friendship in that moment. But for Dean's sake, Xander changed the subject.

"We've got a good crew. Dean is the best of the bunch—of course," he said, not letting him off the hook completely. "Kai and Henry are pretty decent. But I'd say Orion is the only other guy I'd trust."

Dean nodded. "Orion's a good guy. Like, heart-of-gold good."

Dammit.

"Really? What's he like?" I plucked a blade of grass and tried to sound casual as hell. "I mean…out of curiosity."

I looked up to see Dean watching me. I glanced away, more blades of grass dying swift and merciless deaths.

Shut up, shut up, shut up.

"He's funny as hell," Xander said. "Pretends he has an ego, but it's all show."

"Aye, he's a king amongst the Richies but would throw down for us Benders in a heartbeat," Dean said. "Class distinctions mean nothing to him."

I felt him looking at me, but I refused—*refused*—to meet his eye. I had grass to pluck, after all.

"Agreed," Xander said. "If it weren't for Orion and Dean, I'm not sure I'd last very long on crew."

"Cool," I said, and cringed so hard I nearly gave myself a stomach cramp. By now I had a nice little pile of grass sacrificed to my mortification.

The rest of the lunch conversation moved on to other topics. I waited for Dean to bust out with an anecdote about Orion being a recreational arsonist who liked to set fire to Atlas Hall now and then. Or perhaps how he'd once gone on a tri-state killing spree and used his parents' influence to get away with it. No dice.

Face it. He's a good guy too.

Here I was trying to keep Orion at arm's length, and every single thing I knew about him only made me want to draw him closer.

When the lunch bell rang, I jumped up, brushed all the grass off my skirt while avoiding Dean's eye, and practically ran to history. With Orion. Again.

We didn't sit next to each other—that privilege belonged to Tessa Carlyle, a pretty, auburn-haired gal who was a big deal in the Drama department. She sat in the back with Orion while I sat toward the front, my attention split, half listening to Mr. Callister drone on about Mesopotamia and half listening to Tessa whisper-giggle at every witticism that fell out of Orion's mouth. Apparently, there were a lot.

What did you expect? That you were the only one who recognized how gorgeous, funny, and charming he is?

I rolled my eyes into my history book. If my inner voice fawned over him, why wouldn't every girl in school do the same?

"I can't stay," I said, huddled on the aluminum bleachers that had been set up for the inaugural regatta that would take place a few days after the Halloween festival. "I have to pick up my little brother at four thirty."

"It won't be long now," Emery said, leaning forward.

"Remind me why we're out here again?"

"We're here to support my boyfriend and our friend," Emery said, shielding her eyes and looking out over the Bay.

The rowing crew was out of sight, around a bend in the Bend. Their coaches stood on the dock several yards ahead of us, stopwatches in hand, as they watched and waited.

"It'll be Tucker's first regatta as a senior and Xander's first for CHA. It's a big deal."

"Hm," I said, hunched in my old jacket, scanning the horizon for Orion and pretending I wasn't as eager to see him as Emery was to see Xander.

"You mean to tell me you aren't having fun, wasting your afternoon freezing your booty off out here with me?" Emery teased.

I laughed and rolled my eyes. "More fun than I can handle. And don't worry, your secret is safe with me."

"What secret?"

"That the glamorous Emery Wallace is actually kind of a dork."

She giggled, nudged my elbow and, not for the first time, I marveled that this girl was my friend. That I had gotten her all wrong. When I'd met Emery, I was sure she was just another Richie without a care in the world. The Queen Bee in a hive full of drones who worshipped her. But she was kind, sweet, and a talented artist with a tyrant for a father, hell-bent on cramming her into a little life she didn't want.

And she'd listen to you just like you listen to her. Tell her about Orion. Get it out *so it's not chewing you up inside.*

But then Emery shocked the hell out of me by telling me she'd applied in secret to UCLA and how Xander had offered to marry her so she could detach from her parents' money for financial aid.

I blinked. "I beg your pardon?"

"But I don't think I could go through with it," she said. "I don't want to get married unless I mean it. Not until I'm older and can actually do it right. Because it's important to me. And anyway, if I go through with all this, my dad will disown me for sure. I wouldn't have a family."

"Are they really worth keeping?" I asked gently. "I know that sounds terrible, and I don't pretend to know what it's like to have the kind of pressure they're putting on you. But if our own family is no good for us, it's okay to build a new one from scratch."

She smiled sadly. "Easier said than done."

I took her hand. "Xander believes in you, or he wouldn't have made that offer. And I think, deep down, you believe in you."

"I'm trying." She smiled. "In any case, I don't have to worry about it right now."

"Emery—"

"So!" she said brightly. "Who's your date to the Halloween festival?"

I started to argue but there was no arguing with Emery once she put on her Everything Is Okay smile.

"As of right now, no one," I said.

"Any prospects?"

For one wild moment, a fantasy bloomed in my mind of Orion turning to me in chem, no barriers, no caste system, no protective defenses standing in the way…

"I'm waiting for a particular someone to ask me," I said softly, without thinking.

Emery bounced in her seat. "Oooh, who? Tell me! Someone I know?"

"No, forget it," I said, coming to my senses. "It's not going to happen. Not in my lifetime."

Ask me again, Emery, so I can tell you. Ask me so I can say his name out loud and you can confirm everything Aria and Elowen told me—tell me he's a manwhore, a heartbreaker who takes pity on the occasional Bender, and then I can finally stop thinking about him.

But Emery bit her lip, thinking. "Okay, how about Dean?"

"We're just friends."

"What about Xander?" she blurted.

I frowned, confused. "You think I should go with Xander. Your *fiancé*."

"Oh my God, *stop*. And why not? You're in the math club together. You're both super smart. I think you'd make a cute couple."

"You do?"

"Of course!" she said, her smile too wide. "You're both my friend, and I want my friends to be happy."

It was on the tip of my tongue to say no. I could just imagine all the Richie girls in their fishnets, corsets, and glitter while I looked like a frump in a suffragette sash and long skirt. And Orion would be there, looking devastatingly handsome in his costume, even if he came as the Toxic Avenger or put a bag on his head. I should stay home, get a jump on my NoSci entry…

Fuck that.

This school was *not* going to erase me. Plus, if I went with Xander, maybe Emery would finally snap and admit she's in love with him. It would be a strategic kindness.

Petty, but supportive. That's a thing, right?

"Sure. I'd go with Xander if he asked me."

"Great," Emery said, looking like it was anything but great. "I'll talk to him."

"If you insist."

"I do."

Aria, Elowen, Sierra Hart, and Delilah Winslow approached. That was my cue to exit stage left.

I gathered my stuff and slid off the bleachers. "See you, Em."

"Oh, okay. Bye."

I could feel the dark stares of Elowen and Aria stabbing me in the back, but I kept my head up and walked away casually. I was done letting them get under my skin, but that didn't mean I was going to spend one second in their space.

I still had time before picking up Dash and a brutal

ten-page history paper on ancient Mesopotamia coming up, so I went to the library to do some research. When I came out, the light was fading. Autumn was moving toward winter, and the days grew shorter.

I headed to the parking lot, which was almost deserted, and stopped.

My car was gone.

Chapter 12

HARPER

What the hell?

I glanced around, my heart pounding. It had been weeks since any of the Richies had bothered me about my parking spot. I thought that was over. And then I spotted my car near the chain-link fence by the industrial yard, looking slightly off-kilter.

I glanced around again. No sign of anyone, no snickering bully, no message on the glass.

"Okay," I muttered, taking a steadying breath. "At least it's here. No harm, no foul. Right?"

The door was locked. No sign of forced entry, as they say on the crime shows. I climbed in and pushed the button and gas, but the car wouldn't start, and the *check engine* light came on.

"Fuck, fuck, fuck, fuck, no…"

I didn't know the first thing about cars, but I knew it had something to do with the fact that my car was sitting a little bit tilted. I climbed out and peered underneath. Sure enough, a huge, jagged rock had punctured the undercarriage.

They lifted it. They picked it up and set it down on a fucking rock.

Tears came, and this time I couldn't keep them back.

"Harper?"

Orion. He looked fresh from row practice, in CHA athletic pants and a hoodie, and so damn handsome. Somehow, he was both the exact person I wanted to see and also the last person I wanted to see.

I turned my back, quickly wiping my eyes.

"What happened?"

"I don't know. Someone moved my car. They put it on a rock and now it won't start. It's fine. It's fine. I can manage—"

"Slow down, love," Orion said to me gently, even as that dark, menacing expression came to his face again as he glanced around. "Breathe."

"I don't know what to do," I said, panic rising in me as the shock wore off and the implications set in. "This is going to cost a fortune, and I have to get my brother from school…"

"Okay, hold on. One step at a time," Orion said. "The best place in town for repairs is Ralph's on Harbor Avenue. I'll call a tow truck—"

"I can't *afford* a tow truck," I said, humiliation burning my cheeks. "My brother has an afterschool program. I have to get him by four thirty. I have Triple-A. I'll call them. I don't need your help."

Orion stood with his arms crossed. "I'm not leaving you."

I started to protest, but that duality of wanting him yet not wanting him wrapped around my heart. I hated for him to see me like this, and I didn't want him to leave me. I didn't want to do this alone.

I'm so fucking tired of doing this alone.

I called the tow service and thanked the gods of geography that Rhode Island was tiny. It arrived in ten minutes, and a guy in blue coveralls attached my car to his truck. But I'd still never make it to Dash in time.

"I have to call the school," I said. "By the time I get to Ralph's, get the car handled, then call an Uber—"

"Harper," Orion said, his voice smooth, cutting through my frustration and panic. "There's no time. I'll take you to get Dash. The tow will take the car to Ralph's."

"It will? I don't have to go with?"

"No, ma'am," said the tow truck driver. "Call ahead, and they'll get you situated."

"I'll call ahead," Orion said. "You talk to the gentleman here."

"Oh. Okay," I said. "I've never done this before."

"No, worries, young lady," the driver said. "I'll take the car to Ralph's. You do whatever you need to do, then call them when you're ready. They'll run a diagnostic, give you an estimate, then you authorize the work. Got it?"

I nodded. Diagnostics and estimates. I had a credit card with a tiny limit for emergencies, and if it wasn't enough, I'd have to dip into the savings account I'd been dutifully cultivating my entire life. My stomach twisted.

While Orion called the repair shop, I filled out the tow truck paperwork, and then watched as my car was hauled away. That left me with five minutes to get Dash at his school, which was ten minutes away.

"I'm not going to make it."

"Come on," Orion said, giving my arm a gentle tug. "My car is here, and I drive really bloody fast."

We hurried across the campus to the Atlas Hall parking garage. Orion's expression was grim again.

"Do you know who did it?" I asked.

"I have an idea," Orion said. Anger smoldered in his dark eyes.

"Your friends."

"I told them not to."

I nearly tripped. "You knew they had this planned?"

"I'll deal with them later. Let's get this handled first."

I'll deal with them later.

Even in my distressed state, the threat came through loud and clear. The menace was alive in Orion's eyes, but his calm confidence was what I needed more.

The Atlas Hall parking garage was filled with luxury

cars, but to my untrained eye, Orion's was the finest of them all.

Didn't James Bond drive an Aston Martin?

And even though we were in a tearing hurry, Orion opened the passenger door for me, then made up for those ten lost seconds when we hit the road. He hadn't been lying—Orion drove really bloody fast.

The interior smelled of his cologne, leather, and money. I watched, half scared, half turned on (shocked I could be turned on in my present state of anxiety), watching him maneuver the stick shift and pedals, his eyes on the road with that same calm confidence. Orion drove with a wholly masculine authority over the car, commanding and masterful. I bit my lip, watching him, wondering if I were still allowed to be a suffragette for Halloween with these thoughts running through my head.

We made it to Dash's school in minutes, but I was still late. The school was deserted.

My little brother was sitting out front on a bench with a woman who looked to be in her early sixties, with silvery blond hair and a bright smile. If she was annoyed that she'd had to wait, she didn't show it.

Dash ran up to me. "Harper! Harper! This is my teacher, Mrs. Andolina."

"Hi, I'm Dash's sister. I'm so sorry. I had car problems and—"

"Don't you worry at all, my dear," Mrs. Andolina

said. She had a scratchy voice and a thick Boston accent. "These things happen."

"Thanks for understanding. This is my friend, Orion."

Dash stared up at Orion with wide eyes. "Your name is Orion? Like the constellation? We were just learning about constellations! Right, Mrs. Andolina?"

"That's right. Orion the Warrior. The brightest in the sky," she said with a smile. "The constellation lost sailors use to find their way home."

Orion crouched on his heels in front of Dash. "Hey, little man. I've heard a lot about you."

"You have? *My* name means run very fast. Did you know that?"

Orion rubbed his chin. "I might have heard that, but it is true?"

"It *is* true!" Dash said. "I swear."

"Hmmm. I think we need a race." Orion glanced around. "You see that flagpole over there? Do you think you can beat me to it?"

Dash's eyes lit up. "Heck yeah!"

Mrs. Andolina and I watched, her beaming, as Orion and Dash lined up on the sidewalk.

"On your mark, get set…go!"

I expected Orion to give Dash a head start, or to run slowly, but he took off and was soon ten strides ahead. Just when I thought he was going to crush my little brother's heart, Orion pretended to trip and took a roll in the grass in front of the school, tumbling at least three times before landing on his back. He lay spread eagle, breathing heavily. Dash, laughing at Orion's antics, touched the flagpole for the win.

Mrs. Andolina nudged me with her elbow. "Oh, I like him."

I nodded, a heavy ache in my chest. *Yeah, me too.*

"Dash?" Orion called. "What happened? Where am I?"

My little brother came running back to Orion and pounced on his stomach with both knees. Mrs. Andolina and I both winced out of solidarity.

"Orion, I won!" Dash cried. "Are you okay?"

"I was," Orion wheezed. "Until you thrashed my internal organs."

I burst out laughing on a day when I thought laughing was impossible, as the two rolled around in the grass.

Mrs. Andolina smiled at me. "Who *is* this lovely young man?"

"He's… He's…"

I couldn't finish the sentence.

Mrs. Andolina patted my hand. "I see."

Orion held Dash up in the air so Dash could pretend to be an airplane, and the ache in my heart deepened. My little brother had never known a decent male authority figure. One who wasn't drunk, loud, or resentful of a rowdy little kid being in his space, which wasn't even his space at all, but ours.

"We should go," I said, clearing my throat. "I'm sorry we kept you."

"Don't you worry about it. But give them a minute. They're having fun," Mrs. Andolina said, compassion and love pouring out of her. She seemed to be one of those people who was put on the planet to be a teacher. As if her scratchy voice came from years of shouting over loud classrooms of joyful kids, and she hadn't stopped smiling in decades.

"Dash told me you moved here from Pittsburgh," she said, as Orion gave Dash a piggyback ride around the front of the school. "And how has it been?"

I nearly gave her my rote *fine*, but told her the truth instead.

"Not great, honestly."

She nodded. "Moves can be hard. Leaving everything you know and starting over is rough. My husband, Frank, and I moved here from Woburn and have been in Castle Hill for twenty-three years. I've been teaching here all that time. All the parents know me because I love what I do. I love their kids and the kids love me, which is a blessing. Some even still visit me long after they've grown up and gone to the Academy."

I smiled politely, wondering why she was telling me all this.

"Frank and I have a dog. The muttiest mutt you ever did see. His name is Spike, and he has only one eye, but the kids love him." She looked up at me. "Like I was saying, the parents know me, and if they have scheduling difficulties, or if their kids need a little bit of extra help or are feeling a little bit lonely, I'm happy to babysit. Though I don't consider it babysitting, and I certainly don't charge for it."

I glanced at her and she nodded, her smile gentle.

"Dash was telling me that sometimes your mom works a lot, and you're at the Academy, so if you ever need us to watch Dash, I want you to give me a call, okay?"

"Oh. Oh, no, I couldn't ask—"

"You don't have to ask. I'm offering."

My throat felt thick, and I blinked hard as Orion jogged up with Dash on his back, my little brother's face flush with happiness.

"Isn't that right, Dash?" Mrs. Andolina asked. "You've never met Spike."

"No, but I want to!"

"I think it's time to get this one home before my spine gives out," Orion said. His eyes widened slightly to see the tears in mine.

I cleared my throat. "Time to go home, buddy."

Mrs. Andolina took my hand and gave it a squeeze. "My door is always open. Okay?"

"Thank you," I whispered.

"Anytime, darling."

Orion drove to our house—much slower with Dash in the back and no booster seat.

"Come inside, Orion!" Dash said, bouncing out of the car in our driveway. "Come have a snack. We can watch a show and you can see my room."

"Oh, I'm sure Orion has to get back," I said. I was

already embarrassed that our shabby little house looked even shabbier next to Orion's sports car. I'd die of embarrassment if he saw the *inside*.

Orion read my face. "Maybe next time, little man."

Dash pouted. "Why not?"

"I have a lot of homework, and I'm sure you do too," Orion said. He crouched down again and stuck out his hand. "It was a pleasure to meet you, Dashwell."

"Dashwell?" Dash laughed, scrunching up his face.

"Dashiel? Dashopher? Dashraham?"

My little brother was cackling with laughter, the sweetest sound.

"Those aren't my name!"

"No? What's your full name?"

"Dash *is* my full name. Just Dash."

Orion smacked a hand on his forehead. "Silly me. Pleasure to meet you, Just Dash. Until next time."

"When is next time?"

"I don't know." Orion stood to his full height and met my eye. *When is next time?*

Dash tugged at my hand. "Harper, Harper, when can Orion come back? Tomorrow?"

"Um, we'll see," I said, my gaze locked with Orion's. "Why don't you go get a snack? I'll be there in a minute."

"Okay. Bye, Orion!" And then Dash threw his arms around Orion's waist and ran inside.

"Sorry," I said, tucking a curl behind my ear. "He's, um…effusive."

"Doesn't seem to run in the family, does it?" Orion teased, and then his phone chimed a text. He fished it from his back pocket and his eyes widened. "Bloody hell. This can't be."

"Bad news?"

"No, but…I have to go."

"Oh, sure," I said. "But, thank you for today."

Orion's expression had hardened. "You don't have to thank me. I'll find out who messed with your car and—"

"No, please don't," I said. "Leave it. It'll just make things worse."

His mouth made a grim line. "I don't want to leave it. I thought…" He shook his head, frustrated. "I don't like it. This Cold War between us."

"Me neither," I said softly. "But it's been an uphill battle since I got here, and staying in my lane seemed… safest."

"I know." Orion's anger melted into uncertainty. "Harper, do you think—" His phone chimed again. "Shit. This is madness. I really have to go."

"It's okay. Go."

He hesitated, torn. "Let's talk later, okay?"

I nodded faintly.

Orion gave me a last, lingering look, and then put the phone to his ear. "I'm on my way. If you'd have *told* me you were coming…"

His words cut off as he shut his door, and he drove away.

I waited on my front drive in the falling dark until his car was out of sight, my pulse slowing because it had been pounding during the entire conversation.

I went inside, got Dash situated with a snack, and called Ralph's Repair Shop, bracing myself for the worst, but was told they hadn't gotten to my car yet and would call me back before closing.

Time crawled. I made Dash dinner and sat at the kitchen counter to do homework so I could keep an eye on him while he played with his train set on the living room floor.

At seven p.m. my phone chimed with a text, and my heart jumped. But it was Mom saying she was working late and not to wait up.

At quarter to eight, as I labored over a rough draft of my history paper, my phone rang with the repair shop's number.

"God, here we go." I heaved a breath and answered. "Hello?"

"Yes, hi, I'm Martina calling from Ralph's Repair. Is this Harper Bennett? The 2011 Prius?"

"Yep, that's me."

"We just wanted to let you know that the diagnostics have been completed. The oil pan is punctured and needs to be replaced. Our guys will get going on it first thing tomorrow morning, and you should be able to pick it up tomorrow afternoon."

"Wait, wait, don't I need to authorize the work or

something? I thought that was the first step. I don't even know how much this is going to cost."

"Um, yes, there's a note here." Martina sounded like she was shuffling some papers. "The work's been authorized, and payment's been arranged."

"What do you mean? What payment?"

"Orion Mercer? He put a card on file."

"He did *what*?"

I let him call the repair shop. That was my first mistake.

"How much?" I asked.

"Oh, let's see... Including diagnostic, oil pan replacement, damaged fuel line and labor, the total comes to $990."

My face paled. It was more than the limit on my emergency card, but I could figure it out. Withdraw some cash and pay with a combination of cash and card…

"Can you…*not* use his card?" I asked. "I know it sounds weird but—"

Martina chuckled. "There's a note about that too. It says you'll probably ask that, and the answer is no."

Damn him.

"We'll text you when it's ready to be picked up," Martina said brightly.

"Okay. Thanks."

I ended the call and set my phone on the counter and stared at it, split down the middle with emotions. Touched and embarrassed. Angry and grateful. I glanced at Dash, happily playing on the rug. Orion was both infuriating and endearing, and now my little brother was in love with him, and every single door inside me I'd tried to slam closed was wide open.

"I'm paying him back. Every penny."

"What'd you say, Harper?"

"Nothing, buddy. Time for bed."

I tucked Dash in and took my homework to my room. I heard Mom come in sometime after ten o'clock but stayed at my desk. I'd tell her about the car tomorrow, and she could tell me what kind of overtime a dental receptionist put in that kept her at work until ten at night.

Do I even want to know? No, I do not.

I tried to concentrate on my history paper, but Orion and I had exchanged cell numbers early in the semester when we became lab partners. "Later" kept coming and still my phone remained silent.

Finally, at quarter to eleven, my phone rang, and my stupid heart leaped to my throat...until I saw the number.

"Hey, Xander," I said, trying not to sound completely deflated.

"Heya, Harper. Hope it's not too late to be calling."

"No, it's fine. What's up?"

But I already knew what was up. Emery moved fast.

"I was wondering if you had plans for the Halloween festival? Supposed to be a big deal around here."

"Yeah, that's what I hear too," I said slowly. "And no, I have no plans."

"Okay, well… Would you like to go with me? Just as friends. No pressure."

Just friends.

Tears pricked my eyes, and I blinked them away irritably, waiting. As if another call or text were going to come within the next few seconds.

"Harper?"

"Yeah, sorry. Sure, I'll go with you. As friends."

"Great," Xander said, sounding about as enthusiastic as me. Like we were closing a business deal. "Should I pick you up? I can take my dad's car."

"No, I'll meet you there," I said. "I might have to make a quick getaway if my little brother needs me."

"Okay. We can finalize the details tomorrow."

"Yep," I said. "Bye, Xander."

We ended the call, and now I had a date to the Halloween festival.

I set my phone on my desk and got back to work, waiting for it to ring again, with a different boy asking me the same question, proving that I'd been a fool to say yes to Xander. That I should have waited.

But no call came, so I guess I wasn't a fool after all.

Chapter 13

ORION

I DROVE FROM HARPER'S PLACE, MY HANDS GRIPPING THE steering wheel tightly. The last bloody thing I'd wanted to do was leave her. Not when I'd finally managed to melt some of the ice between us but…

Why is he here?

At Atlas Hall, I parked my car and hurried to my floor. Two men wearing all black stood sentry outside my and Easton's door. Security detail.

I rolled my eyes. *Not at all conspicuous.*

"At ease, gentlemen," I said, giving a mock salute.

"Mr. Mercer," one said, opening the door for me.

My bravado might've fooled them, but my stomach roiled. Inside my living space, Father stood at the window, hands clasped behind his back, gold and diamonds glinting off his fingers.

"This is unexpected," I said. "Hello, Father. What brings you here? Business or pleasure?"

"Orion," he said, turning. His mouth was drawn in a grim line. "I'm on my way to New York for a series of meetings. Given the severity of your situation here, I thought it prudent to make a stop."

"Severity," I said. On the coffee table was a manila envelope and an orange bottle of pills. "My next target and the poison to kill them?"

"Always with the jokes." Father sighed. He came around and sat on the lone chair across from the couch. "I've received your mid-semester grades, and they are no joking matter. You're failing or nearly failing everything but piano and chemistry. Piano is meaningless, and chemistry is a B-minus when it should be an A, considering."

It should be an F. I was drowning in my classes, and only Harper kept my head above water in chemistry.

"Then there is the matter of the Novus Science Innovation contest," Father continued.

"Yeah, sorry, I missed the deadline." I hopped up on the kitchen counter that faced the living area. "Slipped my mind."

"It didn't slip mine. I signed you up for it myself after you failed to do so."

"You…?" I felt a headache start to grow behind my eyes. "Why?"

"Why?" Father repeated. "Why would the highly prestigious scion of a science empire not participate in a highly prestigious science contest?"

"Because I don't need the prize. Not the money or the help with college."

"Are you sure about that?"

I gritted my teeth. "Other students could use both much more than I do, and you know it."

"*Other students* aren't my concern. That you are failing to uphold even the bare minimum standards of my expectation is. And now you are failing in your academics as well." He arched a brow. "You may need the help with the college admissions more than you know."

Now *he* was joking. Father had a direct line to the president of Cambridge. I could flunk out of Castle Hill Academy and I'd still get in.

Four more years. I can't do another four years.

"It's too hard," I muttered.

"Say again?"

"I said, it's too hard, Father," I repeated, louder. My heart was pounding, meeting his dark eyes. Admitting it out loud for the first time. "My brain…it can't process the work. I can't read—"

"Nonsense. You read perfectly well. We couldn't get your nose out of a book as a child. You lose focus during exams, is all."

"I can read books, yes. But it's…all mixed up. It's not as simple as losing focus."

"I doubt that," Father said, leaning over his knees. "You haven't been taking your medication, have you?"

"It makes me sick," I said. "It gives me a bad reaction, and it doesn't help."

Father pursed his lips. "I thought so. This is a new prescription. You will take it and you *will* improve your grades. That is your only job. Not crew. Not *piano*." He tapped two fingers on the envelope. "This is a list of formulas Mercer Chem is working on. Simple, basic."

My eyes widened. "NoSci rules state no outside help allowed. That's cheating."

"Don't be gauche, Orion. You will get no help from us. This is merely a list of ideas. Choose one. Choose none, but you *will* participate in that contest."

Father rose to his feet and came to me. I slid off the counter, and he put his hands on my shoulders.

"Your mother and I love you very much. We only want what's best for you. You must know that."

I nodded, a thousand words piling up in my throat, wanting to spill out of my mouth. Only two escaped.

"I know."

"When I was your age, in Year 13, I worked two jobs, and was already building the bones of what would become Mercer Chem. No one helped me, Orion. I had only grit and determination. Those were the bricks and mortar from which I built the empire that will one day be yours."

He clapped his hands on my shoulders and turned for the door.

"Work harder, take your meds, and come up with something brilliant for the contest." He opened the door. "We'll talk soon."

Then he was gone, and the room felt bigger somehow, now that he wasn't filling it with his looming presence. I sat down at the coffee table and opened the envelope and found what looked to be a list of chemistry formulas and ideas, some exceedingly complicated, some simple. Though it made me feel unclean, I could pick the most basic, the most *un*-innovative, the one most guaranteed to *not* wow any judges. Not that I had the mental bandwidth to wow anyone, anyway.

I'll pick the one that won't stand in Harper's way.

"It's still bloody cheatin', innit?"

I tossed the papers on the coffee table and picked up the orange pill bottle, squinting at the label. A different medication than the one I'd been prescribed before. Maybe it'd work…

Or maybe it'll give me a heart attack. That'll be fun.

I set that aside too and rubbed my eyes. First things first.

"Harper."

Just saying her name made everything feel lighter. Better. The headache behind my eyes was driven away by the memory of her smile as she watched me play with that rascal of a brother of hers.

She was *not* going to be pleased that I'd paid for her car repairs, but then again, I wasn't *not* going to pay for them either. Impossible. I might've been a lowdown cheating bastard, but I was still a gentleman.

"Gentleman" isn't the first word she's going to use when she hears I paid the bill…

A grin spread over my lips, just as Easton walked in the door, carrying his motorcycle helmet. He narrowed his eyes at me.

"And how was your day?"

"Smashing," I said. "My father has entered me in that bloody contest I wanted to avoid, is insisting I take medication that might send me into cardiac arrest, and tomorrow I might be expelled because I'm going to beat the ever-loving shit out of someone or someones for bullying the girl I care about. But none of it matters since I'm failing out of school anyway."

Easton listened, nodding. "Makes perfect sense. And you're smiling because…?"

"I'm going to ask that girl to go to the Halloween festival with me, and I suspect she might say yes."

"Of course." He started for our room. "Just don't go having cardiac arrests or getting expelled."

"Why, have you gone and fallen in love with me, Easton?"

"I wouldn't go that far." He shrugged one shoulder. "But…you don't suck."

"I'll take it."

On the way into CHA the next morning, my path dovetailed with Xander Ford's, and we walked along the quad together.

"Xander, my friend, tell me what's good," I said. "Going to the Halloween festival this weekend?"

"Yep," he said, pushing his black square-framed glasses up his nose. "I hadn't planned on it, but I suppose it's the thing to do. Are you dressing up?"

"Of course," I said. "A 1920s gangster."

"Al Capone or…?"

"No. Less *Scarface*, more *Sinners*."

Xander stared at me blankly, and I laughed. The bloke was a certifiable genius in quantum physics but could scarcely name a movie if his life depended on it.

I waved a hand. "The primary objective is to look hot in a suit. What's your costume?"

"A scientist," he said, glancing away almost shyly.

I laughed. "Of course. And which lucky lady will be on your arm?"

"Harper."

I nearly stopped walking. "Sorry?"

"Harper Bennett? She's in the Math and Physics Club with me," Xander said as we crossed the threshold into the Academy's bustling halls. "Do you know her?"

"Yeah, I know her," I muttered, my words lost under the tone of the first bell.

"Gotta run." Xander chucked me on the shoulder. "See you at practice."

I stood in the center of the maelstrom of students, some jostling me on their way to class, while the disappointment sucked at my heart, dragging it down to the vicinity of my ankles.

You waited too long, you bloody moron. You waited too long.

"Yo, Orion!"

Brent Reynolds, erstwhile bow seat from crew, was waving me over from a row of lockers. I wandered over.

"Hey, man! Been a while since we hung out," he said, an eager, almost desperate smile on his face. "Not since that Ford fucker took my seat."

"What do you want, Reynolds?" I asked dully.

"Nothing, just…what are you doing Saturday before the festival? Maybe we could hang out at Cassidy's? Tucker and the rest of the crew don't really talk to me much anymore…"

"Yeah, maybe."

Fuck me. She's going with Xander? Are they an item? Just how late is too late?

"Oh, hey." Brent whacked my shoulder. "Did you hear? I pulled off the senior prank."

My head snapped up. "What did you say?"

"Yeah, so Tucker and those guys said they'd given up on it for some reason, but Rhett told me it'd be funny if I did it anyway."

My teeth clenched. "Did what, exactly?"

Brent frowned. "The senior prank? You know…move

some Bender's car? But that shit was too heavy for just me and Jason. We didn't get very far—"

His words cut off with a choke as my hand shot out and gripped him around the collar, slamming him against the locker. Brent's eyes widened with shock at my sudden ferocity. It shocked me too, the rage that boiled up in me, as if it had been waiting…

"You did that?" I seethed, my face inches from his.

"I thought…I mean, Rhett said—"

"You fucked up her car," I snarled. "Nearly a grand in damages."

"Shit, I didn't know, I swear…"

Brent was staring at me as if I were a stranger. Someone he'd never seen before. I sucked in a breath, forcing the red haze to retreat. Slowly, I let go of his shirt and backed off.

"Jesus, Orion," Brent gasped, jerking his collar back into shape. "What the hell, man?"

I leveled a finger in his face. "You don't go near her, you hear me? Don't talk to her, don't touch one fucking thing that belongs to her. Never again."

"Okay, okay, but—"

"Never again."

I turned and stormed down the now near-empty hallway, inhaling over and over, willing the anger back down as I headed to period one, English. A class where my teacher believed I was cheating because my book reports were exemplary but my exam scores were shit.

My footsteps echoed on the polished floors, and one thought echoed in my messed-up brain.

I can't do this anymore.

Chapter 14

HARPER

"Where were you last night?" I crossed my arms, watching Mom blearily pour herself a cup of coffee from the pot that I'd made. My face was stony. Impassive. But inside my chest, my heart was pounding like a drum. I didn't smell booze, but I'd been here before.

This is how it starts.

"Jesus, Harper, who is the mother and who is the teenager?" She laughed half-heartedly but wouldn't look at me as I took a seat at the counter. She was still in her pajamas—sweatpants and a T-shirt. Blond-gray hair tied in a messy ponytail.

"Well?" I asked as Dash thumped upstairs, getting ready for school. "You don't have work?"

"Because we worked late, I don't have to come in until ten," she said. "Is that okay with you? Does that satisfy the Inquisition?"

"What could you have possibly been doing at a dentist office until nearly eleven p.m. last night? Or do I even want to know?"

"We were filing old patient records, Ms. Nosy," Mom said. "Dr. Hensley's cabinets are a mess, and he decided it was time to upgrade and digitize. I'll probably go back tonight too, which is why I came down this morning. So we can coordinate schedules."

I narrowed my eyes, studying her. She might be telling the truth, but when you grew up on red alert all your life, you learned to trust your instincts. And my gut was twisted into a thousand knots of suspicion.

"Sure," I said. "That makes *perfect sense*. I just hope the good doctor remembers to pay you overtime for all those extra hours and late nights you're putting in."

Mom set her coffee mug down and fixed me with a wide, fiery stare. "Do you have something you want to say to me, Harper Renée?"

"Yes," I said, fighting to keep my voice steady. "My car broke down yesterday. It won't be fixed until this afternoon, so you need to drive Dash and me to school."

Her head jerked. "It what…? Okay. How much to fix it?"

I shouldered my backpack. "Don't worry about it. I got it covered."

"Harper—"

Without taking my eyes off her, I craned to call up the stairs. "Dash, let's go!"

My mother set her coffee mug down and slid off the stool to get her key and slippers.

"What a morning," she said with a light laugh. "You're upset for no reason. Now tell me about the car."

"Later," I said as Dash flew downstairs. "We'll talk later."

She sighed. "Honestly, Harper…"

But she didn't finish her sentence. Dash grappled with his shoes, and she helped him tug his jacket on before we headed out the door. All smiles. But the queasy feeling in my stomach wouldn't quit.

Not again, I thought on the drive out. *Please God, not again.*

In chemistry, Langford was taking his sweet time to arrive, and the seat beside me remained empty too. I had hoped Orion would be early so I could give him the check in my bag before class started without a scene. But when my lab partner showed up, it was like a thundercloud rolling in.

Orion tossed the expensive leather bag that served as his backpack on the table with a slam and took his seat.

"Greetings and salutations, Bennett," he said, his smile tight. Stiff.

I frowned. "Um, *hi*. You okay?"

"Oh, brilliant." He rubbed his eyes. "Another day in paradise."

I tucked a curl behind my ear. "Right. So listen, I appreciate it a lot, but you didn't have to do that."

"Do what?

"You know what." I lowered my voice. "You paid for my car."

"Well," Orion said matter-of-factly. "You shouldn't have said yes to going to the Halloween festival with Xander Ford."

My heart stopped, then took off at a gallop.

"What?" I breathed.

"You heard me."

"You… You wanted to go to the festival with me?"

"Indeed."

"But you didn't ask me."

"I was going to ask you, but you'd made your declaration that we could only be lab partners. Which I honored, until I decided it was bullshit. By then it was too late."

"So…to get me back, you paid for my car."

"Yes."

I blinked. "Your timeline doesn't even make sense."

Orion shrugged again. "Neither do you and Xander, but here we are."

I stared. Every word coming out of his mouth stole my breath, and I went hot and cold all over. It was too much to process. I didn't know what to do with it all, and Langford was going to walk in the door any second.

"I don't understand," I said. "They bully me. They torment me for even talking to you—"

"And if it happens again, I'll make them pay for that too."

"You'll *what*?"

Orion swiveled to face me, his eyes hard. "Don't you get it, Harper? You're the one who doesn't want to be seen together. Not me. I don't care. I never cared. You just didn't believe me. You never gave me—us—a chance."

I sat back in my tall chair, his words whacking me in the heart and sinking in, creating a storm of euphoria and confusion.

"That…that isn't fair," I whispered.

"No?"

"No. I didn't know there was an us. Since when is there an us?"

"There isn't. Not since you drew a line and forbade me to cross it."

I stared, taking in Orion's face as if seeing him for the first time. His rich eyes, broad mouth, perfect skin… And everything about him that wasn't physical—the whole of him—that I couldn't keep out of my mind, and now he was telling me…

We could've been together? For real?

I shook my head, a warmth of possibilities flooding me and then burning away in the next instant.

"Was that before or after Elowen Blake threw herself at you? What am I saying? This is ridiculous. And impossible.

You can't just blindside me… Forget it." I started to reach in my bag. "I'm paying you back."

"No, you aren't," Orion said. "No chance."

"*Yes*," I said, rummaging. "I can't—"

"Harper," he said through clenched teeth, "if you pull money out of that bag, I'm going to scream."

I tensed, every muscle tightening, tears pricking my eyes.

"You can't do that," I whispered. "You can't just say *nothing*. For weeks. And then expect me to guess that you have…*feelings* because we had one moment at the bonfire. It doesn't work that way."

Orion swiveled to look at me, his eyes boring into mine. "I screwed up," he said. "I admit it. I don't know what the fuck I'm doing. But are you honestly telling me you never felt anything? That you don't feel something right now?"

My jaw worked soundlessly, and my mouth went dry, but before I could formulate a coherent thought, Langford breezed in.

"Sorry, sorry. NoSci meeting ran late." He dumped his portfolio on his desk and beamed at Orion. "Speaking of, so glad you joined us, Mr. Mercer! As the deadline approached, I'd begun to worry you were going to skip out."

Orion hunched his shoulders. "Wouldn't miss it."

"That's the spirit. We expect great things from you." Langford's smile on Orion was like a spotlight on the star performer before he moved on to explain today's lab.

"I thought you *were* going to skip it," I whispered.

"That was the plan," Orion whispered back, not looking at me. "Then a surprise visit from Father changed the plan."

So that was his mystery phone call. The tension—that snake that coiled in my guts, sending its adrenaline poison coursing through my veins—struck again.

He's going to win. He's going to win just because of his name…

Screw that. I'd just have to work harder. Later late nights. Weekends…

"No one is going to fuck with you again," Orion whispered suddenly, picking up his bag. "I've seen to that. And I'm sorry for everything that happened already. They're all pricks." He shook his head, the exhaustion falling over him again. "Maybe I am too."

And without another word, he strode out of the classroom.

"Orion?" Langford turned to me. "Something happen, Harper?"

"I…think he's not feeling well."

"Ah. It happens to the best of us. Can you handle the lab alone?"

"Sure."

"Excellent." Langford beamed at me, then bent to speak in a low voice only I could hear. "I'm very much looking forward to the two of you going toe to toe for the NoSci. I have a feeling it's going to be a tight race."

He shot me a wink and started his lecture. I shivered and tried to ignore the itchy feeling I always got around Langford and eyed the door. I wanted to follow Orion, to talk this out properly, but I was pretty sure if I bolted from class, I'd get a summons to the VP office to explain why. And the last thing I needed was a mark on my exemplary record.

I couldn't afford one mistake.

Orion didn't return to chem and was absent in history and piano too. I could hardly concentrate. The events of the last two days were boiling in my mind like some weird stew of good and bad, horrible and wonderful. My busted car and Dash's laughter. My mother's behavior and then chemistry.

Us.

There might've been and now there wasn't.

Because it's impossible, I thought, calling an Uber to take me to Ralph's Repair to pick up my car. I'd go get Dash, because my mother couldn't. Because she was working into the night *at a dentist's office* whose normal business hours ended at five. Because I had a contest to win and a 4.0 to maintain. Because a storm was coming.

I could feel it.

Mom was going to fall off the wagon, if she hadn't already. Or she was having an affair with Hensley, and that was going to crash and burn, and I'd have to pick up the pieces. Another round of her chaos, and it was going to take everything I had to survive it.

Everything.

That night, Mom came home at nine p.m. I was waiting for her on the couch, my oversized coat on, bag on my shoulder.

"Where are you off to so late?" she asked, her smile weak. Nervous. "I see you got the car back. What happened—"

"Are you drinking again?"

"Jesus, Harper, let me get in the door. It's been a long day—"

"Are you?"

My mother took off her coat and hung it on the hook by the door. She wore her "nice" dress, heels, lipstick…or what was left of it.

"Okay, look," she began.

Oh God…

Something inside me died. Again.

She came toward me, and I stood up and moved away, my arms crossed tightly. I looked harsh and unbending, but really, I was barely holding myself together.

"Dr. Hensley—Alan—and I are dating. I didn't want to tell you because it wasn't serious, but it looks like it might be getting serious—"

"Are. You. Drinking?" I demanded, enunciating each word and trying not to shout; Dash was upstairs sleeping.

"I was getting to that," Mom snapped, flouncing on the couch and taking off her heels. "I lied. I haven't been working late."

"No shit."

"He's been taking me to dinner after work. To nice restaurants," she said, ignoring my sarcasm. "Not like the crappy places the losers I used to date would take me to."

Nice restaurants. While I tried my best to cook something healthy for Dash but wound up resorting to frozen dinners most nights, either because I was short on time or we were short on money. Usually the latter.

"He's a nice guy, Harper. He's makes good money—"

"Isn't he married?"

Mom looked away, and I clenched my jaw so hard I thought my back teeth would shatter.

"It's complicated. He and his wife have been having issues for years, and he's going to file for divorce."

"Sure he will," I said. "Any minute now."

"My God, you're snotty," Mom said. "You can't let me have one nice thing."

I thought my eyes were going to explode out of my head, and it was all I could do to keep from throwing the little vase of flowers on the coffee table at the wall.

For Dash. Be cool for Dash.

"So?" My foot was tapping, and my hands were claws on my arms. "Drinking? Yes or no?"

"So that's the thing. Alan thinks it's weird that I don't have wine with dinner. So that's all it is," she added quickly. "Wine with dinner. One glass. Maybe two. No more than that, and I'm fine, Harper. I swear. I can handle it."

I shook my head, waiting for the tears to come, but

they didn't. Not yet. I could feel the lump of dread in the center of me, pulling all the stress and fear and pain and betrayal tighter and tighter.

"There is no third door for addicts," I managed through stiff lips. "Remember AA? There is sober and there is relapsed. That's it."

"Not for everyone," Mom said. "Doesn't have to be."

"Right. You're the exception," I said. "In all of human existence, you're the one exception."

"Harper—"

"I have to go," I said. "I can't do this right now, but we're not done talking about this."

I have to clean things up and close the door on a beautiful boy because it's too messy and we're all full up on messy over here, thanks.

I shouldered my bag and stopped at the door. "Not in the house. If I see any booze in the house, I'm going to lose my shit, I swear to God."

"Of course not," Mom said. "It's not that big of a deal. I promise."

"Promise." I shook my head. "You know, if you repeat a word enough times, it loses all meaning."

And then I went out.

Chapter 15

ORION

We expect great things from you.

Langford's smile had been kinder, brighter than Father's but no less weighted. Pressurized. And Harper beside me…Jesus, could I have fucked that up any harder?

Let's call it a day, shall we?

I'd left chemistry—and the CHA campus entirely—with all sorts of shame tailing me. Shame for my tantrum in chemistry and because Harper didn't know about Father's manila envelope, but so what? Still made me a prick.

"Bare minimum," I muttered as I keyed into my apartment in Atlas Hall. "I'll do the barest bloody minimum for that contest."

A silly vow to make, since the barest minimum was all I was capable of anyway.

I was failing most of my classes, and the skipped classes today would only add to the load. So I sat on the couch in the living area, laptop in my lap, and struggled over the school work, trying to use the hours to get ahead. By dinner, I had a raging headache.

At eight p.m., a text came in from Tucker.

You choked Brent?! WTF? That's hilarious.

It was followed by a bunch of laughing emoji. I put my phone on mute and turned it face down. The Mesopotamia essay for history wasn't going to write itself, but Christ in a sidecar…

My gaze landed on the orange pill bottle. It might work this time, new prescription and all. Fuck me sideways, things couldn't get worse.

I poured myself a glass of water and popped a little white pill.

Back at the couch, I waited for the magic to happen. For the words on the pages to resolve themselves into cohesion. For my brain to stop trying to run away from the mess and just read without me having to jump through hoops to build meaning.

Not for the first time—not by a bloody mile—I wondered if someone, somewhere had gotten it wrong. I knew people who had ADHD. Their meds worked brilliantly without any random, heart-exploding reactions, and they lived their lives. What the fuck was wrong with *me*? But whenever I'd brought it up, Mum and Father insisted the doctors knew what they were doing. My intelligence and keen aptitude were "proof" that if only I'd get my shit together and apply myself, I'd be *just fine*.

"If I apply myself any harder, I'm going to have a stroke."

Or a heart attack.

My heart had began to pound in my chest like a hammer, as if it were trying to break free of my ribs. I suddenly felt both hot and cold at the same time, shivering while breaking out into a sweat.

"No, no, no, bloody hell, not again."

My chest grew tight, and a band of pain wrapped around it, while a sliver of fear worked its way into my thoughts. I'd joked about cardiac arrests and heart attacks but what if…?

"No," I said to the empty room. "I'm fine."

But my breath was coming in short gasps that I could barely get past my throat. Slowly, carefully, I lay down on the couch, willing my heart to slow down. To relax.

Call someone, you bloody fool, before you croak, and Easton comes home to a corpse.

But the idea of sirens, EMTs flooding the halls, me being wheeled out on a stretcher… The whispering and gossip, the negative press, the *spectacle* of it all. And for what? A bad reaction. Mum and Father would hate that. Embarrassment to the family. So much boat rocking…

I breathed, lay still, sipped water, though each minor

movement sent my pulse skyrocketing. Around nine thirty p.m., just when I considered reaching for my phone, the reaction began to subside. Incrementally. I took my pulse and found it to be a cool 170.

"Progress," I croaked.

Ten more hours flat on my back and I'd be right as rain.

A knock came at the door.

Shit.

"Orion?"

Harper.

My eyes fell shut with surprising gladness. Happiness. I didn't want anyone to see me like this. Didn't want to worry her, especially, and Harper Bennett was going to insist I get help. But a small voice from way down in the deeps was calling. Begging for help. To be heard and seen, and this girl…

"It's open," I called, trying to sound normal. Cheerful, even. My voice betrayed me; I sounded like I'd been gargling rocks and washing them down with battery acid.

Harper came in, an expression of concern already on her face that morphed into alarm when she saw me.

"That good, eh?"

She rushed to kneel beside me. "What happened?"

I nodded at the pill bottle on the coffee table. "I tried…" But my throat went dry before I could finish my sentence, and Harper's eyes filled with the worst thoughts.

She grabbed the bottle. "How many did you take?"

I shook my head weakly. "No, no. Just one. Bad reaction. I'm okay."

Harper ignored that and put two fingers to my neck. "Your pulse is racing. I'm calling an ambulance."

"Please, don't," I said, as she fished around in her bag for her phone. "Really."

"I have to. You need help."

"No…I'm fine."

"You're not *fine*," she cried. "You're having a heart attack. Where the fuck is my phone?"

I gripped her wrist. Not hard, but enough to make her stop. "I'm fine. I've had this before." I took her hand and rested it over my chest. Over my heart. "Feel. See? It's slowing."

She held still, feeling my pulse that was calming down. My breaths were coming easier—thank God, or this girl was going to throw me over her shoulder and walk all the way to Newport Medical.

Harper shook her head. "I don't know…"

"I do," I said. "This always happens when I take these fucking meds. They don't work on this bloody broken brain of mine. I should've known better than to try."

"I still think I should call someone. What if…?"

I shook my head from side to side, smiling. "The EMTs will arrive for nothing. They'll say they've never seen anyone in better health than me. I'd both ruin *and* make their night."

Harper sat back on her heels, her eyes falling shut. Tears escaped, rolling down her cheeks.

"Aw, love." I touched a fingertip to her cheek. "Are these for me?"

"Some." She wiped her tears with the heel of her hand and huffed a watery breath. "You. Are. Infuriating."

"I'm fine. Promise. But *I'm dying* for a fresh glass of water."

Harper swatted my arm.

"Too soon?"

She shot me a dirty look and got to her feet. She refilled my glass from the small kitchen. I pushed myself up to sitting, slowly. My pulse kicked up a notch with the small movement, but Harper didn't need to know that.

"My hero," I said, taking the water gratefully.

"I still think I should call someone and have you checked out."

"You can check me out. Any time."

She tilted her head, giving me my favorite glare. Like she couldn't decide if she was going to kill me or kiss me.

"That was weak," I admitted. "But it's the best I could do, under the circumstances."

She sat beside me on the couch. "Why did you take that stuff if you knew it was going to give you a bad reaction?"

"New prescription from my father. Thought they might be different. And because I'm so bloody tired of muscling through."

"Because you have no help. When was the last time you were evaluated—"

I shook my head. "Not tonight, please. I'm exhausted. But I'm happy. Because you're here."

"Don't sweet-talk me. You scared me to death. But you do look better, though that's not saying much."

"There she is," I said softly.

"Come on. You should get to bed. The girl at the desk said I have until eleven to finish my business and get out before curfew."

"You have business?"

She nodded.

"Don't like the sound of that."

Harper's lovely face was still drawn with tension, her eyes shadowed, and a sadness lurked in their brown depths. A deep grief that had nothing to do with me.

Slowly, I got off the couch. Harper hovered near me but didn't touch me. Not a good sign. In my room, she took in the two full-sized beds, one to each side of the spacious room: two desks, two dressers, two closets.

"Your *dorm* bedroom is bigger than mine," she said. "Where is your roommate?"

"Easton? He'll be along shortly. He's a vampire. He can stay up and keep an eye on me, if it makes you feel better."

"None of this makes me feel better," she said while I rummaged in my dresser.

"It's like I said," I said, finding a pair of sleep pants and a T-shirt. I went to the adjoining bathroom, leaving the door open. "Different pill, same shitey reaction."

I changed into a white V-neck shirt and plaid sleep pants. When I reemerged, I didn't miss how Harper's eyes widened slightly, and her pale cheeks—more pale tonight—took on some color. I'd been given a hundred flattering glances, but somehow only hers meant anything to me.

"I've dressed on my own, see? Although, now I'm thinking I should've played this up more." I wagged my eyebrows. "Might've gotten a sponge bath out of it."

"In your dreams." She pointed at my bed. "Get."

"I'll never tire of you bossing me around."

"Someone needs to. What if you were in real danger?"

"But I wasn't."

"But what if you were?"

That was a good question, and if I wasn't so consumed with Harper, I might consider why I'd risked my life rather than embarrass my parents by making a fuss.

Another time.

I climbed into bed, and Harper pulled the covers over me. I settled myself on the pillow, every part of me wanting to reach for her, to pull her under the covers too, and hold her tight. To protect her from whatever pain was hanging over her like a shroud.

But she stood apart, arms crossed, looking as if she were on the edge.

"Hey," I said. "Come here."

Harper shook her head. "I can't, Orion. It's why I'm here. To tell you I can't."

And of all the danger my heart might've been in that night, that hurt the most.

"I suspected as much. At least sit. Tell me."

Harper hesitated, then sat on the edge of the bed. She inhaled a deep, steadying breath. Fortifying herself. Mustering her strength and will…she had so much of both. But I hated that she constantly had to draw on them, again and again.

"What happened?"

"It's my mother. God, it's so fucking…" She bit off her words, eyes shining. "I can't believe I have to do this again. I cannot fucking believe I have to do this again." She looked down, then at me. "She started back up with the drinking."

"Oh fuck. Oh shit, Harper, I'm so sorry."

"Yeah, and with that and everything else I'm dealing with, I just don't think you and I… I mean, I don't know what you were trying to tell me in chemistry today—"

"I was *trying* to say I want to go to the festival with you, but that rat bastard, Ford, beat me to it."

"That's not all you were saying," Harper said quietly. "But also, you never asked me to the festival."

"I wanted to do it in person instead of by phone or text. Because I'm a goddamn gentleman. But it all went sideways, and I'm not, to say the least, an expert at talking about feelings." I mimed a little explosion with my hands. "So they build up and go boom."

"Did you ever take Wolfe up on his offer to play it out?"

"No."

"Why not?"

"Lazy?"

She sighed. "Maybe you should."

"There are a lot of things I should be doing, but we're talking about you."

Harper glanced down again, shook her head. "I don't know how bad it is with my mother, or how far it's gotten. Not too bad yet, I hope. I might be able to get her back into AA. But it's all too much. I have so much on my plate right now. With school, the NoSci—"

"You're not going to get any heat on that from me."

Harper frowned. "Why not? I wouldn't expect you to hold back on my account. In fact, I'd feel like shit if you did."

If you only knew.

"I'm just saying, I'm not exactly acing my classes. Any entry I make for NoSci is going to be half arsed at best."

"Okay, well, in any case, I'm just..." She looked to me, her eyes glittering in the dimness. "Now is not a good time."

I took her hand in both of mine. "For?"

"You know what."

She gently extracted her hand from mine, reached into her bag, and pulled out a check.

My brows furrowed. "Haven't seen one of these in ages. Did you steal this from a museum?"

"Ha-ha," she said. "I couldn't find you on Venmo or Zelle. You can take a photo and auto-deposit… What are you doing?"

I took a bite out of the check and chewed the paper. Then another.

She snatched it back. "Orion, goddammit. We need a clean slate. So that I can deal with all the shit I have to deal with and not have this debt hanging over my head."

"You're not paying me back, Harper. It's the least I could do for all the crap my so-called friends have put you through. *No*," I said, when she started to protest. "I'm not going to hear it. Done is done."

She stared at me a moment more, then let her hands fall in her lap. "Infuriating and…."

"And?" I said, smiling tiredly. "What else am I?"

Harper shook her head, holding my gaze a moment more. Tears stood out in her eyes, and behind them I saw longing. I *felt* it, because it was the same I had for her. I wasn't any good at something real with a girl. I'd never done it before. But I'd wanted to try, and now…

"I should go."

She started to go, but I took her hand. "Are you sure?"

"I'm sure. I made a promise to myself that the next time I got involved with someone it wouldn't be casual. I want something real and solid. Let me finish," she said, when it was my turn to protest. "But that goes both ways. My bandwidth is stretched to the breaking point. I'm not going to be good for anyone right now."

"Why not let me be the judge of that?"

She huffed a breath and wiped her eyes with the heels of her hands. "But it doesn't mean we can't be friends."

"Friends," I said sourly. "Yay."

She pursed her lips. "And as your *friend*, you need help and you're not getting it. Don't argue with me," she added, her expression fierce with anger now. Not at me, but *for* me. The fighter in her turning the battle toward my enemies. An ally. No one had been that for me in a long time.

"I'll help you with your classes if you'll let me. History, at least. You don't need help in piano, though I think you should take whatever Wolfe is offering. It's not every day a world-famous prodigy dumps free lessons in your lap." Harper's expression softened. "You have a gift, Orion. A real gift. And you're not lazy or broken or anything else. But you need more help than a bottle of pills and a shrug."

"Thank you," I whispered. "That's a nice feeling. To have someone who believes in me."

"I do," she said.

"Then stay."

Harper smiled sadly and leaned in to kiss my cheek. "Good night, Orion."

Her lips were soft on my skin, and after, she hovered there. The warmth of her and her scent—wildflowers and cherries—filled my space. Her hesitation was palpable, her eyes shining and dark in the dim light, her lips so close it would be nothing to lean in and capture them with mine.

To taste her and get lost in her and let her get lost in me. To solve this problem of us, consequences be damned.

But Easton fucking Locke chose that moment to step into the room instead of his usual two a.m.

"Oh, sorry. I'll just—"

Harper jerked back. "No, I was just leaving." She gave me a final, lingering glance then turned away. "Easton?"

He nodded.

"Take care of him," she said, and then she was gone.

The next day, I skipped all my classes. I felt like shit. Depressed, tired. A full-body hangover. I'd forgotten about that little bonus to the terrible reaction I had to the meds.

I managed to drag myself out of bed to shower and dress. After the last bell, I made my way to the Arts Wing of the Academy. When I arrived, my pulse was kicking like a jackrabbit, though now I couldn't tell if it was left over from last night or just plain nerves.

I knocked on Professor Wolfe's office door.

No answer.

The syllabus had said I was within his office hours. Maybe I'd gotten it wrong. I nearly turned to leave, but Harper's face floated before my vision. Her faith in me had me knocking again.

A rustling came from inside the office. "Coming, coming."

The door flew open and I was face-to-face with Ezra

Wolfe's bleary eyes. His hair was rumpled, his clothes looked slept in. The scent of an unidentified liquor wafted over me, and cigarette smoke hung in the air.

"Orion." If he was embarrassed or worried I'd rat him out, he didn't show it. Instead, he wore an expectant expression. "You look as bad as I feel. What do you want?"

"I'd like to take you up on your offer," I said, the words sounding rusty, as if I'd never spoken English before. "To work with you on a piece for the concert?"

He crossed his arms. "That was weeks ago. Who says that offer still stands?"

Disappointment whacked me in the chest. I hadn't known how badly I'd wanted this until now. When it was too late.

"Oh. Sorry to have bothered you."

I was five steps away when he drawled, "Do you always give up so easily?"

I turned.

He arched a brow. "Well?"

This was it. A dividing line between one version of my life and another. Once I stepped over it, I had no idea what would happen. No safety net. Wolfe was going to tear me open with a bloody piano. And I wasn't going to be able to hide my struggles from him, either. No chance.

Maybe that's a good thing.

Wolfe must've read my face because a slow grin spread over his.

"It's about time."

Chapter 16

HARPER

Mom held up her phone. "Say cheese."

"Cheese!" Dash said, and pointed his neon pistols at her.

I stood beside him, not quite as enthusiastic.

"Come on, Harper," Mom said. "One smile."

She was on her best behavior, fulfilling her promise to take Dash trick-or-treating, and had been home early the rest of the week. Sober too, as far as I could tell.

I managed a half smile. As soon as the photo was taken, I knelt beside Dash.

"You remember what I told you?"

His head bobbed under his cowboy hat. "If I see any Smarties, grab 'em."

"My hero."

Smarties were, in my opinion, the most underrated candy. Luckily my little brother seemed to agree with the rest of the world that they sucked and saved all of them for me.

I stood up and smoothed my suffragette dress. I had to admit, I was pretty proud of my handiwork—I'd put in a lot of hours making it last year and it had paid off. I looked like I stepped out of the 1880s. Long, icy green, it was fitted at the waist, with billowy sleeves and a sash with the suffragette colors: purple, green, and white. A pin on the bodice read *Votes for Women!*

"You look so beautiful, Harper," Mom said.

"Thanks."

Her mouth tilted at my lackluster tone. "Really?"

"I said, thanks. I have to go. I'm meeting Xander at eight."

"Bye, Harper!" Dash called, waving his little hand.

"Bye, buddy. Have fun. Have the best time." I looked to Mom. "Don't wait up."

"Wow, great costume," Xander said, meeting me at the Bennington Farm parking lot. "Very authentic."

"Thanks, you too."

Xander wore a brown suit and old-fashioned hat—like a scientist from the Manhattan Project. He'd told me he was dressed in honor of his father, Russell Ford, who'd been a physicist of some renown back in Baltimore but was currently battling dementia at their home in the Bend.

My "date" looked very handsome, but my heart ached, wishing that I was on a different boy's arm as we entered the festival fairgrounds.

This is easier and right now I need easy.

At least with Xander, no one would give me shit. After Mom's little revelation the other night, I felt like I was made of blown glass. One more hit and I was going to shatter into a million pieces.

Bennington Farm look to be less like a farm and more like an elegant estate where people held big weddings or parties. The huge backyard had been turned into a Halloween playground. The walks were strewn with hay, and pyramids of pumpkins artfully lined the walkways. Strings of lights glittered between booths of food and drink, and the air was laced with the scents of popcorn and cotton candy. In the center was a dance floor with a DJ on one side and a professional photographer on the other. Tables draped in black ringed the dance floor, each with pretend candles flickering in little orange bowls. Had I been in any sort of a good mood, I might've been impressed. Enchanted, even. No dance back at PS120's gym could compare to this.

But I couldn't help but feel the students at CHA—Richie and Bender alike—paid for this opulence with more than just money.

"Hey, you two." Dean Yearwood waved and joined us. "Wow, Harper, stunning!"

"Thanks. Love the costume, Ferris," I said. I recognized the jacket and leopard-print sweater vest immediately.

"Thank you." Dean smoothed his eyebrows à la Ferris Bueller. "*It is so choice. If you have the means, I highly recommend picking one up.*"

We laughed while Xander stared at us, confused. Dean rolled his eyes and threw his arm around his shoulders. "We have *got* to get this boy caught up. But first…snacks."

The three of us headed toward the food area, Dean chatting, while Xander and I both scanned the crowds, searching for someone else beside the person we came with. His gaze landed on Emery, glowing pink and gold as Barbie. Dean and I exchanged knowing glances. Xander and Emery were in love—it was only a matter of time before they stopped pretending otherwise.

Hypocrite much?

My roaming eye found Orion, and my stupid heart tripped. He wore a dark suit with a red kerchief in the breast pocket and a fedora. Ridiculously handsome as a 1920s gangster. Unfair. Criminal, really.

"He's a damn bandit…"

"Say something, Harp?" Dean asked, following my gaze.

"No, nothing."

I looked away quickly but not quickly enough. Dean smiled in a way that made me feel as if my chest cavity were transparent.

"We should dance," he said. "Let's dance. Xander?"

"No, I…I don't dance," he said, his eyes still glued to Emery, who was on the dance floor with Tucker Hill draped all over her. They looked to be having an argument.

"You mean to tell me you're going to leave this beautiful woman completely unattended? Your loss." Dean held out his hand to me. "Madame."

Why not? It was a party. I could be depressed and stressed out the other twenty hours in the day.

The song was a fast one but immediately slowed as soon as Dean and I hit the floor. Benson Boone's "Beautiful Things" wafted over us.

"Is this okay?" Dean asked, his hands on my waist, mine around his neck. "Don't want to make anyone jealous."

"Xander and I are here as friends."

"I wasn't talking about Xander."

Dean jerked his head subtly to his left. I looked to my right and saw Orion watching us from his table of Richies. A tingle of electricity zipped down my spine at the heat in his eyes. I looked away, my cheeks burning.

"I don't know what you mean."

Dean raised a brow and gave me a gentle smirk. "He asked about you, you know. Right around the time you asked about him. Subtle, you guys are not."

I started to protest, but what was the use? Besides, talking about *him* was like breathing again after a deep dive into a turbulent ocean.

"I can't," I said, my eyes stinging. "I want to, and I think he wants to, but..."

Dean's face lit up. "Really? That's great! What are you waiting for?"

"Will you keep it down?" I glanced around at the

other couples. "My home life is about to implode, and this school… Jesus, this school."

"I know it," Dean said. "The pressure is a lot, but you gotta hope it's worth it in the end. Remember *Shawshank Redemption*? Andy crawls through that tunnel of shit to his freedom. We just have to keep crawling until we get to the good stuff." He leaned in. "But Harper, that guy over there? He's good stuff. More than good. He's one of the *greats*."

Now my vision blurred, and my heart ached with a longing so fierce, it stole my breath.

"It feels impossible, Dean. For so many reasons."

"Such as?"

"For starters, I've been told to keep my grubby Bender hands to myself," I said. "It's humiliating. The old me back in Pittsburgh would've scoffed at the elitist bullshit, but here… It's been nonstop, and I *hate* how small I feel."

Dean's face was a mask of empathy. "I get it. But it doesn't have to be anyone's business but yours and his."

He tilted his chin, indicating I should look where he looked—to the white swan of the black and white pair from *The Black Swan*, sitting at the Richie table. Sierra Hart was her name, if I remembered correctly.

She found his gaze, and for the smallest instant, her eyes lit up under all her makeup. Pure joy, if I ever saw it. And Dean's face… Now I *really* wanted to cry. He looked so happy.

"Protect your happiness, Harper," he said. "Guard it with your life. It might not be a perfect situation, but we don't live in a perfect world. Or, even better, say fuck it—say *fuck them*—and just *be happy*."

"Is that what you're going to do?" I asked gently. "With her?"

He smiled sadly. "She's not ready for that."

"Why not? You're so popular—"

The music swelled at the song's chorus and got loud. Dean leaned in to me.

"I don't live in a house. I live in a trailer at the very end of the Bend," he said. "My dad is on disability after he was injured at work. My mom works two jobs." Dean's gaze found Sierra again and then came back to me, his smile resigned. "Some bridges are too far."

The song ended, and the DJ announced that the costume contest was about to begin and to please clear the dance floor.

"But enough of my sob story." Dean put on a confident Ferris Bueller grin and tugged the collar of his jacket. "Now, if you'll excuse me, I have a trophy to win." He started to go, then turned. "Hey, Harper?"

"Yeah?"

"One of the *greats*."

"Hey, Dean," I called back. "So are you."

"Aw, shucks." He hunched his shoulders, touched, and went to line up with the other hopefuls.

I wandered away from the festivities, listening as the crowd noise grew loud and quiet over and over, like someone messing with the volume on a speaker. I found a relatively secluded spot and leaned against a wooden crate. The late October night was cold and getting colder as winter came on, but the sky was clear and glittered with a thousand stars, like diamonds. The constellation, Orion, was stark and obvious in the night sky.

Et tu, universe?

"We're missing it," said a voice.

That voice. That smooth British tenor that sent butterflies fluttering in my stomach as if I were any other girl with a crush on a boy instead of the one who had to grow up too fast and be the adult in her house. If I just closed my eyes, I could pretend I was that girl and have the fairy tale…

I turned and braced myself for Orion.

Ha. Good luck with that.

He stood in the light from one of the many old-fashioned streetlamps that dotted the farm. It bathed him in a golden light, and up close, him in that suit… It was dark blue with white pinstripes, and tailored to his lean, athletic body. The scarlet kerchief was a red rose blooming out of his breast pocket, and the fedora cut angular shadows on his jaw bone.

"What are we missing?" I said. "Orion…?"

His dark-eyed gaze was soaking me in. "Sorry, I just… You are so incredibly beautiful."

"Oh, um. Thanks." My hands smoothed down the silky front of the dress as I struggled to catch my breath. No guy had ever said something like that to me before. "It's not 'sexy kitten,' but…"

"You made that dress, didn't you?"

"Is it that obvious?"

Orion groaned. He tossed his hat on a nearby hay bale and leaned against the wheel beside me. "What are we going to do with you, Bennett? I was *trying* to pay you a compliment."

"I know," I said. "But I don't know what to do with the compliments, so I deflect with sarcasm. Classic coping mechanism."

"We'll have to work on that. So. Are you having a nice time with *Xander Ford*? Or is it *Dean Yearwood*? You two looked rather cozy on the dance floor."

I tapped my chin. "Remind me who is who again? I have so many dates, they all start to blend together..."

"Hmph."

"Didn't take you for the jealous type."

"I didn't either." Orion glanced at me sideways. "I've found my world rather upended these days."

"Likewise," I said. His cologne tonight was smoky and woodsy and smelled expensive, and he wore just enough to make a girl stupid. "You look...well."

"Do I?" He grinned. "I look *well*."

No, you look ridiculously handsome. More *than enough to make a girl stupid.*

"I meant, you look recovered from the other night."

"Oh, that." He waved a hand. "I knew I would. Still. It was good of you to come and weep over me."

"Oh, hush up."

His gaze softened. "I mean it. I appreciate it more than I can say. And you inspired me."

"You went to the Student Health Office and got yourself checked out?"

Orion made a sour face, his eyes *twinkling* again. "Why would I do that?"

"Right. Silly me. What was I thinking?"

"I paid Professor Wolfe a visit," he said. "Private lessons, twice a week, for that spring concert."

My eyes widened. "Really? God, that's a relief."

"A relief?"

"Absolutely. You not playing the piano in any meaningful way is like owning a Rembrandt and stashing it in the attic."

Orion looked away. "Come on."

I arched a brow. "I'm *trying* to pay you a compliment."

"Well, don't," he said, and brightened as a round of cheers went up from the stage. "Ah, there it goes. Our trophy. That's what I meant by missing it. Someone else just snagged our Best Couple costume award."

Of course, my stomach fluttered all over again at those words, no matter how impossible it all was.

"We're not a couple," I reminded him.

"Sure we are." Orion indicated his suit and my dress. "We matched without even trying. Our costumes are from the same era."

"Give or take forty years," I said.

"Ugh, there is not one romantic bone in your body, is there, Bennett?"

"Not one."

"We'll have to work on that too."

"When is all this work being done? And who is we?"

"We is us. Us is we," Orion said, his voice growing low. Soft.

At those words, every part of me reacted with a warm, aching need, tinged by low-grade panic. I had to stay in control or else my life would collapse around me. But with Orion, I had no control. My emotions were chaotic, deep, and all of them were running straight to him.

I hugged myself tightly. "Orion…I told you the deal with my mother."

"Is it bad, love?" he asked gently.

"It's not good," I said. "Teetering. She's either going to haul herself back from the edge or she's going to fall back into addiction. But so long as she's having an affair with her married boss, my money's on addiction. Bad choices beget bad choices."

I looked over at Orion, so damn handsome and good and…

One of the greats. And I'm going to mess it up.

"I don't want to make a bad choice that will end up hurting anyone in the end."

Orion gazed down at me, as Billie Eilish's "What Was I Made For" played faintly from the dance floor. He stood up and held out his hand.

"Dance with me."

"I thought we weren't going to do this."

"Do what? Dance?"

I shot him a wry look. "I know what you're doing."

He said nothing but waited, letting expectation and inevitability speak for him. I should've resisted. Protested. Stuck to my guns and all that, but what I wanted more than anything was to be in Orion's arms, so I let him pull me to my feet.

He encircled me around the waist, his other hand taking my left and laying it over his chest. His heartbeat was strong, steady. Not the rapid pounding that terrified me the other night. His cologne wafted over me, and his body, so close to mine, was like a promise of safety and protection as much as pure attraction. It took all my will, but I held myself apart, keeping some space between us. My one pathetic rebellion.

"This is a bad idea," I said. "I'm not at your level, socially speaking."

"I told you, I don't care."

"I do. I don't want that kind of scrutiny."

"You're ashamed to be seen with me because I'm rich and popular? That's one I've never heard before."

I shook my head. "The bullying here is next level. I'd rather have a catfight. At least then it's out in the open."

Orion's teasing expression vanished. "They're not going to fuck with you again."

"What are you going to do? Walk in front of me in the hallways all year? I don't want you fighting my battles for me."

"Then we'll keep it on the down low," he said with a shrug.

"You'd be okay with that?"

"Do I have a choice?" His gaze softened. "I just want to be with you."

And that was the last straw. My head fell forward, onto his chest. "God, I'm such a sap."

Orion chuckled. "Not even close, but we'll get there."

I turned and let my cheek rest over his heart. I melted against him, and the world with all its stress and tension melted away too. For a few precious moments, I just let myself exist in that perfect space, as he turned us in small, slow circles.

"For the record," I said. "Being rich and popular are the least interesting things about you."

"Oh yeah? Tell me more."

"Tell *you* more about *you*? Well, you're extremely humble…"

"Obviously."

"You're a good person."

"Am I?"

I nodded against the smooth silk of his suit jacket. "I think, sometimes, you try too hard to make everyone like you."

"Guilty as charged."

"Because you don't have to try at all. You're eminently likable. You have a good heart."

"How do you know?"

"I can feel it. It pours out of you in everything you do. Your words. Your laugh. Your eyes. Most guys…they're not *bad*, but they're a dime a dozen. I would know. But you…"

It's too much. Too good…

I pulled back. Orion's dark eyes were liquid and rich in the dim light. He took my hand that was on his chest and encircled it tighter, clutching it. The arm around my waist tightened too, holding me closer.

"Don't do that," he said, his voice gruff.

"Do what?" I whispered back.

"Pull away. Retreat," he said. "Stay with me. Stay…"

I shook my head. "Ugh, look at me. Look at *you*. You show up in a suit, and I fold like a lawn chair."

He grinned slightly. "That was the plan."

"But I meant what I said the other night. I feel like my life is teetering on the edge too."

"I know," he said. "And I'm all kinds of fucked up, in case you hadn't noticed. But that doesn't mean I want to let you go."

God, everything he said and did was sending me into the clouds, while my brain tried to keep me on solid ground where it was safe.

"Okay, but I need to say the thing that sounds like too much too soon, but I promised myself the next time I got involved with someone it would be something real. Not casual." I looked him straight in the eye. "I don't mean we have to put labels on things right away, or whatever. I just mean—"

"I know what you mean," Orion said. "You mean you want to be taken out on a proper date." He smiled. "I can do that."

"But is this something you want? Something—"

"Serious?" Orion finished. He nodded and brushed a curl off my cheek. "I can do that too. I want to. And I love that you are saying all this. You tell it like it is. No bullshit. That's one of the things I like about you best. You're fierce. Strong."

"I don't feel that way."

"But you are. And for a bloke who grew up in a silent household where no one talked about anything, this is going to be new for me, but let me give it a whirl. You're the only person in this whole bloody school I want to talk to. Or look at. Or stand next to. There's no one else."

"So, it's me by default?"

He gave me a flat look.

"Sorry. Coping mechanism."

"*Incorrigible*," he said. "No, it's you by…what's the opposite of default? Excess? Abundance?" His dark eyes were soft on mine but heated now. "I want an abundance of you, Harper Bennett."

Now both of his arms were around my waist, pulling me closer, and both of my arms were around his neck. My hand went to the back of his head, where his hair was short, before the little springs of his curls began. I'd never touched him there before. His hands had never been at the small of my back. Everything was new, every part of him unexplored and the anticipation was building in me to a fever pitch. I wanted to be allowed to touch his cheek, his jaw, to put my mouth on his neck and kiss him softly there and inhale him.

"You know that feeling where you see your crush from across the room?" Orion asked. "A bittersweet ache. A hunger, almost, that hurts, because you want them so bad, but they're not yours. Not yet."

I nodded, my heart pounding.

"That hunger is tinged with excitement, too. Anticipation for the time when you have that person. When the longing is over." His eyes seemed to darken somehow, his voice rough. "But the ache is so good, so fucking painful in the best way…you almost don't want it to end."

Dear God.

"Do you know that feeling?" he asked.

I nodded again. *I feel it every time I see you.*

But I couldn't speak, could barely move, I was trapped *in* that feeling, and it was just like he said. I was yearning for his kiss in the worst way, and I wanted to stay in the purgatory of almost having it too.

Orion moved away just enough to look at me, his mouth inches from mine. "I've had that feeling before, but not like this. Not like tonight. With you."

A little sigh escaped me. A gasp. My legs turned to sand, and I gripped his arm under his suit, almost dizzy from want of him.

"You're really good at this," I breathed, craning my

chin up. His breath ghosted over my lips, and I nearly moaned. "Orion…"

"Not yet," he whispered. "Just a little more…"

His hand came up and cupped my jaw, his thumb sweeping across my cheek, and then he brushed my lower lip while his eyes searched mine. I was locked in his embrace, his gaze, his space, watching him watch me, but fully present in the moment. My thudding heart sent blood to every nerve ending that was sparking where we touched, waiting and wanting more.

Orion's gaze dropped to my mouth, then back to my eyes, his arm around my waist cinched me in, his head tilted to the side at the same time I craned up for him and our lips met in a kiss. The most perfect kiss of my life.

Soft at first, like a little bomb dropping into the center of me, it grew in intensity. Smoldering, burning, and then igniting. He and I were like a chemical reaction where that needy anticipation found relief. The sweet ache found release.

Orion's kiss, my God… I thought I'd been kissed before, but no. Only a wet mashing of mouths that bore no resemblance to this. *This* was finesse and experience, but I felt the gravity of his devotion too. Lust and yearning and care all infused in his mouth that moved over mine, tongue sweeping, exploring. Gentle, sucking pulls and then harder biting kisses, with our breaths rasping and little sounds of want rising in my throat while deeper groans emanated from his chest.

I kissed him just as greedily, needing to taste and be tasted. My hands slid up his neck, then down his back. Strong muscles moved under his suit as his hands roamed my body, until one hand sank into my hair. He made a fist and pulled gently, angling my head for better access, taking what he wanted.

I fell back against the wheel, Orion's body over mine, looming, but I felt completely protected and safe. Overwhelmed by him in the best way. He kissed me until I was dizzy, then pulled back, sucking my lip, kissing my chin, my cheek, down to my neck, nuzzling and sending shivers of heat across my breasts and down my back. I clung to him as his mouth moved over my throat, to my earlobe, biting gently, then back to my mouth.

I didn't want to stop kissing him. I could've kissed Orion Mercer until sunrise, and it wouldn't satisfy that sweet, heavy ache in the middle of me. One that I already worried had migrated up to my heart and would only grow stronger with every touch, never satiated. More wanting him, not less, until it wasn't wanting any more at all, but something else.

Something so real, I'd never be the same.

"Wait, wait, wait." Orion broke the kiss, both of us breathing heavily. He held my face, brushing the curls off my brow, then slipped down to cup my cheeks, his forehead pressed to mine. "I think, perhaps, we should slow down a bit. We're being serious, after all."

"Did I say that?" I asked breathlessly. "I take it back. Serious can start tomorrow."

He laughed, and his smile was so brilliant it almost hurt to look at him. A different kind of happy than I'd seen before. And I realized I was too, just when I had started to forget what happy felt like.

I kissed him softly, while I still had him there. Once, twice, then smoothed the lapels of his suit I'd been gripping. Holding on for dear life, actually.

"That was romantic, Harper."

"I'll try not to make it a habit."

He chuckled and took both my hands in his. "Well. What do we do now?"

Before I could answer, Dean peeked his head around the corner. "I hate—and I do mean *hate*—to interrupt, but Harper, I need backup."

"Is everything okay?"

"It's Emery and Xander. Things are getting tense. Can you come?"

"Yes, of course."

"Can I be of help?" Orion asked.

"Not this time, my friend," Dean said. "I think Emery would prefer discretion."

Orion turned to me. "Text me when you're done saving the day."

"I will."

He kissed my forehead and let me go.

Dean shot me a quick smile as he led me through the hay-strewn pathways. "I won Best Costume, but that's nowhere near as awesome as seeing you two together. Not that I was peeping, I swear."

"You'll keep it quiet?" I asked. "I prefer discretion too."

"You sure?"

"Right now, it's a bridge too far."

Dean nodded, and silent understanding passed between us. We rounded a bend and heard Xander's low voice, tight with pain and resignation.

"The last thing on this fucking planet I want to do is hurt you. But it will only get worse. For both of us."

A stunned silence, and then Emery whispered, "Okay. If that's what you want."

"That's what I want."

Dean nodded at me. A break in the conversation and we'd eavesdropped too long. We stepped around the corner to see Xander in his suit and Emery in pink, facing each other, both looking heartbroken.

"Hey, guys," Dean said slowly. "Everything cool?"

"I need to go home," Emery said tearfully.

I stepped forward immediately. "I'll take you."

I gave Xander and Dean farewell glances and hurried Emery to my car in the parking lot. Once in the passenger seat, she covered her face with both hands and burst into tears.

"Oh, babe." I wrapped my arms around her as best

I could from the driver side. "Is now a bad time to say I knew it all along?"

"What did you know?"

"You and Xander—"

"There is no me and Xander." She peered at me through mascara-smudged, tear-streaked eyes. "Please, Harper. Take me home."

I followed her directions to one of the biggest houses on the Bay I'd ever seen. Twenty of my houses could have fit into hers. In the driveway, I parked and faced Emery.

"Are you going to be okay?"

She shook her head *no* but said, "Yes." She looked at me with a rueful smile. "Isn't that my way? *Yes* on the outside, *no* on the inside."

"Em, what can I do? Do you want to go somewhere? Talk about it?"

She wiped her face and huffed a breath, looking like someone about to go into battle rather than a girl going home after a dance. "Later. Right now, I just want to get to my room and shut the door on the world for a while, you know?"

"Yeah, I know." I gave her a hug. "Call me anytime."

"Okay." She started to get out then stopped. "Hey, I never asked how your night was."

It was perfect while you were having your heart broken.

"We'll talk later, like you said. Get some sleep."

She smiled gratefully and got out. I watched until she

was safe inside her house, though I'm not sure "safe" was the right word with her tyrant father running her and her brother Jack's lives like a dictator.

Feeling like a selfish asshole, I texted Orion.

Emery's home safe.

The reply came quick.

You're a good friend, love.

I didn't know about that, since I was dying to get back to him.

What now? I texted.

There's that romance again. I'm at your house.

Why?

We just had our first date. I need to give you a proper kiss goodnight.

My heart did a bunch of little flips, and that foreign feeling of happiness flooded me all over again.

At my house, Orion was leaning against his silver Aston Martin like a model in a magazine ad. Mom's SUV was parked in the driveway; she and Dash were home from trick-or-treating. I parked behind her and met Orion at his car.

"You didn't have to," I said, as he pulled me into his arms. "That was a pretty epic kiss already."

"I know, but I did a lot of wooing back there," he said.

"True. That was premium-grade wooing. Professional, even."

"So lest you think I'm full of hot air and pretty words, I want to ask you something. Something very serious."

"Serious? You?"

"There's a party after the Narragansett Bay Regatta. At the Castle Hill Country Club. Supposed to be a big deal," Orion said, tracing his finger over the top of my hand.

"Okay."

"I want you to be my date to it."

I smirked. "What part of 'I'd like to keep us private' did you not understand?"

Orion smiled that charming smile of his, the one that turned persuasion into an art form.

I'm doomed before we've even started.

"I know," he said. "And I'm not trying to pressure you, honestly. But I'm going to put this out there, because I meant what I said. I don't care what anyone thinks. On the contrary, I'd be proud to show off my woman."

"Your woman," I scoffed, even as my heart felt full, every part of me becoming warmer and happier with every word he spoke.

"Yes, my woman." Orion brushed a curl off my forehead. "I would love for you to be my date to that party. To walk down those fancy hallways with you on my arm and dance with you in front of all of Castle Hill." His voice turned low and rough. "I'd like that very much."

I swallowed hard. "You would?"

"Yes, Bennett, I would." He smiled. "So just think about it, okay? And if the answer is still no, and you must insist on keeping our sordid affair a secret, I'll honor that too."

"Orion…"

I looked away before he could see the tears in my eyes, or how thoroughly he'd broken down the defenses I'd built around my heart and marched right in. Or worse, how badly I wanted to keep him there.

"Whatever you decide." He bent to kiss me softly. "I'm not going anywhere."

Part II

Where the heart does not enter, there can be no music.

—Pyotr Ilyich Tchaikovsky

Chapter 17

ORION

"So," I whispered to Harper that Monday in chem, "shall we volunteer to be locked in the supply closet together? I think I'm out of beakers. Are you out of beakers? Let's go get some beakers."

Harper laughed and blushed prettily. "We have plenty of beakers." She tucked a curl behind her ear, not looking at me. "But if there's anyone I'd risk a panic attack for, it's you."

I put my hand on my heart and pretended to almost fall off my stool. "Bennett. That was the most romantic thing anyone's ever said to me."

"Hush," she said, glancing around. As usual, Langford was late to class. "I'm working on it."

"I can see that," I said, a warm feeling flooding my chest. I'd had this feeling for girls before. They typically originated below the belt and rose no further. But this girl…

Kissing Harper Bennett had been more than anything I'd been prepared for. From the moment we touched, something in my heart shifted. Came awake. I'd spoken of physical anticipation, but when we kissed, another hunger had finally been sated. As if I'd been starved and deprived, waiting my entire life and finally, *finally* found her.

And she'd found me. I was exceptionally good at hiding my broken pieces, but no one was looking either. Not my parents anyway. But Harper looked. She saw me. Past the money and the jokes and the mask of *fine* so that when we finally kissed and touched and shared each other's breath, I felt found too.

But this was uncharted territory. I had no bloody idea what I was doing. I'd never cared for anything deeply except survival, and when things got rough, I turned to jokes and laughs. To fix whatever was broken before it got uncomfortable.

She doesn't want that. She wants real.

And honest. And I was a cheating bastard who'd just turned in a proposal for the NoSci, with help from my father's envelope. My theory was that the right blend of polymers could bond to ions in asphalt and make potholes close on their own. It was only a theory, and if by some miracle it passed round one, I'd still have to do all the work. But *self-adhering potholes* was not what prestigious awards were made of.

Father can't say I didn't try.

"What do you have going on today?" Harper asked, pulling me from my guilty thoughts.

"First lesson with Wolfe after school, right before crew practice."

Our first regatta was the next day (the school took a holiday on Tuesday for it) and the entire Academy was hyped the way most schools prepped for football. American *and* European football.

Harper eyed me up and down. "You seem nervous. Regatta or Wolfe?"

"Wolfe. He's going to rip out my guts via my fingers." I leaned in. "Despite the covert status of our relationship, are you coming to the regatta?"

"Wouldn't miss it," she said. "And I was thinking—"

Langford blew in the door, muttering apologies, and immediately began the day's lesson.

"You were saying?" I whispered.

Harper blushed again, looking uncharacteristically bashful. Shy, even. "Nothing."

"I don't have a lot of time," I said, joining Professor Wolfe in the empty auditorium where Advanced Piano was held. "I have crew practice in forty-five minutes."

"Ah, yes, the infamous Castle Hill regattas," Wolfe said, rolling the *r*. "I'll keep our inaugural lesson brief."

Today he wore a long black coat, black pants, and shirt.

He had no detectable odor of liquor hanging around him, and his eyes were clear blue lasers, scanning me up and down.

"First things first," he said, indicating I should sit at the baby grand. He then laid a piece of music on the rack in front of me. "Can you read this?"

I scoffed, even as my insides twisted. "Of course."

"Play."

I obliged, because my brain—for whatever reason—decoded notes with ease. I took a mental picture of the page, set my fingers on the keys, and did as Wolfe commanded.

The piece started with a fast, repetitive series of three notes with my right hand—the music had me envisioning sunlit water rippling along a creek bed. Eventually my left hand joined with a harmony, but Wolfe snatched the sheet music off the rack.

"Stop, stop, stop. What did you just play?"

I shrugged. "Didn't catch the name."

"Ravel's Gaspard de la Nuit."

"Okay."

"How would you describe what your right hand was doing?"

I frowned. "Repeating notes: A, C sharp, and F sharp."

"Rapid triadic ostinatos," Wolfe said. "Do you know what that means?"

"Not really," I said, my neck heating. "I told you, notation isn't my thing."

"So you have facility with the music but no language for it."

"I guess?"

"Have you played this piece before?"

"No."

Wolfe cocked his head. "You weren't reading the notes, you were watching your hands."

"I took a photo of the page." I tapped my temple. "Up here."

The professor's eyes widened slightly. "I see." He dragged a chair beside my bench and sat, crossing one leg over the other. "Change of tactic. Tell me about yourself."

"You want my life story?" I laughed shortly. "Don't see how that's relevant—"

"As pertains to piano. When did you know you had a gift?"

"I don't know," I lied. "I could always play."

Wolfe narrowed his eyes. "For this to work, we'll need to be honest with each other. But since being emotionally vulnerable is new for you, we can quid pro quo, Clarice. I'll tell you something terribly personal about me, and you do the same."

"Is that appropriate, *Professor*?"

"God, no, but that's never stopped me before. But again, only piano-related. Fair?"

"Do I have a choice?"

"No. But if I overstep, feel free to report me to the proper authorities. Get me sacked. Put me out of my misery."

I chuckled. I was growing to like Wolfe, entirely against my will.

"Once upon a time," he began. "there was a boy with such genius that he was overwhelmed by it at a young age. Too many people told him how great he was until the pressure to *be great* was too much. Sex, drugs, and alcohol relieved the pressure. He became a devil, believing they'd leave him alone. But it backfired. The *drama* of it all only made them want him more while draining his bank account. So now I'm forced to pop my head out of whatever den of iniquity I hole away in, play a few concerts, teach at institutions that are far too proud of themselves, collect a few quid and disappear again. But in all the years I've never come across a *you*. Which is to say, a *me*."

"I'm nothing like you," I said.

"True. You're probably better, but it's all locked away for some strange reason that mystifies me. So I ask again, when did you know you had a gift? The truth this time, if you please."

I opened my mouth to joke, to deflect, to tell this bloke he was off his bloody rocker. But what was I here for if not to get somewhere?

"Around the time I started to learn to read," I said. "So, almost two?"

His brows shot up. "That's early."

"I guess. But I remember it well because I didn't struggle with music the way I struggled with reading."

"Why is that?"

"I have ADHD," I said. "My brain doesn't like sticking

with words, and words are... It's hard to explain. But musical notes make patterns. I'm good with patterns and with listening. Then I just...memorize."

"You memorize entire pages of music at once."

"Something like that," I said. "And I can memorize chapters in books, if they're read aloud to me. I can read them myself, but it takes longer."

"You're an auditory and spatial learner," Wolfe said, nodding. "I had a stutter as a child. A speech therapist taught me the different modes of learning," he said, answering my questioning look. "And did you hide your struggles?"

"We hide every struggle in my family," I said, shocked how easily that popped out.

"I had a feeling. Repressed emotional household. I had one of those too. To this day, my mother believes my boyfriends are just *very affectionate friends*."

I chuckled.

"Have you ever composed anything original?" he asked.

"Yes," I said slowly, thinking of how I used to make up songs on the spot. As if the piano keys were singing to me and my job was to help them release the music. But that was nonsense talk. I cleared my throat. "It's been a while—"

"Good." Wolfe tossed the Ravel sheet music aside. "You're going to compose a piece for the spring concert and your Juilliard audition."

"I'm not auditioning for Juilliard, for one thing," I

said. "And for another, that's madness. There's no possible way I can compose something good enough."

"I doubt that," Wolfe said.

"Well...bloody good for you," I said. "But I'm going to embarrass myself. Why can't I play something from the repertoire? I thought you were supposed to be helping me. To dig deep? Tap, tap, tap, and all that rot?"

"And I will," he said. "But if you can play from rote memory, it'll take ages. You're too good at hiding behind your talent. The audience won't know the difference, but I will, and it will drive me mad. The fastest way to feeling the music is to write it yourself. To let it move through you, and write it down."

Write it down. Fucking hell.

"I can't. I mean...I'm not a composer."

Wolfe shrugged. "What do you love?"

"Sorry?"

"What do you love?"

"My family. My brothers. Rowing."

"Boring." He waved a black-nailed hand. "What else? Do you have a significant other?"

"Y-yes."

"Do you love her? Him? Them?"

"Her, but it's new."

"Perfect. First love. Young love. New love. The ideal subject."

My face felt hot, and that twinge of nerves came back. Part of me wanted to get started immediately and part of me wanted to slam the door on this madman and never come back.

"I told you, it's not…that."

"Sure, sure, but she might have potential. What's her name?"

"I can't say. She'd rather we not go public."

Now Wolfe's eyes widened. "Forbidden love, secret love, illicit love… And how do you feel about that?"

"Is this therapy hour?"

"Yes. Music is therapy. Art is therapy. It's the only reason I'm still alive."

The light in Ezra Wolfe's eyes dimmed for a moment. He caught my sympathetic glance and scowled. "Well?"

"I…don't know how I feel about it. It's what she needs right now."

Wolfe sighed. "My God, man. Is there *anything* on this earth that you're passionate about? That frustrates you? That enrages you, or that fills you with ecstasy?"

I struggled for an answer that wasn't betraying my parents over my frustration—and hurt—that they left me to cope with my ADHD alone, but Wolfe flapped both hands at me.

"Don't strain yourself. It's clear we have a lot of work to do. But go. Get to your little boat. God forbid there be any empty trophy space in these hallowed halls. Come back next week, and we'll get to work digging something—anything—out of that lockbox you call a heart."

I nearly told him to bugger off, that this was all

unorthodox and completely out of bounds. (Not to mention, there was the small matter of my handwriting.) I found myself nodding instead.

"Fine," I said. "Next week."

Looks like a storm is brewing, I texted Harper the next morning. The Narraganset Bay Regatta was only hours away. Is your "Orion Mercer is the greatest (and sexiest) 2 Seat in all the Land" sign waterproof?

She texted back. Sign? For what? Is something happening today I should know about?

I grinned. I'll capsize the shell from sheer heartbreak if my woman isn't there to cheer me on. Even if no one is allowed to know she's my woman.

The rolling dots of Harper's reply came and went, came and went. Finally:

"Your woman" again…
My bird? My babe? My doll?

My sign is ready, she texted. "Orion Mercer is a butthead."

I laughed. I gotta run. Coach will have my nuts if I'm late.

I'm so glad you feel comfortable sharing that with
me. Break a leg. An arm?
Both. See you soon. Xo

More rolling dots then, <3

That warm, nervy feeling came back, and I heaved a breath.

This is a good thing. The best thing. Don't fuck it up.

At CHA's parking lot, on the way to the docks, I fell into step with Xander Ford. We clasped hands, and I nodded at the turbulent waters bearded in whitecaps on the Bay.

"Should make for interesting races, eh?" I said. "But hey, check out the crowd."

From this distance, the bleachers were full of colorful blobs—our fans and those from around New England, there to cheer on their team, each represented by a banner in their school colors. Our own black and gold dominated, and a huge sign had been strung up that read *LET'S GO LIONS!*

Xander nodded absently, likely nerves. His first regatta with the Academy. I chucked him on the shoulder. "Let's give 'em a bloody good show."

And we did just that.

Our nemesis, New Haven Prep—who'd whipped our arses last year—narrowly gave us what-for a second time. But Xander Ford turned out to be our secret weapon.

Out on the water, in our black-and-gold unisuits, our coxswain, Dean, shouted at us through his headset. His face was twisted in a snarl, not at all the happy fellow we were used to.

"Come on, fucking pull! Let's go, wind it up!"

We pulled like bastards to Xander's stroke seat pace. He rowed as if he had a personal beef with the entire state of Connecticut. Our shell and New Haven's were neck and neck for a bit on the choppy water, and the sky looked as if it were going to break open and smite us. But somehow, we pulled ahead and crossed the finish line by a meter.

Cheers erupted from the stands, and a different kind of joy found me because I knew one of those voices was specifically for me, even if no one else did.

My hands were curved into claws, stiff from gripping my oar, and my chest was on fire from sucking in cold air as I slumped in happy exhaustion. Kai Thornton, three seat, turned around to share in the win, while Rhett Calloway, behind me at bow, scowled. Stroke seat had been his until Coach Daniels had switched him and Xander.

"Come on, Rhett," I said with a tired laugh. "We won no matter where you plant your arse."

He muttered darkly under his breath, and I shivered as we climbed out into the waist-deep water.

Friends and family greeted the crew as we came ashore, girlfriends kissing my mates. I scanned the crowd for Harper and found her hugging Dean, then Xander. Her gaze found mine, and she gave me a private smile. Xander was eyeing Emery; Dean seemed to be looking for someone else…

Bloody hell, are we all playing different versions of the same messed-up game?

My thoughts were cut off by Elowen Blake hurling herself at me so violently, I was nearly thrown off balance. She planted a lingering kiss on my cheek.

"Congratulations! That was amazing!"

"Fuck's sake, Elowen," I seethed, wrenching myself away from her. "Are you out of your mind?"

She glanced around, chagrined. "I was just trying to congratulate you…"

"Then just say that," I snapped, searching the crowd for Harper, but of all the faces, none were hers.

Elowen glared at me, her cheeks aflame. "You know what, Orion? Fuck you. You're an asshole. I'm done."

She stormed off through the crowd, blond hair flying, straight to Aria and Rhett to tattle on me. I brushed it off, hoping Harper hadn't seen that, and headed for the clubhouse for a postmortem with Coach.

"Gentlemen, you did good. Your time was impressive, given those conditions, and you should be proud of yourselves." He clapped his hands. "Okay, let's go celebrate!"

The locker room erupted into cheers. Tonight, the fancy country club was hosting its annual Regatta Gala, which was sure to be even more epic, thanks to our win. I found Xander and Dean together and slung my arms around them both.

"Bloody hell, Ford. I nearly put out my shoulder trying to match your pace. Good on ya, mate." I gave Dean a jostle. "And Yearwood, no one's a better coxy than you."

"Agreed," Xander said solemnly.

"Nah," Dean said. "You did all the hard work. All I had to do was sit and yell at you. Oh, and steer the boat, but that's not important."

"I hear the Castle Hill Country Club is going all out for this party," I said. "You're both coming, yeah?"

Dean beamed. "Is pi an irrational number? That would be a *yes*."

I laughed. "Dorks, the lot of you."

"I'm not going," Xander said.

"You have to come," I said. "It wouldn't be the same without you."

"I'll think about it," he mumbled.

"That's the spirit!" I said, and went out, but honestly, I wasn't feeling it either. Normally, I'd have been overjoyed at the idea of celebrating the win and the guaranteed pleasure of female company that night. But if Harper wasn't coming, I'd have to fly solo *and* be on my best behavior, all while missing her.

So this is what being responsible feels like. Bollocks.

I headed back to Atlas Hall. Overhead, thunder rumbled as a massive storm prepared to break on top of me. I'd just keyed into my apartment when my phone rang with Harper's number.

I'm in the doghouse already. Damn you, Elowen.

"Hey, Bennett," I said.

"Wow," she answered. "Someone sounds awfully guilty."

"You saw that, eh?" I said, grinning with relief at her

teasing tone. I threw myself on my couch and kicked my feet up. "How much trouble am I in?"

"All of it," Harper said. "You're in all the trouble. So much, in fact…I was thinking about coming to the country club party. To keep an eye on you, of course."

I sat up. "Really? You want to come? But just a few days ago—"

"I know, but…" Harper sounded shy again. "I've been thinking about it all weekend, and how I used to *not* give a shit what people thought about me. I hate how self-conscious I've become, and you're nothing to be self-conscious about. It sucked today, not being able to congratulate you on your win. You were amazing, and you deserve to be celebrated."

"Listen to you. *So* much romance, I can't take it."

"Shut it, Mercer," she said. "And lest you think I only changed my mind and became a possessive, stage-five clinger thanks to Elowen Blake's little performance, I've been thinking about this for a while. I even bought a dress. So…yeah. I'd like to go. With you. If you're cool with that."

My grin widened. "I don't know, I kind of like the idea of you being possessive of me, Bennett. Will you make a scene and claw Elowen's eyes out for touching your man?"

"I'm hanging up now."

"Wait, wait." I laughed. "I want you to come. More than anything. Should I pick you up?"

"No, I have to wait for Dash to get home. His teacher,

Mrs. Andolina? She's driving him from school since I was at the regatta and Mom's at work. As soon as she gets home, I can go. I'll meet you there."

"Sounds good. I'm glad you're coming. And if anyone gives you shit—"

"I know, I know. You'll tell them off, beat them up, caveman sounds, manly bluster, yadda yadda."

I laughed. "Exactly."

"See you soon."

"Can't wait."

I ended the call and rested the phone my chest, onto my "lockbox" of a heart that didn't feel as bolted shut and sunk in the depths at all. It was closer to the surface than it had ever been.

I smiled then jumped, as outside my window, a bolt of lightning tore open the sky, and the rain came down.

Chapter 18

HARPER

I ENDED THE CALL WITH ORION JUST AS THE SKY RIPPED open and the rain started pouring down in sheets.

"That's not ominous or anything," I muttered, and heaved a nervous breath. "I can do this."

I glanced at the dress laid out on my bed and let a small smile flicker over my lips.

I'd told Orion most of the truth regarding my hairpin change of heart. I'd been dead set on keeping us secret, but Sunday afternoon, I'd changed my mind. I'd been strolling Castle Hill's tiny downtown. Amid all the bougie boutiques, antique stores, and fancier establishments was a consignment dress shop. In the window, a white empire-waist dress caught my eye. It had silver embroidery along the seams and intricate diamond-shaped appliqués along its flowing length.

I instantly imagined myself wearing that dress, my hair curled neatly, and maybe even something sparkly in it while walking Castle Hill Country Club on Orion's arm. I imagined dancing with him, celebrating his regatta win proudly instead of hiding us. Hiding *me*.

And why not? Mom seemed okay. She'd been sober at home, and my school stress wasn't going anywhere. I was a tough cookie after all. I could handle more school scrutiny, and Orion was worth it.

Orion…

My pulse kicked up again. I'd vowed not to do casual with a guy again, and *casual* had been left in the dust. It was shocking and more than a little nerve-racking how much space this boy had taken up in my heart, leaving me breathless and utterly unprepared.

And I was *always* prepared.

Trust.

I nearly laughed out loud. In my experience, *trust* was a dirty word.

"I need backup." I punched in Emery's cell number.

"Hey," she said, sounding defeated.

"Hey, yourself." I sat on my bed, next to my dress. "Are you okay?"

"Dad is making me go to the stupid election watch party for Tucker's dad."

I frowned. "The same Tucker you broke up with on Saturday?"

"Yeah, well, apparently Dad didn't get the memo."

I bit my tongue. "Didn't you *tell* him?"

"I did, but he doesn't hear me. And he…he was…"

"He was what?" I asked, my blood running cold.

"Kind to me," Emery said, her voice breaking.

I breathed a sigh of relief, even if it was still fucked up how Grayson Wallace dangled his love in front of his only daughter like a lure instead of just giving it to her unconditionally like a father was supposed to. But my own dad split before he ever knew I existed, so what did I know?

"It's awful," she cried. "But I'm so starved for any scrap for kindness from my own father, I agreed to go to this stupid party. But this is the last one. The last event I do for the Hill-Wallace family alliance, and then I am *done*."

Since knowing Emery, she'd told me that a key element to her dating Tucker had been because his senator father and her tycoon father had business dealings, and it was advantageous to keep the families united. The two men had twisted systems of favor exchanges and backroom dealings, so Grayson used Emery in his schemes like a feudal king from the Dark Ages.

"So after the election, you and Xander can be…?" I prodded gently.

"I don't know, Harper. I'm just trying to get through this night." She sniffed and pulled herself together. "What about you? Going to the regatta party?"

"That's why I'm calling. I was sort of hoping you'd be there for moral support."

It was on the tip of my tongue to tell her about Orion, but I'd planned to do that at the party too, with everyone else. Not over the phone, and not when she was still clearly heartbroken and upset.

"You'll be fine without me," she said. "You're one of the strongest people I know. I wish I had half your courage."

"I don't know about that, but you have courage, Em," I said. "You just have to dig for it."

"Hm," she said, unconvinced. "I have to go. Have the best time. I'm so jealous. Tell me everything after."

"I will."

We hung up, and I heard Dash bang through the front door. I went downstairs to wave goodbye to Mrs. Andolina, got him situated with a snack and his favorite TV movie, then went to get ready for the party.

An hour later, I examined myself in the standing mirror that had once been in Mom's bedroom in Pittsburgh.

For a girl who wasn't too handy with the makeup brush, I thought I did pretty well. The dress was flattering with my pale complexion and dark hair, giving me a Snow White–kind of vibe. (Though if you'd told me a year ago I'd be comparing myself to a Disney princess I'd have slapped myself in the face.)

I blame Orion. The way he looked at me in the suffragette dress…

I wanted to look pretty for him again. And for me. No crime in that.

I'd put on a faint sweep of blush, pink lip gloss, and a little bit of eye makeup. Risking second-degree burns, I'd taken a wand to my curls and tightened them so that they lay in perfect ringlets around my shoulders and used a silvery headband to keep them from my face.

I inhaled yet another steadying breath, and my breasts pushed up from the top of the empire bodice rather prettily.

No crime in that either, I thought, my cheeks heating at the thought of Orion's hands on me, his mouth on me, maybe taking the dress off…

I took a long drink of water from my nightstand and inspected myself in the mirror one last time. Now my eyes were glassy, cheeks flushed, breasts heaving like a character in a Jane Austen novel.

I look *like a character in a Jane Austen novel. I like that better than Disney. More literary.*

God, my thoughts were racing. Like my heart, because I wanted that boy. Bad.

"Down, girl," I muttered, and headed downstairs to wait for Mom to come home.

Dash watched me come down. "Oh my gosh, Harper, you look so pretty!"

"Don't say that, buddy. You'll ruin my makeup."

His face scrunched up. "How?"

I dabbed my eyes with a Kleenex from the coffee table "Never mind. Thank you. That's a very nice thing to say."

Dash beamed and went back to his movie. I sat on the

couch, my delicate shawl and my ugly raincoat on my lap. Waiting.

And waiting.

The country club party started at six o'clock.

At six fifteen, I made Dash dinner, trying not to get any mac and cheese on my dress. I texted Orion that my mother was running late so I was running late, but I'd be there in a few.

Grand entrance? 😊, he texted back. I can't wait to show you off.

My stomach rolled. The last thing I'd wanted was to show up when everyone else was already there. And Orion's swoony words would've sent my heart fluttering, but they couldn't defeat the ugly coil of fear that was taking hold.

I texted my mother. Where are you? I'm late to the party.

No answer.

The storm outside was a wild beast, trying to get in the house, rattling the windows and howling in the trees. Rain pelted the glass like pebbles, and Dash's eyes went wide as the house shook at a particularly gnarly boom of thunder.

"Harper…?"

"It's okay, buddy." I stopped pacing and sat with him on the couch. "Just a bad storm. Mom will be here soon."

It's getting rough out there, came a text from Orion. Maybe I should pick you up.

Guilt whipped me. I hadn't been exactly looking

forward to driving in this mess, even if the country club was a short five minutes away. But the dentist office was farther. Maybe Mom ran into some trouble. I texted Orion that I couldn't leave Dash, and then texted Mom.

Are you okay? Getting worried.

No answer.

At seven p.m., just when I was about to start calling hospitals, headlights splashed the front windows with glaring light. It wasn't Mom's old SUV, but a car I didn't recognize.

Oh God.

"Stay here," I told Dash and went on leaden legs to the front door, to greet the cops that were there to tell me there'd been an accident. That Mom was gone...

I opened the door to find my mother trying—unsuccessfully—to jab her key in the front door with one hand while holding a raincoat over her head with the other. The car idling in our driveway wasn't a police cruiser, but a dark sedan. I could just make out a man in the driver seat. Mustache, glasses. Dr. Hensley, I presumed.

"Harper! You scared me to death." Mom laughed nervously, stepped inside, and my heart cracked in half.

She was drunk. Not falling-down drunk, but more than tipsy. More than "a glass of wine or two."

Instantly, I was three years old and listening to her cackle at the moon while lying on her back on our front lawn.

I was six years old, covering my ears as she screamed and hurled beer bottles at a faceless boyfriend.

I was ten years old, poking her passed-out body, thinking she was dead.

I was thirteen years old, hiding in the closet with Dash as a different drunk boyfriend slammed around the apartment like the storm outside, howling and thrashing to get in…

I shut the door behind her as she came into the house and started for the stairs, giving Dash's cheek a pat on the way, and mumbling something about having to pack. He stared at her, confused, scared, and my heart cracked again.

"Mom," I said. "*Mom.*"

She pretended not to hear me.

"Maeve Bennett."

She turned, and imaginary confusion lit up her eyes. "Oh, Harper. You look so beautiful. Why are you all dressed up?"

"You know perfectly well why. The regatta party," I said, crossing my arms, willing my voice not to falter. For the tears not to come. Because the night was ruined. There would be no party. No dancing with Orion. No standing up for us, or for myself. I couldn't leave Dash alone with her. Not now. But behind me, the lights from Hensley's car were still illuminating our front windows, his car still idling in our driveway.

"What is happening right now?" I asked.

"Oh, honey." Mom's shoulders slumped. "I'm so sorry.

I completely forgot about your party. Alan's taking me to Newport for five days. A spur-of-the-moment thing."

My hands on my arms dug into my bare flesh so hard they'd leave bruises later.

"For five days," I said, and shock cleaned me out. Turned me hollow and cold. My voice sounded empty and dead. "You're leaving in the middle of the week for five days. Just like that."

"I know. I didn't plan for this, and it's not ideal—"

"Not ideal," I repeated. This couldn't be real. There was no possible way this was real…

"Don't give me a hard time," Mom said, heading upstairs, weaving slightly. "I have to. He's my boss. What am I going to do? Say no?"

"Yes!"

I screamed the word. It broke through the shock and erupted out of me on a tide of molten rage. A fury so white hot, it lit me up from the inside, leaving my skin and eyes burning, my throat dry and airless.

Dash flinched. "Harper?"

"In a second, buddy," I managed, teeth clenched to keep from screaming again.

I followed Mom upstairs, to our shared bathroom, where she began stuffing toiletries in a bag from under the sink.

"You can't do this," I seethed. "You can't just leave us for five fucking days. And you're drunk. I can't believe you'd do this to us. To Dash."

"Harper, I can't talk about this right now. I'll be back on Sunday. We'll talk then."

She pushed past me, back down the stairs. I followed on her tail, the fury lighting me up from the inside until I thought I'd combust.

"No, we'll talk now. You can't go. You *cannot.*"

"Harper?" Dash called from the couch. He was standing up, shifting from foot to foot.

"Not now, Dash."

"But…"

I reached for Mom's arm as she pulled clothes from the hall closet that served as her closet and stuffed them in a rolling suitcase.

"No. You cannot do this to us. You cannot. *I will not let you.*"

She tore out of my grip. "I'll get fired, Harper. Is that what you want?"

"Yes!" I screamed. "Get the fuck away from that cheating asshole and find another job. You think that's the only one out there? Just what the fuck is wrong with you?"

"Harper…?"

"Not now, Dash!"

And then he started to cry.

"If you walk out this door, I will never forgive you for this," I ground out, my voice quivering. My entire body shaking. "Never. Do you hear me? *I will never fucking forgive you.*"

Mom stopped at the front door. "Someday, Harper,

when you're an adult and have to make adult choices, you'll understand." She pulled her raincoat over her head and offered Dash a faltering smile. "Be a good boy. Mind your sister. I'll be back in a few days." She turned to me, her eyes shining and glassy. "I'm sorry."

Then she stepped out into the downpour. I stared after her, sure this was a dream. A nightmare. My phone was blowing up. Dash was crying. The rain was pounding…

I can salvage this, I thought wildly. Desperately. Pathetically trying to hold on to a scrap of happiness. *I'll call Mrs. Andolina. Beg her to come back. Yes, I'll ask a sixty-year-old woman to drive into a hurricane to watch my little brother so I can go to a party…*

"Harper?"

I turned. "What *is it*, Dash?"

Sniffling, he pointed one finger up.

I looked up too, to the steady stream of droplets dripping from the ceiling and onto the living room rug in front of the TV. I stared. The heated fury in my body instantly turned to ice. Out of my peripheral, I saw another leak in the kitchen. A third in the stairwell. Like silvery stalactites.

Something in me snapped. My mind went blank but for flashes of traumatic childhood memories that confused then for now, now for then. I was a little girl and I was me. It had happened and it was still happening, and I couldn't escape.

I ran out into the downpour and was instantly

drenched. My dress ruined. My curls flattened. Makeup streamed down my cheeks with rain and tears. The dentist's car was turning around and driving away, and I chased after, screaming as the red taillights grew fainter.

"FUCK YOU! I HATE YOU! DO YOU HEAR ME!? I FUCKING HATE YOU!"

I screamed over and over until the lights faded away. Until the car was gone. Until my voice gave out and I fell to my knees on the hard cement drive. My dress tore and my skin too, though I hardly felt it.

"Harper?"

Somehow under the tumult of the storm and my sobs, I heard Dash's little voice, tear-filled and frightened. It drew me out of the cycle of then and now and into just now.

Pull yourself together. One more time. For him.

But I couldn't stop crying. It was as if something had broken in me after years—more than a decade—of holding myself together, and I was helpless against it. The rage, the grief, the absolute horror of doing another round of Mom's addiction…

I can't do this again. Not again.

I hauled myself off the driveway and staggered into the house. Dash watched me with wide eyes, his own tears streaming. Wordlessly, sobbing, I pulled pots and pans from under the sink and put them under the leaks. The *ping ping ping* of water hitting the metal added to the horrible symphony of this night: a wailing storm of rain, of tears, of water seeping into cracks and ruining everything good and whole, while somewhere, in another life, another me was dancing in a glittering ballroom with a beautiful boy…

"Harper…?"

Dash was still following me as I set out the pans, now and then tugging my hand with his little one. My heart broke for him more than for me, but my sobs wouldn't stop. I shook my head, trying to explain, to comfort him, but I couldn't get the words out. Instead I hugged him close, whispered *I'm sorry* in his ear, and put him in front of the TV again.

Then I sat in the stairwell next to the dripping water and texted Orion.

I had more than a dozen worried texts and missed calls from him that only made me cry harder. I could barely see the phone keys as I typed.

I'm not coming. I'm sorry.

The phone dropped out of my hands, I pulled up my scraped knees—blood and grime and rain stained my dress—and buried my face in my arms. I tried to dive into the black nothing, to make it all go away, but the pounding rain wouldn't stop. The thunder kept booming, and it sounded like the storm was banging on the door, demanding to come in.

Someone *was* banging on the door.

Dash's little voice called my name, and then a deeper one.

"Harper?"

The voice. The accent. The scent of cologne mixed with rainwater. Large, strong hands were on my shoulders, gently bringing me around.

I lifted my head, which felt as if it weighed a hundred pounds, and opened swollen eyes. Beautiful dark ones looked back. Orion knelt in front of me, and I burst into tears all over again when I thought I had none left. Though I was a dirty, sodden mess, ruining his tuxedo, he gathered me to him.

"Oh, love." His voice was low and rumbling in my ear as he held me tight, held me together. "It's going to be all right." He stroked my hair, kissed my forehead. "Everything's going to be all right."

I didn't believe him, but in those moments, encircled in his arms, I pretended he was telling the truth.

Chapter 19

HARPER

"YOU'RE SHIVERING," ORION SAID, HIS HEAD BENT TO MY ear. He pulled away a little and turned to Dash. "Hey, little man. Would you—"

He stopped, and even through my utter, wasted shock and despair, I felt Orion vibrate with fury. I opened my eyes to see him staring at my dress: sodden, dirty, *bloody*…

"Harper," he said through clenched teeth. "What happened? Who did this to you?"

I shook my head, tried to speak, but Dash piped up.

"She fell down in the rain after Mama left," he said in a small voice.

"That's all? No one was here?"

"N-no."

"You're sure?"

"Yes."

Orion eased out a breath. "Okay, then," he said tightly. "No need to fly back into the storm in a murderous rampage, eh?"

"What?" Dash was standing next to the couch, looking lost and so, so small, and hatred for our mother infused me all over again.

"Nothing," Orion said. "Hey, little man. I need your help. I've never been to your house before. Can you bring me a towel?"

Dash nodded, better for having something to do.

"Orion," I said, my voice a croak from screaming. "Please, go. I don't want you to see…"

"No, no. It's all right."

Dash dashed back with a towel. "Is she okay?"

"She's going to be just fine." Gently, Orion wrapped the towel snuggly around my shoulders. "Just sit here for a minute, love." He turned to Dash. "Have you had dinner?"

"Yes."

"Brilliant. More important question: Have you had dessert?"

The barest light flickered in Dash's eyes. "No."

"Well, we'll have to fix that, won't we?"

I hugged the towel around me, still shivering, wanting to shut my eyes and block the world out. But I watched with a detached fascination as Orion moved around my house, sidestepping leaks to take care of Dash.

Humiliation churned in me somewhere, but I was too numb to feel it.

In the kitchen, Orion opened the freezer. "Ice cream?"

"Too cold," Dash said. "My Halloween candy is in the top cabinet. I'm not supposed to know, but I do."

"Clever man." Orion opened the cabinet and found a plastic pumpkin. He handed it to Dash and brought him back to the couch. "Honor system. Pick out three pieces and no more. Can you do that?"

Dash nodded, plopping himself down in front of the TV where *The Princess Bride* was on pause.

He squinted at Orion. "Why are you dressed so fancy?"

"I was at a party. Your sister was supposed to come too. But then your mom left?"

Dash nodded, his lower lip quivering. "For five days with her boss. Harper was really mad. *Really* mad."

"Got it." Orion found the remote and hit *play*. "I'm going to help your sister get some rest, and then you and I are going to hang out for a bit. Would you like that?"

His eyes lit up again, and he nodded vigorously. "Hurry up and you can watch them in the fire swamp!"

"Wouldn't miss it."

Orion rushed back to me. I shook my head, jostling more tears loose. They spilled hotly down my cheeks. "You're so good with him," I whispered. "But I hate that you're here. Seeing this. You should go. Please…"

"Not on your life, Bennett," he said gently. "Come on."

Orion slipped his arms around my back and under my knees and carried me upstairs. The house was small enough that he found my room easily and set me on the edge of my bed.

"This room is very you," he said, glancing around. "Eclectic *and* scholastic."

A bookshelf lined one wall. My desk under the window was a mess of papers, charts, and graphs—the makings of my NoSci entry. Posters for Florence + the Machine and St. Vincent papered the walls…

"And a periodic table." Orion grinned. "Because of course."

I didn't smile. "This is not how I imagined your first visit to my room."

"Don't start with me, Bennett," he said. "Now is not the time for seduction. You need to get warmed up. Are you okay to take a shower? I'll make some tea. Your voice sounds… a bit rough."

Rough from screaming how I hate my mother. Because I do. I hate her.

Orion saw the defeated pall hanging over me. He knelt in front of me and took both of my cold, trembling hands in his large warm ones.

"Hey. I'm here."

I raised my aching eyes to his. "I ruined your tux. I ruined your night."

"You didn't ruin anything," he said. "The party was *so* boring. I was standing around with a bunch of regatta fat cats, being congratulated *endlessly*, and thinking to myself, *I wish Harper would send me an ominous text that sends me out into a typhoon*. That's how boring it was."

I started to laugh, which turned into more crying. He wrapped me in his arms again.

"Take a long hot shower, I'll bring you some tea, and you can tell me everything."

He left, and I moved like a zombie to the bathroom. I took the hottest shower I could stand, trying to drive the cold numbness away. It worked, but exhaustion seeped in to replace it.

I bandaged my scraped knees, dressed in flannel sleep pants and an NYU sweatshirt, and climbed into bed. No sooner did my head hit the pillow than my eyes wanted to close. I felt more than saw Orion return. He set a steaming mug of something on the nightstand, and the bed dipped as he sat beside me.

"This okay?"

I shook my head, hardly able to keep my eyes open. "This is so humiliating."

"You have to stop worrying about that." He ran his hand along my temple. "But love, what happened? Your mother left for *five days*?"

I nodded. "She came home drunk, packed up a bag, and skipped town with her married dentist boss. And the roof started to leak just like I knew it would, because she didn't bother to inspect the house when she bought it, and now we're fucked. The end."

I squeezed my eyes shut. I knew reality was going to come with the dawn. The past becoming prologue yet again. A book I thought I'd finished, only to find it hadn't ended at all, but kept going and going…

I can't do this again…

Exhaustion was dragging me down into merciful oblivion.

"Dash…?" I managed.

"He's fine. I got him."

"I'm sorry, Orion. I really wanted tonight."

"Me too," he said. "But don't be sorry. Just sleep, love."

Gratitude filled me then, driving out some of the awfulness of the night. For this boy who was here, and so effortlessly good, and more noble than I think even he knew.

I tried to tell him, but sleep pulled me under. But it was okay because I knew I was safe.

More importantly, I knew Dash was too.

I woke sometime in the night, no sense of time, only conscious that the storm had slunk away like a wounded beast. The night was finally quiet outside my window. I sat up slowly, my head feeling heavy and achy.

It was a bad dream, that's all. Just a bad dream…

"Right?"

I winced. My throat was raw, and there was a mug of tea on my nightstand that Orion had made me, because it wasn't a dream at all but a living nightmare. I groaned, wanting to sink back under the covers. Humiliation infested me like a fever. God, he'd seen it all. This shitty house, the leaky roof, me completely broken down…

More shame found me because I'd abandoned Dash to my own despair. Failed him when he needed me most. I tossed off the covers and hurried to his room and then sagged in the door. Dash was safe in his bed, fast asleep. Orion was on the floor beside him, his head pillowed on his tuxedo jacket.

He stayed.

He'd stayed with Dash. Stood guard like a knight in a fairy tale until the dragon had gone. My chest tightened with an ache so fierce and so strong, it stole my breath. And despite the outright shitty-ness of the night, my skin burned with heat, my stomach heavy with a different kind of ache.

I crept into the room and gently touched Orion on the shoulder. He stirred and woke. By the light of Dash's *Finding Nemo* nightlight, I put my finger to my mouth and motioned for him to follow me out.

In the hallway, I closed Dash's door and led Orion to my room.

"Should I go?" he whispered. "Or I can sleep on the couch…?"

"God, no," I whispered back. The couch was my mother's bed. "It's two in the morning. You can sleep here. If you want. Unless…you want to go?"

Of course he does. He probably can't wait to get out of this leaky hellhole…

"I'd rather stay," Orion said. "If you're okay with that."

"Oh. Yes. I'm okay with that."

I led him back to my room, shut the door behind us, and turned on the desk lamp. It cast a small warm light. Orion cocked his head from side to side, stretching out a crick in his neck. His bow tie was long gone, the top buttons of his white dress shirt undone, and the shirt itself wrinkled. He slung his equally wrinkled jacket over his shoulder.

"So," he said quietly. The air between us heavy and thick. "Do you mind if I get out of this suit?"

"No, of course not," I said. "Go ahead. I'll just…"

I climbed into bed on one far side of the full-size bed that was always plenty big enough for just me but now felt small. Narrow. Hardly any space at all. I kept my back to him as Orion stripped out of his tux, shut off the light, and climbed in. The bed shrunk again, his big, muscular frame swallowing up his side.

Once he was under the covers, I rolled onto my back. He did the same, and we both stared at the ceiling in silence. I was acutely conscious of his presence, my entire left side humming at the close proximity to his right. A tingling at the nearness, the almost-touching. His arm brushed mine when he shifted, sending little sparks up and down my skin.

"Sorry," he said.

"No worries."

A silence fell, heated and full of electricity. I thought I'd be emotionally wasted and wrung out, but my heart was pounding, and every nerve ending in my body was wide awake and clamoring to be touched.

"I can't thank you enough for tonight," I said, my voice still rough. "For what you did for Dash, especially. He loves you."

"It was nothing," Orion said. His voice also rough, though he hadn't been screaming all night. "He's a great kid."

"Yeah, he is."

Another silence. More staring at the ceiling.

He's just being polite. Staying so I don't feel bad. He'll be gone in the morning, and I can't blame him.

"Well. Goodnight, Orion."

"Goodnight, Harper." He turned his head, a faint smile barely visible in the dimness. "But first...I think you need at least a goodnight hug, yeah?"

"I wouldn't say no to that."

Understatement of the century.

Orion turned toward me and me to him. He pulled me into his arms and kissed my forehead. Then my cheek. Then a tentative, gentle kiss on my lips. Then another... and another, until the gravity—the force that had been pulling at us—gave in and our mouths parted and clashed in a searing kiss.

I moaned with relief, clutching at him, both of us mauling each other, ravenous. A desire I'd never felt before ripped through me like wildfire, burning out the cold of the storm. I'd never *needed* kisses, or rough hands on me, or a body pressed to mine and on top of me. But with Orion, I needed everything. I needed his mouth, his tongue, the perfect clean taste of him. He kissed me as if my mouth were his to take, but I *wanted* to be taken. To surrender to him and let him have me because I'd never felt safer in my life. The masculine power in him was everything I desired, so that *his* desire for me felt right. Good. Safe.

Orion's mouth worked over mine with an expertise that stole my breath, while his hands explored, one slipping under my bulky sweatshirt to find the bare skin beneath my breast.

"Wait, wait," he breathed, wrenching himself way. "I'm an arsehole. You were so upset tonight. We shouldn't."

I hauled him back to me, kissing his lips, his chin, his jaw. "Yes, we should," I breathed. "Don't stop."

"Are you sure?"

"Orion…" I craned up, arching into him, pulling at his shoulders.

He relented and moved on top of me. The glorious weight of him elicited another moan, then a whimper as his hips settled on top of mine. My hands roamed over his back, then slipped under his undershirt to find his smooth skin over hard muscle. There was too much clothing in the way—his shirt, and my sweatshirt, so bulky and unsexy.

"Take it off," I whispered.

In one deft maneuver, bracing himself on one arm

over me, he lifted it off me and tossed it aside. I felt his eyes rake over me, my skin pale in the dim light. One large hand went to my breast, and then his mouth found the small nipple, biting and sucking. I arched into his touch, holding his hair, making a fist in his curls.

"Fuck me, Harper, your tits are perfect," he said between kisses.

Another spark of pure need shot between my legs at the word. Not usually my favorite, but out of his mouth…

He's wrecking me for anyone else…

I pulled Orion to me, tugging at his shirt. I needed his skin against mine. With the same ease, he reached behind his neck for the collar of his shirt and yanked it off. Then he was on top of me again, bare skin pressed to mine. Another first of sorts. Another newness. Most of my "dates" had been sweaty encounters in backseats where only enough clothing was removed to get the job done.

Orion was not that.

His dark gaze drank me up with equal parts lust and appreciation, his hands moving with purpose, to give and take, exploring while leaving little fires in the wake of his touch, and I wanted to give and take in the same way. My hands slid over his shoulders, his neck, the back of his head, then sank into his curls while he kissed me, greedy and deep, leaving no part untouched. He kissed me breathless, then moved downward, to my neck, then between my breasts, then lower. My heart began to pound.

"You've had a rough night, love," he said. "I want to make you feel good. Can I?"

Oh God.

No guy had ever done that for me before. No guy had ever wanted to.

"Do you *want* to?"

"Of course I do," Orion said, tugging at the waistband of my sleep pants. "You'll just have to be quiet," he said, and I could just make out his mischievous grin. "Don't want to wake the boy."

He had my pants off within moments, and nervousness tempered how badly I wanted him. He kissed the delicate, untouched skin at my hip, tongue flicking. My hips bucked automatically. Unbothered, he held me still and moved lower on the bed. My pulse was loud now in my ears, my breath coming in harsh gasps.

"Orion, wait."

He froze. "Yes, love?"

"No, nothing."

"If you want me to stop, I'll stop."

"No, I want this. But…"

Orion came back up the bed and lay beside me. He kissed me softly, caressing my face. "I only want what you want. Have you ever…?"

"Yes," I said. "Just not *that*."

He frowned. "I don't know what kind of lowlife creeps you've been with, but it's childish behavior to sleep with you and not worship you appropriately…" He kissed my mouth, my chin, working his way back down my body. His tongue teased my nipple. "I hope they at least appreciated these glorious tits."

"Will you stop saying that?"

"Oh, pardon me. *Breasts.* Is that better?"

"Actually, no."

He chuckled, moving down my torso to my navel. "You deserve this, Harper. Please allow me to give it to you."

"Well, when you put it that way…"

He grinned, and I saw the white of his teeth, that brilliant smile, and then all thought flew out of my head as his mouth descended. I grabbed a pillow just in time, muffling the cry that tore out of my throat as a pleasure unlike anything I'd ever known shot through me.

Orion, my God… I arched into him, and he held me still, his mouth licking, sucking, even biting lightly until starbursts were shooting across the dark of my eyes. I writhed helplessly but he refused to let me go until he was finished with me. In no time at all, ribbons of pleasure rippled through me in waves, one after another, until finally, the biggest wave of them all crashed over me, leaving me spent, my legs shaking.

He climbed back up the bed and pulled the pillow away from my face. "You can come out now."

"Holy shit," I breathed.

"Ah, there's that romance." He kissed my shoulder, then he sat up and drank the cold tea by my bedside table and leaned against the headboard. "My work here is done."

I rolled my eyes. "You're too much."

"So I'm told," he said with that grin of his that drove me mad. That made me want do things to him…

I didn't think I'd be able to move for days, but I put my underwear and sweatshirt back on, then used the restroom.

"Must you?" Orion asked, giving the sleeve of the sweatshirt a tug as I climbed back into bed. "Cruel of you to deny me a few of my favorite things."

I rolled my eyes but took off the sweatshirt, pulled the covers up, and sat beside him against the headboard, curled against his arm. "You're obsessed."

"Can you blame me? These gorgeous, perfectly shaped pale orbs…"

"Oh my God, stop." I groaned a laugh. "But so long as you don't say 'milky white.' Ugh, I hate that word."

"Milky?"

"*Yuck*, yes. Moist gets a bad rap, but I'll take that over milky any day."

"Fair," Orion said. "I'm not a fan of caramel myself. I've heard that one too many times. I'm not a macchiato, for fuck's sake."

"No," I said, letting my eyes wander over his profile in the dimness, and my fingers trailed up his strong forearm, forgetting myself. "You're so much more than that. Gold and bronze, and warm and good…"

"You're getting much better at this, Bennett." He bent to kiss me softly on the lips.

I took his kiss, let it suffuse me with that warmth that was so him, and then settled back against him.

"I'm not used to…this. I never knew my dad, and my mother's boyfriends were never role models of healthy relationships, to say the least. This new one, included." I peered up at him. "What about you? Are your parents happy?"

He shrugged one shoulder. "Hard to say. They've been together forever. Mum's been with Father from the beginning, when he was an immigrant from Nigeria on scholarship to Cambridge. When he was poor and struggling, starting his company from scratch. She was with him when he had nothing, and she's still with him when he has everything."

"Sounds like true love to me," I said. "Not that I'm the expert."

"I suppose," he said. "They're not overtly loving, but I can't picture either of them with anyone else. They make a good team. Is that romance?" He shrugged again.

"So where does yours come from?"

Orion grinned. "Factory settings. Came with the package."

This boy…

With a boldness I didn't know I possessed, I straddled Orion, my knees on either side of his hips. I took the tea mug out of his hand and kissed him softly at first, holding his jaw in my hand. The other trailed down his chest, down over his pecs, the hard ridges of his abdomen. Every part of him honed from hours in the gym and more hours out on the water.

"You don't have to," he said against my mouth. "You don't owe me."

"I know," I whispered. "This is not a thank-you. This is what I want for you."

My lips hovered over his, kissing him hotly. Then I reached lower, finding him hard in his boxer briefs. I gripped the length of him and squeezed. He hissed in a breath. I breathed it in and began to stroke him.

"Bennett, what are you doing?"

"What do you think I'm doing?"

He brought his hands up on my hips, then slid them up higher along my sides before cupping both breasts.

"This is about you," I said.

"It can't be just about me," he said. "Not when you're like this. Right here in front of me."

His thumbs made circles over my nipples. In answer, I slid into his underwear and wrapped my hand around him.

"Fuck, Harper."

His breath came in shorter gusts. I reached down and tugged his underwear off his hips. A quick glance down in the dimness and my heartbeat quickened. I stroked harder, kissing him, biting his lower lip, while his hands slid down my stomach over my underwear. To the center of me that was still humming.

"This is just for you," I said.

Orion shook his head. "I need something to do with my hands."

Now both of our hips were rocking together as his fingers began to move in slow circles over the silk material of my underwear. I struggled to keep focus on what I was doing.

"Does it feel good?" I breathed.

"Fuck, yes. So good."

The chords on his neck stood out. His breaths sharpened. His grip on my hip tightened. I nearly lost my concentration as another wave, built off the first, tore through me. I moaned. Our kisses became hardly more than a hovering of lips and teeth.

"Harper, I'm going to…oh fuck."

Quickly, I reached to the nightstand and grabbed three tissues from the box. I stroked him through, catching his release, taking all of it, reveling in the pained ecstasy on his face. How the muscles in his abs stood out, the sounds he trapped in his chest and how he shuddered for a long time until finally sinking back against the headboard.

"Fucking hell," he gasped.

I tossed the tissues away and curled up against his chest. Orion's heart was pounding in my ear. He gathered me to him, and we sank back under the covers.

My body hummed with pleasure, both given and received. And satisfaction that I'd stolen back something good from this horrible night, and this guy in my bed had salvaged more than that. I'd been lost and sinking into despair, and he'd pulled me from the brink.

Tomorrow, the work would begin. Again. The hard, heartbreaking work of holding my family together. But these hours with Orion were mine, and I let myself have that happiness, no matter how fleeting it would be.

Chapter 20

ORION

I WOKE THE NEXT MORNING TO WATERY GOLD LIGHT streaming through Harper's window. The storm had abated, the rain had stopped. She slept peacefully, wrapped in my arms, and thank God for that.

Jesus, last night…

While the minutes had ticked by at the country club, I'd started to think she was going to stand me up. That she got cold feet about exposing herself to the vipers. Not that I'd blame her. But Harper was brave and fierce, and my gut told me it was something worse. Even so, the last thing I expected to find was her sobbing and bleeding, abandoned and broken.

The heavy scene had whacked me in the chest. That kind of pure, raw emotion—like a storm raging inside the house just as fiercely as the one without—was shocking. Not something I'd ever witnessed, certainly not in my house. My heart ached to see her so wrecked, and I had to fix it immediately. Put it all back together. Put *her* back together. To make right what had gone horribly wrong so that everything was okay again.

Now, I smiled with relief. The storm was over. The choppy seas had grown calm again.

From somewhere on the floor, Harper's phone rang. She blinked sleepily, smiled to see me, then frowned as last night came rushing back.

"God, it all really happened, didn't it?"

"Yes, love," I said, brushing a dark curl from her pale cheek.

She sighed and bent to grab her phone.

"Emery? It's early." She listened, brows furrowed, then nodded. "Of course I will. Tucker, that asshole. Jesus, Em, I'm sorry I missed your call last night." Harper shot me a loaded glance. "Are you okay?" More listening, and then she smirked. "Thank God, and yes, I can *hear* you smile. Tell Xander I said hi, I told you so, and that I'm proud of him for finally getting his head out of his ass."

She ended the call and tossed her phone aside. "After the election party, Tucker drove Emery out into my neck of the woods and abandoned her when she refused to have sex with him."

"Bloody arsehole," I muttered. "Jesus, I might've driven right past her to get to you."

"It's all right. Xander came to her rescue, and they're together now. As they should be."

"That's my boy."

I kissed Harper's shoulder and pulled her back to me, spooning her, reclaiming her from Emery's crisis. Her eyes were a bit puffy from crying, and her lips were swollen too, from my kisses. I could kiss Harper for hours; she tasted like cherries, her mouth soft but biting too. Everything about her was a contrasting sensation that drove me mad with want. How she was beautifully soft and warm, but strong and fierce too. Warm-hearted but keenly intelligent. Kind but sharp-tongued and witty.

And all of those traits had stirred me to heights of desire so that when she was naked beneath me, I'd felt something I'd never felt before with a girl. Something more than just bodily lust. An attraction to every part of her that had made every kiss, every touch, heightened to a level I'd never experienced before.

And nerve-racking. I'd been handed something precious and fragile and entrusted not to drop it.

"You stayed." Harper rolled over to face me and brushed her fingers over my cheek. "What about your curfew?"

"Atlas Hall blokes watch out for each other. We have a system if we need to get around the curfew. It's how my vampiric roommate comes and goes as he pleases. Think nothing of it."

She smiled faintly. "Wait, what time is it? What about school?"

"I was thinking of taking the day off," I said. "You should too. And the little man. Let's go to Newport. Have some fun. I think you both need it."

"I can't," she said. "Dash needs to sleep, so I'll take the day off, but only to study and get caught up. I have too much work to do. We have that paper due for history on Friday. I have a quiz in Calculus, a poem to write for English, and the Vivaldi that Wolfe assigned that I haven't even looked at." She frowned at me. "Don't you have a lot too?"

"Well, yes, but…I figured after last night you'd want a breather. Let's do something fun and forget all about last night."

Her frown deepened. "I can't *forget*. My roof is about to fall in. And I can't take a breather, either. Especially not now." Harper sat up, pulled on her sweatshirt, and rubbed her eyes. "God, so much work to do, and my mother fucking left. She knows about the NoSci and how much academic pressure I'm under. It's why we came here. And she doesn't care. She doesn't *think*."

I struggled for something to say that would comfort her that wasn't a joke or jest, but jokes and jesting were all I had.

"And the fucking roof." Harper scrubbed her hands through her hair. "I knew it. I knew when she bought this place and didn't do a damn inspection, there'd be a problem. And of course, I was right. She's like a child while I have to be the adult. Again."

Tears welled in her eyes, but she fought them back.

"No, I'm not going to break again. Not for her." Anger colored her words and colored her cheeks. "I have too much shit to handle. Too much of her mess to clean up."

"I'll handle the roof," I said, grateful to have something to *do* that would help. "It's too much for you and…"

My words died at Harper's incredulous stare.

"What?" I asked, feeling like I'd made a horrible mistake.

"Absolutely not." She climbed out of the bed, pulling on her sleep pants.

"Why not?" I said. "You just said you have so much to handle. I can help. I'm happy to help."

"I know you are, Orion, and I'm so grateful for what you did last night. Last night was everything. But I can't let you do that. That's too much."

"It's not too much," I said. "Really."

But the air had changed. Grown colder, and I distinctly felt I wasn't welcome to loiter in her bed anymore. I put on my tuxedo pants, then stood on one side of the room, Harper on the other, the bed between us.

"I appreciate the offer, Orion, but you don't understand addiction," Harper said. "If you clean up my mother's mess, then she won't have to. As much as it sucks, I need this to wake her up."

"But what if it doesn't?"

"Then it's still my problem, not yours." Harper's voice hardened. "You paid for my car and that was plenty. That was already too much. There is no chance I'm letting you pay for this too."

Images from last night flashed in my mind. Harper sobbing and sodden and bleeding…

"I don't like seeing you hurt," I said. "Not like how you were last night. Never again."

"Neither do I," Harper said. "But that's not how life works." She cocked her head. "Are you trying to keep me from being upset for my sake, or because it bothers you to see me upset?"

"Both." I frowned. "I mean…what's the difference?"

"The difference is you being there for me no matter what, and you being there for me in order to keep yourself comfortable."

"That's…ridiculous." I drew on my shirt with a frustrated yank. "I don't understand what the big deal is. This is a huge stress for you. Why not let me make it go away?"

She stared at me. "I just told you why not. Because my mother has to deal with the consequences of her actions. Otherwise, she'll just take and take and fall deeper and deeper into her addiction. Not to mention the small matter of us. How am I supposed to be in a relationship with you with thousands of dollars of debt hanging over my head?"

"Because you won't be *in debt* to me, for fuck's sake," I said. "You won't owe me anything. I would never expect you to pay me back. Jesus, Harper."

"But I'd feel it, Orion," she cried. "An imbalance between us. All the time, every day. I already feel it. I'm already acutely conscious of how *not enough* I am every minute I walk down the halls of that fucking Academy. And you want to add to that?"

"I wouldn't hold that over you and I never have," I retorted. "It's just dollars and cents anyway. Do you know how much money my family has? A roof is nothing to me—"

"It's everything to me!" Harper shouted, then her hands flew to her throat, still raw. She glanced at the door, listening for Dash, then inhaled deep, eyes closed. When she opened them again, she spoke in a low, hard tone. "Thank you for the offer. And thank you for everything you did last night. But the answer is no."

I sighed. "Look, I know I'm not the best at this sort of thing, but I'm trying—"

"No, *you're great* at this sort of thing. Last night, you were just *here*. That's all I needed. That is all I still need. Not you throwing money at the problem."

The words chafed me. I'd heard them a hundred times, and one triggering memory specifically, when I'd overheard a teacher of mine speaking to another in the hallway at Morton. *Orion's parents don't pay attention to his disability. They just throw money at the problem and hope he doesn't embarrass them.*

I ground my teeth, the memory flashing through me like a lightning bolt.

"I'm not *throwing* anything. I'm trying to *fix* the problem. But apparently you'd rather live in a leaking house—and let Dash live in a leaking house—instead."

I regretted the words as soon as they left my mouth, but it was too late to snatch them back. What little color Harper had in her cheeks drained away, and she glared at me.

"Bold of you to assume we don't have the money to fix the roof ourselves," she said, voice quivering. "The poor Bender without a pot to piss in, right?"

"I'm sorry," I said. "I didn't mean… I just want to help, and it makes no sense that you won't let me."

"Yeah?" Harper snapped. "Well, it makes no sense to me that your parents have abandoned you to an ADHD diagnosis when it's so obvious that something else is going on."

I reeled as if she'd slapped me. No, as if she'd taken a wrecking ball to a carefully constructed castle and knocked down a wall. Or ten. A castle built to protect me. To keep me safe. That's locked me in. A prison…

They just throw money at the problem…

"What the hell are you talking about?" I seethed, a sudden deep anger awakening in me. "Just what the fuck is that supposed to mean?"

"You heard me," Harper said, holding her ground. "Something isn't right. And I think you know it. And I think—no, I *know*—you deserve more help than the pitiful bullshit nothing you've been getting."

"Because you're a doctor," I said. "Because you sit next to me in *one* class and so you've made a diagnosis."

"You can be pissed at me all you want, but I'm just saying what I know in my gut to be true."

"Oh, you have a gut feeling," I said, marveling at my ugly tone. The way I was snarling at her, as if this rage boiling up in me had been saving itself for this conversation. "Well, bloody good for you, love. I think I'll leave you and your gut feeling to it, then. Tell Dash I said goodbye."

"I will," she said, her eyes filling now, her lower lip trembling.

I tossed my jacket over my shoulder and stormed out, hating myself for the anguish on her face. Hating the churn of emotions within me, and for what? Because she'd made one observation? Why was this tempest boiling up, hateful and angry? I should stay and try to make it right, but I didn't trust myself. Better to leave and calm down. Better to get somewhere alone and wait until the storm subsided back below the deeps.

I drove back to Atlas Hall over mud-choked roads, my hands gripping the steering wheel.

It's so obvious that something else is going on...

No, the fuck it wasn't. Nothing was *obvious*. Harper was just being defensive because I'd been a dick and crossed a line. I'd said something I shouldn't have, so she'd said something she shouldn't have. Something completely wrong.

I screeched the car into the Atlas Hall parking garage, threw it into my spot, and trudged to my apartment.

Easton was sleeping but woke when I barged in, kicking off my shoes.

"Sorry," I muttered, stripping back out of my tux shirt and pants.

"Long night?" he mumbled.

"You could say that," I replied, tearing off my tux jacket. "I believe Harper and I set a new land-speed record for going from potentially perfect to absolute shit to bliss to absolute shit again in a single night."

"Congratulations," Easton said, sitting up and rubbing his eyes. "What happen—"

I hurled one of my dress shoes into the closet with a frustrated grunt.

"Orion?" Easton said into the silence that was broken only by my heavy breathing. "You good, man?"

"No," I said. "I'm not."

And I'm pretty sure it was the first honest thing I'd said since I woke up that morning.

The next day, I dragged my arse to chem, both dreading and wanting to see Harper. I was a jackass for what I'd said to her but had already dismissed what she'd said in retaliation. It was pure bollocks. We'd had a fight, so what? We could put it behind us and move on. Couples did that all the time.

In class, she arrived and took her seat stiffly beside me. Langford was late. As usual.

"Hello," I said.

"Hello," Harper replied coolly, organizing her materials.

"How's the little man?"

"Fine," she said. "He's resilient. He asked about you." Harper's voice tightened, and she swallowed. "He wants to know when he's going to see you again."

"When is he going to see me again?"

"I don't know," she said softly. "I—"

Langford strode in with a big grin on his face. He held up his briefcase. "I have some NoSci results, and I think I can go ahead and spoil a few of you." His gaze found Harper and me in front of him. "Congratulations, Harper and Orion! Your proposals were enough to impress the judges, myself included. You're both through to round two!"

The class offered a smattering of applause, though I knew that there were several other students in class who had applied for the Novus Prize and were not included in Langford's little announcement. My cheeks burned. My pothole project made it through? On merit? Highly bloody unlikely.

"Congratulations," Harper whispered with sincerity.

"I'm sorry," I whispered back. "I didn't mean…"

My words died at her incredulous stare.

"What the hell did I do wrong now?"

But the answer would have to wait until after class, when I chased her out into the hallway.

"Well?"

"Why are you apologizing for making it to the next round?" she asked as students passed around us in the crowded hall. "Jesus, Orion, can you stop feeling sorry for me for one second?"

"I don't..." I stammered. "My project is shit. Or I thought it was."

Harper crossed her arms. "So you're apologizing because you think you're going to win based on your name alone."

"I don't know. Maybe. I don't understand why you're pissed at me. Again. I want you to win—"

"I want to win too," she said. "But I want to win fair and square. If you work harder or your idea is amazing or it's just plain *better*, then you deserve the prize. Same goes for anyone else. And if that's the case, then I'll be bummed—devastated, even—but I'll take my loss like a woman. But if I lose because your name is on a wall around here, or if I win because you sabotage your project, or you quit, then that's bullshit. Because what most rich people fail to understand is that us *little people* don't want handouts or charity or favors. We've only ever wanted one thing and one thing only."

"Which is?"

"A fair shot."

I stood there like a dope, not knowing what to say. Because my name *was* on one wing of the Athletic Hall, and I *was* trying to sabotage my project, and I *should* be disqualified for accepting outside help in the first place.

I'm a trifecta of dishonor.

The bell rang.

Harper's shoulders sagged. "I have to go," she said, and started to turn away.

"Well, wait." I reached for her arm but pulled back. "What about...us?"

"I don't know," she said softly, hugging her bag to her chest, her eyes filling. "Maybe we're just too different to make this work."

"Are we?"

"Aren't we?" she countered.

"I think that's up to us to decide. Besides," I said, offering a small smile. "You never got your date. You deserve a proper date."

Harper shifted her weight, glancing around. A tear spilled over, and she quickly wiped it away with her shoulder. "Orion..."

"What can I do, Harper? Just tell me and I'll do it."

"I don't want you to *do* anything, except be—"

Second bell rang, and she flinched.

"Now I'm late. To history. And you are too." She shouldered her bag. "I need to get through this week until my mother comes back. Then maybe we can talk, okay?"

And then she hurried down the hall.

I followed after, lead weights dragging my feet, feeling as if I were going to my execution instead of class.

I can't do this anymore.

My new mantra in a school that did accept failure, but expected nothing but perfection.

Chapter 21

ORION

"Ms. Bennett, Mr. Mercer, so glad you could join us," Professor Callister intoned from the whiteboard as Harper took her seat in the front and I took my spot next to Tessa in the back. The pretty actress gave me a friendly smile, but I had nothing in the tank to give back. If Callister played his read-aloud game, I was going to lose my bloody mind.

"I was informing the class that today is the last day for review before your Mesopotamia essays are due on Friday," he said. "You'll all do well to take extensive notes on today's lecture to hone your facts. Fair warning: I'll be running your papers through an AI-detection system. I'll know if you've gone outside the classroom for assistance."

The students pulled out their iPads for notetaking.

I went to do the same and found that I'd left all of my electronic helpers back at the dorms. Because of course I did.

Shit, fuck, bollocks.

I raised my hand. "Professor Callister, I left my iPad back at Atlas Hall. Might I run and grab it? I'll only be gone a minute."

"No, you may not," he said. "You can take notes like we did back in the ancient times: with a pen and paper."

He turned back to his lecture, and I slunk deeper into my seat. Harper glanced over her shoulder, concern in her eyes. I quickly averted mine. Why should she be concerned? There was nothing *obviously* wrong with me, except my handwriting was absolute shit.

"Callister's an ass," Tessa whispered, and passed me a few sheets of notebook paper and a pen.

"Thanks, love," I muttered. I needed to take notes. My term paper, as it currently stood, was absolute shit too, and I was too wrung out to try to memorize Callister's lecture. But writing by hand—never mind my penmanship—wasn't my brain's favorite thing to do.

Because it's hard to focus, that's all. It takes a lot of concentration. I'm a auditory spatial learner, like Wolfe said.

I hunched over, making a protective barrier with my left arm, and put the pen to paper. I tried to follow along to the lecture, my pen scratching away the best I could, but the words came out looking like jagged peaks in a needle-sharp mountain range. Getting them down at all was a supreme effort in forcing communication between brain and hand. Within minutes, I was too far behind and gave up.

Out of desperation, I sketched instead. I drew the images that Callister's words created in my mind: a city-state called Sumer nestled between two rivers that had pioneered most of humanity's biggest breakthroughs, including the wheel, the plow, irrigation, and—irony of ironies—the written word.

When the bell finally rang, I was bloody beat. Exhausted in a way I never felt after a regatta race. I had a strange yearning to talk to Ezra Wolfe but not in his class.

Which I had next.

With Harper.

I had to get out. Get away from fucking classrooms. I hastily gathered my stuff and slipped out the door, to the gym.

There, I changed into workout clothes in the locker room and found a bunch of my crewmates working out on the ergs and lifting weights. In the center of the huge gym, the men's gymnastics team was practicing on the rings, the floor, and Gideon Foster was doing his thing on the horizontal bar, defying gravity with amazing spins and flips.

I joined my mates at the weights just in time to find Xander confronting Tucker about how he'd kicked Emery out of his truck the night of the storm.

"You left her," Xander was saying, getting right up in

Tucker's face but remaining cool as hell. "You fucking left her in the pouring rain."

Tucker had the decency to look embarrassed for half a second, then glanced to Rhett Calloway for back up. I moved to do the same for Xander.

"Back off, Ford, if you know what's good for you."

Tucker started to turn away, but it was a ruse. He came back with a swing and Xander was ready. He ducked Tucker's fist and slammed his left elbow into the bigger guy's nose.

Holy shit, I thought, and did my best not to snicker.

Tucker staggered back, blood leaking from between his fingers, his eyes wide. "I think you broke my fucking nose."

Xander crossed his arms. "I didn't want a physical confrontation, but there needs to be a reckoning."

"A *what*?" Tucker spat a wad of blood on the floor. "I was drunk that night. I don't remember shit."

"I'll jog your memory," Xander said, still cold as ice in his boxy black glasses. "There was a torrential downpour, and you left her stranded on a deserted road."

Tucker scoffed. "So what? You're here to defend her honor?"

"Yes."

"He's challenging you to a duel," Rhett sneered. "Did you see *Hamilton* one too many times?"

"Knock it off, Rhett," I said, my hands clenching into fists, remembering it was Rhett who had told Brent to fuck with Harper's car. I don't know why it had taken me so long to see it, but Calloway was bad news. I hesitated to call anyone *evil*, but…

If the pitchfork fits…

Tucker glowered at Xander. "Pretty fucking bold maneuver, Ford. You know I could kick your ass right now."

"Possibly, given our height and weight differentials, and your amplified propensity for violence," Xander replied. "Regardless, I can't, in good conscience, remain teammates with someone of such low character."

"Low character." Rhett chuckled. "Who does this guy think he is?"

"Shut it, Calloway," I said, and Rhett swiveled his black-eyed gaze to me. I'm sure it was just my imagination, but the gym suddenly seemed ten degrees colder.

"It's cool, Rhett," Tucker said, holding his gym towel to his nose. "Can we have a minute?"

I leaned in to Xander. "I've got your back," I said, loud enough for everyone to hear, and stepped aside, arms crossed.

Xander and Tucker moved a few steps away to have it out. I kept one eye on them, the other on Rhett. He cocked his head at me, eyes narrowed, watching me with a malicious kind of curiosity.

"Got something to say, Calloway?"

"I was about to ask the same of you, Mercer," Rhett said, his tone overly friendly. Sinisterly casual. "You've been different this year. I mean, every year, you've been the Patron Saint of the Benders, but I always assumed it was part of your act."

"My act?" I scoffed, but my hands on my arms tightened. "What the hell are you on about?"

"Your congeniality act. Your Mr. Everybody's Friend act," Rhett said, taking a step closer to me. "But you want to know what I think?"

"Can't wait."

"I think you're a *bloody* impostor with a secret," he said in a mock British accent. "I think you've got the hots for that pretty little Bender with the shitty car. But that's not all. Oh, no. I think there's something else you haven't been sharing with the class."

"Oh yeah? And what might that be?" I asked, striving to keep my tone light. *Congenial.*

Rhett raised his narrow shoulders. "I have a secret of my own. I'm a hoarder. I hoard observations and tuck them away until I feel they might be useful. And I've made some observations about you over the last three years and three months."

A muscle ticked in my jaw, but I said nothing.

Rhett smiled his mirthless smile. The one that didn't touch his dark eyes in the slightest.

"I think, in a family of super smart people—geniuses even, like your brother—you're the stupid one. The intellectual runt of the litter. And when I say stupid, I mean stupid as in, *can barely read.* And you've been trying your damnedest to cover it up by being the guy who makes everyone laugh so that no one finds out you're actually kind of a moron."

I couldn't move. Could hardly breathe. My hands ached, clenched tight into fists. A red haze descended, and all I could see were Rhett's black eyes in his narrow, pale face. A weasel face. All I could hear was my own blood thrashing in my ears. All I could think about was putting my fist through that weasel face until the constant, shameful feeling of not being good enough—of being broken and defective, an embarrassment to my family—went away. I'd beat that knowing smile off Rhett's mouth until it didn't work, and he couldn't tell anyone. Until my fingers broke, and I couldn't play piano. And then I'd have nothing…

Then Rhett broke the spell with a chuck on my shoulder and a laugh. "But hey, it's all good. The crew has never been better. We'll sweep the regattas, and it doesn't take a high IQ to row two seat, am I right?"

My arms dropped to my sides, and I pulled my right hand back, fist ready to fly straight into his jaw, when a bone-chilling howl echoed through the gym. For a split second, I thought it had come from me. Then everyone in the weight room was running past me. Moving like a zombie, I followed Tucker and Xander and that fucker Rhett to the gymnasts.

A crowd had gathered around the mat beneath the horizontal bar where someone was moaning and making strange, hiccuping noises of pure agony. Declan

McConnell, our rings specialist, ran for a trashcan and heaved.

"Gideon," Tucker murmured. He shoved his way through the crowd then stopped, his face going pale. "Jesus fucking Christ, someone call an ambulance!"

My red-hazed vision cleared, and I sucked in a breath.

Gideon Foster was on the mat, sweat-soaked and pale as a ghost. He shivered and trembled, little cries slipping from between his clenched teeth. He sat ramrod straight, staring in horror at his own right leg that was bent in a way no human knee was meant to bend. It stuck out from his body in a hideous, ninety-degree angle, like a broken straw.

My rage morphed into shocked anguish, tinged with no small amount of nausea. Whispers flew all around me that he'd slipped during the dismount, or that there'd been water on the mat. Or he'd just plain landed wrong.

Landed wrong. Yeah, you could say that.

Coaches, trainers, and school security rushed in, the adults ushering us all out of the gym and into the parking lot. Already, the sirens of an ambulance could be heard in the distance, faint but growing louder.

Tucker looked horrified. Rhett stood with him, patting him absently on the shoulder. Not a shred of empathy, only curiosity. I suspected he was itching to go back inside and take a closer look at Gideon's fucked-up leg.

I moved to stand beside Xander. "Poor bastard," I whispered with disbelief. "He was set to go to World's, then the Olympics. Guess that's done."

"That's Castle Hill Academy for you," said Mike Bollanger, defenseman on the water polo team. "It chews you up and spits you out."

I nodded. "First it's Jack Wallace at the bonfire, today it's Gideon. Now we wait."

"For?" Xander asked.

"Strike three," I said absently, watching as Rhett and Tucker moved off. Rhett met my eye and gave me a friendly smile and wave.

He doesn't know anything. Not a damn thing. He's a cold-blooded sociopath. Forget it.

But I couldn't forget it. I'd been angry enough that strike three might've been me beating that fucker to a bloody pulp. And that wasn't me. I wasn't a violent guy, but this year was all turned around and messed up.

And poor Gideon, Jesus...

I stood in the parking lot like a twat, not knowing what to do. The idea of going back to Atlas Hall and trying to make sense of my history notes for that blasted paper only made what Rhett—and Harper—had said echo louder in my head. Instead, I walked straight to Ezra Wolfe's office in the Arts Wing and prayed he'd be there. And sober.

I got lucky on both counts.

"Orion." He peered at me, confused. "We don't have a lesson today. And you look dressed for jock-like activities. I heard someone was hurt at the gym. Glad it wasn't you. More specifically, I'm glad it wasn't your fingers."

"Can we play?" I asked. "I need to play."

He frowned, concerned, but nodded immediately. "Let's go."

"Nope," Wolfe said when I fucked up the cadenza from the Brandenburg No. 5 for the fifth time. "My ears have suffered enough for now, thank you, and you're still holding yourself back." He pulled up a chair next to the bench and sat. "You've had a day. Tell me. How bad was the gym?"

"Pretty bad," I said, thinking of poor Gideon in agony, while Rhett fucking Calloway looked on from a safe distance. "Why do the best people suffer while the arseholes among us sit and watch…?" I shook my head. "Sorry. That's an ungenerous thought."

Wolfe waved a hand. "Pfft. One I've had at least a dozen times per day. Is that all that's bothering you?"

"No." I sat with my hands in my lap, wondering how much to say. Wondering why I felt the urge to say *anything* to this eccentric piano teacher in the first place.

Maybe because it's been forever since someone has asked how you're feeling. Except Harper…

"I fucked it up with my girl."

"Already?" Wolfe's large eyes widened. "That has to be a record."

I shot him a look, though I'd basically said the same thing to Easton.

"Sorry," Wolfe said. "I'm not a pro at this."

"Neither am I," I admitted.

"Brilliant! We'll both bumble our way toward making you feel better, and you'll be so grateful and indebted to me that you'll have no choice but to audition for Juilliard come spring."

"For the last time, I'm not—"

"I know, I know. You're going to waste your God-given, once-in-a-generation talent to go to work for your family's company making toilet bowl cleaner."

After I go to Cambridge. After four more years of school. I can't bloody do it...

"Hey," Wolfe said, his hand gentle on my shoulder. "Now I'm being an arsehole. Talk to me."

"No, it's fine," I said, waving off my self-pitying thoughts. "It's just that she had a very large problem that I tried to fix with my very large bank account, and she didn't like that, and I don't know why."

Wolfe arched a brow. "You don't know why," he deadpanned.

"Is there some big crime in wanting to take care of the girl you...care about?"

"There is if you trample all over her pride and make her feel like a sex worker in the process."

"That is *not* what happened," I said. "The sex worker part, I mean. But maybe the pride part, yes. She has a lot of that. An excessive amount, really. Harp—this girl's a fighter. It's why I..."

"*Care* about her?" Wolfe said pointedly.

I scrubbed my hands over my tired eyes. "But I don't know what else to do. She was wrecked and I couldn't stand it." I looked up at him. "If I see something I can fix, I want to fix it."

Wolfe heaved a sigh. "Relationships with women aren't my forte, but from what I know of the fairer sex, they often don't want you to *fix* anything. It's enough that you're merely *there*. Present. That they feel seen and heard. Isn't that what anyone wants? To feel seen? Understood? And that doesn't take any *doing*. It only takes *being*."

I nodded, remembering Harper had said as much, but what did I have to offer besides my name, a few jokes, and a broken brain that would eventually betray me?

What if Rhett was right?

Wolfe's X-ray vision eyes seemed to see right into my soul.

"Do you fear you aren't enough for her as you are?" he asked gently. More gently than I'd ever heard him speak.

"I've always feared I'm not enough as I am," I said, shocked to say it out loud. Shocked that I let the words out from down in the depths.

"Why is that, Orion?"

"Because…" I shook my head. And that's when I felt it. Something else trying to follow those words out of me. A swell of emotion. Pain. Grief. Years' worth.

That's just because of what Rhett said. I'm not going to let him get to me. Fuck him. Fuck. Him.

"We should get on with the lesson." My voice sounded

rough. Thick. It was hard to swallow. I turned back to the Bach with shaking hands, but Wolfe took the sheet music away.

"Warm-up is over. You're supposed to compose something for the spring concert," he said in a low voice. "Have you put anything down?"

"Not yet."

"Why not?"

"Because I can't," I said, my voice cracking and rising.

"Can't...?"

"I can't fucking write."

"What do you mean?"

"Just what I said," I cried, practically shouting now. "I can't write. The words don't make it from my brain to my hand. They have holes in them."

"Words have holes?"

"That's why I can't do musical notation or tell you it's a fucking ostinato. My brain is broken or...I'm a fucking moron."

Wolfe watched me steadily, without a shred of pity, which was a good thing or else I was going to lose it. "You're not a moron, Orion. In fact, you're quite the opposite. You're a genius—"

"Bollocks," I said, standing up so hard and fast, I knocked over the bench. "I have to go. I have to..."

I started to for the exit, but Wolfe blocked my way, his gaze intent on me.

"Orion, don't," he said. "Don't run away from this

emotion. Don't shove it down or ignore it or pretend like it doesn't matter because it does. This is what's holding you back. Let it out. *Let it go.*"

I shook my head. It was too much. Harper, and Dash, and Gideon, and the poison pills that make me sick and Rhett's poisonous words…

"I'm just having a bad day," I said. "That's all it is. Forget I said anything. I can write just fine. I don't know why the hell I said that."

"Orion…"

"I'll see you tomorrow, Professor Wolfe."

Then I pushed out into the Academy's gleaming halls and headed to Atlas Hall on campus, because there was nowhere else for me to go.

Chapter 22

HARPER

"Ms. Bennett, Mr. Mercer, so glad you could join us," Callister had intoned.

I'd hated being late to history, because anything less that perfection meant I was falling behind, and I was already behind. I'd taken my seat at the front while Orion sat next to Tessa Carlyle. She was beautiful and sweet, and if I lost him to her, I'd probably deserve it.

You bludgeoned him about his ADHD, and that's fucked up.

It didn't matter that he was trying too hard to fix things with his money, at least he was trying to help. Even if he was going about it the wrong way, his heart was in the right place. He was the one good thing I'd had in my life, and I'd probably ruined it by blurting out what I should have said gently. Or not at all.

Yet Orion still wanted something with me. He still wanted to take me out on a date. He still wanted *an us*.

My eyes had stung, and I'd blinked hard to keep my notes from blurring. Meanwhile, behind me, Orion was struggling. Because even if I was wrong to whack him with my suspicions, I knew I was right to have them.

After class, Orion hurried out without a word to anyone, looking completely burnt out, and was a no-show to piano. I felt his absence like a hole in my heart and dragged my feet to the student parking lot when the day was finally over. I spotted Dean heading to his old Camry.

"Hey, Dean."

He had his head down, nose buried in his phone, which wasn't like him.

"Dean. *Dean.*"

He looked up as I caught up to him. He looked nervous. Or guilty. "Oh, hey, Harper. Haven't seen you at the Math and Physics Club lately. You good?"

"Yeah, just…busy. Are you okay?"

"Never better." He flashed a strange, twitchy version of his usual smile and spoke a mile a minute. "But I have to run. Can't talk now. I'm late. Maybe later?"

"Oh…sure?" Before I could say another word, he climbed into his car and drove off. "Good talk."

But my flippant words were only a mask for the worry

for my friend that I now added to the teetering stack of stress that threatened to bury me.

I picked up Dash from school and had a guy come out to give me an estimate about the roof. Nearly ten grand to replace the whole thing, or half that to merely plug the leaks.

"I'd replace the whole thing," the guy said. "If we get another rager like we had last week, you're just going to get new seepage. More seepage means greater the chance of black mold too." He gave me a look. "Is your mom or dad home? Maybe I could talk to them."

"No," I said. "Thank you. We'll be in touch."

I made Dash dinner, and later that night, tucked him into bed.

"Harper, when is Mama coming home?"

"Sunday, bud."

"Why is she gone for so long?"

Because she's an inconsiderate, immature asshole who thinks of no one but herself.

"She just is," I said. "I wish I had a better answer."

Dash nodded, looking so small in his bed. He brightened slightly. "When is Orion coming back? Can you ask him to come over tomorrow?"

Tears threatened, but I pushed them back. "I don't think so. Maybe next week. We'll have to see."

His face fell. "Why? Did you get mad at him too?"

I stiffened. "I…it's complicated."

"Doesn't he like me anymore?"

"Oh, buddy." It took everything I had to keep it together. "It's not your fault. Nothing is your fault. Orion and I are having a disagreement."

"Will you try to fix it?"

"I'll try, but it's not that simple."

Christ, how to explain to a seven-year-old that my relationship with Orion wasn't about him when he was already invested? In love with Orion. I added that guilt to the weight on my back until I thought I was going to crumple.

The only fuel I had left was hatred for my mother. That I had in endless supply.

"Everyone leaves." Dash rolled over on his side, away from me. "*Everyone.*"

"Not everyone," I said. "I'm still here."

But Dash didn't say anything, so maybe that wasn't enough.

The following day, Thursday, Orion was absent from school when I knew he couldn't afford to be absent from school, and a terrible fear began to squeeze my heart. After history class, I shot him a text.

Are you okay? Where are you?

No answer.

My thoughts went back to the night he took those

awful pills out of desperation. What if he'd tried again? Or something worse? The stress I carried on my back was a mountain, but it paled in comparison to my worry for him. If something happened to Orion…

"Harper?"

I turned in the hallway. Tessa Carlyle was petite and pretty in a green dress that highlighted her auburn hair. By contrast, I felt dark and bleak in my black skirt, black tights, and black blouse.

"Can we talk for a second?"

"Sure."

Tessa pulled me aside, out of the flow of traffic. "So this might be out of line, but I think you're the person I should give this to. Not Callister, that's for damn sure."

She pulled a piece of notebook paper from her bag and handed it to me. The top half was a jagged mountain range of words, each letter looking like it was trying to run away from the last. Shaky and uneven. Below that, beautifully accurate sketches of a wheel, a row of crops, and a tablet with strange writing carved into it. As if the two halves of the page were two halves of the same brilliant mind, revealing where it struggled and where it did not.

My heart seized because I knew exactly what this was, and who it belonged to. Then I glanced up at Tessa in a panic.

"It's okay," she said. "I won't say anything."

"How did you know that he and I…?"

"You can't stop staring at each other, for one thing," she said with a giggle. "It's really cute."

"God, is it that obvious?" I asked, my cheeks burning.

"No, but I pay attention. I figure it's my job, if I want to be a good actress. Not going to lie, I was pretty jealous at first, but I got over it. But seems like things aren't so great?" She waved her hands. "None of my business. The point is, Orion dropped this paper in his rush to get out of class yesterday. I was going to return it to him today, but he's not here and…well, it's not the first time I noticed something off. Not in a bad way," she added quickly. "But I think he's struggling and needs help and Callister doesn't care. Or maybe he doesn't know." Tessa bit her lip. "Maybe no one knows?"

I nodded, glancing down at the paper, which blurred in my vision. Because Orion had been working so hard, for so long—alone—and it broke my damn heart.

"No, I don't think so," I whispered.

"So anyway, I don't mean to pry into his business," Tessa said. "I won't say another word or butt in. I just wanted someone close to him to…I don't know. Help? He seems so tired."

I cleared my throat and folded the paper in quarters and tucked it into my bag. "Thanks, Tessa. I appreciate it."

"No problem." She smiled prettily. "And hey, if things get sorted maybe you two will come to my show? We're doing *Les Misérables* this spring. Shameless plug, I know…"

I smiled. "I'll be there."

"Great. And Harper, if you ever want to talk or hang out…" Tessa suddenly looked shy. "This place isn't exactly overflowing with friendly girls. My best friends are the gay boys in drama class. Not that I'm complaining; they're the literal best. But I wouldn't mind having a girlfriend for *girl* talk once in a while."

I managed a smile. "I'd like that."

"Me too." Tessa's own smile was brilliant, and I had a premonition that I was going to see her on the big screen someday.

We parted ways, and I rushed down the hall, not sure where to go, or what to do, except I had to find Orion and…

Do what? Make things worse? And what about Dash? What am I going to do with him?

Anger at my mother for abandoning us flared at me all over again as I walked fast, not paying attention to where I was going, and then I crashed headlong into someone.

"Bloody hell…"

The British accent sent my hopes soaring until I looked up into bleary blue eyes instead of brown ones.

"Professor Wolfe?" I glanced around the crowded hallway, which was nowhere near the Arts Wing of this huge school. "Are you okay?"

"Hm? What?" Today, he wore black baggy pants, a black blouse-like shirt, and a long, light jacket that flowed behind him like a cape, and all of it was tinged with the perfume of old liquor. "Fuck me, I'm all turned around."

Maybe if you weren't hungover all to hell...

"Right," I said darkly. "Arts Wing is that way." I pointed and intended to carry on, but Wolfe looked truly lost. "Do you need some help?"

"Would you mind?" he said. "Being found wandering the corridors in my present condition might be detrimental to my financial interests."

I turned the professor around, and we walked through the crowded hallways like a pair of crows toward his office.

"Why are you in this *present condition* if you know you have classes to teach?" I asked, not too kindly. "Our piano class next period, for instance."

Wolfe glanced down at me. "Have I done something to arouse your anger, Ms. Bennett?"

I didn't reply. We arrived at his office. I saw him safely inside, gestured as if to say, *Voila,* and turned to go.

"You didn't answer my question," he said, slumping onto the couch and stretching out. "Something on your mind? Are you going to tattle on me to President Sterling?"

"No, but..." I crossed my arms. "If you have people counting on you—*kids* counting on you to be there for them, why do you do it?" I shook my head. "Never mind."

"You're her, aren't you?"

"Who?"

"Orion's girlfriend."

I stiffened. "He told you?"

"He let it slip. I pretended not to notice." Wolfe's expression deepened with concern. "It was already a difficult conversation."

"What do you mean?"

"He told me he can't write," Wolfe said in a low voice. "And that words have holes in them. Do you know what he's talking about?"

"I think so," I said. "But…not exactly."

I shut the door and sank down in the chair opposite his couch. Inside my bag, the notebook paper Tessa had given me felt like it weighed a hundred pounds. Orion desperately needed a trusted adult on his side, but it still felt like a betrayal. I'd already been so clumsy and heavy-handed.

"It's delicate, I know," Wolfe said, reading my mind. "But I feel as if Orion has been abandoned or lost in a system that is so busy gazing upon its own accomplishments, it's become blind to anyone who doesn't reek of perfection."

I nodded. Wordlessly, I pulled out the notebook paper and handed it to Wolfe.

He scanned it. The hallway outside was quiet. Second bell had come and gone. Piano class obviously wasn't happening, and I sort of loved Ezra Wolfe in that moment. Because finally, *finally*, Orion had an adult on his side.

Wolfe studied the paper and then folded it and handed it back. "So much of what I'd suspected now makes sense. My old speech therapist taught me more than she realized."

He leaned forward. "Have you ever heard the term 'twice exceptional'?"

I remained in Wolfe's office until last bell, and then shouldered my bag.

"Thank you, Professor."

He waved a hand. "I'm not a good person, but every now and then I get something right. The proverbial broken clock." His brows furrowed with concern. "Do you have an idea where he is?"

"No," I said, rising and heading for the door. "I'll try Atlas Hall first. Once I figure out what to do with my little brother."

"Please let him know I will ensure that this godforsaken institution provides him the resources he needs." Wolfe's expression darkened. "He's been fighting this battle alone, Harper, but it didn't have to be this hard. He won't like to hear that it never had to be this hard." To my shock, Wolfe's eyes grew shiny. "They all bloody failed him."

"Yeah," I said, my voice thick. "They did."

My hand was on the knob when Wolfe said, "Oh, and Harper? The answer to your question is pain."

"Sorry?"

"Why do I drink if I have young people counting on me? That was your question earlier, wasn't it?"

"Oh. Yes." Because I wanted to know. Because all I

had was anger. My own pain. And my mother had never given me any answers, only excuses.

"Every addict is filling a hole of deprivation," Wolfe said. "A need. From the outside, people will label that deprivation attention or fame or money, but those things are just fillers. They're no different from drugs, or sex, or booze. Because the need, when you dig all the way down, is love."

I swallowed hard. "That's what's missing?"

"Indeed. That essential ingredient. Love that was denied or withheld. That hole is always there, so we cover it up with our substance of choice in order to pretend it's not there. But that doesn't work. It never works. Because as soon as the buzz wears off, the hole reveals itself all over again. 'Hitting rock bottom' happens when you fall in." He smirked grimly. "How's that for some two-bit wisdom? I should've been a philosophy professor."

I stood very still. I realized I knew nothing of my mother's childhood. She never told me of her past. I never knew my grandparents; they died when I was little. All I ever saw was a string of shitty boyfriends. Men who used her and left her, one after the other, and the alcohol filling in all those holes where good people should have been.

"Harper," Wolfe said, breaking me from my thoughts. "You have every right to be angry at whoever you're angry at. I'm not going to tell you otherwise. Trauma isn't an excuse to treat anyone like shit. I only said what I said to offer a measure of understanding that it's not your fault. I don't have much to offer except that. Whatever is going on at home, it's not your fault."

I nodded, turned to go, then stopped, clearing the emotion out of my voice.

"Professor Wolfe? You're not a bad person."

"No?" He cocked his head. "What am I? Besides someone with a raging headache and an enduring sense of regret?"

"You're doing your best. You're helping. A lot."

Wolfe smiled wanly. "Perhaps I can do better."

I picked up Dash from school, and we came home to find Mom curled in a ball on the couch. I stopped, my heart stopping too, and then pounding a heavy, clanging beat.

Oh God, now what.

"Mom?"

She rolled over. "Oh, hi, babies."

"Mama!" Dash ran over and threw his little arms around her neck as she sat up. Over his shoulder, she looked tired, her eyes puffy, and it looked as if she'd cried off all her makeup. Her rolling suitcase was by the couch.

"When did you get back?"

"This afternoon," she croaked.

"What's wrong, Mama?" Dash asked in a small voice.

"Nothing, baby," she said. "I…have a cold."

"There were leaks!" Dash held up three fingers. "This

many. Harper was really mad. And sad. Then Orion came over. He's the best. I wish he'd come back. You'd love him."

Mom put her hands to her temples. "Slow down, baby. Who's Orion? What leaks?"

I fixed her with an icy stare. "You miss a lot when you skip town for three days." I turned to my little brother. "Can you go play upstairs for a little bit?"

"Why?"

"Go. Please."

He heard my all-business tone and went upstairs.

"Don't start with me, Harper," Mom began.

My eyes flared, and it took all I had to remain calm. Ezra Wolfe's words about pain and love came back to me. I tried to keep them in the forefront of my mind, but I was still too angry.

And I have to find Orion…

"Why are you home early?" I demanded. "I thought you were gone until Sunday."

"Alan decided that he was going to give it another go with his wife. He called the trip short and fired me." Mom began to cry. "Happy? You got what you wanted. He's out of the picture and I got dumped. Again."

"You think this is what I wanted?" I said, my voice rising. "You think I want any of this? You left us in the middle of a hurricane. Abandoned us for some asshole who—big surprise—abandoned you."

"I know, I know, you had some fancy party to go to. With this Orion person?"

"Forget the damn party, Mom. It's the drinking. It's the fucking drinking."

"I'm sorry," she cried, covering her face with her hands. "I try not to, but it's just so…hard."

"I get that, but you can't *not* try. You have to keep trying, every day, all day, for us. For me and Dash. And for you." My voice quavered, but I fought for calm. "Look at me, Mom. Look at me."

She pulled her hands from her face with a petulant jerk. "What, Harper. What? Tell me what to do, and I'll do it."

"Okay. You're going to get another job. You're going to go back to AA meetings, and you're going to get a sponsor. Someone to be accountable to, because I can't do it anymore. I've been doing it my entire life, and it's not fair."

"Your entire life…" Mom scoffed, then read my expression. "Okay, okay. And? What's this about leaks?"

"The roof needs to be replaced. It'll cost $9,500. We're going to pay for it from savings."

The color drained from Mom's face. "We can't. That's *all* of our savings. I don't have a job. What if I can't find one? What about next month's mortgage?"

"Then you'd better figure it out. If we don't fix it, we could get black mold that will make us sick. Make Dash sick."

"You are not in charge here, young lady—"

"*Yes, I am!*" I screamed, like a slap to her face. I inhaled sharply, calming myself. "You leave me no choice. I'm eighteen. If you don't do everything I say, I'll leave and take Dash with me."

"You can't."

"I'll figure it out."

"Your school…"

"*Now* you care about my school? You didn't care when you drove off with Hensley three days ago. If I can win the NoSci, it'll take care of the debt. But I need you to get your shit together."

Mom stared at me as if seeing me for the first time. "I don't like how you're talking to me right now."

"You don't have to like it," I said. "But you have to do what I say. Because walking out on us was unacceptable." Tears filled my eyes, and this time there was nothing I could do to stop them. I stood up. "I know you're hurting, but so are we."

I went to the kitchen, opening cabinets. "Is there any alcohol in this house?"

"No."

"You swear?"

"I swear."

"Because I have something to do, and I need to know I can leave you with Dash—"

"Jesus, Harper."

I stared, incredulous. "You really believe you can be trusted right now? After the shit you pulled?"

She held my gaze defiantly a moment more and then

gave in. "There's no booze, I swear. And I'll keep it that way. What do you have to do? Where are you going?"

"I'll explain later," I said, and hurried for the door.

"Harper?"

I stopped, shoulders hunched. "What?"

"I'm sorry. I really am."

But the words sounded light and empty. I'd heard versions of them a hundred times, and they never amounted to anything.

"Okay," I said.

"Okay? That's it?"

I turned and faced her. "I love you, Mom, and so does Dash. But that's not enough, apparently, so *okay* is all I have right now."

And then I went out into the November cold, first walking to my car, and then running, to get to Orion.

Chapter 23

HARPER

I DROVE AS FAST AS I DARED WITHOUT RISKING AN ACCIDENT or speeding ticket to Atlas Hall. One perk of living in Rhode Island was its tiny size; I made it there in under ten minutes—about a quarter to five. I checked in at the front desk and knocked on Orion and Easton's door. No answer.

I knocked harder. Then pounded on the door. "Orion!"

"He's not here," said a guy peeking his head out a door from down the hall.

"Do you know where he is?"

"My roommate said he saw him heading back to campus."

"When?"

The guy ran a hand through his hair. "An hour ago?"

"Thanks."

I ran down the path from Atlas Hall, back to the Academy, sure it was going to be locked up. But of course, it was busy with students and their extracurriculars. I'd heard there'd been a terrible accident in the gym the day before, so I nearly skipped it, expecting it to be closed. But it was business as usual, with athletes of all persuasions on the apparatuses. I don't know why I expected anything different.

But no Orion.

I contemplated heading to the STEM Wing to see if he was working on his NoSci project, or maybe the library for his history paper due tomorrow. But I knew in my heart, if he was still on campus, there was only one place Orion would be.

In the Arts Wing, I approached the door to our Advanced Piano classroom slowly and listened. Nothing. My heart sank, but I cracked it open anyway.

Orion sat at the baby grand in a lone circle of light from a small lamp on the teacher's table beside him. No sheet music on the rack. Just him holding his head in one hand, the other hand resting idly on the keys.

My heart dropped again. He looked so utterly exhausted. Defeated. Touching the piano with nostalgia, as if it were some distant thing that was out of reach, instead of the instrument he'd mastered like the brilliant virtuoso he was.

I shut the door and stepped inside. Orion didn't move or speak. I came down the aisle slowly and moved in front of him. He wore jeans, a tight-fitting long-sleeved shirt, and expensive-looking tennis shoes. Every part of him looked elegant and put together.

Because he's still trying. Still trying to live up to some impossible standard…

"Orion?" I said again.

He looked up at me with tired eyes. "Bennett. Greetings and salutations."

"I was worried." I took a seat in Professor Wolfe's chair. "What are you doing here?"

"Not sure," he said. "Wolfe wants me to compose something for the spring concert, but that's rather laughable."

I could've played stupid and asked why, and that would've been my *in* to what I came to say to him. But the last thing he needed was me patronizing him or thinking I felt sorry for him.

I don't, because there's nothing to pity. Not one thing.

"Do you love to play?" I asked instead. A genuine question I wanted an answer to. "What does it mean to you?"

"I don't know," he said, his fingers trailing over the keys. "Sometimes I feel…"

I leaned forward. "Yes?"

"Sometimes I feel like I never gave myself a chance to find out. I've been so busy trying to *not* be an embarrassment to my family."

"You aren't," I said automatically.

He looked up at me sharply. "No? In case you haven't noticed, I'm not doing so hot in the academics department. Not like Odin or Octavian. I'm a wee bit of a failure, love."

"You're not a failure," I said and swallowed hard, my heart pounding. "I think you might have dyslexia."

His head snapped toward me. "I have…?" He stared for a moment and then barked a short, harsh laugh. "No," he said. Petulant. Almost childlike. "No, I don't."

"I talked it over with Professor Wolfe—"

"You *what*?"

"—and you have a lot of the signs. How you said words have holes in them, memorizing lectures, and your handwriting…?"

"I don't have dyslexia. That's ridiculous."

"Why is it ridiculous?" I asked softly.

"Because…it just is," Orion said. "Dyslexia means you *can't read*. Like when you look at a sentence and it looks like hieroglyphics or something. Or the letters are backward. That's not how it is for me."

I inhaled deeply and tried to make my tone as soft as possible. "That's not what dyslexia is. Or that's not all it is. It's a spectrum—"

"That's exactly what it is," he said, practically shouting, his voice echoing in the auditorium. "It's kids who can't read at all, and need special classes in special schools or—"

"Orion, that's a stereotype."

He stopped, staring at me, looking so damn lost.

"Some people with dyslexia can read," I continued. "They can read very well. Especially those with stealth dyslexia."

"*Stealth* dyslexia," he said, as if I were making words up. "Is that what you and Wolfe came up with? Behind my back?"

"He wants to help you. He's the first damn adult who does," I said, and took another breath. "He told me what he knew, and it made sense. So I'll pass it on to you, and you tell me if it makes sense, okay?"

Orion glared at me, eyes hard, but he said nothing, so I continued.

"Some people with dyslexia memorize words by shape instead of decoding them. Or they substitute similar-looking words or their brain fills in the gaps, and they grasp meaning by context. They compensate. And if they compensate well enough, people don't notice right away. Others with stealth dyslexia might not realize they have it at all because they've built a ton of workarounds in order to get by. For years, even. But all these workarounds cost so much energy that they can sometimes burn out." I huffed a breath. "Does any of that sound right to you?"

Orion stared at me a moment more, absorbing all this, then he shook his head. "No. I don't have *stealth* dyslexia. I have ADHD."

"Orion…"

"*No*," he snapped. "If I had dyslexia, I would know."

"Why?"

"Because I cannot have gone this fucking long not knowing!"

I flinched at his sudden rage but stood my ground, sitting calmly in the face of his storm. He was allowed to have it. If I'd been abandoned like he'd been, I'd feel shipwrecked too.

"This is ridiculous." Orion stood up abruptly, pacing the small piano platform like a trapped animal. Then he stopped and stared at me, betrayed. As if I'd ripped out a plank holding up the entire scaffolding of his life. "Why are you doing this to me?"

I flinched. "I only want to help you."

"It's not...*that*," he declared. "I'm just tired. That's all. And you want to help me?" he shouted suddenly. "What is your obsession with diagnosing me? For the last time, love, you are not a doctor."

"That's not what I—"

"Because my parents did that already. They took me to doctors when I was a kid. Tests, evaluations, all of it. The whole Mercer Family Performance Package," he said with bitter sarcasm. "The diagnosis was ADHD. I get distracted. I forget things. I lose focus. That's it."

I shook my head. "ADHD and dyslexia overlap all the time. Misdiagnoses happen—"

"Not this bloody time."

I stared, trying to understand, and seeing a fury in his eyes that was covering something raw. Something old and buried. Not something I created, only unearthed.

"My parents told me. The doctors too, that reading was hard *because of ADHD*," Orion seethed, voice low and shaking. "They said I just needed to try harder. Slow down and apply myself. Focus. And if it's hard, it's because I get lazy. Or I joke around. Or I don't live up to my potential."

My stomach twisted. "Orion..."

"So don't sit there and tell me that after all these years of being told it's one thing, you and Professor Wolfe, *a piano teacher*, for fuck's sake, have decided that it's something else."

He started to go, striding for the door.

I firmed my voice, heart pounding. "What if they were wrong?"

Orion stopped.

"Your parents, the doctors, all of them," I said, my voice quavering. "What if they were wrong?"

For a long moment, Orion did nothing but stand with his back to me. Finally, when I thought he'd continue out the door, he half turned his head over his shoulder, his voice heavy with defeat.

"If they were wrong, then Rhett was right. And I'm a fucking moron."

My eyes flared, those words punching me in the gut. "That is not true. You're not...anything like that. Or broken, or defective. And he's a goddamn piece of shit for saying that."

Orion shook his head. "I am. I'm stupid."

"No—"

"*Yes*," Orion said, turning around, his face a mask of conflicted emotions I couldn't read. "Because if everything you're saying is true, and I was smart, I would have figured it out." He laughed harshly, a horrible, bitter sound. "I'm eighteen, Harper. Eighteen. And I don't even know what dyslexia is. Sounds pretty fucking bloody stupid to me."

I stood up and slowly moved toward him.

"You're not stupid," I said softly. "You believed your parents. Because you were a kid. Because you trusted them. That's what kids do."

He shook his head, his eyes full of disbelief and something like grief. "I study. I memorize. I try so fucking hard. And all this time, all these years, I thought it was just me."

"I know," I said, my voice starting to crack. "You've been working ten times harder than everyone else. Building workarounds no one saw. Because you're brilliant. The memorization, your sketches and your piano... God, Orion, your *piano*. Having dyslexia and ADHD while being that talented… There's a name for that. It's called *twice exceptional.* That's what you are. That's how you were able to keep going and no one knew. Not even you."

"Wolfe told you that?" he said, and I could see him struggling to believe me.

I nodded. "The fact that you didn't know only means you've been doing this alone. *Surviving* alone. And you never should have been abandoned like that. Never."

Orion's head dropped, shoulders bent, on the verge of giving in to the truth.

"I…I think I knew. Deep down, I think I've always known something was wrong. And I didn't question it. I never question *anything*." He shook his head miserably. "Because that's not what we do. My family… We don't *talk*. We keep it all in and we *pretend*, and we just keep going, even when things are messed up, and *I* was messed up, but I didn't want to embarrass anyone…"

Tears filled my eyes, and I blinked them back. "You're not messed up. But you've been compensating your whole life. It's all you know to do. And when something is all you know how to do, then it becomes how you think things are *supposed to be*."

He looked up at me, his eyes full.

"I'm so tired, Harper. I'm so bloody tired of pretending I'm not drowning."

"I know," I whispered, and reached for him, holding his face in both hands. "You don't have to pretend anymore."

He exhaled a long, ragged breath. Finally. I pulled him to me, and he wrapped his arms around me and let go. I held him as best as I could, his large body shuddering, shoulders shaking. I sank my fingers into his hair, the little spirals I loved so much.

Him. I love him—

I tried to cut the thought off before it could dig deeper roots. But it was too big, took up too much of me. So big that I couldn't ignore it. In that moment, it revealed itself, and no amount of my self-preservation could deny it. His pain was my pain. My heart broke because his was breaking. My anger for those who abandoned him ran deep and hot, and yet so did my desire. I wanted to set all this aside and go somewhere and kiss him until we lost ourselves for a few stolen moments. Body and soul, I loved Orion.

You can't. He's moving back to England...

I pushed that thought away too and focused on him. These moments of revelation, because from now on it was going to be different for him. Better. No more struggling alone, unseen.

Orion pulled back, heaving unsteady breaths, and wiped his face with his sleeve. His eyes met mine, and they were as full and dark, mirrors of my own. His mouth found mine in a kiss. One touch, shallow and light. Then another. Deeper. And another. Until the spark lit, and the raw emotion of the night burst forth.

He took my mouth in a devouring kiss, a kiss full of heated need, pent-up pain, and want of me. I felt all of it, consuming and dizzying and powerful, and I let him have me. Let him take what he needed in that kiss, before giving it back. Before kissing him with the same ferocity, because I wanted him just as badly. And I'd never wanted anyone. Never loved anyone—

Stop, it's too much...

He took me down to the hard, thinly carpeted floor, but I hardly felt it. Only his large body on mine, his hands roaming under my skirt, and mine grasping at him, pulling him to me and into me, despite the clothing between us. His hips ground against mine, and I wrapped my legs around him as our mouths clashed in a desperate union of biting, sucking kisses.

"Fuck, Harper, not here," he gasped, pulling back. "You deserve better..."

And I'd wanted better than fumbling encounters in random places. But it turned out I wanted Orion more.

I hauled him back to me, kissed him again, my hands in his hair. "Do you have a condom?"

"I think...yes."

"Then, here." I kissed him again and let my hand slip between us, down to his jeans, and stroked the hard length of him. "I want you. I want this."

He groaned, and that was all he needed. He needed this. A release. And so did I.

Orion attacked my neck, his mouth alternately biting and sucking and licking the delicate skin until I was half out of my mind, every nerve ending tingling and lit up. He moved lower, over my breasts, finding my nipple through the material of my shirt and nipping. But there was no time; we could be caught at any moment, but that only added another layer of urgency to this intensity between us that could not be delayed another minute.

Orion moved off me long enough to find a condom in his wallet, while I stripped out of one leg of my tights and underwear. I helped tear open the button and then zipper on his jeans, and in moments he was ready. With one smooth movement, he used his knee to spread my thighs wide, sending a fresh wave of heated desire all through me, and lay over me.

"Are you sure?" he breathed between kisses.

I nodded rapidly. "This isn't my first time."

"But it's your first time with me." Orion held my face, straining to hold back. "I want it to be what you want."

"It is," I said. "Because it's you."

A heartbreakingly sweet smile flitted over his lips, and he kissed me softly before burying his face in my neck. "I love you, Harper," he breathed, and then we were joined.

I gasped at the perfect, heavy sensation of him, coupled with those words. The gravity of the night, the feel of him, all of it coming together in that moment overwhelmed me in the best way, like a reward I'd been waiting for. Tears stung my eyes but burned away quickly as he began to move. A slow build of heat that grew with every touch that was more perfect than the last.

Little moans were coming from my throat, and Orion kissed me there, then my chin, then my lips as he moved, his hips pistoning slower, then faster, building that heat into a sweet ache that was growing deeper and stronger.

I clutched at his back, over his shirt, then down to the waistband of his jeans that were pulled low enough, until I could find skin. I slipped my hand down, pressing him into me.

"Harper, does it…feel good?"

I nodded mutely, hardly able to speak, and gazed up

into his eyes in the dimness, held his face, then brought it down to mine to kiss. To breathe with him, to taste and revel in him as the pleasure grew into something bigger than I'd ever felt.

"Orion…" I managed and then clenched my teeth, clutched at his shirt, holding him to me, my legs wrapped around his hips. "Oh God…"

The waves rolled through me, leaving me weak and pleasantly heavy, just as his began to crest. Orion reached one hand to grab my hip, the other pressed to the floor. I held his forearm, the other hand snaking into his hair as his face took on an expression of pained ecstasy.

"Fuck, Harper…"

He shuddered, and I watched as the release found him, moved through him and into me. A grunting sound issued from his chest, and then a gasp, both the sexiest things I'd ever heard in my life. Then he collapsed—carefully—on top of me, perfectly heavy. Like a shield. I held him, my hands trailing lazily over his head, into his curls, and down his neck.

"I'm too heavy," he murmured into my neck.

"You're just the right heavy," I said, holding him closer, unwilling to let him go. "But I need to tell you something."

"Hold that thought."

He kissed my forehead, my nose, my chin, then carefully moved off me, disposed of the condom, and came right back, holding me close. And my heart broke in the best way to see so much of that horrible exhaustion and grief had lifted out of his eyes.

They're twinkling again.

"What were you going to say, Bennett?" he said. "Something terribly unromantic?"

"In about ten seconds, you're going to feel so bad for teasing me. Like, *so* bad."

He grinned. "Oh yeah?"

"Yeah." I stroked his cheek, traced his jaw. "What I was going to say is, I love you too."

Orion's smile tilted and became richer. More real, somehow. "I was hoping…so much."

He kissed me then, the most deeply beautiful kiss of my life, before shooting a glance at the door. "Come on. We've pressed our luck long enough, don't you think?"

"Yes," I said. "And you have a paper to write."

We pulled ourselves together and walked back to Atlas Hall. It was early yet, only six o'clock. I called home to check in with Mom, while Orion ordered a pizza.

"What are we doing?" he asked after we ate mushroom and pepperoni slices in his and Easton's dorm apartment, though his roommate was, as usual, nowhere to be seen.

"We're writing your Mesopotamia paper, due tomorrow," I said, and pulled him into his room, to his desk.

"We?"

"You. I'm just here for secretarial purposes." I planted a kiss on Orion's lips. "Can't let Callister have the satisfaction."

"Harper, I can't write that damn paper."

"You're not. I'm going to write it. Well, type it. You dictate."

He frowned, about to protest, but then nodded and tapped his temple. "Yeah, I think I have enough stored in here for something."

He opened his laptop to a blank document, and I smiled into the keyboard, overcome with pride for my brilliant boyfriend.

"Ready when you are."

For the next hour and a half, I typed while Orion paced behind me, dictating his term paper on the impact of Cuneiform, and how writing transformed Mesopotamian government as a tool for the elites, but not the ordinary people.

When it was finished, I did a quick sweep for typos and hit *print*. I handed him the paper. "Callister is going to love it."

Orion shook his head, scanning the paper, then tossed it onto his desk and hauled me to him. "You saved my arse. Twice in one night. How can I ever repay you?"

"Not sure," I said, and disentangled myself to sit on his bed. "But this feels infinitely softer than the floor of the piano room."

He grinned. "Can you imagine class on Monday?" he said as he went to close his bedroom door. "I feel like Wolfe is going to see right through us."

"Probably," I said, pulling Orion to me by the lapels

of his shirt. "But I think it's just the sort of thing he would appreciate."

Orion lay over me, taking me down to his bed. "I think it's just the sort of thing he would find exceedingly hilarious."

An hour later, I lay curled against Orion under the covers, satiated and heavy, humming from being touched in a thousand ways. Being naked with him, pressed against his big, warm body felt perfectly easy and good. I hadn't a shred of self-consciousness but loved how we fit together—my pale skin to his golden brown, my softer curves to his hard lines and muscles. He gazed at me as if I were the most beautiful girl he'd ever seen when he'd been with plenty, and all of them more polished than I ever would be.

He loves me anyway. This poor, stressed-out girl, barely hanging on.

But Orion made me feel like I wasn't alone in my fight, and I hoped I did the same for him. As if he'd read my mind, he planted a kiss on my temple, then shifted to look at me, his expression serious.

"Thank you. Thank you for braving a fucking shitstorm to help me see the truth. No one has ever done something like that for me."

I glanced up at him, my eyes suddenly full. "No one

has ever done what you did for me either. When I woke up in the middle of that awful night and found you on the floor in Dash's room… That was the best thing I'd ever seen in my entire life."

"Oh, love."

Orion kissed me softly, kissed the tears that slipped down my cheeks. "Tonight, you gave it back to me a thousand times over."

"Not just me," I said. "Wolfe helped, and he's going to make sure you have proper accommodations. And I'm so sorry for the way I brought it up at my house the other morning. That was horrible of me."

"It wasn't. I threw your stuff in your face, so you threw mine back at me."

"You were trying to help."

"I was being an arsehole. I just wanted to put everything broken back together and move on." Orion brushed his knuckles over my cheek. "I hated seeing you so hurt. Can't bloody stand it."

He pressed his forehead to mine, and we stayed that way for a long moment. Then he inhaled a breath.

"Well. This was a lot for a Thursday."

I laughed a little. "I know. And though I don't want to move ever again, I should get back home before it gets too late. My mother…she came back early from her field trip with the dentist. He dumped her, so she's a mess. I need to make sure she stays sober. For Dash, mostly."

"God, love. I wish it wasn't so hard for you."

I clung to him, reveling in the safety of his protective embrace. "I'll manage. It's what we do, right?"

With effort, I pulled myself away from Orion, we dressed, and I shouldered my bag.

"Hold on," he said.

He rummaged in the top drawer of his desk and pressed something into my hand.

I opened my palm, and in the dim light found a heavy brass coin about the size of a silver dollar. On it was etched the Orion constellation.

"Odin gave it to me when I first left for CHA," he said. "I kept it in my pocket and held it like a talisman or touchstone whenever I got overwhelmed or homesick."

"It's beautiful," I said. "Why—?"

He closed my fingers around it. "In case things get rough again and I'm not there."

I whipped my head up. "No, Orion. I can't take this—"

"I've never been serious with a girl before. Never loved a girl before. I have no fucking clue what I'm doing. I might mess up again. In fact, I'm quite sure I will. But I want you to know that I'm going to try my best, and this coin is my promise to you." He brushed the back of his hand down my cheek. "My very best, Harper. Because I love you."

My eyes fell shut, sending tears down my cheeks. The coin felt heavier in my hand, weighted with his intention, and a hundred times more precious because of it.

"I don't know what to say," I whispered. "Except that I'll do the same. My very best. And I love you too."

He kissed me then, soft and deep, sparing me from fumbling for more words I didn't have. Except that I vowed to protect his heart as fiercely as the coin in my hand, because he'd entrusted both to me as surely as I'd entrusted mine to him.

And instead of feeling weaker or more stretched thin, I left Atlas Hall, empowered as much by him trusting me as I was by trusting him.

With everything yet to come, we were going to need it.

Part III

Music is enough for a lifetime,
but a lifetime is not enough for
music.

—Sergei Rachmaninoff

Chapter 24

ORION

END OF DECEMBER

"Wait, stop."

Ezra Wolfe leaned over the sheet of music where Rachmaninoff Étude-Tableaux Op. 39 No. 5 in E-flat Minor sat. He tapped the dense collection of notes in the second half of the second measure.

"This is where our friend Sergei locks in the harmony. A static harmony. The opening chords must have weight but not force or volume. No banging. It's heaviness. It's grief. The anger comes later, as predicted by the harmony. Do you see?"

I nodded. "I think so."

Not for the first time over these last six weeks, gratitude washed over me that Ezra had not only abandoned his idea that I compose a piece for the spring concert, but that he was working to teach me the language of music without relying on notation.

"And what do we call this cluster of notes?"

"Chordal ostinato," I said.

"Brilliant. This is where the harmony will emerge from the gloomy textures. Again."

I started the piece over for what felt like the thousandth time since that early November night when Harper had unlocked a door inside me and let in the light. A fresh start and fresh air, like taking a deep breath after being submerged down in the depths.

Ezra liked the Rachmaninoff because it started off melancholy, pitched itself into a rage, and then grew subdued again, all in five minutes of insanely complicated finger work. He was still on a mission to draw raw emotion out of me, but the joke was on him—I was too damn happy.

I played the Étude, concentrating on the intricacy of the piece, my fingers flying up and down the keys, and ignoring the cramp in the tendon of my right thumb. I waited for Ezra to stop and yell at me about my arm weight or complain about my *harmonic tension*. I didn't mind his cranky and unpredictable temper. Somewhere along these last weeks, he'd stopped being Wolfe or even Professor Wolfe and become Ezra. More of a friend and mentor than anything else. Someone who was unlocking a bunch of doors all at once.

A few more than I'm ready to walk through.

I finished the piece, the last, sad note hanging in the air. Ezra had his eyes closed, right elbow resting on his left arm that was across his chest. His black-nailed fingers tapped his lips, deep in thought.

I knew better than to say anything.

Finally, he opened his eyes. "I just wanted to hear the whole thing because *fuck me sideways*, you're a goddamn genius. Even at only half the emotional punch, you're…" He shook his head. "Anyway, we should wrap for the day. You must be eager to spend time with your girl before the holiday break puts an ocean between you."

"Yes and no," I said, bending my aching fingers. "I'm going to ask Harper to come with me."

Ezra's brows vanished into his mop of dusty blond hair. "Really? Taking her to meet the parents. Must be serious."

"Of course it's serious," I said, unable to keep the smile off my lips. "I love her."

"Mm," Ezra mused.

"Something on your mind?"

"She has cracked open the lockbox of your heart, yet you sit clear across from each other in the auditorium." He rubbed his jaw. "Sounds about right."

"*Wrong.* I'm keeping us secret for her protection," I said darkly. "There are arseholes about, one depraved bastard in particular who's fucked with her before. I won't risk it again. God knows what he'll do."

"I know the type," Ezra said. "Evildoers are rare, but a few walk among us." He gathered the sheet music and tapped it on the piano. "Well, I am very much in favor of this union, and even more so of a dose of Harper honesty injected right into the jugular of the Mercer family household."

"That's what I love about you," I said wryly. "You're so shy."

"So I've been told," Ezra said, returning my smile. "And here's more of my reserved, retiring advice. *Tell your parents about your dyslexia.* Because I can't do a bloody thing about accommodations for you without their say-so."

"I will," I said.

He gave me a sharp look.

I laughed. "I promise."

After my revelation with Harper, I saw a private specialist and had it confirmed: stealth dyslexia, dysgraphia, and ADHD—paired with an IQ of 157 and unusually high phonological processing. The neuropsychologist said he'd never seen a case so complex, one that would require extensive accommodations from CHA. With Harper's help, I scraped through history, and the crushing weight on my back finally lifted, making the rest of my classes easier to endure. I decided to wait until the holiday break to tell Father and Mum—when I could do it with my girlfriend at my side.

My girlfriend.

The word made me smile. I hadn't had a real girlfriend before, and Harper was a treasure. I was a better person because of her. Maybe I'd be a better person around my family with her. Maybe I wouldn't feel so *less than* and could untie the knots in my tongue at the dinner table.

"One last thing before we part," Ezra said. "You know I have to say it."

I sighed. "Here we go."

"The time for college applications is growing short."

"Ezra, you know where I'm going."

"Does *she* know where you're going?"

I shifted and glanced away. "We haven't talked about it, but she knows Cambridge is the plan."

"Why is it still the plan?" Ezra asked softly. He gestured at the piano. "Don't you love this? Don't you feel it in your blood, in your bones, in your *soul* that this was what you were meant to do? How else do you explain your innate talent? You're a Mozart. A Beethoven. You're one of those rarest of geniuses, who, for whatever reason, can just *do* this. Don't you want to keep doing it?"

"Yes. But playing for a living is not the same as playing for me. I will always be able to play for me."

"Well, that's just selfish bollocks."

"Selfish? Because I don't want the life you choose for me? How is that any different from living the life my father wants?"

Ezra held my gaze for a moment, and then asked suddenly, "Do you know why I picked this piece?"

"Because it's insanely difficult and emotional?"

"Yes and yes, but *étude* means study, and *tableau* means image. Rachmaninoff is creating an image in the mind of the listener with this music. If you close your eyes and listen, it conjures something. Do you not see it when you play?"

"I don't know," I said. "I'm just trying to not fuck up the finger work."

Ezra groaned and ran his hands through his hair. "You're holding back. Still. And dyslexia has nothing to do with it. I know you can compose something for the spring concert. Or hell, you could even improvise. Just sit down and make contact with whatever is inside you and let it out. It's *aching* to come out, and once you do that, your own tableau will become very, very clear. And it's not bloody chemicals."

"You don't understand," I said, ignoring the flares his words were sending up in my heart. "If I stay with my family's business—"

"You have a safety net," Ezra finished gently. "You will not have to go out into a world that will *not* provide a lick of accommodations. That doesn't care if you struggle. You will not have to sit on a stage, at that instrument, and bleed all over the keys. You will not have to let the world into your heart and soul." He leveled a gaze at me. "Yes, it's terrifying. I'm proof of that, hiding in this school *because* it's so bloody terrifying. But you are not me. You are so much more than me. And the *terrifying* is what makes it great."

His words hung in the air for a moment, and then he snorted a laugh, easing the tension, and took hold of my shoulders.

"All right, I've said my piece. For this month, anyway. I'm not done with you, my friend. But you've earned a break from even my incessant badgering."

He embraced me, and I hugged him back. Tightly.

"Happy Christmas," he said. "I hope you have a wonderful break and that Harper has lenient parents and a valid passport."

I snorted a laugh. "You don't quit, do you?"

"Me? Never," Ezra said. "It's part of my charm."

"Charm, sure." I grinned. "Let's go with that."

—

I left the Arts Wing and passed through the center of the Academy, near the gym. Tucker and Rhett were headed toward me.

"Mercer!"

Tucker clasped hands with me while Rhett eyed me coolly. I eyed him right back.

"I feel like I haven't seen you in ages," Tucker said. "What are you doing for the break? Heading home?"

"Yep. You?"

"Same ole. But let's not slack on our training," he said. "Two regattas left, and the season is ours."

"Oh, *physical* activity has never been Orion's problem," Rhett said. "Mental exertion, on the other hand…"

Tucker frowned. "Huh?"

"But I envy you, Orion," Rhett continued. "To never be burdened with *overthinking*."

Weeks ago, his insults would've gotten under my skin. Now, I smiled brightly, showing all my teeth.

"Well, Calloway, it's not as though thinking has enriched your personality." I cocked my head. "How's the family business going? Still bringing in a steady pipeline of souls down below?"

Tucker snorted. "Damn, Mercer."

I beamed and chucked Tucker on the shoulder. "Happy Christmas, gents. See you next year."

I continued down the hallway, just able to make out Tucker saying, "What the fuck was that all about?" and Rhett's muttered reply.

Not that I gave a shit. Tucker's first and foremost concern was sweeping the regattas, and Rhett knew it. He wasn't about to jeopardize that by saying something that might make a crewmember—me—quit. Not when we had the best team CHA had had in years.

I left the campus humming Myles Smith's "Stargazing" all the way to Atlas Hall.

"*You were right there all along*," I sang as I keyed into my and Easton's dorm. I found my roommate on the couch, laptop on his lap, a duffel bag at his feet.

He glanced at my dopey grin and rolled his eyes. "You get worse every day."

"Insufferable, aren't I?" I said and flounced into the chair across from him. I pulled out a small gift-wrapped box that had been burning a hole in my jacket pocket all day.

Easton eyed the box. "What is that?"

"Her Christmas gift. I'm taking her out tonight to ask her—" I burst out laughing at Easton's shocked expression. "I'm asking her to come with me to the UK for the holiday break, you knob. And the ring isn't the ring you think it is."

He shook his head. "You never can tell these days."

I gave his bag a nod. "Where are you off to?"

"Somewhere my parents aren't," he said, snapping his laptop shut and standing up. "Right now, actually."

I stood up too. "Well, happy holidays and safe travels—" I made to give him a hug, but he ducked out of reach. "Oh, sorry…"

"No, it's fine," he said quickly, looking away. "I…don't like to be touched."

"Apologies, mate. I should've asked."

"All good. I gotta go. Have a nice time." He shot me a smile. "Hope she says yes to your *proposal*."

Easton gave a small wave and a half-hearted smile, and then he was gone. Worry swooped in. He was so young, and there was no doubt in my mind that his avoidance of his parents and being touched were connected. I ran for the door and peered into the hallway, but it was empty.

I half wondered if he was going to come back.

I arrived at Harper's house at 7:30 p.m. No sooner had I climbed out of the car than Dash came flying out of the dark at me. He threw his arms around my waist, squeezing tight.

"Orion!"

"Hey, little man. How have you been?"

"I'm so glad you're here! I made an entire castle and a dragon with my LEGOs. Come see, come see!"

I let him pull me up the sidewalk, breathing a nervous sigh about meeting Harper's mother for the first time. I had no idea what to expect. Harper had told me she'd been going to meetings and was sober, but I felt like an intruder who possessed more information about her private life than I should.

The woman who met me at the door looked nothing like her daughter, blond hair going gray pulled into a ponytail, and tired eyes that widened to see my Aston Martin and then again at me in my dark-gray suit and maroon tie.

"So, you're Orion," she said. "Harper didn't tell me you were so handsome."

"Hello, Mrs. Bennett."

"*Ms.* Bennett," she said, shaking my hand. "Harper is still upstairs. Come in."

The house was warm in the chill December air and smelled like cinnamon. A small Christmas tree stood in the corner, decorated and strung with yellow lights. Harper was self-conscious, but her house felt homey and warm compared to the castle-like monstrosity that was my childhood home.

Maybe she'll bring some of her coziness with her.

"Over here, Orion." Dash pulled me to his LEGOs on the coffee table.

"Wow, impressive, little man. You did this all by yourself?"

"Yep! It only took me three days."

"Amazing."

"He's really taken with you," Ms. Bennett said tightly. "You must've made quite the impression on him last time you were here."

"No, it was nothing," I said lightly. "We just watched *The Princess Bride*. His favorite part is the Rodents of Unusual Size. Isn't that right, Dash? Because *you* are a rodent of unusual size who must be vanquished by me, the Dread Pirate Roberts."

I tackled him to the floor and tickled him while he laughed and kicked and squirmed, until I caught sight of Harper at the top of the stairs.

My breath stuck in my throat. "Holy shit."

Dash, breathless and red-faced, giggled. "You said a bad word."

Harper came downstairs in a dark-blue dress that brushed the floor. The top was low cut and revealed enough of her cleavage to make the blood flow straight to my prick. Her hair was piled up on her head, leaving a few curls loose and exposing her neck and shoulders. I now had the insatiable urge to bite and kiss and lick...

"Oh, Harper, you look lovely," her mother said. "Where are you two going?"

Her mother, *you wanker. Get it together.*

"Newport," I managed, and stood up when it was safe.

"Orion's taking me out for seafood," Harper said. I noticed for the first time that she carried a shoebox-sized gift, wrapped in red paper and tied with a green bow.

"That's her favorite," Dash said. "My favorite is Applebee's. Will you take me to Applebee's?"

"Dash." Harper said. "Don't be rude."

"I'll take you to Applebee's, I promise."

"Yay!" Dash stuck his tongue out at Harper, who flared her eyes at him.

"Have fun, you two," her mother said. "Don't stay out too late."

Harper gave a faint smile as I helped her put on her coat; the tension between them was palpable. She ruffled her little brother's hair and then we went out. At my car, I went to open the door for her but stopped.

"You are beautiful."

"Yes, I heard, thank you. Teaching my little brother some naughty language." She smiled and straightened my tie. "But *holy shit* is what I thought when I saw you. You are…devastating."

"Why, thank you."

I kissed her and tasted the plum flavor of her lip gloss and the sweetness of her mouth, like black cherries. The kiss threatened to become more than kissing, her need and mine always burning hot whenever we came together. I pulled away with effort, our breaths pluming in the cold under the streetlamp.

"Is that a very big present in your hand, Bennett, or are you just happy to see me?"

She rolled her eyes. "Will you get in the car? I'm freezing my butt off."

I burst out laughing. "Romance!"

I'd made a reservation at the Chart House, the most expensive restaurant in a town full of expensive restaurants. Our table had sweeping views of Narragansett Bay—the water was a swath of black velvet in the wintry dark December, glittering with the lights of yachts and sailboats outside the window.

Harper picked up the menu, and her eyes widened at the prices.

"I don't want to hear one word about it, Bennett," I said. "Not one."

She rolled her eyes, but a small smile betrayed her. "Fine. Just this once."

"Absolutely not *just this once*. You have to let me indulge every now and again. Splurge on my woman."

"There you go again with this 'my woman' business."

"Well, aren't you?"

Her pale cheeks blushed, and I declared victory. To myself anyway.

The waiter arrived, and we ordered sparkling water, calamari appetizers, halibut for her, swordfish for me, and then it came time to exchange our gifts.

"Let me go first," Harper said.

"Why?"

"Because I'm going to feel inadequate and ridiculous after your gift. The diamond necklace from the *Titanic* or something."

"Oh damn, you guessed it," I said.

She laughed nervously and placed the shoebox-size present on the table in front of me then gave it a small push. "Merry Christmas, Orion."

She bit her lip and watched as I unwrapped the paper. The shoebox wasn't a shoebox but an antique wooden box with a hand-painted grand piano on the lid, set against an ivory-colored sheet music background. Black notes drifted behind the piano like birds.

"This is amazing," I said. "Stunning."

"There's more," she said, still nervous. "Inside."

I opened the latch, and my damn heart clenched. "A protein bar."

"It's the second one that Bandit spit out the day we met," Harper said.

"You kept it," I said, marveling at the implications. "Because you knew even then…?"

"Maybe." She smiled, tucked a curl behind her ear. "It's stupid, I know…"

"No, it's perfect," I said. "Because that moment was perfect."

And we both knew it.

Harper cleared her throat, still shy. "There's more, of course."

Under the protein bar, wrapped in tissue paper, was an antique brass metronome in two parts. I took it out of the box and put the two parts together, then set it in motion.

"Holy shit again," I said.

"I thought this would be a good way for you to keep time, since it's not the easiest for you to find on the page. And also, I just thought it was really beautiful."

"Where did you find this?"

"Antique store downtown." She bit her lip again. "Do you like it?"

"It's absolutely perfect. Thank you, Harper."

"There's one more."

I shot her a smirk. "Now who's going overboard?"

The last item in the box was a piece of paper folded into a square and tied with a thin red ribbon. I untied it to see sheet music. "Chopin's Nocturne. It looks handwritten."

"It is," Harper said. "One night I was working late, and I overheard you play this at the Academy. And it was just one of the most beautiful things I've ever heard, and so…I don't know. It's meaningful to me, and I wanted you to have it too, so I wrote it by hand."

"You wrote this?"

She nodded. "I don't know why I did that, but…"

"I love it," I said, my throat thick. "I love all of this.

These are the most thoughtful gifts anyone has ever given me. Thank you, love. Truly."

I leaned over the table to kiss her, then sat back, staring into the box—a treasure chest. My own chest felt heavy and full, and Harper was so beautiful in the candlelight, and I never wanted to sit across from anyone else, and Ezra's words about the end of the year came back to me…

Fucking hell.

"Our food is taking forever…" I said loudly and pretended to tear into the protein bar.

Harper's eyes widened with a laugh. "What—"

"I'm kidding, I would never."

I put it back in the box and closed everything up and put it away for later.

Later. I don't have to figure it all out right now.

"Your turn." I reached into my pocket and pulled out the very ring-shaped box.

Her eyes widened again. "I knew it. The *Titanic* diamond." With trembling fingers, Harper unwrapped the box and opened it. She gasped, her hand flying to her throat. "Oh my God, Orion."

She pulled the ring from the box—eighteen-karat gold with a two-carat square peridot, surrounded by four round pearls alternating with four round amethyst gemstones.

"It goes here," I said, and touched the middle finger of her right hand.

"It's so beautiful," she murmured. "Suffragette colors."

I nodded. "I saw it and it made me think of how strong

you are and how you fight for what you believe in. How you fought for me," I said softly. "I really wanted those pearls to be diamonds, but I restrained myself, so there..."

Harper put the ring on her middle finger, where it fit perfectly. "I've never had something this nice before. I don't even know what to say."

I reached for her hand across the table. "Say you'll come with me to the UK."

She looked up sharply. "What? When?"

"Over the break."

"But...I can't leave my mother and brother for Christmas."

"After, then. We're off school until the first week of January. Plenty of time."

She stared, absorbing this, thinking. "If I can go—*if*—it can only be a little while. I don't trust my mother. But maybe for a few days? Maybe I can ask Mrs. Andolina to check in on them?"

"So will you?"

"You want me to meet your family?"

"More than anything. You'll love my brothers."

"And your parents?" Harper looked uncertain. "I'm not...what they're used to."

"You're perfect," I said. "Please, come. A stamp in your passport."

"Okay," she said, her dark eyes lighting up with the idea. "Yes. I'll see what I can do."

"Brilliant."

Harper shook her head, disbelieving. "I love you... and...I love this damn ring." She looked up to see my triumphant smile. "And oh my God, you can take that smug, victorious look right off your face."

"No," I said, laughing. "I don't think I will. I think I'm going to wear this for the rest of the evening, thank you."

She laughed too, and we ate our expensive seafood and went back to my place, and I took her to bed where the ring was the only thing *she* wore for the rest of the evening.

Chapter 25

HARPER

On the last day before winter break, Dean, Xander, and I left the Math & Physics Club meeting and stepped out of the Academy into a quiet afternoon under a cold gray sky. The walkways were scraped of snow, and most students had gone home already.

Dean and I observed a moment of silence for Xander; the club had asked him to host the Christmas party, and he'd been touched by everyone's eagerness to meet his physicist father, who was falling further into dementia.

"So, how are things with Emery?" I asked eventually, as we crossed the parking lot. "She gives me a stellar report about you. You're really nailing the whole boyfriend thing."

That coaxed a smile from Xander. "Good to know."

"And?" Dean said, wagging his eyebrows. "How goes it on your end? I haven't had a chance to have some manly man talk with my best bro in a while."

I rolled my eyes, but secretly I was glad to see Dean acting a little bit more like himself today, and not nervous and twitchy, or with his nose buried in his phone.

"Things are fine," Xander said. "Perfect, actually, except—"

"Except you can't tell anyone or go anywhere where people will see you," I finished. I knew the drill, and kept my right hand securely in my pocket, away from Xander's observant eyes.

"Yes, that," he said.

"Her dad is a piece of work," Dean said. "But hey, in a few short months, she'll be eighteen and can tell him to fuck off forever."

Xander shot me a silent plea to keep his secret. He hadn't told anyone—not even his best friend—that he'd promised to marry Emery to help her escape her family if it came down to it, while Dean knew about Orion, and I knew about Sierra. I wondered, not for the first time, how many secret relationships were floating around this institution.

A goddamn smorgasbord of Romeo and Juliets.

"What about Christmas gifts?" Dean asked. "Last year, we did a white elephant for the club. That was a hit, even if I ended up with a wall hanging of a singing fish."

"Sounds good. And speaking of gifts, I need to pick

out something for Emery. I have an hour to kill before she comes over."

"Want some help picking out a gift?" I asked. "*I* have an hour to kill before I become Emery's alibi for coming over to your house."

Dean laughed. "Such a tangled web of deceit. I'd be happy to help, but alas, I have plans." He chucked Xander on the shoulder. "We'll have to save our man talk over brewskies for another time."

"Can't wait." Xander hugged Dean goodbye, then turned to me. "Shall we? Do you have shopping to do?"

"Nope," I said, smiling to myself. "I'm done."

Xander drove us to the little village of Castle Hill that looked like a scene out of a Hallmark Christmas movie. Six months ago, I would've rolled my eyes, but now…I recalled the look on Orion's face when he opened my gifts to him. I'd worried they hadn't been enough; my constant worry was that *I* wasn't enough for someone who could have anything—and anyone—he wanted. But his smile had been unlike any I'd seen him wear. So genuine and…

Happy. He looked happy.

That brought to mind Dean's face at the Halloween festival when he'd spied Sierra, and my worry came swooping back.

"Dean's acting weird," I said as Xander pulled into a parking space behind a Christmas tree lot.

"How so?"

"He's been jumpy lately. Manic, even. You haven't noticed?"

Xander frowned and shut off the engine. "No. But like he said, I haven't seen much of him lately."

"There's that too," I said. "He always has 'other plans' and spends a lot of time on his phone. He used to hardly touch it, now it's in his hand constantly."

"I've been so wrapped up with Emery, I haven't been paying attention. Maybe he's stressed about finals?"

"Maybe," I said. "I have a bad feeling."

"Now I do too. He's so private," Xander said. "He's one of my best friends, and yet I've never been to his house. He's never mentioned his parents or anything about his home life at all."

"Me neither. But I have the feeling he's under a lot of pressure."

"Really? But he's…"

"A Bender?" I retorted. "So are you. So am I. You don't feel the pressure this school—this entire fucking town—puts on you to be something worthy of walking its hallowed halls?"

"I see your point," he said. "You and he aren't…?"

"No, just friends," I said, and nearly told him the truth. But that would derail the convo that needed to be about Dean, not me. "And he's the same mix of open and completely closed off with me as he is with you." I turned to face Xander in my seat. "I know you have enough on your plate with your dad, but can you talk to him? Have that 'manly chat' but for real?"

"Of course," he said. "I'd turn the car around and do it now if I could." He gave me a reassuring smile. "I'll make it happen, I promise."

—

After helping Xander pick out a beautiful locket for Emery, he drove me back to the Academy so I could grab my car and head to Castle Hill Elementary to pick up Dash. Mrs. Andolina was waiting with him, just as she'd agreed, so I could tell her everything that was happening at home. Not just to ask her help so I could take this trip, but to ask for *help*. Because I knew she'd understand and wouldn't make me feel embarrassed or ashamed.

"Oh, honey," she said, after I'd spilled my guts. She took my hands in hers as Dash bashed a tetherball around a pole. "You're not the first family to deal with this around here. Wealth doesn't inoculate anyone from addiction. Rich or poor, it can strike any household. I'm sorry it's come to yours. Has it been this way a long time?"

"Ever since I can remember."

"I'm so sorry, Harper."

"I wanted to ask a favor, and this is going to sound like emotional blackmail after my sob story."

"It's not a sob story, dear. It's real life, and I already told you, I'm happy to help any way I can."

I told her about Orion's offer to visit his family after Christmas. "It would only be for a few days. Mom's okay right now. No steady job, but cleaning Airbnbs regularly and not drinking. But I'm scared to leave."

"Would you like me to check in on Dash while you're away? Or if she has to work, I can babysit. He can play with that mutt of mine all the livelong day."

"Would you? I know it's a lot—"

"It's not a lot. You're five minutes away, and it sounds like you could use a break." She patted my hand. "And because I know you're a tough girl with a lot of pride, consider it my Christmas gift to you, if that helps."

I blinked hard. "That helps a lot."

At home, I told Mom the plan.

"December 29th to January 3rd," I said. "Mrs. Andolina will help out with Dash."

My mother frowned over a cup of coffee in the kitchen. It was four in the afternoon, but she'd been drinking black coffee by the gallon since she started AA meetings again.

"Are you telling me or asking me?" she said. "Because it sounds like you're *telling* me you're flying clear across the Atlantic to be with your boyfriend I've met *one* time, to stay with his parents I've met *zero* times, and that you'll be gone for *five* days."

"Yes, that's what I'm telling you," I said, facing her

from the living room, arms crossed, as Dash watched, wide-eyed from his LEGO set at the coffee table. "I've been busting my ass, working late on my NoSci project every night, while trying to maintain my 4.0 GPA, and I'd like to have this. This one thing that—"

"Really? Because it seems to me like you're going out to fancy dinners and coming back wearing expensive jewelry," Mom sniped, gesturing at my hand.

In the dim light of our living room, the ring glittering on my right hand was like a beacon. I stuffed my hand in my sweater pocket.

"I went to a fancy dinner *one* time, and the ring is none of your business."

"None of my business?" Mom snapped. "You're my daughter. Who you're dating—who you're *fucking*—is absolutely my business."

My entire body stiffened, and Dash's little gasp was loud in the sudden silence.

"Go upstairs, okay, buddy?" I told him in my lightest tone. "Please?"

He nodded, eyes shiny.

Goddamn her. Goddamn her to hell.

When he was upstairs, I whirled on her and seethed in a stage whisper, "What in the actual hell are you thinking?"

"What am *I* thinking?" she spat back. "You think you can come and go as you please? That what I say doesn't matter anymore?"

"Will you lower your voice?" I hissed. "Think of Dash for one goddamned second. Think of literally *anyone* but yourself—"

"Me? You're the selfish one, leaving us to live it up in some castle with your billionaire boyfriend." She snorted. "Oh, he's such a charmer, isn't he? Such an English gentleman."

I went cold all over. "What the hell is that supposed to mean?"

She smacked her mug down with a *thud*, sloshing coffee over her wrist. "If he was really such a great guy, he'd do more than buy you jewelry. I mean, doesn't he know what a mess we're in? I'll be lucky to clean enough houses to make mortgage."

"That is not his problem," I said stonily. "That is our problem."

"*Our* problem," she said snidely. "I'm sure you'll be thinking of *our* problem while flying off to his mansion on his private jet." She stormed from the kitchen to the couch and snatched up the remote. "Now if you'll excuse me, I gave you the bedroom, so I don't have a place to be alone. Would you please get the hell out of my face for a few hours?"

She turned on the TV—volume up—to one of her afternoon talk shows, while I stood trembling with rage even as my heart felt like it was going to shatter. Without a word, I stomped upstairs to find Dash waiting for me.

"Harper?" he said tearfully. "Are you leaving?"

"It's okay, buddy." I gathered him in my arms. "I'm not going anywhere."

I can't take the chance. Not anymore. Another trip, ruined.

But that same night, Mom was apologetic and almost cheerful. She'd changed her tune and told me she was excited for me to go.

"I'm so sorry, baby," she said. "When you told me you were leaving, something ugly came out of me. It's what Angela, my sponsor, calls, 'self-will run riot.' I was focusing only on what I wanted, and I tried to control the situation in thc worst way. Do you forgive me?"

I stiffened, wary. "You're okay with me going? Just like that?"

She nodded and came into the kitchen where I was making spaghetti for dinner.

"What I said was completely out of line. You've been working so hard. You deserve this trip." She took my hand in both of hers and admired my ring. "That is just beautiful. Orion has great taste."

Later that night, I went upstairs and Googled *self-will run riot*. It was a real thing, and common in the AA world. Maybe she was telling the truth. I remained on high alert for the next few days, but Mom seemed okay. Sober. Working, and insistent I have a great time in England. Orion had already flown back to the UK for Christmas when I texted him.

I can come.

The reply was nearly instant. Brilliant! Sending flight details now. <3

I smiled, excited. A stamp in my passport. And even though a tiny voice in the back of my mind whispered something wasn't quite right, it was drowned out by another voice that told me it was okay to have this one thing for myself.

So I took it.

Chapter 26

HARPER

I STEPPED OFF THE JETWAY AND HEADED TO BAGGAGE claim, where I was greeted by Orion holding a sign that simply read *Bennett.* The smile that appeared on his face when he caught sight of me was worth a million pretty rings.

He tilted the sign from side to side and waggled his brows. "Well? How was your flight?"

"How was my first-class flight on a world-class airline? Let me think..." I tapped my chin, pretending to think. "I hated it. It was awful. Torture." I gave him a playful shove on the chest that didn't budge him in the slightest, then pulled him to me for a kiss. God, he was so handsome.

Hot. He's so hot, I amended. As if he'd somehow become even more good-looking over our separation. But it was the essence or substance or whatever made him, *him* that I'd missed the most. Nine days without Orion had felt like nine weeks.

"I missed you," he said softly.

"You read my mind," I said, still holding the lapels of his lightweight designer jacket, not wanting to let him go yet, into the bustle of London.

Orion brushed his thumb over my cheek and kissed me again. "Come on. You have a lot of my country to see and not a lot of time to see it."

He helped me with my one bag and led me to a black SUV and a uniformed driver.

"Morton, this is Harper," Orion said as we climbed in.

He tipped his cap. "Miss."

"Hello, Morton."

"Did you want to eat before we get going?" Orion said. "It's about a forty-minute drive to Surrey."

"I thought you lived in London."

"Nope. But don't worry. We'll come back and sightsee."

He took my hand and gave it a kiss as the car moved out of Heathrow and headed south along a highway called the M25. I checked in with home for the second time (the first being the second the plane touched down and I could turn off airplane mode) and let myself relax a little. The scenery was mostly barren: winter trees over grayish-brown land, but beautiful in my eyes because it was entirely different. We passed quaint little villages and not-so-quaint estates that grew bigger and bigger, until

Morton drove us down a long, private road. A sign read, *Ademere House.*

"Ademere?"

"*Ade* means 'crown' or 'royalty' in Yoruba," Orion explained. "*Mere* is old English for 'body of water.' When he bought the estate, my father wanted to pay homage to his roots. The name means *Crown by the Water.*"

"That's lovely," I said. "Where's the water?"

"Behind the house. You'll see," Orion said, peering out the window. "We're here."

Ademere House was enormous. A fairytale castle, with actual towers and turrets, but more imposing. It sat back from the long, circular drive, on miles of wooded land, like a miniature city unto itself. It was a lot of house for a family of five when five hundred could probably fit within the pale stone walls. For the first time, I had an understanding of what *billions* meant but couldn't wrap my brain around so few people possessing so much.

"The baby boy returns from Heathrow with the Girlfriend," said a deep, laughing voice as Morton set the luggage on the curb.

"Do *not* call me that and do not call her that," Orion scolded, but his grin was wide. "Harper, this is Odin. Oldest, but not wisest, brother."

"No, that would be Tav, though nowadays, that's debatable," Odin said grimly, then put on a cheerful smile the same way Orion did when dismissing unpleasant thoughts. He stuck out his hand. "Pleasure to meet you, Harper. Welcome to our *humble* abode."

"Thank you." Odin had the same charismatic optimism as Orion, only in a bigger package. I liked him immediately.

"Of all his many ladies, you're the first Orion has brought home," Odin said to me. "You must be special."

"Can we not?" Orion said, glaring.

"What?" Odin blinked innocently. "It's a compliment." He gestured up at the house. "What do you think, Harper? They don't make them like this in the States, do they?"

Orion whacked him on the shoulder. "Quit putting her on the spot."

"I just meant, it's three hundred years old," Odin said.

"I like it," I said. "It's very *Saltburn*."

Odin burst out laughing. "Oh, I like her."

"Me too," Orion said, gazing at me.

I smirked. "You sure? You have so *many* ladies…"

"Yes, but I like you the most. Ow!" Orion laughed as I elbowed his side and we headed toward the huge manor. "Ah, there's Tav."

Orion nodded his head at the entrance. A slender young man—slightly shorter than his brothers—dressed in all black, came out from behind one of the entry's immense pillars, shoulders hunched, hands stuffed in his pockets. He had the same loose curls as Orion, but they brushed his shoulders and fell over his eyes, which were a striking green against his darker skin. Everything about Octavian was quiet and subdued, where his brothers were boisterous and lively. He greeted me with a soft-spoken voice, and then we all stepped inside.

Immediately, the energy shifted. Odin's and Orion's brilliant smiles vanished, and they stood straighter. Stiffly. It was warmer in the grand entry but not by much, and the silence was like a living thing that ate our words and made our steps echo.

Orion read my face, "Intimidating, I know, but you get used it."

I smiled faintly. *Do you?*

I'd never felt so out of my element in my life. As if I'd been dropped into a king's castle without being trained in the etiquette.

A liveried butler approached and took my bag up one of two stairways that led to different wings of the house, while another indicated we all should follow him to where Mr. and Mrs. Mercer waited.

As we moved through the manor, I stared up and around at the high ceilings and enormous rooms decorated for the season with garlands, bouquets of red and white flowers, and a Christmas tree in almost every room. But beneath the festive decor were classic portraits, modern abstracts, and West African bronzes and sculpture, all complimenting each other in expert arrangements.

"Our mother's handiwork," Odin said, noticing my awed expression. "She's a gallerist in London."

"It's incredible," I said. "She's so talented."

"Isn't she?" he said. "It's all so varied; you expect nothing to work, but it all works."

We passed through a huge room with a sleek black grand piano, and I gave Orion's hand a squeeze. "This must be where you spent a lot of time."

He wore a smile I couldn't read, and my stomach tightened. I tried to imagine Orion in this house as a little boy and reconcile him with the man beside me—someone who made jokes, laughed easily, and filled spaces without trying. I pictured him at the piano in that mausoleum of a room, his music swallowed by high ceilings and closed doors, and failed. But he'd struggled in silence for years, and somehow emerged with the best parts of himself still intact.

I was somehow prouder of him and loved him more, even though I didn't think that was possible.

We entered a more modern-looking sitting room where Mr. and Mrs. Mercer were waiting.

"Mum, Father, this is Harper," Orion said, his accent sharper and more refined than I'd ever heard him use.

They both stood up, her arm linked in his. Rockwell wore a suit; she was in a violet dress. The sense of meeting royalty came over me again, and I wondered if I should curtsy.

"Hello," I said. "Very pleased to meet you."

"Pleased to meet you, dear." Celeste Mercer was beautiful, with blond hair, green eyes, and diamonds glittering on her ears and fingers. But it was immediately clear she was not a trophy wife. Aside from having her own career, it was obvious these two were partners. Equal in all things, and I remembered that Orion had told me she'd been with him since the beginning.

"I trust you had a pleasant flight, young lady?" Rockwell intoned. He was large, big around the middle, with an intimidating bearing. A mountain of a man because he'd *built* a mountain out of nothing with his bare hands and expected every ounce of respect and deference he'd earned while amassing his vast fortune.

"Yes, sir," I said. "Thank you."

I felt them both watching me, sizing me up. Not cold or cruel, only practical. Controlled. There was a slight hum of tension in the air, everyone wearing pleasant smiles, and I got the impression that the worst thing I could do in this house was start screaming at the top of my lungs or maybe burst into tears.

After some pleasantries, a different servant appeared to show me to my room so I could rest before dinner. Orion came with me and loosened up the moment I closed the door to my huge suite, which was complete with private bathroom and a balcony that overlooked the grounds.

"My room is just next door," Orion said, taking me by the waist and waggling his brows. "Just FYI."

"I can't imagine anything worse than your parents catching us having sex."

"They wouldn't dream of coming up here in a million years."

"Why not?"

"Because the very last thing *they'd* want to do is catch us having sex. The scandal!"

I pulled away from Orion to sit on the four-poster bed. "They're intimidating as hell, but nice. Even if they both scare me shitless, I can tell they're good people."

Orion grinned. "Sounds exactly right."

"Odin seems fun. Can't get a read on Octavian."

"Neither can I," Orion said. "Not anymore. He's changed. The monochromatic color scheme is new. Maybe there's a goth craze sweeping Cambridge."

I glanced at Orion sideways. "So, you're going to tell them tonight, right? At dinner, about your dyslexia? And the spring concert?"

He stiffened. "I will."

He sounded as if I'd asked if he wanted to get dental surgery followed by a colonoscopy. I reached for him and pulled him so that he stood between my knees. "Is it hard to talk to them about this stuff?"

"It's hard to talk to them about anything."

I gave his hands a squeeze. "I'm here for you."

"I know." He bent and gave me a kiss. "That's the best part."

Orion's confidence vanished again as soon as we stepped outside of the room and headed down to dinner. I learned there were three dining rooms: a formal dining room that could hold over a hundred people, a smaller dining room for half the number of people, and the "family" dining room for tonight. It was smaller—slightly bigger than my entire house—with high ceilings and cool air despite the fireplace burning in one wall.

A team of servants served a seven-course meal. Rockwell and Celeste hadn't seen their sons in months, all of the boys being at their respective schools, but the conversation remained light, jumping along from topic to topic on the surface like a skipped rock. I waited for Orion to tell them about his diagnosis, or more importantly, his *misdiagnosis*. How he'd been suffering in silence for so long, struggling and working so hard to keep up, and how brilliant he was. I *needed* them to come listen to him play at the spring concert. Maybe they'd all finally understand—Orion included—what was at stake.

But course after course was served, and he said nothing. Finally, as dessert plates were being cleared away, Orion shifted in his seat, looking like he was facing a firing squad.

"Mum, Father, there's something I need to tell you," he said stiffly.

Celeste lifted her a glass of red wine. "What is it, darling?"

"Father probably told you, but I've been struggling academically."

The tension in the room tightened.

"Now, Orion," Rockwell said. "There's no need to bring up a private matter at the table."

I stared. *Private matter? Among family?*

"But there's a reason, Father, and Harper helped me find it. My piano teacher too, and I…well…"

I bit my lip and wished we'd been seated next to each other so I could take his hand. Odin sat frozen, his gaze ping-ponging back and forth, while Octavian watched the scene with wide eyes.

Orion heaved a breath. "I have dyslexia."

"Oh." Celeste's hand went to her throat. She looked to Rockwell from her end of the table. "H-How do you know?"

"I was evaluated. Privately," he added when their eyes widened in alarm.

"And what did they say?" Celeste said when her husband remained quiet.

Orion explained his diagnosis in full, and a tense silence descended.

"You have ADHD," Rockwell said finally, frowning, as if he preferred his conclusion to everything his son had just explained.

"Yes, but dyslexia too," Orion said uncertainly, and every fear he'd had about feeling *less than* or stupid or not enough were loaded into those four words, so much so that I *did* want to scream at the top of my lungs or burst into tears.

"But…you read so well, dear," Celeste said. "In fact, of all your brothers, you read more books…"

"Yes, I can read, but it's a struggle," he said. "I need

context. Shorter text gives me a hard time, which is why my test scores are so bad. I can do better—perform better academically—if I have help. Accommodations. My teacher can help me—"

"I don't understand," his father said. "Dyslexia, as far as I understand it, is a learning disability. People with it are not…" He shifted his large frame.

"Smart?" I said, unable to keep my mouth shut a moment longer.

The entire table looked to me. Orion shook his head almost imperceptibly, but I ignored him. I couldn't help myself.

"There is no correlation between intelligence and dyslexia, Mr. Mercer," I said, as if I were giving a formal presentation. "It is a learning processing condition, in which one's brain organizes and codes information differently. That's all. People with dyslexia are no different intellectually from anyone else and can land anywhere on the spectrum. But Orion happens to be brilliant. So brilliant, in fact, he's designated as 2e, or twice exceptional. For dyslexia and his high intelligence and musical aptitude."

Rockwell pursed his lips. "*Musical aptitude* isn't the point," he said. "It's—"

"*It's exactly the point!*" Octavian shouted suddenly, shocking the room like a bolt of lightning.

"Octavian—" his mother began mildly.

"*Twice. Exceptional*," he said, banging his fist on the table with each word, knocking his water glass over.

"That's enough, son," Rockwell said, unperturbed as a servant hurried in to clean up the mess while another replaced his water glass.

"Forgive Octavian, Harper," Celeste said with a tight smile. "He's under a lot of school pressure himself, aren't you dear?"

Octavian gazed at his mother from under his curls but said nothing. He quietly excused himself from the table and left the room. There were a few beats of nothing, and already I was beginning to understand the silence in this house was frequent and came in a hundred shades and flavors.

Finally, Celeste turned to Orion. "Darling, you're certain about…this?"

"Yes, Mum," he said, still looking to where Octavian had gone. "It explains everything."

Celeste looked to Rockwell, and a silent dialogue passed between them. Finally, Mr. Mercer steepled his hands. "Very well. We'll ensure the Academy provides you with proper accommodations."

"Thank you."

Odin breathed a sigh of relief only I could hear, and Orion looked visibly relieved. Octavian's outburst was already forgotten, as if it never happened. The tension at the table loosened, except mine. I waited for Orion's parents to apologize to him. For one or both to show any kind of remorse for all the silent suffering their son had endured for *a decade* under a misdiagnosis.

Nothing.

Celeste reached over and gave Orion's hand a squeeze. Then she looked to me. "Now, tell us, Harper. How are you liking Castle Hill?"

"That's it?" I hissed, later in my room. "That's all they're going to say? They'll get you accommodations but nothing else?"

Orion shrugged. "That's how it is in my family."

"But…aren't you angry? Don't you want to tell them about how hard it's been and how hard you've worked and—"

"What for? To make them feel guilty? It won't change the past. And it would only embarrass them in front of you. It's out now. That's all that matters."

I shook my head, a hundred arguments at my lips.

"It's out but not resolved. And what about Octavian's outburst? And us?" I said, pacing. "They didn't ask one question about how we met, or one question about… anything. Nothing of depth or—"

"That's just not their way," Orion said. He shrugged at my incredulous expression. "It just isn't."

"You've suffered a lot. Alone. Don't you want to sit down and explain that? Make them understand how it's been for you? You didn't tell them about the spring concert, either."

"I will," he said. "I *will*," he repeated, reading my

dubious expression. "We still have time. I'll tell them that it's important and that I want them all to come."

I shook my head. "It all seems so superficial. Like everything floats on the surface. Don't you want to have a deeper or more meaningful relationship with them?"

Orion sighed, frustration creeping into his tone. "Because that's so easy? That's how they are, love. They're not going to change. I wouldn't even know where to begin."

"Maybe by telling them the truth?"

"Which is?"

I frowned. "Oh, I don't know. That it's totally sucked for you for the last *ten years*? That you nearly had a heart attack with the ADHD meds? That Callister is a dick to you because he has no idea—"

"And what good would that do aside from making them feel like shit?" He ran a hand through his curls. "Look, I appreciate you being on my side. I haven't had that in a long time. But let me handle my family, okay?"

Every part of me wanted to push past Orion, march down the hall, find his parents, and scream at them for how my boyfriend had suffered. But he was right; it was none of my business. I couldn't *fix* it the same way he couldn't fix my mother.

With supreme effort, I nodded.

"Oooh, you hate that, don't you?" Orion said, grinning and moving toward me.

"Don't make jokes," I said, letting him encircle me in his arms. "And yes, I hate it."

"That's because you're fierce," he said, kissing my forehead, my cheek, down to my mouth. "My warrior woman."

"You're just trying to seduce me out of being pissed off," I breathed, my lips brushing his.

"Absolutely," he said. "Is it working?"

"No."

"Good," he said gruffly. "Take it out on me…"

He kissed me, and of course I melted into him. Surrendered. My body suffused with that perfect, needy ache that only he could satisfy. I kissed him back. Hard, biting kisses, my hands grabbing at him, doing as he'd said, letting my fiery anger morph into heated want of him.

I didn't know where else to put it.

Chapter 27

ORION

I KISSED HARPER, SILENCING HER WORDS, DEFLECTING like I always did because she was right about everything.

Later. I'll deal with it all later.

That was fast becoming another mantra, but all thought was burning up in my desire for her. How she'd stood at my side tonight—even from across the table—brave in the face of my intimidating parents, to explain in succinct terms my complicated diagnosis. I'd seen grown men cower under my father's hard stare, but Harper…

My girl is unafraid…

We were nearly at the bed when three soft knocks came at the door, followed by one harder one. The secret code.

Harper froze. "Oh shit."

"It's okay. It's one of my brothers."

I answered the door to Odin. "It's Octavian. Come quick. Backyard."

The look on his face was enough for me to not waste time with questions. "I have to go," I told Harper. "It's Tav."

"I'll come too…"

"No, stay here," I said. "Stay warm and safe. Please."

She started to argue but nodded stiffly. "Text if you need me."

"I will."

I ran next door to my room, grabbed my coat and galoshes, and followed Odin downstairs and outside. My heart clanged faster and heavier with every step to the immense grounds behind the house.

"I tried to get him to come back," Odin said, "but he insists on talking to you."

"Come back from where…?"

The word trailed away like smoke. I could just make out a dark figure in the middle of the white ice of the lake.

Oh fuck.

It was cold in Surrey, but not that cold. Not cold enough to freeze the lake all the way through.

"Tav," I called, trying to keep the panic out of my voice. "I'm here. You can come off now. *Now.*"

Octavian stood with his hands in the pockets of his sweatshirt, his breath like a chimney, underdressed for the cold.

"Come on, Tav, you've made your point," I called while

Odin pulled a long branch off one of the dead trees that surrounded the lake. "We're all sufficiently scared shitless."

I heard the ice crack, and the eerie, high-pitched whining sound went straight down my spine.

"I didn't come out here to scare anyone," Tav said. "Or maybe I did. But this feels…honest?"

He was too far away to make out his face, but I could tell he was looking at me.

"Honestly terrifying?" I called. "If you don't come back, Odin and I will be forced to belly crawl to you, and I don't want to get my favorite shirt wet."

"Always with the jokes," Tav said with a sigh and rocked on his heels as if he were waiting for a bus.

Odin dragged the branch to me, and we exchanged helpless glances.

"Come on, Tav," I said. "I…I don't want to lose you."

"That's better, thank you. I don't want to lose you either."

"You're not going to lose me," I called.

"I might," he called back. "When you said you had dyslexia, I thought, *Thank God, now we're getting somewhere. This ghost of Mozart, who's been haunting our house forever, is going to be what he's supposed to be.* But you're going to tell me you're going to throw it all away to work for Father's business?"

"That's what this is about? Jesus, come inside and we can talk about it."

Silence. I tried again.

"Has a certain Ezra Wolfe been in contact with you, by any chance?"

Odin punched my shoulder.

"All right, all right," I muttered, then louder, "You're right, Tav. I had a straightforward path, and now I can't see where I'm going. Okay? Happy? Now will you get the fuck off the ice?"

Octavian stood still a moment more. "Okay."

"Okay?"

But he was already walking back toward us. I held my breath, listening to the ice crack and whine as my brother made his way back to shore. I aged a hundred years waiting for him to reach us. Odin wrapped a coat around him, and we three stood together, our breaths pluming, clutching each other.

Octavian grinned at me from under his curls. "Not knowing your path is better than locking yourself up in a box and throwing away the key."

"So glad you approve," I muttered. "Can we go in now?"

"Yes, let's. It's quite cold out."

Odin and I exchanged incredulous glances, and we hurried inside, into the family sitting room. Odin lit a fire. Tav sat on the floor, warming his hands. I slumped on the couch, adrenaline leaving me drained, and shot Harper a text.

All good. Be up soon.

Glad to hear it but hurry, she texted back. Pretty sure I just saw the Headless Horseman.

I grinned. I will.

"She's great," Tav said, watching me. "Keep her. *Marry* her. God knows, this family could use ten more just like her."

I put my phone away. "We can talk about my love life later. First, what the bloody hell was that?"

Odin nodded. "That wasn't funny, Tav. What's with you, lately?"

"Given what I have learned over the last year, I felt it necessary to impinge upon Orion the severity of the situation," Octavian replied.

"Sure, what's a little emotional blackmail among brothers?" I muttered. "You scared the crap out of us."

"Good. But I knew the lake wouldn't break. I saw an elk walk across this morning."

Odin and I exchanged dubious glances. The whining crack of ice told us otherwise, but we were too glad he was home safe to argue.

"Besides," Tav continued gravely, "sometimes it takes a brush with death to learn what's at stake."

"What do you mean?" Odin said, joining me on the couch.

Our brother's green eyes—our mother's eyes—gazed into the fire. "A friend of mine died by suicide three months ago. No, that's not true. He wasn't a friend. He was my boyfriend."

Odin and I exchanged wide-eyed glances, identical bolts of shock running through us. Neither had known our brother was gay, or however he identified, but that wasn't the point.

He was alone. Alone in who he was, and alone in his grief, just like me. Because we don't talk about anything. Not a bloody thing.

"Tav…" I whispered. "I'm so sorry."

"Me too," Odin said gruffly.

"I'll tell Mum and Father. I planned to this very night, actually, then you upstaged me with your announcement." Octavian smiled into the fire. "But I'm not afraid. That's what losing Skyler…" He stopped and looked at us, his eyes full. "His name was Skyler."

Immediately, and at the exact same time, Odin and I slipped down to the floor, one to each side of our brother, and put our arms around him.

"That's what losing Skyler did for me," he continued, his voice thick. "You realize what is valuable and what is bollocks. I'm not going to follow in the business. I'm going to wander around Europe for a while and figure out who I am and what I want."

"Okay," Odin said. "You do that." He looked to me. "And if you want to play, play. I'm going into the business. I *want* to go into the business. I want to follow in Father's footsteps. Always have."

My gaze jumped between my brothers, both of them looking at me expectantly. "I…I don't know. I've always planned on going into the business too. Piano was always just…"

"Something you loved," Octavian said, and Odin nodded. "You loved it until they told you enough times it was just a hobby. Nothing serious. Nothing you could actually *do* and make them proud. Right?"

I swallowed hard. "Maybe," I whispered. "I don't want to be an embarrassment. If I go out in the world like I am…"

"There's nothing wrong with who you are," Odin said and looked between us, like the big brother he was. "None of us."

"Orion…" Octavian smiled through his tears. "Don't wait until someone falls through the ice to find that out."

We went our separate ways to bed, and I passed by my mother's favorite drawing room and heard voices. Mum and Father were sitting by another fire—our estate had thirteen or fourteen chimneys; I could never remember—and talking in quiet voices. It was clear they hadn't heard our commotion outside.

"You'll take care of him, won't you?" Mum was saying, sipping a tiny glass of port. "If it's true about that dyslexia, we need to protect him."

I froze, listening, and suddenly I was ten years old again, listening as my first diagnosis was handed down and discussed.

"I will," Father said. "It's more important than ever to keep him in the family business."

"But what about Cambridge?"

"If he wins the Novus Science prize, we can claim he's precocious enough to skip it. He won't have to struggle out there or embarrass himself. And no one needs to know."

"I like that," Mum said. "It's a private matter, and he'll be safe. Thank you, dear."

The issue settled, he took her hand in his, and they smiled stiffly at each other and watched the fire.

I headed back upstairs slowly.

Protect him.

He won't have to struggle or embarrass himself.

He'll be safe.

No one needs to know.

In my room, Harper pulled me into bed. "Everything okay?"

"Yep," I said, grateful for the dark hiding my expression. "All good."

Chapter 28

HARPER

I SPENT THE REMAINDER OF MY VISIT BEING WHISKED around London and the quaint little village closest to Ademere, and then it was time to go home. Orion still had a few more days with his family, so he and his brothers saw me off to the airport.

"Lovely to meet you, Harper," Odin said, engulfing me in a hug. "Come back anytime. *Anytime.*"

Octavian gave me a small bow and a formal handshake. "I wholeheartedly second that."

Orion walked with me as far as he could. "You survived."

"So did you," I said, ringing my arms around his neck. "Next semester is going to be so much better for you."

"Hopefully for both of us," he said. "Especially when you win the NoSci. Because you're a brilliant chemist."

"Will your parents come listen to you play at the concert?"

Orion's grin tilted. "Maybe. Looks like the NoSci award ceremony is the same weekend. So they might be there by scheduling default."

"I'll take it."

We kissed for as long as I could stand before becoming self-conscious in public, then reluctantly let him go.

"Thank you for coming," he said, brushing the back of his hand over my cheek. "For being there, that night."

"Thank you for the trip," I replied. "And the stamp in my passport. And just for being you."

"I love you," he said.

"Love you too."

"Hey, Bennett," Orion called as I headed toward security, his smile brilliant. "You're nailing this romance thing."

A dozen smart-ass remarks came to mind, but I decided not to ruin the moment. I smiled back. "You make it pretty damn easy."

He staggered back, clutching his heart as if he'd been shot by Cupid's arrow, and I smiled, a warm glow infusing every part of me.

I took that warm feeling with me all the way back to Rhode Island, where it stayed with me until I opened my front door and found my mother passed out on the living room floor and Dash nowhere in sight.

"Oh fuck."

I dropped my bag and the handle to my rolling suitcase and fell to my knees beside her. I checked for a pulse, but she was already mumbling something wetly. Stale wine was on her breath and coming out of her pores. The coffee table was littered with three empty wine bottles and a pizza box, only one slice eaten.

"Dash?" I called, grabbing for my phone. "Dash!"

No answer.

The phone nearly slipped out of my hands as I yanked it from my pocket. I searched fruitlessly for missed calls and texts until I realized it was still on airplane mode.

"God*dammit.*"

I switched airplane mode off and watched my screen populate with a missed call and a text from Mrs. Andolina, both from this morning. The text told me to call her, so I sat back on my heels, my eyes falling shut. I put the phone to my ear and listened to the message.

"Hello, Harper. Your mother has had a bit of a relapse, I'm afraid. I checked in every day, but yesterday things took a turn, and it seemed best if I took Dash to stay with us. He was confused at first but is having fun playing with Spike. Yesterday he made a snowman with Frank. I didn't see the point in telling you since you're coming home today, but… anyway, I hope this reaches you before you arrive home. Perhaps you can come over here first? We can talk about how we can help you and Dash going forward. I'm so sorry, sweetheart. I hope you had a lovely trip."

My hand dropped to my lap. Yesterday? What happened

yesterday? What set Mom off? But I knew in my heart the truth.

Nothing. It wasn't yesterday. It was the minute I left. She just hid it from Mrs. A until she stopped caring about hiding it.

"Self-will run riot," I muttered.

I hauled myself off the floor and texted Mrs. A that I'd be over in half an hour, then cleaned up the coffee table. I threw out the empties like I used to when I was a kid, when the sound of glass bottles *clanking* together inside a garbage bag had been the soundtrack of my youth. And here I was again.

I straightened the living room, erasing the signs of Mom's bender, then hooked my arms under hers and hauled her onto the couch. I was bigger and stronger now; I could do it like a pro. She muttered and mumbled but didn't wake up. I covered her with a blanket, set a glass of water and three Advil on the coffee table. I grabbed my car keys, my other hand going to my pocket where the constellation coin Orion had given me lived. It lived in every pocket of every outfit I wore. I rubbed my thumb along the stars while doing some math. Because doing the math, horrible as it was, was better than dwelling on what I'd come home to.

The NoSci prize money is $25,000.

It's awarded in the beginning of April which is four months away.

Our mortgage is $1,400 per month.

$1,400 x 4 months is $5,600 plus late fees…let's say $10K total, to be realistic.

Worst-case scenario, if my mother didn't get her shit together—which, let's be honest, seemed probable—we'd be in the hole for ten thousand dollars, and the bank would foreclose until I won and paid off the debt.

"*If* I win," I said, getting in my car.

But losing, I decided, wasn't an option.

Because it couldn't be.

Part IV

I will seize Fate by the throat;
it will not bend me completely
to its will.

—Ludwig van Beethoven

Chapter 29

ORION

MARCH

I STEPPED INTO THE PIANO ROOM AND SHUT THE DOOR behind me. Ezra had left the light on at the baby grand and promised no one would bother me at six on a Friday night. I sat and set the box Harper had given me for Christmas beside me. I took out the metronome, snapped the pieces together, and placed it on the piano. Then I unfurled the Nocturne she'd written and set it on the rack.

Her handwriting was clear and sharp, and my chest ached that she'd taken the time to write it out instead of printing it. The notations were harder to read, but I'd played this before. I set the metronome to 4/4 and fixed the pages in my mind.

Music made patterns my brain could follow. More than that, something inside me understood them. I'd always kept my feelings locked away, but music pulled them out, with the familiar fear of going too far, of getting lost.

But Harper unlocked something in me. She broke the wall down.

I closed my eyes and let the sound carry me, and when I finished, I sat in the feeling it left behind—the same one that rose when I thought of her. Love. I loved to play. Octavian had said I always did. I'd just been told too often that it was only a hobby, that I was meant for something more important.

The accommodations since December had helped a little. Callister was off my back, and my testing was more structured. But the real world wouldn't be like this. Wouldn't *feel* like this. At my father's company, I'd be protected. Beyond that? I pictured myself on a stage, an orchestra at my back and counting on me not to fail. I didn't speak the language of music. I only felt it. How would that ever be enough?

I took my hands from the keys and shut off the light.

I picked Harper up at her house at seven p.m. She didn't like me coming to the door anymore. She didn't want me to see her mother, so I texted from the driveway that I was there. Dash came running out first.

I picked him up and swung him around. "There's my little man."

"Can I come too?"

"Not this time, Dash. Next time, for sure."

"Okay," he said, disappointed.

I'd taken the three of us to Applebee's several times, or to parks, and once to a hideous pizza place where scary animatronic animals suddenly came to life and sang songs like possessed stuffed animals. But Dash loved it.

The light is going out in his eyes, Harper had told me, and that fucking killed me.

She came out looking stunning in a black dress. Simple but beautiful.

"All good?" I said.

"Yes. Mom's okay right now, but I'm not taking any chances." She ruffled Dash's hair. "Mrs. Andolina is on her way. Be good for her, okay, buddy?"

"I will," he said, and threw his arms around Harper's waist. "I love you."

"I love you too."

"*I love you, too*," I echoed, and Dash made a face.

"Yuck!"

But he laughed, and that was everything.

I took Harper to dinner at an Italian restaurant and held her hand across the table, the ring I'd given her glinting in the candlelight.

"How long do I have for this date?"

"Depends," Harper said, arching a brow.

"On?"

"Is Easton home? I prefer privacy if we're going to pull an all-nighter."

"What do you take me for, some kind of amateur?" I scoffed. "And *all-nighter*? Really?"

She laughed. "I like it better when you're the romantic one."

"*Clearly*," I said. "Good thing I'm a natural in that department or we'd be hopeless."

After dinner, we drove to the Academy. Harper headed up the walk, toward Atlas Hall, but I tugged her hand toward the school itself.

She frowned. "Because we don't spend enough time in there?"

"Hopeless, Bennett," I said, laughing. "*Hopeless.*"

I led her to the Arts Wing. Her eyes widened as she took in the Nocturne and the metronome sitting on the piano. "Am I getting a private performance?"

"Is that completely cheesy and big-headed of me?"

"Are you kidding?" She swatted me on the arm. "This is all I've ever wanted. Why do you think I gave you the Nocturne in the first place?"

I laughed. "All right, all right, don't make me self-conscious."

Harper sprinted to Ezra's chair, sat ramrod straight, arms folded in her lap. "Ready."

"That's not where you're supposed to sit." I scooted over on the bench. "Come here."

Her face softened, a side of Harper very few people got to see. Her romantic, soft, sweet side. And so beautiful because it felt like it was just for me.

Slowly she sat down beside me as if awed. I couldn't understand it, couldn't wrap my brain around the fuss that people made over my playing, her and Ezra and Octavian. I pushed it all aside. This was just for her.

"When did you set this up?" she asked softly.

"Earlier today. I've been practicing."

"As if you need to practice."

"Shut it, Bennett. My neck will not hold my head up if it gets any bigger. Now, if you please..."

I cleared my throat and adjusted the sleeves on my suit and set the metronome to 4/4 time. Then I laid my fingers on the keys and played.

I played just as I had earlier that evening, only this time Harper was sitting beside me and it was ten times more powerful because it was for her.

When it was done, the last notes hung in the air, wavering, then faded away. Harper was quiet, and I looked over. Tears stood out in her eyes. She was staring at the keys, then my hands, then me.

"I thought it was beautiful the first time," she said, shaking her head. "Orion, do you not want to do this forever?"

Instead of answering, I kissed her. I drew that feeling around us, infusing my kiss with it, and sending it to this girl I loved so much. As if it could speak for me. As if it could sort out the tangle that was the future and make everything work out perfectly without anyone getting hurt or upset or disappointed.

Somehow, we made it back to Atlas Hall where, true to my word, I'd already ensured Easton would be nowhere in sight. I took Harper into my room and shut the door, kissing her luscious lips, sharing her breath, her heartbeat… It beat with mine—a cosmic metronome had set them to the same time. It had put this girl in my path, and my life had never been the same since.

My hands were in her hair and then down her back. I found the zipper of her dress and slid it down, then pulled it off her shoulders, all the while kissing her. It slipped off her body to pool at her feet, leaving her in her bra and underwear. Both black lace. I took a moment to drink her in, the beauty of her pale skin against the black, while she pushed my jacket off my shoulders and undid the buttons of my shirt one at a time.

Her eyes met mine in the dimness, dark and rich, and full of thoughts and questions and hope. The same fear I had of letting down my family also wondered if I could be enough for her, this extraordinary girl who was so strong and brave. Who walked a tightrope with no safety net, carrying her mother and brother on her back. Who deserved everything. But if I stepped off that ledge into the unknown, without the Mercer name and money, I might be nothing but a failed musician she'd have to carry too.

But that was later. We had right now; what I wanted right now was her.

Our kisses became ferocious. Needy. Our clothes stripped away, and then she was in my bed and I was over her. She was soft and curvy to my hard angles. I wanted to be gentle or soft, but there was a power between us that I could not deny. A force that was too strong, and I know she felt it too.

It had never been like this with any other girl. Never been this complete, where lust and love were there in equal parts because there had never been love. Never been this undeniable feeling that I didn't want there to be any other girl ever again.

When the pleasure burned through her, I reveled in it almost as much as I reveled in my own, which came moments later. Shuddering, I collapsed over her, my face pressed into the crook of her neck.

I started to move off her, but she held me close. "Stay," she whispered. "Please, stay."

I kept my face buried in her neck, my eyes shut, because I knew what she was asking the only way she knew how.

And I didn't have an answer.

Chapter 30

HARPER

The next morning, light streamed over Orion and me, neither willing to haul ourselves out of bed.

"How are we feeling, love?" he asked, his fingers trailing lazily in my hair.

"Perfect because I'm here. With you," I said with a smile. "At home, it's the same old, same old. Mom gets her butt off the couch every now and again and cleans a house or two, but it's not going to be enough."

"You know I'm here…"

"I know," I said. "But between her sponsor and me, we're trying to motivate her with very scary bank notices." I shook my head. "Anyway, I don't want to talk about it. I have to get going to work on my NoSci. What do you have for today?"

"Same. Plus, crew practice and a lesson with Ezra."

The schedule was getting packed—the Head of the Bay Regatta was this Friday, while the Novus Science projects presentations were the following Thursday, winners announced at a big ceremony on Saturday, and the spring concert on Sunday.

He gave me a squeeze. "How are the old Ugly Buckets coming along?"

"Don't make fun of my Ugly Buckets," I said, laughing at his affectionate nickname for my water-purification project.

"Hey, your Ugly Buckets are going to save the world. My pothole glue is going to save an axle or two. Definitely not in the same ballpark."

"We'll see," I said, and last night came back to me. The dinner, the sex, all of it floating on the sound of Orion's incredible Nocturne.

He shifted under my heavy gaze. "What?"

"Nothing," I said. "I just realized I have a little bit of time before I need to get to work."

"Oh. And?"

I shrugged one shoulder. "And. . . ." I kissed his lips, his chin, his neck, and then started moving down.

"What are you doing?" he said tightly.

"Just something I feel like doing," I replied.

My mouth was now on his chest, over one small nipple. I bit it, and he gasped sharply, so I sucked and licked the pain away.

"Harper," he said through gritted teeth. "You don't have to."

"I know." I moved lower. "I want to." I stopped and cocked my head. "Unless you'd rather I didn't."

"I never said *that*."

The following Monday at school, Tessa Carlyle fell into step beside me in the hallway, a Starbucks in hand. "Now that is a ring."

"Oh, thanks," I said, and covered my fingers self-consciously.

"You do ***not*** have to hide that beauty from me," she said, grabbing my hand and admiring it. "From Orion, right?"

"Yes. Christmas."

"Oh my God. I'm so jealous. I'm sorry, I shouldn't keep saying that, but he is *so* hot and, according to you, the world's best pianist, *and* you get to have sex with him on a semi-regular basis."

I laughed. "He spoils me, honestly. The other night we went to a beautiful restaurant, and then after, he played the Nocturne for me."

"Kinky."

"Indeed. He was rewarded generously."

"Oh? Do tell. Like I said, I'm surrounded by gay boys and have zero prospects. I need to live vicariously through you."

I don't know what possessed me; usually I never kiss

and tell, but once upon a time, back in Pittsburgh, I'd been a bold, give-no-fucks kind of gal.

I shrugged and said coyly, "I may or may not have gone down on him until he came so hard, he forgot his own name."

"Jesus, Harper!" Tessa had been lifting her Starbucks to her mouth. "I nearly spit out my coffee."

"Huh. I don't really have that problem."

"Oh *my God*." She laughed harder and shoved me in the arm. "You are terrible. I love it."

We rounded a corner, and there was Orion standing with a bunch of his Richie friends.

"There he is," Tessa said. "Girl, look at him."

Orion shot me a wink as we passed, and Tessa just about fainted.

"He's so charming," she said. "He's *Prince* Charming, surrounded by Tucker the meathead, Rhett the serial killer, and Blake, Blake, and Blake."

"That's a lot of Blakes."

"Those guys are all the same. So boring. Orion is the only good one," Tessa declared. "You lucked out."

"Yeah," I said, my smile fading.

"Oh no." She peered up at me; she was a petite little thing. "What just happened?"

"Nothing. Things have been great. My home life is a complete shit show, I'm stressed to the max, but he's the best. But the end of the year is racing toward us, and we haven't talked about what happens after."

"Oh," she said. "What's the plan?"

"He's supposed to go back to the UK and go to Cambridge, and I'm hoping the NoSci will get me into MIT or NYU with a bunch of scholarship help and some prize money."

"Are you going to NYU?" Tessa bounced up and down. "That's my dream school. Did you apply?"

"Yes, but I've almost forgotten all about it because I don't have a prayer of paying for it, and I don't know what I'm going to do about my little brother."

"What do you mean?"

I waved a hand. "Nothing. Long story."

"Well, I hope it all works out. You're brilliant and it would be so wonderful if we went there together, even if we're locked away in different departments. And maybe you should just sit down with Orion and talk it out?"

It sounded so simple when she put it that way. The best I could do was a whispered *stay...*

"Yes, but..." I bit my lip and decided to be really honest. "This is exactly the situation I wanted to avoid. I didn't want to be with somebody and really..."

"Love them?"

I nodded. "Unless it was real. And this is real, but every time the subject of him playing piano instead of working for his father's company comes up, he deflects or makes jokes. I think we're both just afraid to have that conversation because what if it's the end? I mean, we're in high school." I touched the ring on my hand. "It's not like I can demand a different kind of ring. I can't demand forever."

Tessa bit her lip, thinking. "Well...why not?"

I made a face. "Because who does that?"

"People who are in love?" She shrugged. "I'm not inside your relationship, but I've been in a lot of plays and musicals, and they're all stories. And all stories are love stories. Every single one. Maybe I'm just a hopeless romantic, but if he loves you and you love him, then there's no reason why your story can't go on forever."

"Thanks, Tessa."

"Anytime," she said brightly. "Go have your talk, and then have more sexy times so you can tell me all about it. That made my day."

"Happy to be of service."

She left, and I thought she took her optimism with her, but then I noticed Bandit, the vending machine, across the hall.

Maybe...

Chapter 31

ORION

I POINTED MY IPHONE CAMERA AT THE GROUND, HIT *record*, and narrated.

"Now, we pour the polymer into sample number three of our experiment, and watch the magic happen."

Keeping the camera trained on the ground with my left hand, I poured my concoction. It oozed, thick and grayish-black, into the hole in the ground.

"Voilà. The pothole magically begins to close," I said. "As you can see, the ionic bonds create a chemical 'grip' with the oxidized asphalt already present in the road. No need for heavy machinery or road closures, and the polymers will dry within an hour. You can refer to the project report for my materials list and experiments detailing the steps I took to arrive at these conclusions. Thank you very much."

I shut off the camera. "Bollocks. It worked."

Well, it was a vanity project as far as science experiments went. Nothing compared to Harper's water-purification system that would actually benefit communities and save lives. Even if she had to work with cheap "ugly buckets" while I had access to all the world-class materials I could ever want. I was confident mine was enough to please my parents that I'd tried, but not enough to wow the judges for a win.

Lush greenery just brushing off winter's white and birdsong surrounded me. Harper's house was just down the street and around the corner in this Bend neighborhood where the potholes were plenty. I thought about popping in, but I didn't want to interrupt her work or embarrass her if she was having a bad day. Instead, I packed up my equipment and headed back to the Academy for my lesson with Ezra.

I headed into the STEM Wing to stow my NoSci project equipment and then headed to the Arts Wing. Ezra was waiting for me in the Advanced Piano room. He had a strange smile on his face, and he was rocking back on his heels, hands in the pockets of his black coat.

"What are we so happy about?" I asked, dumping my bag on the piano bench. "Did the Academy renew your contract for another year?"

"God, no." Ezra's smile turned into a grimace. "Do you think that would be cause for celebration? No, the Orchestre de Paris has invited me to be a featured soloist across multiple programs in the fall, and the Accademia Nazionale di Santa Cecilia has pinned me down as their resident concert pianist in the spring. I'm a kept man."

"Congratulations!" I said. "That *is* cause for celebration."

"Thank you, but that's not why I'm smiling," Ezra said. "This Friday, at one o'clock, the chair of the Piano Department *and* the associate dean of music from Juilliard are coming *here* to listen to *you* audition for their illustrious institution."

I froze. A dividing line seemed to draw itself in the sand right before me. The *later* I kept putting off was suddenly here, and all the fear and uncertainty and *not enough* I'd been harboring for years came roaring up. I couldn't do this. I wasn't good enough. I could barely write. I was an embarrassment… It all hijacked my mind, and I felt like a passenger on a speeding train, wanting to get off and too scared of where I might land if I did.

"Ezra…"

"I know, I know," he said, waving his hands. "You haven't decided, and I'm not trying to bully you, despite all evidence to the contrary. Just think of it as insurance. Keeping your options open, though it's not every day those important people are willing to travel on the word of a miscreant like me. But honestly, Orion, your Étude is perfect, and the spring concert is one week too late for their schedule. Now is your opportunity, and you must seize it. Harness that incredible talent of yours and show it to them."

"Ezra, even if I agreed with your *questionable tactics*, the Head of the Bay Regatta is on Friday. I have to row."

He stared at me for a moment, then ran his hands over his face. "Oh, bloody hell, I forgot."

"You *forgot*? The entire school's been talking about nothing else for weeks. I've mentioned it at least a hundred times."

"Well, perhaps it slipped my mind because sitting in a thin little boat, pushing a paddle back and forth is nowhere near as important as Juilliard."

"Or perhaps it slipped your mind because you're drunk all the damn time."

His eye's widened, his tone stiff. "Cheeky, aren't we?"

"I'm sorry," I said, waving my hands. "That was uncalled for."

"To put it mildly."

"But you can't just make these kinds of decisions for me."

"*Well, someone bloody has to!*" he shouted. "Are you telling me you're going to walk away from your craft? From that life?"

"What life?" I shouted back. "*Life* is not going to *accommodate* me just because I can play. I don't speak the language of music. I can't write. I'm going to embarrass myself."

"Who told you that?" Ezra said incredulously. "Who… what lies are you listening to? Because it's bollocks." He leveled a finger at me. "You were abandoned for ten years, and you're still abandoned. Even now. And so you're scared. I get it, Orion. But—"

"I'm not *abandoned*," I retorted with a snort. "I'm not *scared*."

Terrified, maybe…

"No? How about this," Ezra said. "Are you going to walk away from Harper?"

I stared, fumbling for something to say.

"You don't get it, do you?" he continued. "Do you know why your Étude is brilliant? Because of her. Because of *love*. She has cracked open your heart, and you're going to walk away?"

"I…haven't decided yet."

"Yes, yes, yes, you haven't decided yet." He flapped his hands, storming for the door. "When is yet? When is later? When is soon? Because there will come a time, Orion, when *yet* and *later* and *soon* become *too late*."

I went to crew practice down by the docks under a gray sky and cold air, my mood just as gray and stormy, muttering and cursing under my breath, telling myself that Ezra Wolfe had no right to talk to me like that. He was a piano teacher, not a therapist. He didn't know what the fuck he was talking about.

Because it's just so simple to upheave your entire life. To leave your family's empire and everything they had planned for you to play little songs for a living.

But the thoughts rang hollow. Empty. Which only infuriated me more.

Rhett sneered. "Who pissed in your Cheerios, Mercer?"

"You can fuck all the way off, Calloway."

"Whoa, whoa, whoa." Tucker stepped between us, while Xander and Dean watched, ready to intervene. "Now, guys, let's be cool. We got the Head of the Bay in five short days, and we're going to kill it. Once we do that, we only have one regatta left and the season is ours."

Rhett shrugged narrow shoulders. "Sure, sure," he said with a snide smile. "Just make sure Mercer has someone help him read the road signs. Wouldn't want him getting lost on the way to the docks."

Instantly, a red haze fell over my vision and I lunged at him, but Tucker held me back and then gave Rhett a not-too-gentle shove. He took me by the shoulders. "You okay, man? Don't listen to Calloway. He's just blowing off steam."

"Sure he is," I said, while Tucker was doing anything and everything to keep the peace in order to get his win.

"Hey," he said. "Speaking of blowing off steam, I was thinking after we win this thing, we have a big party. A rager. We haven't had one in a while."

"Yeah, okay," I said absently, my mind still in the piano room. A Juilliard audition right there in my hands, and instead I was going to be here, with Rhett Calloway sitting behind me, rowing a little stick…

"Cool," Tucker was saying, "but the party can't really be at my house 'cause my parents are in town. In fact, everybody's parents are in town."

"Yeah. And?"

"Well…your parents are *not* in town. In fact, your parents are clear across the Atlantic. What about having it at Atlas Hall?"

I nodded, thinking. "Yeah, I could do that. I could totally do that."

The school wouldn't care. I was a goddamn Mercer. I was Big Five. I could do whatever the fuck I wanted.

"Sure," I said. "I'll hire somebody and get it rolling."

"Fuck yeah!" Tucker said. "We're going to win this thing, and then we're going to celebrate in style."

"One hundred percent."

Because screw Ezra Wolfe. He didn't get to decide my life for me. No one did but me.

And Harper…?

But Coach Daniels and the assistant coach were heading toward us to start practice.

I turned to Rhett. "Hey, if you're a good boy, Calloway, I might let you come to my party."

Chapter 32

HARPER

At my desk in my room, I placed the turbidity and pH test strips in the water samples that had been filtrated with either sand, gravel, cheesecloth, or charcoal layers, and then noted the results. I noted the best reduction in sediment and the drinkable pH, then moved on to bacteria testing. A tired grin spread over my lips.

"Thank God." My results were as I predicted. Drinkable water…which wasn't bad considering I'd had to budget like a madwoman for the materials.

I hastily wrote up my results and set them on my desk. I'd leave the formal write-up for next week and start rehearsing my presentation for next Thursday.

My phone chimed with a text from Tessa.

Check your mail???

I frowned. No. Why?

Um hello???

A photo popped up of a college acceptance letter from NYU.

"Oh, shit."

In all my Mom drama, I'd started to think I couldn't do any college without the NoSci. Not a poor Bend kid like me who'd need the gross GDP of a small nation in student loans to pay for any of it.

Congrats!!! I typed. I'm not surprised.

Thanks but Go. Mail. Now.

I headed downstairs, my stomach queasy. Mom was on the couch napping. Or passed out. Hard to tell these days. Dash was watching cartoons.

"Hey, buddy," I said. "Did you hear the mailman?"

"Yep," he said without taking his eyes off the screen. My little brother used to get ridiculously excited about the mail. He used to get excited about a lot of things. I shot my mother a dagger glare.

I'll never forgive her. Never.

I went to the mailbox. Amid envelopes stamped with

scary things like *open now* and *urgent* and *final notice,* there was a thick manila envelope from NYU.

"Holy shit."

I brought it all inside on shaking legs. At the kitchen counter, I opened the envelope. Inside was a brochure and some paperwork, but on top was a letter with NYU letterhead.

Dear Ms. Bennett,

It is our greatest pleasure to inform you…

The letter fell out of my hand, and I gripped the counter. Tears blurred my vision, and joy ballooned in my heart. It wasn't MIT, my first choice, but NYU was a world-class school, and they wanted me. Me.

I have a home…

"Harper?" Dash asked. "Are you okay?"

"Fine, buddy. Got some good news, actually."

"What is it?"

"I got into college. In New York."

Dash's face fell. "You're going to move to New York?"

My mother stirred and sat up. "Who's moving to New York?"

"Harper," Dash said, crying now.

"Well, wait," I said, my elation deflating. "I just got accepted. I don't know…"

"Isn't that nice for you," Mom said, smiling thinly. "With *Orion*? Is he going to buy a penthouse in the Upper East Side for the two of you while we lose our house?"

"Wow, okay," I said, letting the letter fall to the counter. "I guess a *congratulations* is too much to ask for. And I don't know what Orion is doing after graduation, now that you mention it."

Now that I *mention it. Out loud. For the first time.*

Tears sprang to my eyes.

"But thank you *so much* for taking this happy moment and completely fucking it all up." I snatched the letter and waved it. "This is what we came here for. So I could get into a good college. Which I did, no thanks to you. And if you're so goddamned concerned about this house, then get off your ass and get a job."

"How dare you—"

"Come here, Dash," I said, holding out my hand. "We're going to Mrs. A's."

He nodded, sniffling. I came around the counter, into the living room, with the rest of the mail.

"A really smart man once told me that lack of love is one reason people drink," I said, standing over my mother, my voice trembling. "Well, here we are. Your love." I slammed the unpaid bills and notices into her lap. "But if you keep going, this is all you're going to have instead."

And then I walked out.

—

I spent the rest of the week concentrating on school and taking care of Dash. Mom and I rarely spoke, though I noticed she was taking more shifts and going to more AA meetings. But if she wanted a kudos, she'd have to do more than that.

I didn't spend time with Orion either, or even share my news about NYU. Texting him about it didn't feel right, and the only time we saw each other in person was in class, where he was strangely distant after our beautiful Nocturne date. I told myself it was because we were both busy with the NoSci, and he had the upcoming regatta and a party he was throwing at Atlas Hall right after.

And his upcoming performance at the spring concert?

He hadn't said one word about it. Every time I thought about Orion playing at that concert, a strange feeling filled my chest. Hard and heavy, like a boulder of words built from everything we couldn't say. Everything we *didn't* say about the future. *Our* future, if we had one. I'd been too afraid of being hurt, and he'd been too afraid to step out of his family's protective castle to consider something different for himself beyond this year.

We're way past that. Aren't we?

Friday afternoon, I was on my way to join Emery to watch the Head of the Bay Regatta, when I spied Ezra Wolfe walking to his car in the staff parking lot, adjacent to the marina.

"Professor Wolfe!" I called and hurried to catch up to him.

He stopped, his long black coat nearly brushing the ground. "Ah, Harper," he said, smiling sadly. "How can I help you?"

"It's been a shit sandwich of a week, but I got some good news and haven't had a chance to tell anyone. But you've been really great this year, and so I want to tell you." Of course, my stupid eyes had to go and tear up again. "Dammit. I swear I've cried more these last six months than I have my entire life."

"I know the feeling." Wolfe put a black-nailed hand over his chest. "I'd be honored to hear your good news, Ms. Bennett."

"I got into NYU. I thought I'd have to win a certain science contest—and I do, because I desperately need the money—but, yeah. They accepted me. And if I say that one more time—accepted—I'm going to really cry."

"You go right ahead," Wolfe said. "I've heard it told that weeping happens when a soul feels an emotion that is too big for the body to contain. Congratulations, Ms. Bennett. I, for one, am not surprised in the least."

I wiped the heel of my hand over my eyes. "Thank you for that. And for listening." I heaved a breath. "Not going to the regatta?"

"No," he said, strangely flat. "But tell our mutual friend good luck."

I started to go when Wolfe stopped me.

"It's interesting, isn't it? Juilliard and NYU are both in Manhattan, a short subway ride away."

"Yes," I said slowly. "Why?"

"No reason," he said grimly. "Except I'm a terrible person. I meddle and manipulate and stick my nose in where I shouldn't because I *cannot* imagine that boy pushing numbers behind a desk when..." He bit off his words and shook his head. "Forgive me. Ask *him* to forgive me, and tell him that I was wrong. Tell him it's never too late. Never."

With Wolfe's cryptic words ringing in my ears, I'd joined Emery Wallace on the bleachers, smashed in with the rest of the Academy, to watch the Head of the Bay Regatta. Colorful flags and banners decorated the marina, as our Royal Pride rowing crew took on three different schools in half a dozen different races.

We'd already watched the singles, twos, and the fours win their races, and now Xander and Orion's race, the men's eight, was underway. Emery had my arm in a death grip as we waited for the boats to come from around the Bend. Her cheeks were flushed and her blue-green eyes were sparkling.

"You look positively radiant," I said. "What gives?"

"I didn't get into Brown," she said, not taking her eyes off the water. "Isn't that great?"

"Uh, congrats? Wait, did your dad flip his lid?"

Her tyrannical father had been adamant Emery attend Brown when she wanted to go to a different school. Have a different life with Xander.

"That's the best part," she said. "He didn't seem all that pissed. I think maybe he's coming around."

"Or he's got a plan B. Em, are you sure—?"

"Here they come!"

The crowd on the bleachers got to its feet, cheering on their guys, while the teams on the dock pumped their fists for their boys.

Our boys wore black-and-gold unisuits and iridescent sunglasses, their bodies moving in perfect synchronized precision as they fought for dominance against two other schools. Emery's eyes were glued to Xander, closest to Dean as coxswain. She was practically drooling.

"Girl..."

She giggled. "I know, but can you blame me?"

I found Orion, second from last at the head of the boat, moving with catlike grace and beauty...

"No," I told Emery. "I can't."

The crowd grew louder as the race got close with the finish line only a few meters away. But our guys pulled as if their lives depended on it while Dean bellowed his commands with an aggression I'd never seen from my friend before.

Emery gripped my arm tighter as the race came down to the finish.

I wasn't into sports, but I was into Orion. I let the

electric hum of energy from the crowd infect me too, and then I was jumping up and down, adding my voice to the crowd, hoping my energy would find him and give him the extra support he needed.

The boats were neck and neck until ours pulled ahead just as they crossed the finish line.

"They won." Emery had me by the shoulders. "They won!"

"Yes, I see that."

But I was laughing too, caught up in it. We joined the crowd running to the crew as their boats were pulled ashore. Every man was exhausted but happy, slumped over and patting each other on the back.

I ran to Dean and threw my arms around his neck. "Congrats!"

"Thank you, thank you," he said, grinning tiredly. "For the only guy on the shell who didn't row, I'm surprisingly exhausted."

His smile tilted, and I watched him meet eyes with Sierra. She smiled shyly and wiggled her fingers at him surreptitiously, before laughing loudly with a group of popular Richies.

"Still a bridge too far?" I asked, my heart aching for him.

"Yep." He smiled ruefully. "Eh, what can you do?"

I hugged him again. "Hey. I love you."

"Aw shucks. Love you too, my friend, but why so serious? It's just a boat race."

"Nothing. Life. You know how it is." I shook my head and then watched, shocked, as Emery threw her arms around Xander's neck and kissed him in front of everybody.

"Well, what do you know," Dean said. "There's hope for us Benders yet."

I searched for Orion in the crowd. He'd always maintained that he never cared what anyone thought about us. Maybe I'd be brave too and throw myself at him, and tell him about NYU and how I didn't want him to leave…

But when our gazes clashed, he smiled and waved and turned away, celebrating with his team.

"Harper?" Dean said, breaking me from my thoughts.

"Sorry, what?"

"You're coming to the party tonight, right?"

"I suppose."

"You don't sound enthused."

I smiled grimly. "Let's just say watching a bunch of people I care about get drunk out of their minds isn't my favorite thing right now."

"Orion's not a big drinker, at least," Dean said. "And I promise to behave."

"You're the best." I gave another hug and a kiss on the cheek. "Congrats again."

I got lost in the crowd and headed back to my car. In the driver's seat, I texted Orion.

Congrats on the win.

I was at home, in my room, when the reply came.

Thank you, love! Got swamped after the race with team stuff, but I can't wait to see you at the party. We'll kiss in front of the whole bloody school so I can show off my woman, proper.

My thumb touched the gorgeous ring on my middle finger as Wolfe's words came back to me, along with that unpleasant feeling. That mountain of words unsaid between us. But over text was not the time, and Orion had just won his race.

Tonight. We'll find some time tonight.

I'll be there. <3

Chapter 33

ORION

After the post-race wrap-up from Coach, I showered and changed into designer plaid pants in brown and beige, and a cream-colored Loewe hoodie, and then hurried back to Atlas Hall to oversee the party prep in the center courtyard and connecting lounge. The caterers, decorators, and DJ I'd hired were all hard at work, setting up tables of food and drink, stringing up lights and sound systems, and lighting up the fountain in the center of the courtyard with a rainbow of changing colors. As I'd predicted, my last name meant that the Academy administration turned a blind eye to all of it, and our regatta win sealed the deal.

Because we'd done what was expected of us: We'd won.

The crate of booze I'd gotten from a guy who knew a

guy, however, was discreetly kept out of sight. No need to push it, after all.

I usually didn't partake much myself, but after the adrenaline rush of the race had faded, a lot of *thinking* had swooped back in, and I wasn't in the mood for thinking. Time was racing out from under me just like the Narragansett waters, carrying me to my future.

Not bloody yet, thank you very much.

So as the partygoers began to trickle in, I began to sample the product. For quality-assurance purposes, of course. The punch was sickly sweet and yet bitingly strong with vodka. I downed one Solo cup of the concoction and then another, and that was all it took for me to become buzzed enough that *thinking* could bugger off for the night.

My crewmates surrounded me, and Tucker wasted no time passing around a flask that he'd already half drained.

"Orion!" he shouted, draping a heavy arm over my shoulders. "Thizzparty is the shit," he slurred. "You've outdone yourself."

Rhett eyed me coolly, saying nothing. On his best behavior lest I toss his arse out. Before I could reply, Xander Ford strode right up to Tucker, snatched the flask from his hand, and turned it vertical.

Then he handed it back and wiped his mouth. "Thanks. I needed that."

I met Tucker's glance, and then we both busted out laughing.

"Ford, you're a goddamn madman. This is the best fucking crew in CHA history!"

Xander was jostled and hugged, and more drinks went around. I tossed back another just as Harper approached slowly. Warily. Watching the boys as if they were a pack of hyenas. She looked so beautiful in a green dress with small red flowers, her hair falling softly around her shoulders.

My goddamn heart.

"Harper!" I said, and she flinched and studied me, disappointed. "I'm shouting, aren't I?"

"Just a little."

"Apologies. I've had a wee bit to drink." I drank *her* in, drank her up. "God, you are…so fucking beautiful."

"Thank you," she said. "You look amazing too, and your race was incredible. But I've hardly seen you all week. I was hoping we could talk, but I guess not."

She glanced down, and I wasn't too drunk to notice the sadness in her eyes. The uncertainty and the questions and everything we'd left unsaid needing to be said. I owed Harper so much; I owed her more than jokes and deflections, and now I was too bloody drunk.

The guilt bit me hard and sharp, and so of course, I got silly. Stupid. A selfish jackass, still clinging to *later*.

"Tonight is supposed to be fun. Come, come," I said. "Have a drink."

"No, thanks," she said as I fumbled for a Solo cup at the punch table.

"But it's a party."

"I said, no thanks. My mother does enough drinking for the both of us."

"Oh, right." I set down my cup and pulled her to me. "What's wrong? You have a line. Right here. A cute little worry line…" I traced the little furrow between her eyes with a finger. "Let me guess. Bills piling up."

Harper's eyes flared, and she shoved away from me. "Will you keep your voice down? Jesus, Orion."

"I'm sorry, love," I said. "But I hate how hard everything is for you. I know, I know, you don't want me to help, but let me cover whatever you owe. You have your pride, but what's the alternative? You become homeless?"

She stared at me as if she couldn't believe what she was hearing. *I* couldn't believe what I was hearing, the words spewing out of me on a tide of vodka and defensive nonsense. She crossed her arms, tears standing out in her eyes, but her gaze was unwavering.

"Oh, we're doing this right now? Okay, let's say I let you help me, Orion," she said. "Then what? How long will you continue to pity me, long after you and I are nothing? Will you deposit money into my account every month? For years? Until you get married? I can't imagine your wife will approve."

"My wife… What are you talking about?"

"You're going back to the UK at the end of the year, aren't you?"

I took a step back, pushed by her words.

You bloody wanker, you're fucking it all up.

"So what happens to us?" she continued. "Who am I to you when we graduate? The girl you once dated? Your charity case? You and I will be finished, but I'll have this debt hanging over my head. Just what the hell am I supposed to do with that?"

"No, I..." I stammered like a fool. "That is not how..."

"All this time," she said, her voice hard but quavering. "All this time with the *I love yous* and the romance and the taking me to meet your family, and I was such an idiot. I told myself not to let anyone in. That I didn't have the bandwidth to deal with my mother's bullshit, and the pressure, and everything else to give my heart away. But I thought, 'No, he's different. This is going somewhere, and he's too talented to give up his music. He won't...'" Her voice cracked. "'He won't give me up.'" She tilted her head up. Defiant. Strong. "But I guess I was wrong."

"Harper..." I said helplessly.

"Have a nice life."

Then she turned and walked away.

I stared in drunken incapacity, watching her go. I didn't know anything. Not my future, not what was going to happen next week, or what I was going to say to my parents or Cambridge or Juilliard or any of it. The only thing I knew was that the best thing in my life just walked away.

I started after her when a scream ripped through the noise of the party. A bloodcurdling scream that made hearts stop and the DJ cut the music.

Sierra Hart was on the ground with Dean, his head in her lap. For a strange, panicked second, my brain told me that he was sleeping or had passed out. But I already knew in the deepest part of me that was a lie.

No…

A crowd had started to form, and Xander Ford collapsed on his knees beside our friend. My incapacity vanished, and terror like I'd never known lit me up from the inside, burning away the alcohol. I shoved through the people, screaming for an ambulance. I lay Dean flat and started chest compressions. There was no thought in my mind, nothing but adrenaline and denial. Because this couldn't happen. I would *not allow* this to happen. I could not let Dean be dead.

But he is. Oh God, help me, he is…

Xander grabbed Dean's jaw and gave him a shake, demanding he wake up. He blew air in his mouth while I pressed both palms over his heart, but Dean wasn't unconscious, and we both knew it. Xander met my eye and for a second—he and I were locked in the same helpless communion. An understanding of the truth and a fierce rejection of it at the same time. I shook my head, and Xander made a sound I never wanted to hear again in my entire life. An agonized cry erupting from deep in his chest.

"*No!*" he bellowed, and slapped Dean across the face and blew more air while I pressed on his chest until my shoulders ached. Finally, help arrived, and we were pushed outside the circle. Helpless. Sierra was screaming. Harper was in Xander's arms, clinging to him, crying in his shirt, while I watched the EMTs work on Dean. Cold. Numb.

Because it was too late.

He'd fallen through the ice.

Chapter 34

ORION

The funeral was a blur.

My brain held on to snapshots. It was sunny out; I remember that. Xander gave a eulogy, the words a beautiful stream of noise floating through me. Dean's parents were in the front row, shell-shocked and pale. Sierra was behind them, sobbing into her hands. Harper had tears streaking her cheeks like silver.

The day before, Coach Daniels had asked me to say something. "A little bit of humor can't hurt, Orion."

I'd stared at him blankly. Xander had accused Rhett of murder. He said he'd seen Rhett give Dean a pill at the party. My party. The pill had been laced with fentanyl. One unlucky dose. I thought I'd be overcome with murderous rage for Rhett. That just the sight of him would have me tackling him to the ground and beating him until his face was unrecognizable. Until my fingers were ruined, and I'd never play piano again. That's what I deserved because it was my fault. My party.

Is that what Coach wanted me to say?

"Dearly beloved, we are gathered here today because I know how to throw one hell of a rager."

People started getting up from their seats, which meant the funeral was over. Harper stuck close to Emery. She wouldn't look at me, much less speak to me. Not that I blamed her. I'd been drunk that night but not drunk enough that I didn't remember what I'd said.

Another layer of shame and guilt and pain. A tsunami of emotion churned below, but I felt none of it. I was cold. Frozen. As if I'd been locked in a block of ice and it hadn't thawed out.

I didn't go to the reception. The reception was for shaking hands and hugging Dean's loved ones and telling them how sorry you were that he was gone, as if you weren't in on it. As if you were just a bystander. That wasn't me.

Tuesday. The NoSci presentations were the next week, Mum and Father were flying in for the award ceremony, then came the spring concert, and none of it made any bloody sense. The way that life just kept going, as if nothing had happened. It didn't give a shit that an extraordinary person had disappeared off the earth but expected you to just go about your day, business as usual.

And growing up in my house, my childhood, we didn't have big emotions. I had no idea where I was supposed to put all this grief. This enormous boulder of pain that I didn't want but was forced to swallow anyway.

Dean? Dean Yearwood? What is wrong with this world?

And I'd thrown the party.

That little tidbit was piss icing on the world's biggest shit cake, and if I thought about it too hard, I'd go mad. It had to stay down in the depths while I wandered the surface, cold and detached and numb.

"Orion?" Easton said, as I moved like a zombie through our dorm. "Are you okay? I'm so sorry about your friend..."

"Oh, I'm bloody brilliant," I said flatly, heading for the door. "I have crew practice. Can you believe that?"

"Hey, man. You don't have to go."

"What else am I going to do?"

Easton only frowned, concerned, but I didn't have anything in me to care.

You're going to go sit in the shell where Dean sat not four days ago? Brilliant!

But the mindless emptiness had me trudging like a sleepwalker down to the marina.

Rhett was there with Tucker, looking like a guilty little weasel. Again, I wondered why I didn't fly at him to beat him bloody, but that would require emotions, and mine were locked down tight. Xander Ford arrived, looking like the walking dead. He stared at Rhett as if he couldn't believe what he was seeing.

Coach huddled us up. "I know this is going to be a tough day. We've lost one of our own, and as hard as it is…" His voice cracked. "We have a season to finish, and I'd like to think that Dean would want us to finish strong. To make him proud."

We all headed for the water, quiet, solemn, and climbed into the shell. Rhett was like a wraith behind me. A shadow. My skin crawled and broke out into gooseflesh.

What are you doing here? Instead of being with Harper? Or sitting at a piano? Or doing literally anything else that is honest and real.

Ahead of me, Xander muttered under his breath, "Jesus fucking Christ," and tossed his oar into the water. He climbed out and sloshed through waist-deep water toward land.

Coach Daniels, on the shore, tried to stop him. "Now, hold on, son…"

Xander knocked his hand away. "Don't fucking touch me."

Yes. Xander. He's doing it right. Follow him.

I clambered out of the shell and caught up to him. "Xander, wait. Talk to me."

Tell me how to do this…

He spun around, and his eyes widened at Rhett behind me. Xander pushed past me, back into the water.

"He killed Dean," he said, then again, his voice rising. "He killed him! He fucking killed him, and we're all just going to pretend like nothing happened? Business as fucking usual?"

"Now, hold on, man," Tucker said, climbing out and moving between him and Rhett while Coach Daniels and I held Xander back.

"Get off me," he snarled, and ripped himself out of our grip. "What the fuck is wrong with you?" he screamed at all of us. "Did he mean *nothing* to you? Whatever it takes, eh? Win at all costs. Win no matter what. Put him back on the boat like nothing happened. As if Dean were never here at all."

"Now, son—" Coach began.

"I'm not your son. I'm not on this team. I'm done. Done with this fucking place."

I watched him stalk away.

Coach shook his head at me. "Orion. Don't."

Tucker glared at me. "Mercer, don't you dare. We're one win away."

A win? It made no sense. Didn't they get it? Xander got it. We'd already lost.

I walked away too.

Chapter 35

HARPER

The Saturday after Dean's funeral, Orion and I stood as witnesses at Emery and Xander's wedding, because somehow that was life now. The best people died while others got married to separate—Xander marrying Emery to free her from her parents' money so she could leave the state, not so he could be with her.

I couldn't look at Orion. Admittedly, I'd freaked out at him at the party. But for all I knew, he was still going across the ocean, and I couldn't think about that now. My mother barely left the couch. The light was going out in Dash's eyes, and he spent more time with Mrs. Andolina. I had to stay focused on NoSci—because we needed the money, and because if I stopped to breathe, I'd lose my mind.

Because Dean. Oh my God, Dean.

That sweet, kind boy who saw the best in everyone, the first person to welcome me to this snake pit of a school, was gone. Erased.

He'd been taking amphetamines—provided by Rhett—to keep up with his two jobs, school, and taking care of his parents. One had been unknowingly laced with fentanyl. It was so unfair I could barely breathe.

But I had to keep moving. Give my presentation. Try to keep my family from falling apart.

Last night I packed a duffel with my materials and made two trips to the car with buckets and samples. This morning—Thursday morning—was do or die.

I pulled on a deep-green dress scattered with tiny wildflowers, a mustard corduroy jacket, scuffed brown lace-up boots, and my battered leather satchel. I drew a breath, hoping I looked professional. Serious.

Dash was with Mrs. Andolina again. Mom was on the couch, smoking cigarettes—an old habit she'd recently renewed—a mug of coffee in one hand, the TV remote in the other, and last night's wine bottle and glass arrayed before her. She didn't bother hiding the drinking anymore, and AA meetings were a distant memory.

"You look nice," she said tiredly. "Where are you off to?"

"The Academy," I said. "NoSci presentations are today, remember?"

"NoSci?"

"The Novus Prize for Scientific Innovation," I said through gritted teeth. "The one with the $25,000 reward."

"Oh, right, right," she said. "Yeah, we need that money. The Airbnb business has been pretty dry lately."

Her choice of words had me biting the inside of my cheek.

"Okay, so… I'm off," I said at the door.

"Good luck, baby," she said, her eyes glued to the TV.

"Thanks," I murmured and went out.

At the Academy, in the STEM Wing auditorium, a table was reserved for each of the contestants for our presentations. Hopeful students, about twelve of us, stood in a semicircle at their tables or spoke in animated but hushed tones. On the stage was the award itself and space for the judges, press, and dignitaries from various universities. It all became really damn real.

I went to my table where my Ugly Buckets, sample containers, and laptop were ready. We would each have access to a PowerPoint, and tech wasn't my strong suit; I wanted to ensure my slides were perfect.

Orion was at his table with his Gray Ooze experiment. His table looked neat, professional; his materials were top of the line while mine were cheap as hell.

It's fine. It's the content that counts.

Our eyes met. He looked tired but blank. His eyes completely devoid of any *twinkle*. I know he blamed himself for Dean because he'd thrown the party, and what was left of my shattered heart wanted to go to him. To tell him it wasn't his fault. But I had almost nothing left in the tank.

Get through this presentation, and then…

But I couldn't see beyond that. My future rested on the cheap plastic filtration system I'd devised that may have looked ugly but actually worked. And worked well.

After a few minutes, the judges entered, and the auditorium went silent.

"Good afternoon. I'm Dr. Milford Hargrave, head of our STEM department," said a tall, thin man with a gray beard. "You know Dr. Ian Langford, and it is my honor to introduce to you, Dr. Regina Chen from MIT. We are your judges for today's presentations."

My heart began to thud as Hargrave explained the procedures, and my eyes found Orion. He smiled faintly. Sadly. And then the contest began.

I watched as the three judges made the rounds.

After what felt like an eternity, the judges made it to Orion's table. Orion was entirely checked out but came to life like a performer putting on a show to explain his Gray Ooze self-closing pothole polymer. The judges seemed enchanted, impressed, and laughed loudly at his jokes. Even stiff Dr. Hargrave.

And then it was my turn.

"Right now, the system is designed for contaminated freshwater, especially in flood zones, using layered filtration and activated carbon to remove particulates, chemicals, and organic compounds. I've achieved 98 percent clarity. Additional cleansing comes from sunlight, which heats the water, causing it to evaporate. The vapor condenses and is collected here. It doesn't require electricity, only heat and time, so it could be scaled for disaster zones or remote communities. The filtration unit can handle debris and pollutants, but I see no reason why, potentially, it can't be expanded for desalinization too."

The judges took notes, seemingly impressed. Langford wore an expression I couldn't read and asked a bunch of questions—far more than I heard him ask anyone else. I was prepared and answered everything thoroughly. The judges took more notes, and I saw them take in the cheapness of my materials. My cheeks reddened, but I held my head up.

"In times of sudden disaster, or in underserved communities, people can't wait around for billion-dollar industries to swoop in and provide clean drinking water," I said. "But they can start with an ugly bucket and a little bit of sunlight."

The judges exchanged glances, and Dr. Langford laughed. "Bravo. Well said, Harper."

I eased out a breath as they moved on. Orion approached slowly.

"That was brilliant," he said.

"Thanks, but I don't know. We'll see," I replied, hating how awkward and terrible and fucked up everything was now. "Yours sounded well-received."

"Mine is crap. I just did it to keep my parents happy, that's all. I'm not going to win shit."

I bit my lip. I wasn't so sure about that, but it was out of my hands. I'd done my best. That was all I could do.

His phone chimed a text. He glanced at it, frowning. "Mum and Father. They're here for the awards ceremony tomorrow. They want to go to dinner."

"That's nice. They're supportive—"

He barked a harsh laugh. "It's a farce that I'm even here. I should have dropped out a long time ago. But they came all this way, and I blew off the audition, and Dean..."

"Audition? What audition?" I said, my pulse jumping.

He only looked at me sadly. Strangely. "Good luck, Harper."

"Orion, wait."

But he was already gone.

My classes were cancelled due to the NoSci presentations, but the last thing I wanted to do was go home. Emery was busy preparing her prom decorations, and Tessa was in rehearsals for *Les Mis,* so I loitered at school until I couldn't loiter anymore. And then I remembered I'd left my laptop in the auditorium for the PowerPoint section of my presentation.

The auditorium was quiet, dark. I moved to my table to put my laptop in my old leather satchel and ran a hand over one of my "ugly" filtration units.

Come on, Universe. For Dash.

"Ms. Bennett. Working late, I see."

I jumped, instantly tense all over. "Oh. Professor Langford. Hi."

He wore khaki pants and a blue button-down shirt from earlier today but without his blazer. He flashed me a grin, his teeth white under the fluorescents as he approached.

A lot of the girls in school thought he was handsome, with his big blue eyes and swoop of thick gold hair. I guessed he was about the same age as Ezra Wolfe—late thirties—but I'd never felt comfortable with him. Just being in Langford's space made me itchy.

"Your presentation was very good today," he said, perusing my materials. "Impressive. The most impressive, honestly."

"Professor Langford, as a judge, are you supposed to be telling me that?" I asked carefully. "Before the announcement, I mean."

"You're a bold young lady, aren't you, Ms. Bennett? I like that. I like that a lot."

He moved closer until he was right behind me, looking over my shoulder, his breath wafting over my neck. I suddenly wished I wasn't wearing a dress. And that I hadn't taken my jacket off.

"Your water-purification system is ingenious. I had a feeling you would pick something *noble*."

The front of his thigh was now brushing the back of my leg. I took a step to the left. "I think I should get going…"

"I take it you adhered to all the rules stringently?" he asked. "No outside help?"

"Of course not."

"I thought so," Langford said. He leaned his hand onto to the table, half caging me in. "It's just a little on the cheap side. Hargrave couldn't get around that."

I took another step away. "Excuse me?"

He stood up and crossed his arms, facing me. Standing close. "I've heard about your family's plight."

"Our plight?"

"Castle Hill is a very small town, Harper. People talk. My dentist, for instance. He told me all about a woman who was harassing him. A former employee named Maeve Bennett. She was begging for her job back because her roof had caved in. Causing a stink and making threats about exposing an affair." He smiled. "Some people will say anything when they're desperate, won't they?"

"I…I have to go."

I took a step back, my back hitting the edge of the table. He took a step forward and ran a finger down my bare arm. A cold shiver ran through every part of me.

"What are you doing?" I asked over the lump in my throat.

"You're a very beautiful young girl, Harper. I've thought that since day one. The way you sit in the front of the class, with your luscious body on display in your poor little dresses. But you know what you're doing, don't you?"

My blood iced over as he moved closer, towering over me, pinning me between himself and the table. I was frozen, a strange tingling adrenaline running through me that locked me in place. Hardly able to breathe and unable to move but for my heart that was kicking in my rib cage like a trapped animal.

"I've watched how you ogled Orion Mercer all year. He won the contest, you know."

My breath froze in my chest. Shock and fear and dread all falling over me like an avalanche.

"His parents give too much money to the school for it to go any other way. Not to mention his chemistry pedigree. And you came in at a valiant second place. But I can change that. I can help you, Harper."

His other hand came up, holding me by the shoulders, then he touched my cheek, cupped it, and ran his thumb over my lower lip, then down my neck toward my chest.

"Your project is the one that matters," he said. "That's why I'm trying to help you. I can sway Hargrave...if you cooperate. Because I believe in you. I can ensure that that prize money you need so badly is yours."

"No," I said, barely a whisper.

"Now, don't be like that..."

"No," I said, louder. "Stop touching me."

I pushed his chest with both hands, but it was like pushing a tree trunk. The placid smug smile on his face instantly turned into an ugly, angry sneer.

"Do not say no to me," he snarled, and then in the next instant, the smile was back. "You need the money. You deserve it. Why not just relax and let it happen?"

My breath was coming in short panting gusts, my thoughts racing.

Is this happening? Is this really happening? This cannot really be happening.

And it might've happened if one thought out of the blue hadn't come to me: Dean Yearwood, smiling at me and holding out a clipboard.

Answer me these questions three…

My frozen panic snapped. I drove my knee into Langford's groin. He made a strangled sound and folded in half. I shoved him back, drew my arm across my body, and snapped it out. The back of my hand cracked against his cheek—my middle finger smashed between Orion's ring and Langford's jawbone. Pain flared, sharp and heavy, but I barely felt it. I shoved past him and bolted for the door.

"Harper, *do not* run away from me," Langford intoned.

I had no idea where to go, or what to do. I ran in a blind panic out of the lab. I tried to call for help, but my throat had gone completely dry, and I couldn't bring air any deeper than my throat.

The hall was empty and quiet, but behind me, Langford was coming, and my mind fractured in two. I was me in that hallway, and I was also ten years old, running from a drunk boyfriend of my mother's. A monster who was bigger and faster than me, and who was going to hurt me. I had to hide.

Without thinking, I ran to the chemistry storage closet and keyed in the code with trembling fingers. I hauled open the heavy door, ran inside, and shut it behind me then shut off the lights.

The stupidity of my plan came at once, as the childhood memory faded, leaving me with the terrible *now*. The darkness and smallness of the space closed in on me, adding to my terror and panic. Surely Langford had seen me. I was trapped. Cornered. My chest constricted until I thought I would pass out. I huddled in the corner, pulled my knees to my chest. A small *clank* came from my side. The brass coin Orion had given me with his constellation on it had fallen out of my pocket. I snatched it up and rubbed my thumb over the stars over and over again, calling to him in my mind.

Find me, Orion. Please…

Nothing but silence. The darkness tried to swallow me whole. My bag with my phone was still in the auditorium, so I sat huddled in the corner, my face hot and dry, rubbing the coin, trying to breathe but remaining as quiet as possible. To make myself small. Invisible.

Finally, the adrenaline drained out, leaving me limp, wrung out, and then the tears came. Great hiccuping sobs. I tried to keep them muffled, but I couldn't help it. I cried for Dean, for my mother, for Dash, and for me. For what had just happened… And then I screamed as the door opened.

"Miss?" A janitor stood there with a mop in hand. "I thought I heard something…"

I scrambled to my feet and pushed past him, back to the auditorium that was dark and empty. I grabbed my bag and jacket and ran to the parking lot where I stopped short. There were only two cars in the parking lot: mine and Langford's. And Langford was leaning against his and glancing around. Waiting for me.

The fear gripped me all over again.

I turned and ran the other way. To Atlas Hall. I tore past the gal at the front desk and pounded on Orion's door.

He opened it, and I threw myself at him, clinging to him.

"Harper? What's going on?"

I heaved several deep breaths to calm down.

Orion held me at arm's length, studying me with growing alarm. "What happened?"

I raised my tearstained face. "Langford."

Chapter 36

HARPER

FOR THE BRIEFEST SECOND, DISBELIEF FLASHED ACROSS Orion's face, but he blinked it away, and anger swept in. "Tell me everything."

After I did, Orion's jaw clenched. "I'll kill him. I'll kill him right now."

"No," I said, calmer now. "I'm going to handle this."

"How?" Orion said, pacing across his place. He wore an undershirt and sleep pants, and looked haggard, wrecked by grief for Dean. "What are you going to do?"

"I'm going to tell the school exactly what happened." I read Orion's face. "I know what you're thinking. His word against mine. They're not going to believe me."

"Maybe, I don't know. He's super popular. When you said his name..."

"I know. I saw it."

Orion's head whipped to me. "Harper, I believe you. You know that, right? I believe you one hundred percent, but it's this fucking system. It's this whole thing… It's the school. I saw it today at a crew practice. It was business as usual, and I was there. I was a part of it. I went down there and I sat in that goddamn boat…" He shook his head angrily. "This is not about me. I'm just saying, they might fight back. *He* will fight back, but I'll be there with you. I'll drop out of the contest."

"No," I said, feeling strangely calm. Clear-headed but exhausted. "You cannot drop out."

"Why not?"

"Because it's just more charity. It'll just look like I can't fight my own battles or that the only reason I won is *because* you dropped out. I have to tell them the truth and see what happens. We have to let it play out and hope that they do the right thing."

"Okay," he said slowly, "but I *should* drop out. There's something I need to tell you."

"Not now. I really can't. I'm so tired. Please. I need to sleep."

Orion looked conflicted for a moment, and then he nodded. "Take the bed. Do you want me to sleep on the floor?"

"No," I said. "I don't know where we're at right now, but I need you. Your coin. It saved me. I hid in the storage closet until the janitor found me. I would've probably lost it even more if it wasn't for you."

"I'm glad," he said. "But I wish I'd been there. I would've killed him."

"Then this would be an even bigger mess than it already is."

Orion's face was unreadable as he took my hand. I kicked off my shoes and lay down in the bed.

"What do you need?"

"Hold me, Orion. Please?"

Wordlessly, he climbed into bed and held me to him, my back to his chest. He wrapped his arms around me and held me tight. I thought I would pass out immediately, but my hand ached where I'd hit Langford, and the memory of his leering face and his touch kept coming back to me. Every time I dozed off, I felt his fingers on my skin or his breath on my neck, and I'd bolt awake.

"It's okay, I'm right here," Orion whispered every time I jerked awake. He never seemed to sleep. "I've got you, love."

Finally, I slept and stayed asleep.

The next morning, I woke in Orion's arms, and for one soft, stupid moment, I thought the whole thing must've been a terrible nightmare. Nothing bad had ever happened. Nothing bad *could* ever happen when I was with him…

Then it all came flooding back, and my stomach clenched.

I sat up and nudged Orion's arm.

"I have to get going," I said, and climbed out of bed.

I wanted to get home and shower and change and never wear these clothes ever again.

"Do you want me to be there?" Orion asked. "Should I call someone? Just tell me what you need, and I'll do it. I'll do anything."

"I have to do this on my own," I said. The memory of Langford at his car, waiting for me, sent a shiver running down my spine. "But will you walk me to my car?"

"Of course."

It was early yet; the student parking lot was empty.

At my car, Orion's brows furrowed. "Call me or text or…I don't know." He scrubbed a hand down his face. "I'm sorry, Harper. I'm sorry things got all cocked up and that I'm such a bloody mess. Because there's something I still need to tell you."

"Later," I said. "Please. I'm barely hanging on. I have to get home, and…then I have to do what I have to do. Okay?"

He nodded finally. "It's something I should handle on my own anyway. Something I should have handled a long time ago."

"Thank you."

He pressed a kiss to my forehead. "I'm sorry. It isn't worth shit, but I am sorry."

"Me too. We'll talk later."

I got into the car and drove home, my mind too tangled to touch what *we* were. That would have to wait. I had to gather every bit of strength I had, because this wasn't just for me. From the start, something about Langford had felt wrong. Now I knew why. I wasn't the first he'd tried this with—not by a long shot. Other girls had come before, and even if I failed, I had to stop him, so no one else would come after.

At home, my mother was asleep on the couch. Good. I didn't have any energy to deal with her. I bundled my dress and coat in a garbage bag and threw them away. Then I showered and got dressed in black pants, a black sweater, and my motorcycle boots, and headed back to school, to the administrative offices.

At President Sterling's office, his secretary looked up from her desk. "Can I help you, dear?"

"I need to speak with Dr. Sterling."

"Do you have an appointment?"

"No, but it's extremely urgent."

"You can't see him without—"

"Professor Langford sexually assaulted me last night."

The secretary's face went white. Without taking her eyes off me, she pressed a button on her phone. "There's a student to see you, Dr. Sterling."

"These are quite serious accusations, young lady," Dr. Sterling said ten minutes later, after I'd told him everything. "Professor Langford is a popular teacher with a stellar reputation. You're quite certain this is what occurred?"

"Yes," I said through gritted teeth, cheeks burning with humiliation. "I'm *quite certain*."

Dr. Sterling rubbed his angular jaw. "The NoSci award ceremony is tomorrow afternoon. Press is here. Parents. University representatives. The timing is…unfortunate."

"My apologies for the inconvenience."

He frowned. "The appropriate thing to do is allow Professor Langford the opportunity to tell his side of the story tomorrow morning, prior to the ceremony. I would like to see both of you here at nine a.m."

What was left of the blood in my face drained out. "You're going to make me sit in the same room with him?"

"Young lady—"

"My name is Harper Bennett."

"Miss Bennett. This is a very serious accusation. I must hear his side of things. And if what you say is true, then your story should be able to stand up to scrutiny."

"Or I could just go to the police. I came to you first because I thought…" I swallowed hard. "I thought you'd do that for me."

Sterling's expression softened, and he leaned forward. "What you've described is serious, Harper. I want you to know I know that. It took great courage for you to come here."

My throat burned. I nodded.

"But if we involve law enforcement right now," he continued, "this matter leaves the school's hands immediately. It becomes public. Parents, press, lawyers. Things like this tend to move fast, and not always carefully. Or *quietly*."

Parents. He meant Orion's parents. It was all over his face.

He sat back in his chair. "We'll open a formal inquiry and document in writing everything you've told me."

"And then?"

"Give us until tomorrow," he said gently. "We'll have a meeting. You may bring an advocate. A trusted adult. But if that still doesn't satisfy, you're absolutely within your rights to go to the police. No one here will stop you."

No one will stop me.

I could read Sterling well enough to know he was praying I'd keep this an internal matter. But I didn't want to go to the cops either. I didn't want to drag Orion's name into something loud and public. I didn't want to sit alone in a cold police station and explain to a row of men how I'd been hunted and touched and threatened—only to be told it *wasn't that bad.*

His word against mine.

"I just want to make him stop," I whispered, hating how small my voice sounded.

Dr. Sterling smiled. "We'll get to the bottom of this. I promise."

The next morning, I met Ezra Wolfe outside his office door.

"Are you sure?" he said. "About me, I mean. 'Trusted'

is a new one for me." He tapped a black-nailed finger to his chin. "So is 'adult,' now that I think about it."

I glanced up at him, big, tall, imposing all in black. But also one of the best people I knew. "I can't think of anyone else I want with me for this."

His teasing smile faded. "I can't say enough how sorry I am, Harper."

Yesterday afternoon, after leaving Sterling's office, I'd gone straight to Ezra to ask him to be my advocate. It was humiliating, having to tell him the whole sordid story, but I thought telling it again might make it easier.

I was wrong.

He heaved a breath. "Ready?"

"No. But…yes."

We began the trek through the Academy to Sterling's office.

"If it helps at all, I haven't had a drink since we last spoke," he said. "Since you gave me a good talking-to all those months back."

"Really? That's wonderful."

"It's been less wonderful and more awful, terrible, and very bad. But thank you." He shook his head. "And that you can find it in your heart to be glad for me at a time like this speaks volumes about you, my dear. How is your mother?"

"Not as well as you," I said. "But one crisis at a time, if you please. I only *look* like I have my shit together right now."

Because on the inside, my stomach roiled, my heart clanged, and every time I let my thoughts wander, the memory of Langford's touch or his body caging me in came roaring back, and I flinched as if someone had shocked me.

We passed through the Arts Wing to the STEM Wing, where I noticed the students talking in clusters. Every single one of them stopped to stare at me as we passed, whispering to each other, most with snide looks on their faces.

"Now what?" I said to Ezra as two students gave me the stink eye, and one muttered "Fucking Bender" as we passed.

"I haven't the faintest," Ezra said. "But it certainly brings back schoolyard memories when I was the only boy in my class who wore eyeliner and the occasional skirt."

Tessa Carlyle hurriedly fell into step next to me. "Oh my God, Harper, what is happening?"

I glanced around and then at her, a ball of dread dropping into my gut. "You…you heard?"

She nodded. "It's bullshit. It has to be right?"

"Bullshit? Wait, what are you talking about?"

"Langford," Tessa hissed. "There's a rumor going around that you lost the NoSci and freaked out in the auditorium. That you threatened to make up an assault unless he gave you the win. When he refused, you filed a false complaint."

I felt faint. "Oh my God…"

"Bloody hell," Ezra murmured.

Tessa looked between us. "I know that's bullshit…but what actually happened?"

"The opposite," I said, my face on fire as we passed a cluster of students, all of them stopping to watch us pass. "He…he threatened me, saying that Orion won, but if I did what he wanted…" I couldn't even say it. "So I made a complaint."

"Oh God," Tessa said, her eyes filling with tears. "Oh, Harper, I'm so sorry. Everyone loves Langford. I'm not even in the science department and I know that. All these people…" She threw her arms around me. "I have rehearsal I can't get out of but… Is there anything I can do?"

"No. Thanks," I said, sounding shell-shocked to my own ears.

"Okay, call or text when you can."

She reluctantly left, and I clutched Ezra's arm.

"Who told them…?" I breathed.

"Langford," Ezra said darkly. "He's trying to get ahead of it. Come on. Let's take a detour."

He led me out a side door into blinding sunshine.

"He's a piece of steaming shit, but this is a lot, Harper. Too much, maybe. You tell me what you want. Keep going or…?"

I sucked in a breath. "Keep going."

Ezra and I were ushered into President Sterling's office where half a dozen people were pacing, agitated, including Sterling.

They all stopped, and an array of faces stared back at me—I barely registered Orion's parents were among them—because my blood had gone cold at the sight of Langford.

"It's abhorrent that she should be in the same room with him," Ezra declared, tattooed and pierced amid all the suits. "We all know that, right?"

Dr. Sterling held up his hands. "Professor Wolfe, if you please. No one has been formally charged. Keep that in mind." The man next to him, his lawyer presumably, nodded. "Please be seated."

Ezra turned to me. "You don't have to do this. We can leave right this bloody second."

"It's okay," I said so only he could hear. "Let's get this over with."

Moving on stiff legs and looking anywhere but at Langford, I sat in the chair farthest from everyone else, Ezra beside me like a buffer.

"We're just waiting on Orion, then," Sterling said, with a deferential nod to his parents, who sat near the window, perpendicular to the desk.

Ezra and I shared shocked glances.

"What for?" he asked.

"This is an internal meeting regarding a faculty concern, and the integrity of the Novus Prize for Scientific Innovation," Dr. Sterling said. "Orion's name was brought up, and because his parents are here and such valued members of our Academy family, we thought it best to include all involved parties."

"I see," Ezra said with biting sarcasm. "I thought we were here to discuss a student complaint against a faculty member. Silly me."

A knock came at the door, and Orion was ushered in. He looked just as appalled as Ezra that Langford was here.

"What the hell…?"

"Orion, hush," his father said placidly. "Sit."

Orion didn't want to sit. He looked ready to murder Langford. I shook my head at him, and he reluctantly took a seat with his parents, hands gripping the armrests of his chair.

"Now that all parties are present…" Sterling said, and nodded to his lawyer, who turned to me.

"Miss Bennett, if you would."

I swallowed, sat up straight, chin up defiantly, though my heart was jackrabbiting in my chest.

"Last night, I went to the auditorium to retrieve my laptop around six p.m.," I began, only the slightest quaver in my voice. "Dr. Langford arrived and told me that Orion had won the contest because of his family's influence, but that he—Langford—could change the outcome if I… cooperated."

"And what did you take 'cooperated' to mean?" the lawyer asked.

"That he wanted me to have sex with him," I stated clearly.

Sterling and the Mercers visibly flinched while Orion's face was a mask of rage.

"And what gave you that impression?"

I clenched my teeth against the tide of humiliation and said in a rush, "He touched me inappropriately on my arms, my face, my neck. I told him to stop. He refused. He had me caged in." My voice was beginning to break down. "I fought him off and ran. I hid in the storage closet until a janitor found me and then I left. To Atlas Hall."

"Why didn't you go home if you were so distraught?" the lawyer asked.

"Is that relevant?" Ezra interjected.

"I'm merely trying to get the whole picture," he said.

"I went to Orion. Dr. Langford was waiting for me in the parking lot," I said, and everyone shifted uncomfortably. "I told Orion everything, and then—"

"And then spent the night at his place?"

"Bloody hell, man," Ezra snapped.

"Professor Wolfe." Dr. Sterling placed a hand on his desk. "You will have an opportunity to ask questions momentarily."

"*Yes*," I said. "Because I was exhausted and scared. The next morning, I immediately came here."

The lawyer and Sterling conferred, and then Sterling said, "Dr. Langford, would you like to give your version of events?"

My entire body stiffened. Froze. As if it were in the auditorium all over again. I kept my eyes straight ahead, at a fixed point on the wall.

"I was in the auditorium last night, wrapping up NoSci

business," Langford said. "Harper was there, and she was upset about the committee's decision. She expressed a dire need for the prize money. I told her I couldn't change the outcome or influence the other judges, nor would I try. The conversation became emotional, so I removed myself."

I wonder how it must be to lie so easily. Without a shred of remorse or hesitation.

The lawyer for the school nodded, made a note. "There was no further interaction?"

"That's correct. It was a very short conversation. As for waiting in the parking lot, it's true, I lingered. I was upset. Unsure about the threats she had made and what might happen to my reputation. If there is security footage, I'm certain that's what it will show."

Ezra snorted. "So thoughtful of you to bring that up first."

Sterling and the lawyer conferred, and then Sterling folded his hands on his desk. "Well, this seems rather inconclusive, I'm afraid."

I went cold all over. That was it? Nothing more to say or do? They were going to drop it, and he was just going to get away with it? And do it again and again...

My hands twisted in my lap, and I winced. My middle finger was swollen and red around the ring Orion had given me after I had struck Langford last night. Ezra's gaze flickered down at my hand, then over at Langford, but he remained silent, eyes narrowed, like he used to do when he was listening to us play in piano class.

"Inconclusive?" Orion burst out. "That's it?"

"Without evidence or corroboration, there isn't enough cause to take any further action."

"You can't afford to suspend your precious award ceremony, you mean," Orion said, disgusted. "This was never about getting her a fair hearing. It was about damage control."

"Orion, please," his mother chided.

"Be that as it may," Sterling said, "I have an institution to run. Rumors are flying—"

"Rumors *he* started!" Orion thundered, jabbing a finger at Langford.

"Orion, that's *enough*," his father admonished.

"No, this can't be all." Orion shot to his feet, glancing around at everyone, and I loved him for it, even as I sat, dumbstruck and defeated. "I thought we were here for Harper. For *her*."

"Yes, and she told us her story," Sterling said.

"Her *story*?"

"But some things are bigger than one student," he said, not looking at me. "This is the first Novus Science prize, and it was years in the making. It'd be a black mark on the Academy to have it fall apart at the eleventh hour. I propose we proceed as scheduled. Orion accepts his award and then—"

"The fuck I will," Orion snapped.

"*Orion*," his father scolded. "My God, that is quite enough."

"No chance," he said, shaking his head. "I'm not getting up there and accepting an award I don't deserve."

Sterling scrubbed his hands down his face. "And why not?"

"Because I cheated."

My head snapped up. I looked again to Ezra, but he only watched and listened.

"Cheated?" Celeste Mercer said with a small laugh. "Darling, please."

"I did. I got outside help. An envelope of ideas from Mercer Chemicals, and I used one to make my project. I didn't win anyway. Langford himself said Harper did. The prize goes to her." He turned to me. "I'm so sorry, love. I should've told you a long time ago. I never should've entered in the first place." His voice thickened. "Maybe none of this would've happened."

He straightened and faced Sterling.

"You can't give it to me, and if you put me on the stage and hand me that award, I'll tell everyone what happened and pass it right on to her."

"Now, that won't be necessary…" Sterling began.

"It is necessary," Orion said. "All of it is *necessary*. She is the rightful winner. Not only because I cheated, but her project is better. She deserves it."

Sterling's mouth made a grim line, and he conferred with his lawyer. I risked a glance at Langford, who sat back, a smug smile on his face. Forgotten. Off the hook. Free to do what he did to me to someone else.

"Very well," Sterling said finally. "Harper will accept first prize, and Orion will be disqualified."

"Now, hold on," Rockwell began. "Is this the right solution?"

"Forget the bloody prize, what about Langford?" Orion demanded. "What about what he did to her?"

"Sit *down*, Orion…"

"This meeting is over," Sterling said, his voice rising. "After the award ceremony—"

"Did you tell Harper the outcome of the competition?" Ezra Wolfe asked Langford smoothly, his voice cutting through the mayhem.

Silence fell.

Langford cleared his throat. "Excuse me?"

"You said she was upset about the committee's decision, but the announcement hadn't been made yet. How did she know she lost?"

"Oh, well…she must've assumed."

"She *assumed* that she had lost the prize and *got emotional* and started throwing around accusations and threats?"

The Mercers and Sterling exchanged glances. Orion resumed his seat, listening intently.

"I'll ask one more time," Ezra said, his voice deadly soft. "How did she know she lost?"

I refused to look at Langford, but I heard the desperation creeping into his voice.

"I—I don't recall. I may have said something about the way the discussion was leaning."

"Ah," Ezra said. "I am but a mere pianist, but it strikes me as odd that you discussed the committee's deliberations with a student."

"Vincent," Langford appealed to Sterling. "This is ridiculous..."

Sterling pursed his lips. "Answer the question, Ian."

Langford's chair creaked. "I was trying to manage expectations."

"I see," Ezra said. "It sounds like you had a lengthy conversation when earlier you said that it was a short interaction."

The mood in the room had shifted. Sterling was regarding Langford with a sour expression.

"I have one more question," Ezra said. "What happened to your face?"

"My...?"

"Face. You've a wee cut on your jaw. It looks fresh."

His hand flew to the small cut on his right jawline. "Oh, I...I must've cut myself shaving."

I examined my ring closer. There was dried blood on the pearls, maroon staining the white. I hadn't even noticed, my body had been so hijacked by fear and anxiety from being in the same room with my attacker. Hope flared in my chest.

"That's not from shaving," I said. "I hit him."

Dr. Sterling turned to me. "Come again?"

"I fought him off," I said. "I kicked him in the groin and backhanded him. My ring hit him in the face. You can still see the blood."

"That's ridiculous." Langford scoffed. "This whole thing is utterly ridiculous."

Sterling frowned. "Was there a physical altercation, Ian? Just how close were you to her?"

"No, I… If she struck me, I don't recall. Or she did, but I didn't consider it relevant."

"You didn't consider it *relevant*." Ezra laughed darkly.

"That'll do, Professor Wolfe." Dr. Sterling sighed and ran his hands down his face. He consulted with the lawyer again and then nodded, resigned. "Given this new information, I have no choice but to suspend Dr. Langford without pay, pending a full inquiry."

"Vincent, please—"

"Ian, this conversation has crossed into a legal matter. I'm going to ask you to excuse yourself while we determine the next course of action."

Langford slowly got up, straightened his tie, and stepped out. The instant the door closed behind him, a tight band around my chest loosened. Ezra reached over and patted my hand. I grabbed his and held on tightly.

"Miss Bennett, this is all deeply regrettable," Sterling said. "We will conduct a full inquest, but I hope that presenting you with the Novus Prize will be the first step in making things right. Today at the ceremony."

Ezra snorted. "Of course. The show must go on."

All eyes turned to me.

"Sure," I said. "I'll take it. I am, after all, desperate for the money."

My sarcasm was lost on Sterling, who sighed with relief. "Thank you. Now, if there's nothing else?"

"May we speak with our son privately?" Rockwell said stonily.

"Yes, of course," Dr. Sterling said. "You may have the room."

Ezra and I stood, and I met Orion's gaze. For the first time since Dean's death, there was life in his eyes. A spark. And in that spark, love for me. I held it carefully, like something precious that had survived a storm, and went out.

In the hallways of the Academy, safely away from that horrible office, I turned to Ezra. "I don't know how to thank you."

"You don't have to thank me for a thing," he said. "I admit, I'm surprised that you took Sterling up on his offer, but I have a feeling you have your reasons."

"I do. I—" I began and then felt a light touch on my arm.

"Harper?" came a watery voice.

"Sierra?"

Sierra Hart's face was tear-streaked, her eyes red and swollen. "Can we talk?"

Chapter 37

ORION

Sterling and his lawyer cleared out, and a short silence fell, heavy and full. The kind of silence that would have crushed me before.

"Orion," my father began. "That outburst was completely uncalled for. Cheating? Why would you say that? You've brought embarrassment—"

"Good," I said. "I didn't win. I cheated. *We* cheated."

My father blustered. "It wasn't cheating; it was *accommodation*. You have…a disability."

I stared at him, and the last piece of numbness blew away. The last anchor holding it all down lifted, and the words came pouring out.

"Dyslexia," I said. "I have dyslexia. You can't even say the word. And I wasn't diagnosed with dyslexia when you gave me that envelope, remember? I was still struggling under a *mis*diagnosis that was ten years old."

"Well, that has been rectified—"

"Nothing has been rectified. I need to say something, and you both need to listen."

I stood up to pace, to feed off the energy surging through me.

"Ten years," I said. "I spent ten years thinking I was broken. Thinking I was defective. That asking for help was shameful. But I am not broken. Music is how I exist in this world. I speak it fluently, and all this time, I've been fighting it and burying it and pushing it down because *we don't talk about anything!*"

My mother flinched. My father only stared at me, his eyes hard.

"But I'm done," I said. "I lost my friend. I may have lost Harper too. She was put through a nightmare—and for what? I shouldn't have thrown that party. I shouldn't have rowed in that bloody race. I should've been at the piano, auditioning for Juilliard. Fighting for a visa. Fighting to stay here. With her."

"So it's about this girl," my father said, frowning. "She's quite poor, isn't she?"

"In some ways," I said. "But rich in all the ways that count. And she doesn't want my money."

Shame bit me, thinking of all the times I'd offered Harper money in lieu of something she really wanted—for me to stick around. To be there for her. To be honest with myself. To be honest about my music. Everything Ezra had been telling me since the beginning.

"I love her. That's what it's about. I love her and I love to play."

My parents exchanged uncomfortable glances. I wanted to scream. To force words out of them. Anything.

"If you want to cut me off, then do it," I said. "I hope you don't, because I love you. But I can't be in the family business, Father. You built something from the ground up. From nothing. Now I have to start from nothing. It's going to be terrifying. I might embarrass myself. But at least it'll be honest. And I'm sorry if I've disappointed you. I've disappointed myself, and I let down the one person who didn't deserve it. I may have lost her. But I'm going to try to fix everything that I broke and hope it's not too late."

They exchanged a glance. A nod. A silent understanding.

"You're a grown man. You have to do what you feel you have to do," my father said gruffly.

"That's it? That's all you have to say? After ten years? A *decade*—"

"It's too difficult to talk to you like this," Mum said. "Maybe when we've all cooled down, we can speak later."

My father nodded. "I think we're done here."

I stared in disbelief as they rose from their chairs. My mother's eyes were glassy, her hand locked in his as they walked out. The door clicked shut behind them, and my heart cracked in two.

The safety net was gone. There was nothing under my feet now but air because I was no longer down in the depths.

I was free.

I went to the STEM auditorium. Every seat was taken, so I stood in the back instead of one of the chairs onstage with the other hopefuls—Harper among them. Whispers followed her name about "false accusations," and I saw nods at Langford's empty chair at the judges' area.

My hands curled into fists. I wanted to shut them all up myself. But Harper was strong and brave. The bravest person I'd ever met. She didn't need me fighting her battles for her. Only at her side, like she'd been at mine.

Please let it not be too late.

The press snapped pictures of the students, the dignitaries, and the judges—Dr. Hargrave, Dr. Chen, and Dr. Sterling sitting in for Langford. The speeches rolled on about how extraordinary the Novus Prize was. All I could think about was the price Harper had paid for this show to keep going.

Finally, after a video presentation of each of the experiments (except mine; bloody fast editing, that), the awards were announced. Fifth. Fourth. Third. Second. Dr. Sterling lifted a glass flame trophy with a gold leaf at its heart.

"First prize, for her portable and sustainable water-purification system…Harper Bennett!"

My girl rose, head high, to scattered applause. Dr. Sterling looked relieved as he handed the trophy to her.

"Congratulations, Miss Bennett," he said into the mic.

"Thank you for this award, Dr. Sterling," Harper said, and then she handed it back. "But I can't accept this."

The auditorium broke into murmured talk.

"Every time I look at it, I'll be reminded of how I was assaulted by one of the judges, Ian Langford."

Talk surged louder now. Dr. Sterling went pale. My heart swelled with pride.

That's my girl. My warrior.

"The only reason I'm standing here is because a good person told the truth and was disqualified," Harper said. "He did what he did because of pressure. Pressure from parents. From the school. From the administration. One of the best people we know is dead because that pressure crushed him under its relentless fist."

Her voice faltered. She kept going.

"I don't actually know if I won this award," she said. "I'll wait for the results of the inquest into my assault. And that inquest is only going to happen because Ezra Wolfe believed in me." She looked out at the crowd. "He believed in me when a lot of others here didn't and still don't. But I'm not alone. Another of Langford's victims is coming forward."

Gasps rippled, and the talk grew loud.

"Unlike me, she's not a Bender," Harper said. "She's given me permission to tell you that. Because it's not about money. It never was. It's about fairness. And now it's about justice. If you've been harmed by Ian Langford and don't feel safe coming forward, I understand. Because power protects its own. But the other victim and I will make sure he never touches another girl again. Thank you."

Harper resumed her seat on the stage and folded her hands in her lap.

Silence.

Then a single clap.

Another.

They rose to their feet in a standing ovation. The press surged forward. Camera flashes lit the air like lightning. Harper didn't flinch.

"Goddamn," I whispered, clapping until my hands ached.

Someone stepped beside me. "Don't hurt those precious instruments," Ezra Wolfe said. "You've got a performance tomorrow."

I smiled, my throat thick. "Yes, I do."

Chapter 38

HARPER

I THOUGHT I COULD GO HOME AFTER THE AWARD ceremony, but two police officers were waiting for me with Dr. Sterling as I stepped off the stage.

Fear shot an icy dagger into my heart as the image of my mother, dead on the couch, filled my head.

"What is it?"

"Langford," Dr. Sterling said. He looked like he had a headache. "He's making this worse for himself. If you would come down to the station to answer some questions? Miss Hart is already there."

Before the ceremony, Sierra had told me that Langford had tried to assault her under the guise of comforting her over Dean's death. He'd found her weeping in the room where our Math & Physics Club met. She'd only escaped because Kevin Huang, our president, had walked in. He was willing to corroborate her story too.

I went to the Castle Hill Police Department to make a statement with Sierra, the two of us holding hands tightly in the public lobby, waiting for our turn to be taken to separate interview rooms. There, I told my story again, they took photos of my injured finger, and then I was free to go. In the parking lot, I hugged Sierra tight.

"I'm so sorry about Dean."

"Thank you," she said, still crying. I bet she hadn't stopped since the night of the party. "I never should have tried to hide us because, *God*, it's all so stupid. Meaningless. It's like, he's gone, and now it's all so clear what really matters, you know? And it wasn't any of that stupid shit that I used to care about."

"I know," I said. "But he was happy. You made him so happy."

Sierra lifted her tearstained face. "I did?"

"Yeah," I said, my own voice cracking. "I saw it, every time he looked at you. It was amazing to see."

"But I...kept us hidden. Like I was ashamed."

"I know, but I think that was Dean's superpower: He saw us all for who we are and what we could give. He didn't ask for anything more."

"I know," she said miserably. "That's why I loved him." She wiped her eyes. "My parents are waiting for me. Thank you, Harper. What you said helped a lot. More than anything."

She hugged me and went to her waiting parents. I had Dr. Sterling waiting for me.

"Miss Bennett." He cleared his throat. "That was quite the speech you gave at the ceremony."

I crossed my arms. "The public needed to know he's a threat."

"Yes, of course, that is our priority as well."

"Is it? Because it seems like protecting the Academy's reputation is your number one."

"The two matters are not mutually exclusive," he said, shifting his weight. "Going forward, perhaps a different approach would be in order?"

This was new, having the Academy's proverbial balls in a sling.

"I'm listening."

"We are prepared to offer you a settlement. Obviously the $25,000 Novus Prize is yours, but I feel a substantial financial offer would not be inappropriate given your pain and suffering. Especially if you're willing to make a statement to the effect that we handled this situation expediently."

I tapped my foot, thinking of my mother and Dash. Dash, especially.

"I'm willing, Dr. Sterling," I said. "But only if Langford faces real justice for what he's done to me, to Sierra, and anyone else he's harmed. If he gets off on some bullshit technicality because you didn't do everything you could to support us, I'm going to go apeshit on social media."

"Uh, yes," he said. "That sounds…fair."

He stuck out his hand and I shook it, wincing. Dr. Sterling turned my hand over and examined my injured finger.

"I am sorry, Miss Bennett. Truly. The rest is just business."

"I know, Dr. Sterling, but what everyone in *business* seems to forget is that there are real people behind the numbers." I took my hand back. "Remember that when you write my check."

I went home. Mom was on the couch as per usual, an open bottle of wine on the coffee table, the TV on.

"You're home late," she said with a wan smile. "How did it go?"

I stood for a moment in our little house, in the haze of cigarette smoke. Dash's LEGOs were pushed to one side to make room for wineglasses and takeout food containers. The nightmare of the last few days joined the years that had come before. All of it. The bullying, the storm, the bills piling up, Dean, Dash's fading light, Langford… My face crumpled, eyes stinging and throat burning.

Mommy…

"Oh, baby," Mom said. "What's wrong? What happened?"

I dropped my bag and rushed to the couch. I sat in her lap, threw my arms around her, and buried my face in her neck.

She stiffened, shocked. "Baby… What—"

I cried, clinging to her. The smoke and wine and the scented detergent I hated surrounded me in the dark of my eyes squeezed shut, and I cried harder. She rocked me back and forth, stroked my hair, and kissed my temple, while I cried and cried.

"I need you," I said between hiccuping sobs. "I can't do this alone. I just *can't*."

I braced myself for excuses. Apologies that went nowhere or more empty promises. But my mother nodded, swallowed hard, and sat up straight.

"Okay, baby." She gathered me to her and held me. Her arms strong and tight. "I got you. I'm here. I'm here now and I got you."

I didn't know if I could believe her. Or trust her. I couldn't see the future; it was a dark, murky path. But for those moments, I let the anger and hate go, and found love beneath. It was still there, and if she had chance to make it, it was love that would see her through.

And if she fell down again, it was my love for Dash that would see *me* through. And we'd be okay.

Somehow, we'd be okay.

Sunday night, I stepped into the Performing Arts Center Auditorium. It held thirteen hundred people, and I was amazed to see that almost every seat was filled. I smoothed down my black dress and took a seat in the middle back, amid the parents and students who were murmuring and perusing their programs.

The light dimmed, and Ezra stepped out into the center of the stage where there was a lone spotlight over him and a sleek black grand piano.

"Welcome to the spring concert. My name is Ezra Wolfe, Advanced Piano instructor, and if you're wondering how in the bloody hell I got here, you're not alone."

A smattering of laughter rippled through the auditorium.

"I am so proud of these ten performers you're about to hear. They've worked hard all year, having survived my unconventional 'teaching' style." He put *teaching* in air quotes. "Thank you all for coming and showing your support for these talented artists."

I glanced at my program. Orion was last, playing Rachmaninoff's Étude-Tableau Op. 39 No. 5 in E-flat minor. I smiled to myself.

Showoff.

Ezra introduced each performer, and finally, it was Orion's turn. I put my hand to my chest, over my heart, as he came on stage. He wore a black tuxedo, no tie, the top buttons undone. He would always be the most handsome boy I'd ever known, but now his face looked even more beautiful somehow. His smile was soft and real. No mask. Just himself. And his true self was breathtaking.

He shook Ezra's hand, and Ezra whispered something to him. Orion nodded, gave a small bow to the audience, and then sat down at the piano. He laid his hands on the keys, and I held my breath.

Silence.

The silence stretched.

Orion took his hands off the keys and rested them in his lap. The audience members around me began to exchange glances.

My heart began to pound.

Then Orion lifted his head. "This is for Dean."

He put his hands back on the keys. There was another moment of silence, and then he began to play.

Not the Rachmaninoff. Not anything I've ever heard from the classic oeuvre. Not anything I've ever heard before. Not anything *anyone* had ever heard before.

And it was only moments into his performance when I understood what he was doing.

He's playing the year.

The music started out light, almost jaunty, but was a complicated weave of overlapping harmonies that danced and sang together like laughter. It then mellowed into something romantic, bringing to mind a moonlit night and a crackling fire. A bonfire.

My hands were clasped tightly over my heart, and I was half in that auditorium, half back on the beach, with his jacket around me under all that moonlight…

The melody deepened and so did the night, becoming velvet and dark and rich before the thunderous lower notes of a storm began to build. It stole my breath that

Orion was creating this as he went. Improvising. Weaving a tapestry out of notes from moment to moment, on the spot.

The storm built and built into a raging tempest, and I was back in my house, listening as the rain came down. Orion's left hand thundered along the piano's lower octaves, while his right hand trilled the upper notes like raindrops *plinking* into pans…and then sunlight.

Both hands moved into the upper octaves as the melodies began to sing and tell a story. A love story.

Our story.

Then they grew dark again, descending into the pounding, modern beats of a house party. The house-party beat became a heartbeat, Orion's left hand alone forming a chord and hitting it over and over. A pulse. A heartbeat that beat faster and faster, and then stopped.

A split second of silence where the entire auditorium held its breath…and then melancholy swept in with gentle but relentless refrains. I wiped tears away as fast as they came, as if they were impeding my ability to listen, because the sorrow…the beautiful sorrow of Orion's music was breaking my heart until the sun came out. Softly. A few higher notes amid the melancholic lower phrases, and I was back at Dean's funeral where the sun shone, beautiful and gold and full of hope.

But Orion didn't leave us there. He finished his piece with the last notes hovering, not quite cheerful, not despairing, but something in the middle. Something that was like a question being asked and waiting for an answer. A future unseen, but with the hopeful harmonies echoing faintly behind, until the last note faded to silence.

Orion took his hands off the keys. There was another quiet in the auditorium. No one moved or even breathed before the first smattering of applause. That applause became its own storm—an ovation unlike any I'd ever heard before. The crowd got to its feet in an uproar. I looked around me, people wiping their eyes, shaking their heads at each other as they slammed their hands together.

Orion stood, gave a short bow, and exited the stage. It didn't matter. The audience applauded the empty circle of light until Ezra brought him back. He gently nudged Orion into the spotlight and stepped aside. Orion shook his head, humbled, took another bow, and then searched the audience. There was no possible way for him to see me amid the hundreds of faces in the dark and with the spotlight in his eyes, but I thought maybe he found me anyway.

And hope burned in my heart. We could find each other in the darkest storm or in the bleakest night. We could find each other anywhere.

Chapter 39

ORION

After the concert, I was surrounded. The other performers, parents, students, all shaking my hand, patting me on the back and telling me how amazing my performance was.

Ezra stood beside me like a proud parent. Bittersweet, until I saw my own parents, Octavian, and Odin, making their way toward us.

"What are you guys doing here?"

"Are you kidding?" Odin said. "We flew in yesterday." He engulfed me in a hug. "Bloody hell, little brother. I knew you were good, but *that*? That was—"

"That was a miracle." Octavian threw his arms around me. "I have no words."

"Thanks, Tav." I turned to my parents. "Mum, Father.

This is Ezra Wolfe, professor and world-famous pianist. He's been my mentor this year."

They looked him up and down: tattoos, eyeliner, bracelets, nail polish.

"Very pleased to meet you," my mother said, shaking his hand. My father did the same.

"Impressive," my father said. "Getting that performance out of my son."

"I take no credit," Ezra said. "And that wasn't a performance, that was a creation. A work of art. A maestro painting a masterpiece as we watched. Or listened, as it were."

I shot him a look.

He batted his eyes. "Too much?"

"Just a bit."

"Not enough," Ezra countered and shook his head, marveling. "I'll give you a moment."

Odin and Octavian gave me knowing smiles and moved off to talk with Ezra, leaving me alone with Mum and Father.

"Most impressive," my father stated. "What is the name of that piece? I don't recall ever hearing it."

"He made it up on the spot," Mum said. "Isn't that what Professor Wolfe implied?"

"I did."

My father's eyes widened. "Extraordinary. It seems this is your calling."

My mother kissed my cheek. "We're so proud of you."

"You are?"

"Of course, darling."

A short silence fell, and I waited. Because I'd said everything I'd needed to say to them, and I'd just bled my heart and soul all over those keys. Expectation—*my* expectation—hung heavy in the air, waiting, and they both knew it.

My father rocked back on his heels, lips pursed. Finally, he cleared his throat.

"When I emigrated to Britain, it was not easy, to put it mildly," he said stiffly. "It was quite difficult for me. Where other men had to be good, I had to be great. Where other men had to be great, I had to be perfect. Greatness is a shield from struggle, or so I believed. I wanted to protect you and your brothers from the struggles I endured. But to armor you in greatness meant there could be no weakness. I did not intend to create hardship, only to spare you taking the road I had already walked." He coughed. "Nevertheless, I'm quite proud of you, Orion, and will always be. No matter where your path takes you."

I looked between my parents.

"Does this mean…?"

"It means that we'll support you in whatever you want to do, darling," Mum said, her eyes full. "We knew you were talented, but that was extraordinary."

Another silence fell, in which I stared blankly. A blank slate before me, and instead of scared, it was the same as when I'd decided to scrap the Rachmaninoff and just play—both terrifying and exhilarating.

Then Ezra stepped forward. "I don't mean to eavesdrop, but I was just eavesdropping."

My mother laughed while my father looked mildly amused.

"I caught that last bit about support. On the subject of Orion's future, I recorded his performance and will be sending it to the Juilliard music department this very night."

My head whipped up. "I thought I missed that audition."

"You did. But Juilliard was intrigued as to why I would not shut up about you, and so they have agreed to assess tonight as an audition, in absentia. I feel very strongly that they will offer Orion a place in their department this fall. An O-1 visa will be required to stay in the country, and I'd be honored to sponsor Orion on that front."

Father and Mum exchange glances.

"Juilliard," he said. "That is an esteemed institution, is it not?"

"For the arts, there are few higher."

"Wonderful. We look forward to hearing what Juilliard has to say. Let us know how we can be of service. Now, apologies, son, but we have to get back. Our jet is waiting."

"Already?"

My mother took me by the face and kissed my cheek. "Marvelous, darling. Just marvelous."

My father shook my hand. "Well done, son. We'll be in touch."

My brothers rejoined me. "I thought I was going to be…"

"Cut off forever?" Odin laughed. "That would be far too much drama and conflict for our parents."

I laughed lightly. "I guess so. But you just got here. You flew all that way just to hear me play?"

"Wouldn't have missed it for the world," Odin said, engulfing me in a hug.

Octavian hugged me too. "*Exceptional.*"

"Thank you for everything," I whispered, holding him tight. "And stay off that goddamn lake."

After they had left, I turned to Ezra. "You're a liar. You're not a world-famous pianist."

"No? What am I?"

"A guardian angel in disguise," I said. "I can't thank you enough. For what you did for Harper, and for what you did for me. But especially what you did for Harper. If you hadn't been there for her, I don't even want to think about what might've happened. Except I *know* I would've punched Langford in the face and messed up my hand. Though it would've been worth it."

"It would not have been worth risking your career for that tosser. And besides, she did for me more than I did for her. Trust me." He grinned. "Now, if you'll excuse me, I have a video to process."

He hugged me and held me at arm's length.

"It's been a privilege, Orion. A privilege."

Finally, the last well-wisher departed, but I wasn't ready to go back to Atlas Hall. I hung around until the auditorium cleared out, and then I sat at the piano and ran my hands up and down the keys.

"I have a complaint," said a voice coming down the aisle. My favorite voice. "My program said Rachmaninoff. That wasn't Rachmaninoff."

Harper was stunning in a black dress, her hair piled up with little curls brushing her pale cheeks.

"Hello, love."

"How in the world did you do that?" she said, moving into the circle of light.

"I thought about Dean. It felt like he deserved something. A tribute." I shrugged. "I don't know, I wasn't really thinking."

"That's what made it perfect," Harper said. "Scooch."

She sat down next to me on the bench.

"Careful, Bennett. If you keep bossing me around like that, I'm going to fall in love with you." I brushed a curl from her cheek. "Are you okay?"

She nodded, then shook her head. "Yes and no. I'm fine, but I'm not okay, if that makes sense. I'm not hurt, but I feel like I've been wounded in some deep, unalterable way, you know? And I'll wear the scar forever."

My heart cracked with pain for her and flared with such hatred for the man who did this to her. Who'd cared more for his own sick needs than about the human being in front of him.

"What you did, Harper, was the bravest thing I've ever seen," I said, my voice thick. "And while I hate that it happened to you, and I'd erase that night if I could, you were extraordinary long before it. I'm so fiercely proud… If I can say that without sounding like a patronizing arsehole."

She smiled faintly. "I'll allow it."

God, this girl.

"I'm proud because, thanks to you, that fucker is going to jail, and he's not going to hurt anyone else." I held her cheek now in my palm. "I know that doesn't make it easier…"

"But it helps," she whispered. "It helps a lot."

I leaned forward and kissed her forehead, and we stayed that way for a long minute. Then Harper sat up and huffed a breath.

"In other, better news," she said, wiping her eyes. "Ezra tells me you're going to Juilliard."

"He's sending them tonight's performance. That's not a guarantee—"

"So you're going to Juilliard. And I'm going to NYU."

"Oh?" I said, playing it cool, while joy suffused every part of me. "So we'll be in the same city."

"Seems so. After I figure out what to do with Dash. But the Academy is trying to buy my cooperation, and I think things are going to be okay with my mom."

"Really?"

"I'll be able to afford rehab and family counseling, so I have hope. And if things still aren't okay, we'll figure it out. That's what we do, right?"

"That's what we do." I glanced down. "I'm sorry, Harper. I'm sorry I cheated and stayed in that damn contest."

"I understand why you did."

"I know. Your speech at the NoSci was the best thing I've ever heard in my entire life."

"Your performance tonight was the best thing *I've* ever heard in my entire life. I could feel Dean all around me."

I nodded, glanced away.

"Hey." Harper touched my cheek so I'd look at her. "If he didn't take that pill at your party, he would've taken it somewhere else. Because he was doing his best to keep up like all the rest of us. You can't blame yourself."

"But I do."

"I know, but…" She bit her lip. "I think maybe guilt is a way that we torture ourselves. The tragedy is so big and so painful, so we try to take a piece of it and give it a reason or assign blame because otherwise it feels so meaningless. But you can't take it on yourself, Orion. Dean would hate that. *God*, he would hate that."

"Yeah, he would."

Her words made sense, and someday, when the grief didn't have such sharp, biting teeth, I might believe them.

I took Harper's hand in mine and kissed her injured finger. "I have a suggestion."

"And what is that?"

"I hear the rents are pretty rough in New York. And since we'll both be living there, and you'll have all kinds of Academy hush money..."

She frowned. "I saw your parents were here. Did they cut you off?"

"No, I just thought it'd be nice to have a sugar mama—Ow!" I laughed and rubbed my arm where she'd swatted me.

She laughed too, shaking her head. "*Incorrigible.*"

My laughter faded. "I want us to live together, Harper. In fact, I don't want to live a single day without you." I cupped her cheek. "Because I love you. You're the reason I did what I did tonight. You're the reason I can play."

"No..."

"*Yes*, Bennett. Now hush up and let me be romantic a minute. It's because of you I'm able to choose the piano. My love for you. You make me want more, and that's what playing is. It's more emotion and pain and grief and joy and all of it. Losing Dean..." I swallowed. "He showed me what it's all for. You, Harper. And music. And love. They're one and the same. Loving you is music."

A tear rolled down her cheek, into my hand that held her.

"So what do you say?" I said thickly.

"Yes, Orion," she whispered. "I'll be your roommate."

I stared for a moment and pretended to nearly fall off the bench. "Dear God, Bennett. You're just killing me."

"Sorry, let me try again," she said, meeting my gaze, unwavering. "I love you. With every bit of my heart, I love you, and I don't want to spend one single day apart from you." She smiled and touched my cheek. "I want an abundance of you, Orion."

"I see what you did there."

"I learned from the best."

I kissed her softly, laid my lips on hers. My girl, my warrior. Her mouth parted for me, soft and warm, sweet and good. The best kiss of my life because it was with this girl who saw me. All of me. And the part of me that has been searching for a place to put my true self had found its home.

We broke the kiss, and I grinned. "You know what we've never done?"

She arched a brow. "Is this about to get super inappropriate?"

I rolled my eyes. "Way to ruin the moment."

"I'm just trying to stay consistent."

"We've never done a duet. You're a hell of a piano player, yourself."

"Oh, please," she said. "I'm a toddler compared to you."

"That is not true. There will be no Bennett slander in my presence." I gave her elbow a nudge. "Come on."

"What are we going to play?"

"I don't know. There's bound to be a duet that we both know. And if there isn't, we'll make it up as we go along."

"Make up a duet," she said. "Because it's just that easy."

"No," I said. "It's bloody hard as shit, but that's what makes it fun."

Harper studied me. "Your eyes are twinkling."

"They're what?"

"Nothing," she said, smiling to herself. "Okay, Orion Mercer." She put her hands on the keys next to mine. "Let's play."

Epilogue

HARPER

A symphony must be like the world. It must contain everything.

—Gustav Mahler

10 YEARS LATER, BOSTON

"It's strange how everything happens all at once," I murmured.

And yet it felt like it took forever to get here.

I ran my hands over the embossed diploma cover from MIT for the hundredth time.

Dr. Harper Bennett, PhD.

"What's that, baby?"

Mom sat on the couch, applying lipstick in her compact mirror. She looked beautiful in a long blue dress, her hair almost entirely silver now. Pale pink and gold light spilled over her from the living room window of my Boston townhouse. The sun was setting over the city, casting it and my mother in a warm glow.

"I was just thinking it's funny how I defended my

dissertation and got my PhD just as Orion finished his tour. Chapters closing at the same time."

"Well," Mom said, "chapters close so new ones can open."

She shot me a wink. I smiled back.

Maeve Bennett knew something about opening new chapters. What had happened to me with Langford all those years ago had been the slap in the face she needed. My shocking million-dollar payoff from Castle Hill Academy paid for her rehab, but it wouldn't have worked if the desire to get sober hadn't come from her.

Ten years later, and she hadn't touched a drop. I knew it was a struggle for her every day, but she kept going, fighting for me, for herself, and for Dash.

I glanced over at my brother, sprawled on a chair, all gangly arms and legs in a suit, blond hair neatly combed—for a change—scrolling on his phone.

He felt my eyes on him and glanced up. "Yeah?"

"Speaking of new chapters," I said. "I can't believe you graduated high school."

"Believe it, sister."

"Nope. You're not allowed to be seventeen. I forbid it."

He snorted. "Then I have bad news for you. I turn eighteen in two weeks."

"Stop it."

He shot me a grin and went back to his phone.

The light is back in his eyes.

It had flickered, dimmed, and nearly gone out, but

my money had paid for counseling for the three of us before I left for NYU. Between Mom's sobriety and Mrs. Andolina's care, Dash had thrived. He didn't go to Castle Hill Academy—I made damn sure of that—but a high school in Providence. He'd been an honor student, and was now on his way to Brown to study psychology.

"Well, I'm ready," Mom said, snapping her compact shut. "Don't want to be late for your husband's big shindig."

My husband.

Six years after the wedding, and I still got butterflies thinking of Orion as my husband. We'd had a little ceremony right after I graduated from NYU and he finished his studies at Juilliard. I didn't want a big fuss, but something small and intimate. But because Orion could not be contained, the reception was anything but small and intimate. I smiled just thinking about it.

Everything about *my husband* made me smile.

After Juilliard, concert halls and symphonies across the world clamored for him, but I was going to Boston, to MIT for my post-grad, and so he chose to play for the Boston Philharmonic to stay close to me.

But the world kept calling, and I wasn't about to keep his star from shining. He'd just finished his first major tour all over Europe and the States. I'd skipped my graduation to see him play in the finale a week ago, and it was worth every minute. To see him center stage, surrounded by nearly one hundred musicians, playing beautifully, brilliantly, and playing with so much heart, it left the audience in tears.

"It was my best concert," he told me, "because it was the last one before I got to come home to you."

Home. That's what Orion wanted more than anything. To have a family. I'd seen it with Dash—how he was so natural and loving. Bursting with love and anxious to share it. But he'd waited patiently until I'd gotten my degree, until we were both established in our fields.

He's waited long enough.

I smiled to myself and gathered my little clutch handbag. I wore an emerald-green dress, satiny and slippery, that slid over my skin like liquid mercury. I smoothed it over my stomach.

My mother gave me a funny look.

"What?" I said.

"Nothing. You look…radiant."

"I'm happy," I said, not meeting her eye. "Happy that Orion is home and I graduated, and we can…be together."

"I'm happy for you too, baby. But you graduated from *MIT* with a doctorate in chemical engineering and water conservation or whatever, and you didn't even walk in the ceremony."

"The timing didn't work out," I said. "Plus, I don't need the fuss."

"You heard her, Ma," Dash said. "She doesn't need the fuss. Now can we *go* already?"

"Okay, okay."

We headed down to the street. Orion had sent a car service to take us to the hotel. My mother's eyes widened as the driver opened the door for her. She'd never gotten used to the sudden wealth in our family. I hadn't either, but I'd used my CHA money to pay for school—mine and Dash's—and Orion had earned his way in the music world on his own.

I won't pretend it wasn't comforting to know his parents would support him should he fall, but Orion didn't fall. He soared. Now someone, somewhere, was always learning his name.

At the Belmont Concert Hall, we stepped into the lobby, and I almost smacked right into Tessa Carlyle.

"Tessa!" I said, stunned.

"Oh, shit, hi," she said, then threw her arms around me. "It's been too long!"

"What are you doing here?"

"Shooting a movie," she said, her smile bright. A Hollywood smile.

"What a coincidence," I said. "Mom, Dash, this is Tessa Carlyle. We went to school together at Castle Hill and NYU."

Dash gaped at the world-famous actress, practically drooling. He'd seen her latest movie with the megastar, Zachary Butler, three times already. She and I had managed to keep in touch despite her meteoric rise to fame, which I'd predicted a long time ago, and she and Emery had been bridesmaids at my wedding.

Tessa was dressed elegantly, her petite frame wrapped in a deep-purple dress.

"We look like we're dressed for the same occasion," I said. "Rooftop party? Orion is celebrating the end of his first major concert tour."

"I hadn't heard," she said. "But I've been following his career. Unreal. And you! Congrats on the degree, *Doctor* Bennett. Or is it Dr. Mercer? Or Bennett-Mercer? I can't remember what you decided on."

"Bennett," I said. "Harper Mercer sounded weird, and Orion doesn't care."

"I'm sure he doesn't."

"You should come up. Say hi. I'm sure he'd love to see you."

Tessa smiled. "I think I will."

"Great," I said, and reached over to close Dash's mouth.

The elevator door opened to a warm June night on a rooftop terrace above one of the city's oldest concert halls. Like most of Boston, it was all historic brick and grand columns, but with glass railings running the perimeter. Warm lights were hung in gentle swoops overhead, and there was a bar, tables, music, and a dance floor. Dozens of people—friends, musicians, and musical directors from Orion's tour, I presumed—filled the patio in their finery, talking and laughing in clusters.

"Wow," Mom said, glancing around. "This is lovely.

Whoever planned this party has amazing taste." She scanned the crowd. "Where's Orion?"

"He had some things to wrap up," I said. "Should be here any minute."

Tessa wore her Hollywood smile again. "I'm going to the bar. Can I bring anyone anything?"

"Soda water with lime?" Mom said. "If you're offering."

"Same," I said.

Tessa held out her hand. "Dash, help me carry?"

I thought my brother's eyes might pop out of his head. "Uh, sure. Yeah. *Yes.*"

She took his arm, and they made their way through the crowd.

Mom turned to me. "No champagne? You don't have to abstain on my account."

"I know, I just…" I stammered. "Oh, there's Orion."

My breath caught like it always did at the sight of my husband, and his face when he saw me…

He's going to make me melt into a puddle one day with that smile of his.

Orion was blindingly handsome in a tuxedo, black tie, red flower in the lapel. He approached and gave my mother a peck on the cheek.

"Nice to see you, Maeve. Lovely, as always."

"Thank you, honey," she said.

"And you…" Orion encircled me in his arms. He bent and kissed me softly. "You are stunning, love."

"Speak for yourself," I said, kissing him back and pretending my knees weren't weak. I straightened his tie. "What is this all about? You don't wear a tie unless you're performing or you're up to something."

"Then I must be up to something," he said, then shook his head. "Nah, there's a good chance I'm going to be asked to play, so..."

I frowned. Nope. He was up to something.

Orion signaled to someone, and an announcement came over a mic for everyone to gather at the small makeshift stage.

"Come on," Orion said, taking my hand and offering my mother his arm. "I have to give a boring speech, and then we can start this party, proper."

We moved through the crowd. I thought I recognized some cohorts from MIT, and a pair of blue eyes rimmed in eyeliner met mine and then vanished.

"Wait," I said. "I could've sworn I just saw..."

"Hm?" Orion said, rushing us through the crowd that had gathered around the small makeshift stage where a lone microphone stood.

"Never mind."

Orion directed my mother to the front of the crowd. "Maeve, if you would. No, not you," he said when I moved to stand beside her. He engulfed my hand in his. "You're coming with me, Bennett."

"No, no, no. This is your celebration. Your spotlight."

"Not tonight."

My husband took the stage and dragged me up beside him. I sighed fondly.

He cannot be contained.

"Thank you all for coming," Orion said into the mic, and a crowd of fifty or so stared back at us—at *me*, it seemed—smiling and glowing. "The tour was amazing and I'm so grateful to have been a part of it. A wee bit of background, I have a very complicated case of dyslexia. Ten years ago, a team of specialists helped me unravel its twists and turns and found proper medication that works for me. Until then, I didn't think it would be possible for me to go out into the world and do what I do. To have so many talented musicians surrounding me and counting on me to not cock it all up."

A smattering of warm laughter from the crowd.

"But I am here, and it's because of this woman, standing at my side."

I shook my head immediately, but Orion's hand tightened on mine.

"I had the help of an incredible teacher, but Harper… she saw me when no one else did. She saw through my jokes, my deflections, and my excessive amount of charisma."

More laughter, but Orion's tone grew serious. His voice thick with emotion.

"She helped unlock the chains around my heart so that I can play the way that I do. My *love* for her is why

I can play the way that I do. But she doesn't like being fussed over. She doesn't like attention or being called inspiring." Orion looked to me, his eyes rich and deep. "A pity, Bennett, because you are…so inspiring."

Orion took the mic off the stand and faced me, holding my hand.

"What are you doing?" I whispered, my own throat tight.

"What you deserve," he whispered back and then spoke into the mic again. "Harper once told me she wondered if life might slingshot her into the ground or into a beautiful life of her own making." My husband's jaw worked, and he paused for a moment. "I predicted the latter. And I was right."

I bit the inside of my cheek. "Orion…"

"She went to MIT," he continued, "and did what Harper always does: She outworked everyone in the room. She earned her doctorate and is now about to build a career where her genius will provide communities with clean water. She's going to help so many people who will never know her name." He looked to me, his eyes full of pain and pride, and memories that were years old. "Again."

A sob tried to choke me. I knew what he meant. Langford had been charged with sexual battery and might've gotten off with a slap on the wrist for a first offense had Sierra and three other girls not come forward. The prosecutor, backed by the full weight of Dr. Sterling and the Academy, argued Langford had a pattern of predatory behavior and deserved jail time. He was sentenced to twelve years in prison, stripped of his teaching credentials, and would be listed on every sex-offender registry until the end of his life.

It had been a bittersweet victory, and while the memory of that horrible night grew older and its darkest shadows dispelled by the light of therapy, the scar was there. It would always be there, but Orion never let me forget that our scars didn't define us. They weren't what made us beautiful or strong. They were signposts on the roadmap of our lives, telling us where we'd been.

And how far we'd come.

Overcome by my husband's bottomless heart and endless love, I looked to the crowd, and found my mother's eyes streaming too. Dash's jaw was clenched, and Tessa dabbed her cheeks and eyes. And then I saw them. Colleagues from MIT…*and* Emery and Xander Ford, Odin and Octavian, Rockwell and Celeste Mercer, and Ezra Wolfe…

Ezra. Oh my God…

"She is the bravest person I know," Orion said, his voice thick and his eyes so full of love and pride, I could hardly breathe. "And so tonight, I want everyone here to know her name too. It is my great honor and privilege to introduce my wife, Dr. Harper Bennett, PhD."

The applause hit me like a wave, and I pressed a hand to my mouth. Orion replaced the mic and pulled me to him. He held me close while a handful of his musicians procured violins and a cello and played "Pomp and Circumstance."

"Congratulations, love," he whispered.

"I can't believe you did this," I managed. "This was supposed to be your night. Your first tour..."

"When was it ever going to be your night?" he asked, holding me close. "You skipped your graduation because I had a bloody concert. You spend so much time cheering me on, and the rest of your time in the lab. You deserve this. More than this." He cupped my cheek. "You deserve to be celebrated."

Orion kissed me softly, then grinned. "Now, come on. There are a bunch of people dying to see you."

We stepped off the stage, and I was surrounded by everyone I loved best in the world.

Emery Wallace and Xander Ford came first, my best friend with tears in her eyes. Orion and I had been a bridesmaid and best man at their official wedding five years ago. Their two-year-old daughter, Aurelia, was perched on Xander's hip. The toddler's golden hair was the same as her mother's, but she had her father's brown eyes. Or one of them—Xander had heterochromia. But it had been more than a year since I'd seen them last.

I shook my head. "How...?"

"Orion's been planning this for months." Emery threw her arms around me. "Congratulations, babe!"

"Thank you, Em. God, I missed you." I turned

to Tessa, who'd snuck up to join us. "And you. What a *coincidence*."

"Some actor I am," she said, rolling her eyes. "I panicked because Orion worked so hard on this. I was so scared I'd blown it."

"I never would have guessed," I said.

"Which worked in my favor," Orion said. "Come here, angel." He plucked Aurelia out of Xander's arms and held her as if he'd been born to do it. My own stomach fluttered, my heart full of the sweetest ache.

"Dr. Bennett," Xander said, pulling me from my thoughts. He offered his free hand with mock formality.

I shook it with a grin. "Dr. Ford."

Xander had also done his post-grad at MIT in quantum physics, though our paths hadn't crossed as often as we'd hoped, while Emery had broken free of her tyrannical father to make her own way. She now ran a successful design business.

I froze and then glanced around. "Wait. You did this," I said to my best friend. "The decorating and planning. Didn't you?"

Emery beamed. "Guilty as charged."

I swatted Orion's arm. "How on earth did you plan this while on tour?"

"It wasn't bloody easy, I'll tell you that. Was it, sweet pea?" Orion cooed at Aurelia and then grimaced as she grabbed a handful of his curls.

Dash and my mother approached, my mother wiping

her eyes. "You wonderful man," she said, kissing Orion on the cheek as he relinquished the baby back to his best friend. "I had no idea."

"I did," Dash said, beaming proudly.

"I needed the manual labor," Orion said, ruffling his hair. The two smiled fondly at each other, Dash with something like adoration for my husband. Though he was only eleven years older, Orion was the first decent father figure Dash had ever had.

Because Orion was made to be a father.

"How did you keep it a secret?"

I jumped. "What?"

"I was asking your brother how he managed to keep it a secret." Mom's brows furrowed. "Are you okay?"

"Yep. Fine."

"Dr. Bennett," came a voice. Ezra Wolfe and his husband, Matteo Ferraro, joined us.

"Let me guess," I said, trying not to burst into tears. "Matteo did the catering."

"Correct!" Ezra said, pulling me in for a hug. "Congratulations, my friend."

"I'm going to kill Orion," I said into his shoulder. "I'm going to kill all of you."

"No, you're going to be celebrated tonight, just like your hubby said." Ezra pulled back to look at me, a thousand emotions exchanged between us without a word. Most of them gratitude. And love. So much love. "I know," he said, sniffling. "Me too."

Then he and Orion hugged tightly, and my husband's eyes fell shut with something like relief. Because it was possible to have more than one soulmate, and Ezra was ours.

"Look at you," Ezra said, holding Orion by the shoulders. "It's been too long."

Orion scoffed, but his voice was thick. "A few weeks. As if you weren't texting me after every European performance at two in the morning, complaining about my arm weight."

"Well, if you'd stop laying on the piano as if you're about to take a bloody nap on it, maybe I wouldn't have."

Matteo and I exchanged glances and laughed. I kissed him on both cheeks.

"Ciao, bella," he said. He was shorter than Ezra but built, with a handsome angular face softened by an inherent sweetness. They'd met during Ezra's appointment at the Accademia Nazionale in Rome. Matteo was a chef, and Ezra had wandered into Matteo's bistro after a performance.

"He come in, very tired," Matteo had said when we'd first been introduced three years ago. "But he has music in his bones, sí? I can hear it. Very beautiful."

"I'd just performed," Ezra had explained. "But I was alone. *Lonely.* He put down a bowl of pappardelle that I didn't order, sat down across from me, and said, 'Eat until you feel better.' I felt better immediately, but I kept coming back. Just to be sure."

I'd loved Matteo in that instant too.

"Ciao, Matteo. Thank you for being here."

I turned to Orion and gave him another incredulous look. He shrugged, the picture of innocence, and then I was engulfed in Odin's bear hug.

"There she is, my favorite sister-in-law."

I laughed and kissed his cheek, then Octavian, who looked happier, brighter. Odin was thriving at Mercer Chemicals as his father's number one man, and Tav was a writer living in Paris.

"Congratulations," Tav said in his thoughtful way.

"Thank you," I said. Though he was older than me, I'd always felt a big-sisterly protectiveness for Octavian. Seeing him happy was another gift piled onto this night when I was already spoiled rotten.

Their parents followed, and a hush trailed in their wake as people stepped aside. Neither had lost that regal air about them. Rockwell stood with his hands clasped behind his back. Celeste was stunning all in silver.

"Dr. Bennett," Rockwell said. "Congratulations. A tremendous achievement."

In ten years, he'd never become less formal, less closed in, but he'd never treated me like an outsider either. Celeste was warmer, as if the years had thawed the cool, collected front, and let more of herself shine through.

"Marvelous, darling," she said, giving me a hug and light kiss on the cheek.

"Thank you both for coming. This is such a surprise."

"Orion told us how much it meant to him," Rockwell said, "and because you mean so much to him…"

"And because you make our son so happy," Celeste added, "we had to be here."

"Thanks, Mum," Orion said, and looked to me. "It's true. I've never been happier."

Challenge accepted.

"It's so lovely to see you all," I said and took his hand. "But I need a word alone with my husband."

"Uh-oh," Orion said. "How much trouble am I in?"

"All of it."

We went to the far edge of the terrace, where the city lay strewn below us and the night had fallen, rich and dark. I tucked my arm in Orion's, and we stood with the sky's canopy above and the city's below.

"You didn't have to do all this," I said. "But thank you. It's the greatest gift."

Orion held me close. "And here I thought I was getting a lecture about putting you on the spot."

"I don't need the attention. It's the thought you put into it. And your speech." My throat thickened, and I wondered just how I was going to do this. Then I glanced upward, and it all fell into place.

"There." I pointed to Orion's constellation. "That's you."

"No…"

"*Yes.* Remember what Mrs. Andolina said? Those are the stars lost sailors use to find their way home."

Orion nodded. "I remember."

We both were quiet for a moment, thinking of the beloved teacher who'd passed away last year. And thinking of Dean. Always Dean.

"Ten years ago, I was lost," I said finally. "I kept my heart locked away because I'd been hurt too many times. But then I met you. You showed me the way home."

"Awfully romantic, Bennett," he said gruffly, and brushed a curl from my cheek. "And I've had that same thought about you so many times, I've lost count."

"We both wanted a real home for so long. One that was whole and warm and full of laughter and tears too." I swallowed hard and took his hand and placed it over my lower belly. "I want that with you."

Orion stiffened, his head shot up. "What?"

"I was going to tell you later," I said. "Then you ambushed me with this party. But...yes."

His stunned eyes went to our hands, then back up to me. "But...we were going to wait. We..."

"You've been waiting," I whispered. "I know you have, and I've never felt more ready."

"Harper," Orion whispered. "Really? You're sure?"

I nodded. "Yes, Orion. I'm sure."

"I'm going to be a father," he said, as if he needed to hear it out loud to believe it.

I slid my hand to his face, cupping his cheek. "You are."

He laughed—one sharp, disbelieving sound—then

hauled me to him. "I'm going to be so good at it," he said against my hair.

"You don't say," I said, laughing and crying.

"I'm serious," he said fiercely, pulling back enough to look at me. "I'm going to work so hard because I want to be…" His voice faltered. "I want to be everything we never had."

"I know," I said. "That's why I know you're going to be the best father to this baby. I don't have a single doubt."

Orion stared at me a moment longer and then held my face in both hands.

"I love you. I love you so much, there isn't enough music in the world to express it. But I'm going to try. Every time I play, it's for you. And…"

"Him," I said, my hand over Orion's on my stomach again. It was far too soon to tell, but I knew anyway. "Your son."

"My son." Orion laughed again and then shook his head, his eyes overflowing with love and *twinkling* with incorrigible mischief. "No. *Our* son. Our son, Bandit."

Oh my God.

"Of course," I said. "To commemorate how we met."

"Exactly."

"Over my dead body."

Orion laughed, and his smile was the most brilliant, purest smile of joy and love I'd ever seen. "We'll put it in the *maybe* column."

He turned me so my back was to his chest, his hands

resting over my belly. Behind us, the party continued, all the people we loved best in one place and those we had lost above in the stars, maybe, where Orion's constellation burned bright. The brightest in the night sky, waiting, like me, to guide the lost home.

The End

AUTHOR'S NOTE

While this is a work of fiction, the issues and traumas are very real, and it is always my goal to treat them with the utmost respect and dignity, and with the fervent wish that readers feel seen and know they deserve to be loved. If you or someone you know is struggling, please reach out.

Suicide & Crisis Support

U.S. 988 Suicide & Crisis Lifeline—https://988lifeline.org
International Helpline—https://findahelpline.com/

Sexual Assault Support

RAINN—https://rainn.org

Alcohol Abuse Support

SAMHSA National Helpline (U.S.)—
https://www.samhsa.gov/find-help

International Alcohol Support—
https://www.aa.org/find-aa/world

Read more from the world of Castle Hill

Prologue

XANDER, AGE TEN

It was the Fourth of July, and my mother was walking out on us.

"I'm leaving you."

She said it to my dad, but it was a plural *you* that included me too. The words traveled from Mom's mouth to my heart at the speed of sound ($v = 343$ meters per second). I thought it must have been faster than that given how hard they punched me in the chest. Faster than the speed of light, even. Einstein's Theory of Special Relativity states that nothing in the universe travels faster than light ($c = 186{,}282$ miles per second), but surely this was an exception—a bullet in my heart, shattering my insides.

My mind turned the chaotic pain into a manageable equation:

F—M(Pd) = *e*^∞ *(D* + *C)*

Whereas, after she had an affair with a Parisian diplomat (*Pd*), our family *(F)* had now lost one mother (*M*), resulting in emotional devastation raised to an infinite power *(e^∞)* for both dad (*D*) and child (*C*).

In plain English, it meant my mother didn't think her only son was worth sticking around for.

People had told me I'd inherited my genius from my father. But that morning, he was slow to catch on when I'd already done the math.

"Oh, come on, Sharon," Dad said wearily. "Not this again. It's just one week."

Every summer, we'd drive the six hours from our little home in Gaithersburg, Maryland, to Dad's family house in Castle Hill, Rhode Island. Mom hated these trips. The Rhode Island house was too small, too dark, too full of Dad's books and papers, and crammed with my grandparents' antique furniture Dad inherited after they passed away. Mom would always try to talk Dad out of these trips, then threaten to stay home, then finally give in and complain the entire time.

That morning, my father believed she was keeping to tradition, until he finally analyzed the situation: He and I were packed and ready to go, the Buick loaded with our luggage for the week. A sleek black sedan idled next to said Buick. Mom's luggage was in the front entry. She was dressed up in a dark skirt suit, pink blouse, and heels with her makeup done. Then there were all those hushed phone calls and late nights with her "colleague" at the State Department that past month, hanging over us like a black cloud.

Mom bent and touched her fingertips to my cheek. "It won't be forever."

I stared at her from behind my black, square-framed glasses. What did that mean? She was coming back? When? At some future date between today and forever? It was a statement made of inconclusive data, which was worthless. It was her walking out the door but leaving it cracked behind her, trapping me in a perpetual state of mystery as to when (or if) she'd ever walk back through it.

I sort of hated her for that.

Then she turned to Dad. "I can't do this anymore." Mom shouldered her big bag and took the handle of her rolling suitcase.

Whatever "this" was remained an unknown too; I wouldn't ask, and my father couldn't. He stared at my mother's retreating back as she stepped out the front door and slipped—long-legged and elegant—into the diplomat's waiting sedan and drove away. Then Dad turned to me with a fixed, shell-shocked smile.

"We'd better hit the road if we want to beat traffic."

I hardly felt a minute of the six-hour drive to Castle Hill. Philadelphia flew past me in the west, then New York City in the east, without notice. Next came the green of

Connecticut, which gave way to the endless bridges and shorelines of Rhode Island. All those miles slipped out from under me as the shock of my mother's abandonment jolted around my brain, animating thoughts like Frankenstein's monster:

I did this.

It's all my fault.

She doesn't want me.

These were the facts as I saw them, since moms don't leave—but mine did.

"Look, there." Dad pointed out the windshield to a park straight ahead of us where several families were having a Fourth of July party. We'd arrived in Castle Hill. It was the first time he'd spoken in more than an hour. "There're a bunch of kids. How about you go play with them for a while?"

"What…?" My heart that had been thudding with a dull, heavy clang, sped up. "*Now*? Aren't we going to the house?"

"Sure, sure. But I need to go alone for a bit first."

I stared at him. "You're going to leave me here? Dad, I don't know those kids. I can't just walk up and invite myself…"

But he was already pulling the Buick into a parking spot. He rested his pale, long-fingered hands on the top of the steering wheel, his gaze on the party in front of us but not really seeing it. "I need to get some numbers on paper before I lose them. You understand that, right? If I don't write the figures down, they might—whoop!" He made a fluttering motion. "Fly straight out of my head, never to return."

My father was a physicist at the National Institute of Standards and Technology. This was supposed to be his summer vacation. But I was in the front seat where Mom should have been, so it wasn't a vacation at all.

"What do you say, buddy?" Dad turned to me, almost pleading. "Looks like a fun party. I see some kids your age. Some girls, even. It'll be good for you to practice your social skills in that department before Langdon."

The Langdon School was a private academy for gifted boys that I'd be starting in the fall. It was in Bethesda, a twenty-minute drive from our home and Dad's work at the NIST. But I already knew I'd be taking the bus: With Mom gone, the chances that Dad would pick me up from school every afternoon were infinitesimally small.

I faced forward, swallowing hard. I recognized Brenton Park from past summers. Parents sat at picnic tables while kids, ranging from toddlers to preteens, threw Frisbees, played tag, or ran along the banks of a small pond. I knew there were fish in that pond—catfish, carp, and fathead minnows—and even a few turtles.

"We just got here," I protested weakly. "We've been in the car for more than six hours. I want to go to the house and—"

"Oh, look. Those boys are playing ball." Dad mustered a weak smile. "Doesn't that look fun?"

It did not. How could anything be "fun" ever again?

"They don't know me, Dad," I said. "They're not going to want to play with me."

"You never know until you ask. You could make some new friends."

I doubted that. I had no friends back home. Why would it be different here? I was "a major nerd" and "a freak from another planet." Those would remain constants no matter how many state lines we crossed.

I chewed my bottom lip. Brenton Park was at least a six-mile walk from our house, and there was no bus. "When are you going to come back and get me?"

"I'll be back soon. Before dusk," Dad said. "A few hours, son. That's all I ask."

My father's eyes—blue, like one of mine—were glassy. His lip quavered, reminding me of the neighbor kids back home when they scraped their knees. Dad didn't need to work; he needed to cry about Mom. Fine for him. I wasn't going to give her the satisfaction, even if she never knew it.

I looked straight ahead, jaw clenched. "You'll come and get me at dusk? You won't forget?"

"I won't forget."

"Okay." I climbed out of the car. Dad gave me a little wave, like he was sorry but that he couldn't help it, and drove away.

I put the odds of his coming back on time at sixty-to-one against. It wasn't that he was a bad parent; his mind just didn't work like everyone else's. Mine didn't either, but where I was sharp, organized, and remembered everything, Dad was scattered. Nervous. He could calculate hundreds of probabilities for quantum interactions but couldn't remember to close the garage door. It's part of why Mom left, I knew. I'd heard the fighting.

"If your head wasn't screwed on, Russell, it'd roll right off!"

She didn't say it in a funny way but in an angry way. Over this last year, she'd been angry a lot. I guessed she'd done her own calculations and concluded it wasn't worth it to stay.

It won't be forever.

My mind wouldn't leave her cryptic words alone, turning them over and over, round and round, like a Rubik's Cube but with missing color squares. An equation I couldn't solve, and there was nothing worse than that.

Dusk was coming fast—light's longer wavelengths dominated the sky in shades of red and orange as the sun sank toward the ocean. I figured I had less than an hour to kill until I'd know for sure if Dad forgot me.

Standing alone in the parking lot, I observed the party from a safe distance. In the clearing by the pond, kids were laughing, chasing each other, and throwing bread at the ducks and minnows. From the grill, the humid air trapped the scents of barbecued hamburgers and hot dogs. The grown-up men wore khaki pants and polos (like the uniform I'd wear at Langdon) and the women were in blouses and jeans with designer sandals. Richies of Castle Hill.

Castle Hill was south of Newport on a peninsula shaped like a shoe, where the Atlantic Ocean poured into Narragansett Bay. It was filled with Richies who lived in big houses on the water. They all had luxury cars and yachts, and they all belonged to the Castle Hill Country Club.

Not us.

At the top of the shoe, the land jutted up, then curved back down, like an elbow. The elbow was called the Bend, which was code for "poor." Dad's little house was on the Bend. He may have been a genius—a little famous even, for his work in particle physics and electromagnetic spectroscopy—but Mom was always complaining he didn't publish enough papers in the right journals, so we were always on the "edge of ruin."

I glanced down at my worn shoes and my jeans with the holes in the knees, then pushed my glasses up higher on my nose. I was a Bend kid all the way. No one—certainly not a Richie—was going to let me play with them.

I wouldn't know how anyway.

An anvil-shaped boulder surrounded by weeds and tall, spiky Atlantic manna grass rested near the edge of the parking lot. I sat down on it and waited for dusk while the kids played and the grown-ups drank their wine and grilled their food.

My stomach growled. It had been three hours since the gas stop in Connecticut. The scent of the ocean, the grill, and the sounds of kids laughing carried memories of other, better Fourths of July. Now I was just a boy, sitting on a rock, wondering what I'd done to make my mom leave.

"Hi."

I jerked out of my poor-me thoughts and looked up. My breath caught like I'd been punched in the gut.

It was a girl.

Not just any girl. *The* girl.

I couldn't stop staring. She didn't seem real. She *couldn't* be real; she was too pretty—Alice in Wonderland in a pink dress instead of blue, her thick blond hair curling in long ribbons around puffy sleeves. Big blue-green eyes watched me with curiosity, and her smile included the whole world. It included *me* when I'd never felt more alone in my life.

But she was obviously a Richie, and I was from the Bend. Once she knew that, this perfect girl would walk away. Or I'd drive her away. It only took most kids a few minutes of talking to me to decide I was too freakish to be friends. I'd learned the hard way it was better not to try. Better to be a jerk and save us all the trouble.

"Hey," I answered finally, tearing my eyes off of her and training them on my ratty shoes.

"What are you doing here by yourself?"

The girl's voice was high and sweet, mine full of bitterness.

"Nothing. Sitting. Is that allowed?"

She jerked a thumb to the kids playing behind us. "I saw you from over there. You looked so sad and lonely; I thought I'd say hi."

I scowled. "I'm not sad *or* lonely."

The girl scuffed her shoe in the dirt. "Oh, okay. Sorry."

I felt bad. *She* looked sad and lonely but covered it with her pretty smile. She wasn't dressed for the park in her fancy dress and shiny black shoes, either. More for a family photo or special occasion. She even had something pink and glittery painted on her lips. This girl looked made-up, like a little doll.

Or maybe this is how Richies go to barbecues at the park.

"Sorry," I mumbled. "Bad day."

"Yeah, me too." She brightened and held out her hand. "I'm Emery Wallace."

Slowly, I took her hand, certain my hair was going to stand on end when our skin touched. "Xander Ford."

"Pleased to meet you, Xander."

ACKNOWLEDGMENTS

It takes a village to write a book and I'm so grateful for mine. People who've been with me from the very beginning, and some just entering my life and making dreams come true. I'm so grateful for all of you.

Thank you to my amazing beta readers, Terri, Joanne, MJ, and Annette for your wonderful thoughts and critique, and your beautiful words in support of my messy ones. Love you all.

So much gratitude to my agent, Georgana, to Christa, my wonderful editor at Bloom, and to the entire Bloom and Seymour Agency families. I still think I'm dreaming.

To my wonderful assistant, Melissa, my right-hand gal and keeper of memories. I love you, always.

To Robin for seeing the raw mess of the book and holding my hand through every neurotic crisis of faith. Love you.

Huge thanks to Dr. Diana Naranjo, PhD, Clinical

Professor of Pediatrics at Stanford University for ensuring the details of Orion's condition were accurate and authentic, although any errors are mine. Also thanks to the International Dyslexia Association website for their resources and expertise.

Thank you to Denise Leora Madre at Prose Without Thorns whose resources were invaluable to me as I wrote my beautiful Orion.

A big thank you to Suanne Laqueur for lending me your brilliant eyes when certain chapters weren't behaving themselves. #labu

And thank you so much to my readers, all of you, new and old. You are the reason I get to do my dream job every day. I'm so grateful. Much love.

ABOUT THE AUTHOR

Emma Scott is a *USA Today* and *Wall Street Journal* bestselling author and Pushcart Prize nominee, whose books have been translated into eight languages and featured in *Buzzfeed*, *Huffington Post*, *New York Daily News*, and *USA Today*'s Happy Ever After blog. She lives in the Bay Area with her husband, daughter, and her dog, who won't stop barking. If she's not at her desk writing her latest ugly-cry romance, she's probably playing *Baldur's Gate 3*. Tell her to stop it and get back to work.

Visit: emmascottwrites.com

Subscribe: bit.ly/2nTGLf6

Hang Out: facebook.com/groups/906742879369651

Follow: facebook.com/EmmaScottwrites

Contact: emmascottpromo@gmail.com